About the author

Thomas E. Lightburn served for twenty-two years in the medical branch of the Royal Navy, reaching the rank of chief petty officer. He left the service in 1974 and obtained a Bachelor of Education Degree (Hons), at Liverpool University. After sixteen years teaching at Liscard Primary School, Wallasey, he volunteered for early retirement. He then began writing for the Wirral Journal during which time he interviewed the late Ian Fraser, VC, ex Lieutenant RN, and wrote an account of how he and his crew in a midget submarine, crippled the Japanese cruiser, *Takao,* in Singapore. Thomas is a widower and lives in Wallasey, pursuing his favourite hobbies of soccer, naval and military history and the theatre.

BATTLE ENSIGN

Also by Thomas E. Lightburn

The Gates of Stonehouse
ISBN 978 184386 203

Uncommon Valour
ISBN 978 184386 203

The Shield and the Shark
ISBN 978 184386 301 2

The Dark Edge of The Sea
ISBN 978 184886 400 4

The Ship That Would Not Die
ISBN 978 184386 463 9

The Summer of '39
ISBN 978 184386 5612

A Noble Chance
ISBN 978 184386 647 3

Beyond The Call of Duty
ISBN 978 184386 714 2

The Russian Run
ISBN 978 184386 840 8

Deadly Inferno
ISBN 978 184386 736 4

Mission into Danger
ISBN 978 184386 994 8

The Hidden Enemy
ISBN 978 178465 132 9

Triumph Over Fear
ISBN 978 178465 5327

All published by Vanguard Press

Thomas E. Lightburn

BATTLE ENSIGN

Vanguard Press

VANGUARD PAPERBACK

© Copyright 2021
Thomas E. Lightburn

A CIP catalogue record for this title is
available from the British Library.

ISBN 978-1-80016-073-6

*Vanguard Press is an imprint of
Pegasus Elliot MacKenzie Publishers Ltd.*
www.pegasuspublishers.com

First Published in 2021

**Vanguard Press
Sheraton House Castle Park
Cambridge England**

Printed & Bound in Great Britain

Dedication

This book is dedicated to Ex Able Seaman John Dennett, Legion d'honneur, and the men who served in the landing craft during the Second World War.

Acknowledgements

I wish to thank the team in the research department of the Imperial War Museum and the British Museum for their help over the internet. My gratitude to the staff of Wallasey Library for their help. I have used Robin Neillands's excellent book, *The Dieppe Raid,* Phillip Zieglar's *Official Biography* and *Malta Convoys* by David A. Thomas for references. Finally, I am most grateful to Gale Pumford for her computer expertise.

A BRIEF HISTORY OF THE BATTLE ENSIGN

In the Royal Navy, the Battle Ensign is the name given to a large White Ensign hoisted to the mainmast or yardarm just before a battle at sea was imminent. In the 17th and 18th or 19th centuries, if a warship surrendered the flag, it was known as, 'striking the colours'. This is the origin of the phrase, 'to nail ones colours to the mast', showing a determination not to surrender.

The Battle Ensign was seen as an important element for the morale of the crew, and was held in high regard. If a warship was sinking, the flags of battle ensign would be taken off before the ship sank and entrusted to the senior surviving officer. In the British Museum there is a battle ensign taken from the Spanish warship, *Ildefenso,* captured at the Battle of Trafalgar.

CHAPTER ONE

Lieutenant Commander Hugh Manley stood on the open bridge of HMS *Helix,* one of several Hunt-Class destroyers built in 1939. Manley was twenty-eight, fair haired and single. He stood six feet two with intelligent, dark-blue eyes, set in clear-cut, angular features. Whenever he smiled, the small dimple in his chin appeared larger, a trait that added to his overall attraction to most women. After obtaining a first in geography at Oxford, he joined the navy in 1939. In doing so, he was following in his father's footsteps, who commanded a destroyer in World War One. Whenever he was on leave, he stayed with his parents, Harold and Martha. Both of them were in their late forties and ran a florist in Seven Oaks. *Heli*x was Manley's third ship; the first two being a minesweeper followed by a D-Class destroyer. After successfully completing a gunnery course at Whale Island, he was appointed to *Helix* as her first lieutenant.

Manley was very proud of his ship. He clearly remembered the first time he saw her. It was shortly after 1200 on Monday 1st May, 1941. A dark blue utillicon, nicknamed a 'tilly', met him outside Portsmouth Harbour station. After a quick drive through the dockyard, they arrived at Fountain Lake Jetty where *Helix* was tied up.

After climbing out of the tilly he stood on the cobbled wharf, and with an experienced eye, took in the ship's pennant number, H60, painted in black, standing out against her gaudily camouflaged hull. The sleek sharp bows, long narrow fo'c'sle and A and B twin, Mk XV1, 4-inch guns, mounted in front of the open bridge. Then came a single, slightly angled funnel, and close by, slung inboard, rested one of the two ship's clinker-built sea boats. Further along, two Carley floats lay at an angle, attached against the starboard side of the after deck. Either side of the after deck house was a moon shaped searchlight, two quadruple 2-pounder pom-poms and a 20 mm Oerlikons, each protected by a circular steel shield. Finally, secured to either side of the quarterdeck, were two as depth charge throwers, ready to launch one of the 21-inch depth charges. As his eyes watched the White Ensign, fluttering proudly from the ship's stern, Manley recalled stepping onto the gangway, feeling a deep-seated feeling of pride.

In a remarkably short time, he got to recognise the face of every officer and rating on the ship. They were a mixed bag; some were RNVR or RNR, others were HO (Hostilities Only), the remainder were regular navy. After a strenuous five-day work-up, the ship's company became an efficient, coherent fighting unit, ready to face the enemy.

The time was 2200; the date, Wednesday, May 10th, 1942; the place, mid-Atlantic on convoy duty. High above, angry dark cirrocumulus clouds, scudding across the inky black sky, failed to prevent the luminous rays from the anaemic moon casting a silver sheen on the waters of the high rolling sea. For the umpteenth time, Manley blew into his gloved hands and watched a cloud of vaporised breath billow around his face before a blast of bitterly cold northerly wind swept it out of sight. With every roll and pitch of the deck, he grabbed hold of anything at hand to prevent falling over. Nearby, officer of the watch, Lieutenant Peters, a tall, rangy RNR officer with blue eyes and fair hair, Petty Officer Podge Hardman, quartermaster Knocker White, did the same.

Meanwhile, *Helix*'s captain, Commander Penrose, was sat, hunched up on his high chair, deep in thought, seemingly oblivious to wind and weather. Like Manley, he and the others wore woollen balaclavas under hooded duffel coats, mufflers and gloves which, silhouetted against the ghostly light, made them look like Trappist monks.

Henry Penrose was born in Tavistock, Plymouth, the birthplace of Sir Francis Drake, in 1908. He was married to Jean, his childhood sweetheart, and had a twelve-year-old daughter called Janet Penrose. He was a little over six feet tall, sturdily built, with dark hair, greying at each temple. His sharp, pale blue eyes, set in a heavily tanned, angular features, presented an imposing figure that commanded instant attention. Anticipating the Blitz, Penrose moved from London and bought a small bungalow in St Albans. Jean obtained a part-time as a receptionist for local solicitors, Barnet and Cross, and Janet attended St Albans Grammar School.

Penrose's father was a retired naval captain who commanded a cruiser at Jutland and was mentioned in dispatches. His grandfather,

Admiral Sir Thomas Penrose, fought at Sebastopol and was awarded the Victoria Cross for outstanding bravery under fire. With such an outstanding pedigree it was not surprising that Penrose was determined to add another cluster of gold leaves, on the peak of his cap.

On the morning of May 11th, *Helix,* plus *Stork, Pelican, Samphire, Deptford, Gardenia* and *Marigold,* five flower class corvettes, plus the CAM freighter, *Dorset* and a rescue ship, MS *Beachy,* relieved five Canadian destroyers and two American frigates, all of whom had reached their endurance while escorting Convoy SC94 from Nova Scotia and had to return to Canada. Unlike *Helix* and the British corvettes, the Canadian and American warships didn't have HF/DF or the new ten-centimetre radar[1] [2]. Consequently, since leaving Canada, the convoy had been constantly attacked by U-boats and had lost two merchant ships.

The following morning, *Helix* and the escorts were at defence stations. Buster Brown, a small, thick-set able seaman from Doncaster, was sat up in the *Helix*'s crow's nest. Despite wearing a balaclava, gloves, two sweaters and a woollen muffler under his duffel coat, he continued to shiver. Ignoring the steady sway of the mast, he could see the dark shapes of the three rows of merchant ships and escorts sending up frothy bow waves as they cut through the silvery sea. Suddenly, he saw a bank of fog lying like a black wall, blotting out the horizon.

Picking up the bridge intercom, Brown shouted, 'Fog, fog, sir, directly in front of us roughly five miles away.'

'Thank you, Brown,' said Manley. Although fog was almost impossible to detect on radar, on the bridge, Penrose and Manley and the others had already seen it, looking like a swirling wall of dense mist.

In a matter of minutes, the convoy was engulfed in a miasma of swirling grey murkiness.

'Jesus Christ, sir,' said Knocker White, peering into the dense mist. 'It's a real peasouper. I can hardly see me and in front of me.'

Manley leaned over the front of the bridge and blinked. All he could see was great wafts of impenetrable greyness and the tips of the twin

---

[1] CAM freighters are fitted with catapults, enabling them to launch aircraft

[2] H/F, known as 'Huff Duff' refers to high frequency direction finder, an electronic system detecting short wave messages between U-boats and the surface up to ten miles away.

four-inch barrels of A and B guns, twenty feet in front of him; nothing else, no ships, no sea, not even the ship's bow. It was like moving in a world of dank, churning clouds. The mournful drone of dozens of sirens of the merchantmen added to the surreal atmosphere as the convoy, one by one, disappeared into the churning greyness that seemed to go on forever.

The thirty-four ships were spread out, five miles apart, in three lines. Commodore Bradley in the cargo freighter, *Trehata,* occupied the middle of the centre column. *Deptford* and *Marigold* protected the starboard section with *Samphire* bringing up the rear. As senior officer, Penrose commanded the escort group. *Helix* led the way with *Stork* guarding the convoy's port side. Many ships didn't have radar and were perilously close together. Therefore, the danger of telescoping into one another drew continual siren blasts, hoping the fog would lift

'At least this pea soup will keep the bloody U-boats away, eh, sir?' PO Podge Hardman said to Manley while staring into the grey abyss. As his nickname suggested, Hardman was two badge seaman petty officer whose prodigious girth and ruddy complexion displayed his love of beer and food.

'I suppose you're right, PO,' Manley replied, feeling the damp, coldness of the fog sneak down the sides of his muffler onto his neck.

At that moment, without moving his head, Penrose, stirred himself, and in his unmistakable West Country burr, said, 'Anything on radar or asdic, Number One?'

'Radar reports several merchantmen are scattered around, sir,' Manley answered. 'Asdic reports contact submerged roughly two miles on the far side of the convoy.'

'I expect the escorts in that area will have picked the contact up and won't need me to tell them to investigate,' said Penrose, peering through his binoculars. 'I'm sure our turn will come soon enough. Reduce revolutions one third, slow ahead.'

Suddenly, three intermittent blasts of a siren could be heard echoing through the gloomy atmosphere. Prior to sailing the convoy, Commodore John Bradley had informed all ships, including the escorts, of a series of siren signals he would use to alter the convoy's course in the event of an attack or inclement weather.

'Three blasts, sir,' said OOW Sub Lieutenant Milton, glancing at Penrose. 'That means the convoy, including the two escorts, are to alter course to port?' Milton was a tall, dark-haired RNVR officer, who, before the war, was stock broker.

'Quite correct,' came Penrose's muffled reply. 'Port ten, I only hope the other ships have heard it over the racket their sirens are making.'

'Port ten, sir,' repeated Leading Seaman Sammy Lee from the wheelhouse, situated directly below the bridge. Like many ratings Lee was HO.

Throughout the morning the convoy crept carefully through the fog. At 1130, '*Up Spirits, cooks to the galley,*' was piped.

The issuing of rum began in 1655 when the British captured Jamaica, with its rich sugar plantations from which rum is derived. Until then, beer, which often became sour, was the staple drink. However, in 1740, Admiral Vernon, known as "Old Grog" because he wore a distinctive red grogram cloak, introduced rum into the navy. From that date, the daily ritual of issuing rum in warships and shore bases all over the world began.

The neat rum was kept in a large oak barrel, ornately decorated and reinforced with brass bands. One of which had the words, "The King (or Queen) God Bless Him (or Her). Under the watchful eyes of the duty PO and OOW, the duty rum bosun from each mess collected the precious liquid, mixed two measures of water to one of rum, in an aluminium basin, called "a fanny". Any rum left over after each man had his "tot" was referred to as "The Kings (or Queens)" and shared out. "Sippers" or "Gulpers" were given to messmates in return for favours rendered.

Shortly after midday, Able Seaman Ben Lyon, climbed down the metal stairs leading into the seamen's mess. In one hand he carried the "fanny". The other hand held onto the stair rail, steadying himself against the roll of the ship. The dank smell of sweaty bodies, mingling with tobacco smoke, attacked his nostrils as he entered the mess.

'Here it is, me lucky lads,' said Ben, placing the fanny on the well-scrubbed mess table. *Helix* was Ben's first ship. He was a tall, fair headed twenty-year-old lad from Hull. Some men were playing uckers, a modified game of Ludo. Others played cribbage, gin rummy, or wrote letters. All of them wore blue overalls and kept their life jackets handy in case of emergencies. They stopped what they were doing and looked up as Ben came in.

'I hope you haven't spilt any,' joked Bud Abbot. Bud was the "killick", of the mess, so called because of the single fouled anchor he wore on his left sleeve.

'So far, so good, Bud,' Ben replied, wiping beads of sweat from his brow with the back of his hand.

Men quickly lined up alongside the table. Using one hand, each man in turn, placed a glass tumbler in the fanny and filled it with rum. He then poured it into a Bakelite measure, returning what was left in the tumbler into the fanny. He then poured the contents of the measure into a separate tumbler, and by naval law, was supposed to down it in one. However, some poured the rum into a bottle to be either drunk later or used as barter for favours.

Taff Hughes, a stocky one badge able seaman, appeared at the top of the stairs carrying a large aluminium tray containing dinner, covered in grease-proof paper. Immediately, the mouth-watering smell of food filled the air. Hughes was the duty cook. This task, carried out daily on a roster basis, was to collect the midday meal from the galley and take it to the mess. In harbour this was relatively easy, but at sea, in rough weather, it could be precarious, to say the least.

'Someone give me a hand before I spill this lot,' cried Hughes.

Straight away Pincher Martin, and using a hand to support the tray, helped Hughes down the stairs and placed the tray on the table. Hughes then left the mess and returned, holding a smaller tray of pudding. While Hughes was away, men grabbed a plate from the cupboard, and stood in line as Bud Abbot dished out the food. It was said, that the after-effects of their rum, increased the sailor's appetite.

Throughout the middle watch, (midnight to 0400), the fog gradually dispersed, and by "*Call the hands*" at 0600, a pale sun peaked though a dull, overcast sky. During the morning, *Helix* and the rest of the escorts, were kept busy, rounding up those merchantmen who had strayed out of the columns and were now scattered around some miles away from the convoy. Then, just after 1100, Leading Asdic Operator Dusty Miller's strident voice came over the bridge intercom. 'Two undersea contacts five miles to port, bearing red two oh, sir, and closing'

'They must be the same buggers that were reported earlier,' said Penrose, who, sitting in his chair, immediately trained his binoculars away to port. 'Sound action stations, Number One, it looks like we're in for a busy day.'

A few minutes later, from the Gun Direction Platform situated above the bridge, gunnery officer, Lieutenant Ted Powers, also RNVR, reported all gun's crews closed up. In the sick bay, situated on the port side of the after deck house, Harry Bamford, a slightly built, fair haired sick berth attendant, was in the process of placing a large a large kidney dish full of surgical instruments into the steriliser when Surgeon Lieutenant Latta arrived. 'All prepared as usual?' he asked Bamford, sitting down at his desk.

'Yes, sir,' Bamford answered confidently, closing the steriliser lid.

In the canteen flat, the first aid team, led by PO Steward Sandy Powel, a tall, pasty-faced man with deep set grey eyes, was made up of NAFFI manager, Ted Grainer, a small balding man with grey hair; Jack Jones, a small, slightly built Leading Writer; Lofty Bensen, a tall, dark, six-footer and tiny "Dick' Turpin", so called, because before the war he was a jockey.

On the bridge, Penrose, sitting on his chair, looked carefully at his wrist watch, then, glancing approvingly at Manley, said, 'Four minutes, not bad, Number One.'

At that moment a tanker, roughly five miles away to starboard, exploded. This was quickly followed by a tall pall of flickering yellow flames, clearly visible some ten miles away to port. A few minutes later another detonation occurred in the same area. In a matter of seconds, a mixture of scarlet and yellow flames and swirling clouds of grey smoke bellowed upwards, momentarily blocking out the sun's weak rays. Throughout the day everyone on board *Helix* could hear the intermittent *thud, thud,* coming from the far side of the convoy as *Deptford, Marigold,* and *Semaphore* launched salvo after salvo of depth charges in an effort to either sink or prevent the U-boat from further attacks.

In *Helix*'s engine room, Lieutenant (E) Derek Logan, RNR, was engrossed, checking the temperature gauges. Logan was twenty-nine, tall and single with a mop of perpetual untidy fair hair. Before the war, he worked for Cunard and was second engineer on the SS *Antonia,* before being called up from the RN reserve in 1941. Logan was a fanatical about engines. His pasty complexion bore witness to, too much time he spent, even when off duty, ensuring his precious engines were in tip-top condition, something that irritated his staff.

Standing next to him on the steel platform was Dolly Gray, a tall, muscular, HO stoker. Like the rest of the stokers, his once dark blue overalls, now a shade of white, caused by constant washing, was open to the waist, displaying a pale, sweat-stained, hirsute chest. 'Any idea what's going on up top, sir?' asked Gray.

Without taking his eyes of the gauges, Logan simply shook his head slightly and replied, 'Your guess is as good as mine.'

'What about you, Chief?' Gray said to Chief Stoker Harry Johnson, a tall, pale-faced, slightly round-shouldered man whose bald head, surrounded by grey hair, gave him a monk-like appearance. Had it not been for the outbreak of war in 1939, he would have completed twenty-two years of pensionable service and be at home with Ethel. He and Ethel had been married for twenty years. They lived in Gosport and had a son, Bert, who was killed at Dunkirk. 'I expect the captain will tell us what's going on,' said Johnson. 'Now stop worrying,' he added with a toothy grin, 'and keep a weather eye on them there oil gauges.'

Just then the tall, stocky figure of Chief ERA Paddy O'Malley came in through a hatchway. 'Be Jesus, how's it going, Harry?' he asked Johnson, using an off-white handkerchief to dab away beads of sweat from his heavily lined pale face. Even though the stokers had been in action several times before, each man knew if the ship was torpedoed, or hit by shellfire, their chances of getting away before they drowned was greatly reduced compared with their shipmates up top.

'To be sure, this racket is driving me and the lads in the engine room round the bloody bend.' O'Malley hailed from Londonderry and joined the navy the same time as Johnson. O'Malley was a widower, his wife, Mary, having died of a heart attack five years ago. They had a twelve-year-old son called Patrick who lived in Londonderry with Mary's parents. When the ship was in Portsmouth, Johnson often invited him for a few beers and a meal at his home in Gosport.

'I know what you mean, Paddy,' Harry replied, 'I wish the old man would tell us what the fuck's going on.'

As if reading Harry's mind, the tannoy clicked into action. 'This is the captain speaking,' said Penrose. 'The fog has now cleared and the convoy is under attack from a U-boat. Two merchant ships away on the port side have been sunk. The escorts in that area are dropping depth charges. The rescue ship is doing her best to pick up survivors. *Helix* is to remain in the van. Remain at defence stations. That is all. I'll keep everyone informed.'

'I should fuckin' well hope so,' muttered a stoker, standing near Harry checking fuel gages.

From his vantage point in the crow's nest, Buster Brown had already witnessed the sinking of two cargo ships. Now, with horror etched in his eyes, he saw men from an oil tanker jump overboard and splash into the water. He looked anxiously as the bulky shape of the rescue ship gradually approached the area, close enough to pick up survivors swimming in a sea which was now a flickering mass of flames, set alight from the oil spewing from the bowls of the tanker. Suddenly, the tanker disintegrated into a mass of swirling black smoke and flames and disappeared under the sea. Another vessel carrying ammunition blew up and quickly sank, taking most of the crew with her. 'My God,' Brown gasped as he slumped back into his wooden seat, 'how many more ships will we lose before we arrive home?'

Everyone on *Helix*'s bridge stood in silence, and like Brown, saw palls of black smoke and flames coming from the port column of the convoy.

Lowering his binoculars, Manley gave a worried sigh, then looking at Penrose, said, 'By my reckoning, sir, that leaves twenty-nine ships left.'

'Quite so, Number One,' Penrose replied soberly. Glancing thoughtfully at Sub Lieutenant Baker, a tall, dark haired, twenty-five-year-old RNR officer, he asked, 'What's our ETA Land's End, Pilot?'

'Roughly 0700 in two days' time, sir,' replied Baker. After obtaining a second in military history at Liverpool University he became an assistant manager at Barclay's Bank, Wallasey. He and his girlfriend, Janet, who he had met at grammar school, had been engaged for nearly a year, and hoped to marry whenever circumstances allowed.

'Hmm…' Penrose muttered, giving Manley a sideways glance. 'As you know, Number One, that's where the convoy will split up.'

'Yes, sir,' Manley replied. 'As I recall, *Stork, Pelican,* and *Marigold* will escort ten ships to Glasgow; *Samphire,* and *Deptford* are to take ten to Bristol, leaving ourselves and *Gardenia* to accompany the remaining nine to London.'

'That's correct, Number One, so here's hoping we don't lose any more ships,' Penrose answered guardedly. 'Stand down from action stations.'

The time was 1400. The sea was choppy, and high above, the ugly, dark cirrostratus clouds promised rain. No sooner had Penrose finished speaking than Buster Brown's voice in the crow's nest came over the intercom. 'Submarine on the surface about ten miles on the port beam, sir,' he yelled excitedly.

Almost at the same moment, Pincher Martin, a small, stocky, ginger haired able seaman, reported a small black line appearing on his pale green radar screen, and added. 'It's a sub, sir, and it doesn't appear to be moving.'

Everyone on the bridge trained their binoculars away to the right. Sure enough, the dark outline of a coning tower, 8.8 cm deck gun and snub-nosed bow could be seen silhouetted against the grey sky.

Baker lowered his binoculars. Nearby on his desk was a copy of "Jane's Fighting Ships", a detailed compendium of all the world's warships. He picked it up and quickly found what he was looking for. 'It's Type VII, sir,' he cried. 'They carry five torpedoes, four in the bows and one in her stern.'

'Thank you, Pilot,' said Penrose. 'I think the blighter's probably recharging her batteries.' Glancing warily at Manley, he went on, 'Hands to action stations, then signal *Stork.* Give the sub's position and tell them to remain on station. Better inform Commodore Bradley in *Trehata.* Say, "I am investigating. Do not break formation".' Penrose then unhooked the ship's tannoy. 'A U-boat has been sighted some distance away,' he said calmly.

Minutes later everyone was closed up. These included Lieutenant Barry Goldsmith, a tall fair hired twenty-three-year-year-old old TAS,

(Torpedo, Anti-Submarine) officer, and his four-men team, manning the depth charges throwers on the quarter deck.

'Sub's beginning to dive, sir,' Manley cried. Like the others he saw a cloud of white bubbles appear on the side of the U-boat.

'Yes, I can see,' Penrose replied, glancing warily at Manley while gritting his teeth. 'The bastard's blowing her ballast tanks.' Straight away he contacted Lieutenant Logan in the engine room. 'There's a U-boat on the surface, Derek,' he said, feeling his heart thumping a cadence in his chest. 'Open her up and give me everything you've got. And don't worry, I'll take responsibility for any damage to your precious engines.' With his binoculars still clamped to his eyes, he snapped, 'Hard a port, revolutions one five.'

In the wheelhouse, Digger Barnes repeated the order which was relayed to Lieutenant Logan in the engine room who adjusted the main engine throttle. Almost immediately the ship heeled steeply to the left forcing everyone on the bridge to grab hold of anything at hand. After righting herself, *Helix* bounded through the sea sending up a gigantic frothy bow wave curling over the fo'c'sle.

Throughout the ship, the tension was palpable. In the engine room everyone listened to the *thud, thud* of the waves thumping against the bulkhead. A few stokers nervously licked their lips; others simply stood and felt lines of warm sweat running down their backs, while, on the quarter deck, Lieutenant Goldsmith stood by the telephone, anxiously waiting for the order to set his depth charges at the required depth in readiness to fire.

Stoker Dolly Gray, shot an apprehensive glance at Lieutenant Logan. 'Fuck me, sir,' he gasped, 'if we go any faster the rivets will burst.'

'And what about the engines, sir?' asked a pale-faced stoker. 'Do you think they can cope with this speed we're going?'

'Oh, do shut up,' Logan answered confidently. 'I can assure you my engines and boilers can deal with anything the captain requires, now,' he added, looking impassively at CERA O'Malley, 'so, everyone relax and keep calm.'

The first aid party mustered outside the NAFFI. 'Everyone, check your first aid bags and make sure you've got plenty of shell dressings,' said PO Powel, opening his small, brown canvas bag.

'Oh, bloody hell, PO,' growled Bensen, 'we've done this a dozen times before.'

'Then do it again, and pipe down,' Powel replied bluntly.

Meanwhile, the ship continued to cut through the high rolling sea, sending a spumescent curling bow wave over the fo'c'sle. On the bridge, all eyes were focused on the U-boat.

'Do you want to open fire, sir?' said Manley, noticing a determined glint in Penrose's eyes. 'We're only about a half a mile away and the bastard will be gone soon.'

Baker and everyone on the bridge heard Manley's question and waited anxiously for Penrose to answer. 'No,' Penrose grunted. 'At the speed we're going we should hit the conning tower before it disappears underwater.' A few seconds after Penrose had finished speaking, he suddenly felt a sudden pounding in his chest. Making a conscious effort to conceal his discomfort from Manley, he quickly put his hand in his jacket and fiddled with a small box and took out a white pill. 'Heartburn,' he said to Manley, popping it into his mouth. The pill was Digoxin, prescribed by Doctor Peter Smyth, his local GP and personal friend, when he was on leave. He had felt his heart rate increasing on several occasions before but was reluctant to report sick as *Helix* was due to sail. After a careful examination, Smyth told him he was suffering from what he called, "chronic arterial fibrillation," a rhythmic disorder of the heart that could, if left untreated, be extremely serious. Penrose was only too aware that if the navy knew of this, he would be given a desk job or, at worst, a medical discharge, and not receive the fourth gold stripe he coveted so much. He therefore kept his condition not only from the ship's doctor, but also his wife as he knew she was worried enough with him being away so much. Therefore, he took a pill whenever he felt his heart rate increase.

Manley gave Penrose a defiant glance. 'But what do you intend doing, sir?' he asked impatiently.

Penrose clenched his teeth. 'Do, Number One?' he grunted, 'I'm going to ram the bastard!'

CHAPTER TWO

In a flash, Manley realised the implications of his captain's intention. Ramming an enemy ship was always a last resort, especially when every other method of attack had failed. He was also aware that the damage *Helix* could sustain might result in her sinking and possible loss of lives. Feeling the blood drain from his face, he turned and faced Penrose. 'Ram, sir!' he shouted, 'Why not use depth charges instead?'

Feeling the thumping of his heart gradually subside, Penrose replied, 'Too bloody late now, Number One.' He and the others saw the top of the conning tower, roughly two hundred yards away. Penrose unhooked the tannoy, and doing his best to sound calm, said 'In a few minutes we will ram the U-boat. All hands steady themselves.'

The captain's warning sent alarm running throughout everyone. Lieutenant Goldsmith ordered his depth charge crew to secure and get below. Chief GI Bob Shilling told the guns crew to stand down while on the bridge. Petty Officer Len Mills, a weather-beaten, six foot, thick-set Cornishman, held onto the binnacle. QM Sammy Smith grabbed the side of the captain's chair while the two lookouts quickly caught hold of a stanchion. In the wheelhouse, Digger Barnes increased his grip on the wheel while QM Chalky White, a tall, pale-faced able seaman grasped a nearby stanchion. Leading Seaman Chats Harris cast a worried glance at Bud Abbot, his opposite number on B gun. 'Bugger this for a fuckin' skylark, Bud, my old gash bucket,' Harris gasped. 'We never practised this during our work-up.'

'That's because there weren't any soddin' subs to practice on, yer daft bugger,' Bud sarcastically replied. 'Now shit in it before we all end up in the oggin.' In sharp contrast to Harris, who was tall, muscular with thick brown wavy hair, Abbot was small and stocky, whose pugnacious features made him resemble James Cagney.

In the crow's nest, Buster Brown felt his stomach contract with fear. Watching the U-boat's conning tower and tall periscope some twenty yards away from the ships bows, he realised it was too late to leave his post. By the time he clambered down the rattling rigging onto the bridge, the ship would have hit the top of the conning tower and he might be thrown overboard. 'Sod, it, he muttered nervously, 'I'll stay here and take my fuckin' chances.'

On the bridge everyone held their breath as *Helix*'s sharp bows crashed into top of the conning tower as it was about to sink under the water. A tremendous shock wave immediately vibrated throughout the ship. A shuddering, grinding noise quickly followed this as *Helix* slowly stopped.

Penrose held desperately onto the sides of his chair. Baker managed to grab hold of Manley before he fell backwards. The others lost their grip on whatever they were holding onto and tumbled over. Below, in the engine room, Dolly Gray staggered against the bulkhead and sustained a two-inch gash on his forehead. In the engine room, CERA O'Malley slipped on the steel grating and twisted his ankle. Other stokers were thrown against the panels and dials, bruising shoulders and arms. Chaos reigned in the galley as pots, pans and trays left the security of their shelves and flew everywhere.

'So much for the toad-in-the-hole,' cried Chief Cook Dai Evans, doing his best to pick his bulky, five-foot six frame off the galley deck, while watching two trays of under-cooked sausages fall onto the deck. Peering, wild-eyed, at the four cooks who were holding onto parts of the galley equipment, he shouted, 'Well, don't fuckin' well stand there gawping,' he yelled, 'someone help me up.'

'To be sure, Chief,' said Spud Murphy, a tall, ginger-headed HO chef from Londonderry. Letting go of a table and taking hold of the chief's arm, he grinned and added, 'We could always wash 'em and make those Yankee hot dogs.'

'Get this fuckin' lot cleared up,' snapped the chief, glaring angrily at his staff. 'Or I'll make hot dogs of all the lot of you.'

In the sick bay, situated in the after deck house, directly over the seaman's mess deck and under X gun turret, everything rattled. Doors of the medical cabinet flew open, scattering bottles and tins everywhere. Tiny flakes of asbestos fluttered from the overhead pipes like confetti. Sick Berth Attendant Bamford managed prevent himself falling over by tightly clasping the metal rail of one of the cots. Surgeon Lieutenant Latta wasn't so lucky; he was sitting at his desk and toppled backwards bumping his head on the deck.

'Bloody hell, sir,' said Bamford as he helped the doctor to his feet. 'I think we'll have a few bods with bruises after this lot.' Bamford was from Cheapside and spoke with an unmistakable cockney accent.

'Och, and a few broken bones,' the doctor added, rubbing the back of his head.

As the ship passed over the spot where the U-boat sank, everyone on the bridge watched in awe as a widening circle of frothy white bubbles erupted in the sea. This was quickly followed by a dull, rumbling noise. With the exception of Penrose, who remained in his chair, everyone stood in silence, only too aware what was happening in the sea below them.

'She must be breaking up, sir,' Manley said quietly, staring at the ever-widening ripples of water.

Penrose didn't reply. He had been in action before and had witnessed death and destruction whilst on convoy duty. Therefore, the realisation that he was responsible for sending over a hundred men to their death was met with equanimity. 'Slow astern,' he said calmly. 'Better check for damage and injuries, Number One, and stand down from action stations.'

Seconds later, the crew listened intently as he told them what had happened. After Penrose had finished speaking nobody cheered or clapped each other on the back. Instead, they stood in sombre silence, lost in thought. Not so long ago, many of the crew were civilians, engaged in a variety of jobs, far removed from the situation they now faced. Now, for the first time in their lives, they had witnessed death, and even though the victims were the enemy, it pricked some consciences and made many of them uneasy. In the seaman's mess, Bud Abbot, frowned then gave Sammy Smith a sombre look and said, 'Poor bastards. What a way to go.' It was a sentiment shared by everyone on the ship.

The time was 1600. Lieutenant Tim Sherwood, the ship's electrical officer, came onto the bridge. After obtaining a second at Manchester University, Sherwood joined the navy. He was twenty-two, tall with a mop of untidy ginger hair.

Behind Sherwood stood Chief Bosun's Mate, Charlie Jackson, wearing a pair of dirty blue overalls and a wrinkled, well-worn cap. Jackson was a small, powerfully built man with intelligent blue eyes and weather-beaten features. Like Chief Stoker Harry Johnson, he was overdue for his pension.

'How badly are we damaged?' Penrose asked, looking warily at Sherwood then Jackson.

'The electric supply to the for'ard mess decks and chain locker are out, sir,' Sherwood said, taking off his cap and wiping his brow with the back of his hand, 'but I'm sure it can be fixed.'

'And part of the bows below the waterline are staved in and shipping water into the paint store, sir,' Jackson added, breathing heavy. 'And the port side of the bulkhead is partially staved in but so far it hasn't leaked.'

'Any injuries?' asked Penrose.

'The chief ERA has injured his ankle and a stoker has a head injury,' Manley replied. 'The doc is looking after them.'

'Just how serious is the damage to the bows, Chief?' Penrose asked Jackson, nervously stroking the bristles on his chin.

The chief removed his cap revealing a shiny bald patch in amongst greying dark hair. 'At the moment the water is ankle level, but if the ship increases speed over ten knots the vibrations could make things worse.'

'And the port side bulkhead, will it hold?

'We'll do our best, sir,' Jackson replied confidently.

'Thank you, both,' Penrose replied. 'Carry on. I'll try ten knots, so keep me informed.'

'Aye, aye, sir,' Sherwood answered curtly, then he and Wilson left the bridge.

Glancing at PO Telegraphist Jack Frost, Penrose said, 'Signal *Stork* and inform the rest of the escorts, plus Commodore Bradley, C-in-C Portsmouth and Plymouth.' Anticipating the order, Frost stood ready, pad and pencil in hand. Frost was a slightly built, two badge man whose hooded dark blue eyes and leathery features gave him a slightly sinister appearance. Penrose went on, say, '"*U-Boat, pennant number U21, rammed and sunk*",' 'Give its position and add, '"*no survivors*".' Penrose paused momentarily, then went on, '"*Damage to* Helix's *bows. Bulkhead shipping water, but might make ten knots. Stork to detach from convoy and assist if necessary.* Marigold *to take* Stork's *position. Convoy to proceed as arranged. Will make for Plymouth. Request dry dock".'*

Frost finished writing down the message and left the bridge, then returned five minute later. 'Signal from *Stork,* sir,' *"Convoy continuing as arranged. Will join you soonest".'*

'Thank you, PO,' said Penrose. 'How far away is the convoy, Number One?'

Manley lowered his binoculars and looking through the azimuth ring on the compass repeater, said, 'about twenty miles on our starboard beam, sir.'

PO Frost arrived on the bridge holding a small sheet of paper. 'Signal from C in C Plymouth, sir, it reads, *"Dry dock unavailable, damaged by bombs. Can you make Portsmouth?"*

Turning to Baker, he said, 'the damage to the bows will definitely slow us down. So what will our ETA in Portsmouth be if we manage ten knots?'

Baker turned around and using his dividers did a quick calculation, then, looking over his shoulder he said, 'three days, sir.'

'Thank you, Pilot,' Penrose replied. Penrose glanced thoughtfully at Frost and said, 'Reply to C in C's signal, give our ETA in Portsmouth, and add, *"Providing bulkheads holds. Will keep you informed".'*

A few minutes later Frost arrived. 'Signal from C in C Portsmouth again, sir, it says, *"Number 9 dock available on arrival. Good luck to you and Stork".'*

Penrose gave Manley an anxious look, then said, 'Engines half ahead, speed ten knots, revolutions ten and let's hope for the best.'

The ship gradually increased speed. During the next hour everyone on the bridge listened intently to steady throb of the engines. The buzz of the intercom broke the tension.

'Captain,' said Penrose.

'Logan, sir,' came the reply. 'I'm glad to say, so far, the bulkhead is holding.'

'Thank you, Derek,' Penrose replied, nervously running his tongue along his upper lip. 'Well done to your team. Let me know immediately if there's any change.'

Just as Penrose had finished speaking, "Scouse" Johnny Morris, the captain's steward arrived on the bridge holding a steaming mug of kye and a plate of sandwiches. 'Thought youse could do with these, ser, the chef told me you liked chicken, seein' as how yer missed yer tea.' Before the war, Morris, a small, twenty-year-old, heavily built lad, from Toxteth, Liverpool, worked as waiter in the Adelphi Hotel.

'Thank you, Morris,' Penrose answered, accepting the mug and blowing across the top, 'that's very thoughtful of you.'

'*Stork* approaching on starboard quarter, sir,' shouted the starboard lookout. Everyone on the bridge looked to the right and saw the sharp bows of the flower-class frigate sending up a frothy bow wave as she ploughed through the sea. In a matter of minutes, she slowed down and was roughly fifty yard away from *Helix*. Using a loud hailer, her captain shouted. 'Do you need a tow?'

Accepting a loud hailer from Manley, Penrose, holding his half empty mug, shouted, 'No thanks, can safely make ten knots. Grateful for your company. Remain on present position.' Turning to Manley, he finished his drink then added, 'Revert to defence stations, Number One.'

The time was 1800. Dusk was fast approaching. A fine vail of drizzle reduced visibility to a less than half a mile. In the seamen's mess, the warmth of the atmosphere exaggerated the sour smell of stale tobacco, smoke and bodily odours. Tansey Lee, Sammy Smith and Dusty Miller were playing poker. A small pile of matches lay in the centre of the table. Close by, Swampy Marsh, a thick-set HO rating with dark curly hair, was playing uckers (ludo) with Pincher Martin. Bud Abbot and Spud Murphy were writing letters. Others were cocooned in their hammocks, which, with every gentle roll of the ship, swayed in unison as if manipulated by a puppet master.

'Fuck me,' cried Marsh, giving Pincher a suspicious look. 'That's the second time in a row you've thrown a six.'

'Bollocks,' Pincher replied as he casually moved his disc another six places. 'It's all in the wrist movement,' he said, picking up the small, brown Bakelite cup and waggling it about. 'And don't forget, that's sippers you owe me.'

During the night, the convoy and escorts went ahead of the two warships and gradually disappeared over the horizon. As dawn broke the two warships, now alone and vulnerable to enemy attack, either by air or sea, slowly cut their way through the high rolling waves of the Atlantic Ocean. High above, a full moon peeped through the mass of dark altostratus clouds. Except for the steady beat of the engines, and the gentle roll of the ship, all was quiet. On the bridge, Penrose sat hunched up in his chair. Both eyes were closed and his hands, clad in woollen mittens were curled around a hot mug of kye. Nearby, Midshipman Morgan was aware that the captain had been on the bridge all night and was asleep. Morgan was tempted to take the mug away, but frightened in case he woke Penrose up, decided not to. Instead, he stamped his feet and grimaced as a gust of bitterly cold northerly wind attacked his face. A year ago, eighteen-year-old Henry Morgan, a tall, fair-haired lad with intelligent brown eyes, was a junior clerk in his father's law firm. Shortly after Christmas 1941, against his parent's wishes, he had joined the service. Two months later, after passing out from Dartmouth, he joined *Helix*.

Both vessels had darkened ship, but Morgan could easily make out *Stork*'s black silhouette and froth white wash some two hundred yards away on *Helix*'s port beam. Suddenly, the tranquillity of the scene was broken by the sound of Penrose's mug hitting the deck. Penrose opened his eyes and sat up, blinked and wearily shook his head.

'What time is it, Mid?' he asked, stifling a yawn.

'0320, sir,' Morgan replied. Then plucking up courage, went on. 'Why don't you go to your cabin, sir? Lieutenant Milton has the morning watch and he'll be here soon.'

'Hmm…' muttered Penrose, 'perhaps you're right.' He slowly pushed his burly frame off his chair. Noticing the bits of broken mug lying nearby, he gave Morgan a tired look. 'Sorry about that, waste of good kye.' As he spoke the moonlight caught Penrose's face, allowing Morgan to see how drawn and exhausted his weather-beaten face looked. 'Call me instantly if the leakage from the bulkheads increases. Understand?'

'Yes, sir,' Morgan answered.

Steadying himself on the arm of the chair, Penrose rose slowly and left the bridge. By the time he arrived in his cabin, his heart was thumping like a drum. He immediately took out a small pill box from his jacket pocket, and feeling his hand shake slightly, picked out a Digoxin tablet and quickly swallowed it. Too tired to even take off his duffel coat, he wearily pushed himself onto his bunk and immediately fell asleep.

A few minutes before 0400 Sub Lieutenant Ray Milton, a small, stocky, RNR deck officer with dark, wavy hair, took over the watch from Morgan.

'How's the bulkhead holding?' he asked Morgan, while tucking his woollen scarf around the top of his duffel coat. Before the war, Milton was a maritime architect. He was twenty-one, single and joined the navy in 1940. *Helix* was his first ship and he was now one of the ship's two deck officers.

'So far, so good,' Morgan answered with a sleepy sigh. 'The captain has just gone below and has asked to be contacted if the leaking increases.'

During the night, the convoy and escorts disappeared over the horizon. Shortly after 0500 both warships were less than one hundred sea miles off the southern tip of Ireland. High above the dark clouds promised rain and the high rolling Atlantic waves continued to batter both ships. (A nautical mile is 1,852 metres, a land mile is 1,609metres.)

At precisely 0600, on Monday the 14th, the tired voice of duty QM Knocker White came over the tannoy. 'Eave oh, eave oh, lash up and stow. Cooks to the galley.'

Bleary eyed and yawning, those ratings who, despite the dangers of being tossed out of their hammocks, grabbed hold of the iron bar attached to the deck head directly above and heaved themselves out of their hammocks onto the deck. Others slept on the deck or table, while some preferred to use the tops of the metal lockers enclosing their mess. Except for footwear, all had slept fully dressed.

'Boiled eggs and hard tack for breakfast, I suppose,' grunted Sammy Smith, sitting on the table bench and pushing his stockinged feet into his shoes. (Hard tack was a simple type of biscuit made from wholemeal, vitamins and flour.)

Meanwhile, Able Seaman Hooky Walker, in the crow's nest, wiped the lens of his binoculars and peered into the misty sky and saw a black dot in the sky. Walker was an HO able seaman with a swarthy complexion, with perfect twenty-twenty vision. With his binoculars still clamped to his eyes, he contacted the bridge. 'Aircraft bearing red 040, approaching on port beam, sir.'

Sub Lieutenant Milton acknowledged and unhooked the captain's intercom. Seconds later Penrose's tired voice answered. 'Captain. What's the problem?'

Milton told him. 'Sound action stations,' snapped Penrose, 'I'll be up straight away.'

Glancing warily at PO Len Mills, Milton repeated Penrose's order. Straight away, he, Mills and QM Jock Forbes, a tall, dark, muscular able seaman from Dundee, trained their binoculars to the left and saw the black crosses clearly visible on the underside of the grey wings and distinctive red nose.

'It's a ME109, sir,' cried Mills, 'and it's losing height.'

At that moment, Penrose came onto the bridge. A few minutes later Manley and Sub Lieutenant Baker arrived, and like Penrose, immediately trained their binoculars away to the left. By this time, the ship's company were closed up at action stations.

Above the bridge, in the gunnery direction platform, Lieutenant Powers wiped the mist from his binoculars and peering through the grey gloom, reported, 'It's coming in too low, too low to use the 4.5s sir, however, the pom-poms and Oerlikons should deal with the bugger.'

'The sod's heading straight for *Stork,* sir,' cried Powers.

'Bloody hell, sir,' Manley shouted to Penrose, 'if the blighter puts *Stork* out of action, we'll be sitting ducks.'

The warning wasn't lost on Penrose, who, furrowing his brow, calmly replied, 'Not only for him but for any U-boat that happens to be in the vicinity.'

Meanwhile, Leading Seaman Dutch Holland, had manned the port pom-pom. One eye was pressed against the single circular gunsight while his right hand hovered near the firing button. In front of him three gunnery ratings waited to feed rounds of two-pounder ammunition into the breeches of each of the four, gun barrels. On and on came the fighter, yellow flames of cannon fire flickering from the edges of each wing.

For a fleeting second, the ME109 came into Holland's sight. With lightning reflexes, he pressed a button. Immediately a sharp rattle of gunfire rent the air, sending streams of bullets arching into the air. The deafening cacophony of noise was increased by Leading Seaman Dicky Bird and his gunners on the starboard pom-pom, joining in the attack. To this nerve-jangling cacophony was added spine chilling *rata-tat-tat* of the Oerlikons. For a moment the fighter was obliterated by lines of cross fire from both ships.

On *Helix*'s bridge everyone else watched in horror as the fighter came in low and raked *Stork* with ferocious cannon fire. Seconds later, the plane pulled away into the cloudy grey sky.

'Signal *Stork*, Yeoman,' said Penrose, 'say, "*any casualties? Can we help?*"'

A few minutes later came the reply. '"*Two ratings killed, one badly wounded. Thank you for your offer. Suggest we proceed as arranged*".'

The remainder of the day passed peacefully as the two warships continued their lone sojourn. During the night, Penrose ordered both vessels to alter course to ten degrees to starboard. By 0600 the next morning, both ships were fifty miles off Land's End.

At 0900 Penrose ordered the lower deck to be cleared to witness *Stork* burying their dead. The sky was dull and overcast and a bitterly cold, northerly wind churned the sea into a heaving mass of white-topped waves. Over the tannoy, Manley called the ship's company to attention. A hundred yards away they saw rows of *Stork*'s ship's company, bareheaded and standing to attention. Nearby, facing aft, stood the officers. A pair of ratings, each carrying an army type canvas stretcher walked slowly onto the quarterdeck. On each stretcher lay the body of one of their comrades, strapped in a hammock and draped in a white ensign. The captain, holding a bible, read a short prayer then, under the guidance of an officer, each stretcher was carefully lifted onto the edge of a guard rail. The dull dong of *Stork*'s bell, barely heard over the howling wind echoed around. Seconds later, each body slid from under the flag and splashed into the sea.

Two hours later both warships entered the English Channel and by "Up Spirits," the verdant coast of Hampshire could be seen a few miles away on the ship's port beam. Shortly afterwards the flat terrain of the Isle of Wight hove in to view. On *Helix*'s bridge, Penrose, relaxing in his chair turned to Manley, and in a tired voice, said. 'Home at last, eh, Number One.'

'Yes, sir,' Manley replied, nodding slightly, 'but for how long.

CHAPTER THREE

Shortly after 0600, on Tuesday 15th May, with *Helix* in the van, the two warships cruised slowly into Portsmouth harbour. The special sea duty men of both vessels were fallen in on the fo'c'sle and quarterdeck. The chin straps of their caps were down and the shiny black oilskins they wore protected them against the blustery cold, westerly wind, while, in the distance, dozens of bulging barrage balloons hovered over the city, like silver sentinels. Away to port, two submarines lay alongside HMS *Dolphin,* the navy's main submarine base. Behind the base, the grey slated rooftops of Haslar Hospital could be seen glistening in the early morning mist. Further along, the houses of Gosport were barely visible, while across the harbour, South Sea common, dotted with gun batteries, commanded the approaches to the city.

After passing Fort Blockhouse the ships sailed passed a light cruiser and two destroyers. All three vessels were camouflaged in dark green and black.

'Attention on the upper deck. Face the starboard,' was piped. At the same time, Penrose and Manley stood on the starboard wing and returned the salutes from the duty officers on the bridges of the cruiser and destroyers.

The same ritual was carried out as the two ships cruised past Semaphore Towers, a large imposing building where both captains knew the admiral of the dockyard would no doubt be carefully scrutinising each ship for any lack of discipline or an open scuttle.

'Signal from *Stork,* sir,' PO Frost said to Penrose, 'it says, "*Will leave you to berth alongside Dockyard Wharf. Good luck*".'

'Reply, "*Thank you for your company. Deeply regret the loss of your two ratings. God speed*".'

Everyone on the bridge gave a friendly wave as *Stork* slowly pulled away to starboard, heading towards the wharf. Ten minutes later *Helix* approached North Corner Basin situated further down the harbour.

'Starboard five. Slow ahead,' snapped Penrose.

'Five a starboard wheel on, sir,' replied Chief Barnes from the wheelhouse.

'Special sea duty men fall out, Number one,' said Penrose, 'and make sure they have a good breakfast.'

Helix gradually turned to the right and entered he calm waters in the wide basin at the end of which were two large, oaken dock gates leading into the dry dock. Seawater would eventually be let into the dock. When it was at the same level as that in the basin, the gates would slide open, allowing *Helix* to enter.

'Stop engines,' said Penrose.

'How long before the dry dock is flooded, sir?' Sub Lieutenant Baker asked Manley. Baker had relieved Milton and was OOW.

'About an hour or so,' Manley replied, stifling a yawn. 'I expect the dockyard engineers will let us know.

Shortly after 0900 a message from the engineer informed Penrose the dry dock was now flooded. Everyone on the bridge watched as the giant dry dock gates slowly slid open.

'Slow ahead, revolutions five,' said Penrose, sitting on his chair, sipping a mug of tea. Meanwhile, on both sides of the dock a crane waited. With the help of dockyard workers wearing yellow waders, the cranes would lower thick wooden planks to support the sides of the ship as the water was slowly drained away. It was a slow onerous task, requiring careful timing and skill.

When *Helix* was in the middle of the dock, Penrose ordered the engines to stop and all hands to keep clear of the upper deck. Almost immediately, the ship began to roll gently as buoyancy was lost. As the water level was reduced, the steep slippery concrete steps around the sides of the basin slowly came into view. Dockyard workers on either side of the basin ensured the stout wooden supports were firmly in place against the ship's side. By the time the water had drained away ship was resting on the grating. On the quarterdeck, Sub Lieutenant Milton turned to deck officer, Sub Lieutenant Jock Jewitt, a tall, gangly faired Sub Lieutenant from Dundee, and said, 'All those struts against the ship's side make them look like oars from a Viking raider.'

'Och away with you, man,' Jewitt replied. In doing so his dark blue eyes and weather-beaten complexion creased into a wide grin. 'I'm afraid you've got an over-developed imagination. What you need is a good run ashore.'

By midday, a metal gangway leading from an exit in the basin to the quarterdeck, was in place, along with the ship to shore telephone.

'Up spirits, cooks to the galley, mail is now ready for collection,' was piped.

Leading hands of messes hurried to the coxswain's office where the "postie", Slinger Woods, a tall, dark haired able seaman from Hull, handed out bundles of letters.

Shortly afterwards, the sound of envelopes being torn open accompanied raucous laughter and ribald comments echoed around each mess.

'My missus says she's two weeks overdue,' said Lofty Day, staring wildly at his letter, 'and wants me to increase her allotment.'

'Never mind, mate,' said Dutch Holland, 'maybe it's a false alarm.'

'Or a grudge baby?' grinned Jock Forbes, placing his letter in an envelope.

'What the fuck do you mean by that?' Day replied angrily.

'Someone's had it in for you while you've been away,' Jock answered, grinning like a Cheshire cat.

'Fuckin' sheep shagger,' grunted Day as he threw a boot at Jock.

In the wardroom, Sub Lieutenant Baker felt the blood drain from his face as he read a letter from his fiancé, Janet It was brief and quickly came to the point.

Dear David,

I am writing to tell you that while you've been away, I have met and fallen in love with someone else. I realise this will come as a shock and upset you, and I'm terribly sorry for that. However, I hope we can remain friends.

God bless you and take care of yourself.

Affectionately yours,

Janet.

'Are you all right, laddie? You look as white as a sheet,' asked Lieutenant Logan, who was standing nearby drinking a cup of tea.

'Not really, Jock,' muttered Baker, who, feeling as if his world had suddenly collapsed, slowly left the room and went to his cabin.

Penrose was sat behind his desk in his cabin. The two letters from Jean telling him Janet and her were keeping well, lay on his desk. Sitting opposite him was a stocky, dockyard official with a heavily lined face and rheumy grey eyes who had introduced himself as Joseph Pendleton. Next to him, Manley relaxed back in an armchair and crossed his legs. Unlike the dark blue, oil-stained overall worn by Pendleton, those worn by Penrose and Manley were pristine white. The three men had just returned from examining the damage sustained when the ship rammed the U-boat.

'As you saw, the cracks below the waterline on the port side of bows are severe.' He spoke with a pronounced Hampshire accent. 'Luckily, the damage to the paint store isn't so bad.'

'How long will it take to repair them?' Pentose asked, somewhat anxiously.

'Let me see now,' Pendleton replied while pensively stroking g his chin. 'The bulkhead will need a new plate, but the cracks in the paint store could be welded, so I'd say a week at the earliest.'

With a tired sigh, Penrose replied, 'Thank you, Mr Pendleton.' Then, glancing at the wall clock, went on. 'Perhaps you'd care to join my first lieutenant and myself in a drink?'

'A whisky would go down nicely, sir,' Pendleton answered, 'and a few packets of Players would be most welcome.

Half an hour later, Penrose and Manley accompanied Pendleton to the brow. 'Thank you for the drink,' said Pendleton, shaking their hands. 'And err… I'll see if I can hurry up the repairs,' he added, smiling wistfully while touching the small brown paper parcel tucked under his arm.

'Bribery and corruption, sir,' said Manley, watching Pendleton walk unsteadily down the gangway. 'I hope it is worth it.'

'We'll just have to wait and see, Number One,' Penrose replied.

'The ship's company are due ten days leave, sir,' said Manley. 'May I suggest we ask for a dozen volunteers who live locally to remain behind, and send the rest on four days leave.'

'I agree, Number One,' Penrose replied. 'They can have the other six days when we leave dry dock, providing we're not required to go to sea.'

'What about you, sir?' asked Manley, noticing the dark rings and bags under his captain's bloodshot eyes. 'If you don't mind me saying so, I think you could do with a rest.'

'Not at the moment, Number One,' Penrose replied, 'later, after the repairs are completed. In the meantime, I suggest heads of departments remain on board to order stores. This will enable Lieutenant Logan to overhaul his engines, and I want Baker to check with the oceanic department in barracks and bring his charts up to date. The doc and the deck officers and midshipman might as well go on leave.'

The prospect of leave was greeted by the crew with alacrity; the seven creases in bell bottoms were neatly pressed, white fronts and shirts ironed and shoes polished. That evening, a small contingent of engineers and dockyard workers invaded the ship. Throughout the night the constant hammering and ear shattering sound of welding kept everyone awake.

'That fuckin' noise is driving me nuts,' growled Tansey Lee from under the cosy confines of his hammock. 'What time are those coaches taking us to the station tomorrow?' The time was 2330. His question was directed at Pincher Martin in the hammock a few feet away.

'0900,' came Pincher's muffled reply. 'Now shit in it and let me have a quiet wank.'

In his cabin, Lieutenant Baker lay in his bunk. For the umpteenth time since receiving Susan's letter, he asked himself how she could have done this to him, and who was the "someone", she had met. Was he in the armed forces or exempt service, or maybe a conscientious objector? With a weary sigh, he switched off his bedside light and stared blankly up at the pipes and cables in the deck head. 'To hell with it,' he told himself before eventually falling asleep. 'I'm not giving up. As soon as I can, I'm going to sort them both out.'

CHAPTER FOUR

At 0900, on Thursday 17th, the crew left the ship. Each rating carried a "pussers" green suitcase, and boarded a coach that took them to Portsmouth Harbour station. (Anything naval, is referred to as "pusser".) Shortly afterwards the officers climbed into a tilly waiting on the wharf, and left the dockyard. While in dry dock Penrose, Manley, Logan and Jewitt would be billeted in the wardroom in barracks. The twelve volunteers were allowed to draw their "tot" and go ashore at 1600, leaving four ratings to share a twenty-four-hour telephone and security watch. Penrose and the other three officers left when it suited them.

Among the twelve volunteers that remained behind to man the ship were Chief Stoker Harry Johnson and ERA Paddy O'Malley. Standing by a guard rail on the quarterdeck, O'Malley glanced sideways at Johnson, and said, 'To be sure, four days isn't long. I hope they make the most of it.'

With a smile, Johnson replied, 'That reminds me, Paddy, Ethel's met someone called Joyce, who lives in the next road. They play bingo together and she has a phone. Her hubby, Jack, is in the army and was captured at Dunkirk and is now a POW. Anyway, I managed to phone Ethel to tell her I'm coming home and I was bringing you with me, and to bring Joyce. I also asked her to make my favourite, rabbit stew, tonight.'

Paddy threw his head back and gave a hearty laugh. 'And, to be sure, she's now playing matchmaker, eh, Harry?'

'Oh, pipe down and give me a ciggy,' Harry replied giving his friend a playful dig in the ribs.

During the morning, the grating noise of welding and banging of hammers echoed around the ship. Canvas mats were laid down on the passage ways to protect the deck from the hob nailed boots worn by the dockyard workers. Penrose sat in his cabin and caught up with reading signals and writing reports. Manley wrote a letter home, then, along with

Engineer Lieutenant Logan and Lieutenant Powers, conducted a tour of the ship making sure all departments were secure.

Because the boilers, engines, heating and ventilation were shut down, the atmosphere throughout the ship became muggy and eerily quiet. All sounds became exaggerated with the air damp and dusty. A warm westerly breeze blew down river while the sun, hidden by stratocumulus clouds, promised dry, dull, weather. With their gas mask satchels and steel helmets hanging over their shoulders, and wearing their number one uniforms, Harry Johnson and Paddy O'Malley cadged a lift in a coach, that dropped them off at the harbour station. Both men carried small brown suitcases containing "nutty" — a term used in the navy, covering sweets and chocolate.

Along with a crowd of civilians and dockyard workers, they walked down the metal slipway, and stood behind a stout wooden barrier while watching the tug-like ferryboat slowly chug alongside the jetty. An elderly deckhand then left the vessel and jumped onto the jetty. Using thick manila rope, he secured the vessel by quickly tying a figure of eight pattern around two steel bollards. After this he undid part of the ferry boat's guard rail while another deckhand drew back the barrier, allowing each person to carefully step aboard.

An all-night shuttle service, consisting of two ferryboats, ran between Gosport and Portsmouth. The journey across the harbour to Gosport took just over ten minutes. From a small open bridge, the captain, a grey-haired man with a white beard, expertly manoeuvred the ferryboat passed an aircraft carrier, two destroyers and a frigate. After passing her sister ferryboat, the captain cut engines and slowly hove to alongside the Gosport jetty. A guardrail was removed and a wooden gangway allowed the passengers to leave. (In 1963, these ferryboats were superseded by two modern double decker vessels.)

Paddy and Johnson joined the passengers and walked up the concrete slipway at the top to the bus station. 'That number ten stops not far away from Richmond Road, where I live,' said Johnson, pointing to one of several double-decker green busses parked nearby. Johnson paid both their fares to a small, stout, female, "clippy", then, along with a few other passengers, took their seats. The bus drove up a busy main street road stopping a few times to allow passengers to leave and board.

'That's the White Hart, said Johnson, pointing to a large white-fronted pub on the left side of the road. 'When I'm on leave, that's our local.'

The bus stopped at the corner Gordon Road and Stokes Road. After a five-minute walk they turned into Richmond Road, a wide thoroughfare consisting of rows of red bricked terraced houses.

'Here we are, mate,' said Johnson, stopping outsider number twenty. 'Home sweet home,' he added, glancing nostalgically at the house. There was no garden, only a single step leading up to a pale-green, oak door, painted by Johnson a few months ago. In front of floral-patterned curtains, folds of dark, blackout curtains could be seen, gathered at each corner of the bottom bay window and two top windows. A thin trail of grey smoke eddied from a chimney stack, and like all the widows in the road, they were criss-crossed with white tape.

Johnson was about to press the doorbell when the door opened, revealing a medium sized woman with a round, pale, fleshy face and bright blue eyes. Her thick legs were bare and she wore a pair of fluffy brown slippers. Over a pink blouse and black skirt, a polka dotted apron was tied loosely around her ample waist.

'Well don't just stand there, Harry,' she said, showing a set of even, slightly tobacco-stained teeth, 'come and give me a hug.' Harry immediately threw his arms around her, and lifting her off her feet, gave her a huge bear hug, then kissed her hard on the lips. 'Put me down,' she cried, turning a deep shade of red, 'or you'll have the neighbours talking, so you will, and I take it this is your friend,' she added, looking at Paddy as Harry lowered her onto the step. Having been born and bred in Portsmouth, she spoke with a distinct Hampshire accent.

'This is Paddy O'Malley,' said Harry. 'And, needless to say, this is Ethel, my long-suffering wife. Do you think he could use Bert's old room?' he added tentatively.

'Of course,' Ethel replied, 'I'm sure Bert wouldn't have minded if...'

Paddy quickly interrupted her. 'I hope I'm not putting you to too much trouble?'

'Nonsense, Paddy,' Ethel answered, warmly shaking his hand. 'You're more than welcome.'

As they walked down a well-lit hallway, the peppery smell of cooking permeated the air.

'Hmm…' murmured Harry, sniffing the air. 'Don't tell me, love,' he said putting his arm around Ethel's waist and giving it a quick squeeze. 'Rabbit stew.'

The house, like those in the area, was a typical two-up, two-down with an upstairs bathroom. The walls of the small kitchen were whitewashed and the floor tiled in a deep red. In the middle a pristine white tablecloth covered a small table and two chairs. A few dishes lay stacked on a wooden drain board and one of two shiny brass taps dripped into a deep stone sink. In one corner, next to a cupboard, was a metal ice box and an assortment of cooking utensils hanging from a shelf. A kettle lay on an unlit gas stove above which an assortment of plates slotted into a metal rack. A door and two steps led onto a sloping backyard and a brick-built toilet with a flat slate roof.

Ethel opened a door, allowing Harry and Paddy to enter the parlour. The rays of the late afternoon sun, beaming through the window highlighted the patterns on the pastel-coloured wallpaper and sent dark shadows onto the low slung, cream coloured ceiling. A thick green carpet covered the floor. A coal fire crackled below a narrow marble mantelpiece on which rested a large clock, set in a shiny wooden frame. Above this was a large round mirror attached to two tiny silver chains hanging from the wall.

'Now, sit yourselves down and I'll be back in a minute,' said Ethel who, smiling warmly, hurried away.

Paddy slid off his gas mask and steel helmet off his shoulder and sat down into one of the two well-worn, brown leather armchairs. Harry followed suit and plonked himself down into the other armchair.

'Is that your son?' Paddy asked Harry, nodding towards a framed photograph of a young, fresh-faced lad in khaki, resting next to a few family portraits.

'Yes, that was our Bert,' Harry replied, taking out a packet of Woodbines and offering one to Paddy. 'He was with the BEF and he would have been twenty in a week's time,' he added, lighting both cigarettes with a match. (BEF refers to the British Expeditionary Force sent to France in 1940.)

'He was a fine looking, lad,' said Paddy, taking a deep drag of his cigarette.

'Aye,' Harry sighed as he flicked ash into a brass ash tray, 'we're very proud of him.'

Just then, Ethel came in holding three glasses and three bottles of Guinness and placed them on a nearby small, glass-topped table. 'I was just telling Paddy how proud we are of Bert,' said Harry.

Ethel didn't reply. Instead, she nodded and poured out the drinks. 'Harry tells me you've asked a friend of yours to come for a meal,' said Paddy, sensing the pain in Ethel's eyes. 'Er... what's she like?''

'You'll find out,' Ethel answered quietly, 'now finish your drink then you can both take your gear upstairs.'

At six o'clock Ethel switched on the wireless and they sat in the front room, smoking while listening intently to the sonorous voice of Alvar Lidell on the BBC, announcing more shipping losses in the Atlantic and the shortage of food on Malta.

'Those poor Maltese,' Ethel said, with a sigh, 'they must all be starving.'

'They won't be if our convoys manage to get through,' said Harry, exhaling a steady stream of tobacco.

A few minutes later the doorbell rang. 'That'll be Joyce,' said Ethel. She quickly stubbed out her cigarette in an ash tray and left the room.

'Have you met her, Harry?' Paddy asked, feeling slightly nervous.

With a mischievous glint in his eye, Harry replied, 'Yes, I do, and believe me, she's a corker.'

Muffled female voices could be heard coming from the hallway. The sounds suddenly became louder when the front room door was opened. Harry and Paddy stood up as Ethel and Joyce came in. 'This is my good friend, Joyce,' Ethel said to Paddy.

Harry was right. Joyce really was a corker. A few yards away stood a tallish woman who Paddy judged to be in her late thirties. She had an attractive, oval-shaped face and short blonde hair and carried a small black handbag. Under an open, knee-length, brown coat she wore a fawn sweater and a white, open-necked blouse.

'Nice to meet you, Paddy, isn't it?' She asked, shaking hands. She spoke with a broad Hampshire accent. In doing so, the corners of her pale blue eyes wrinkled into a warm smile.

'And you,' Paddy replied, feeling how soft her hand was in his.

Harry and Ethel gave each other a surreptitious glance, sensing the immediate attraction between Joyce and Paddy.

'Come on, m'dear,' Ethel said, 'let me take your coat. Supper will ready shortly.'

After a few drinks they went into the kitchen and sat down. The atmosphere, as they enjoyed Ethel's steak and kidney pie, was warm and friendly. Joyce told Paddy about Jack, her husband. 'The Red Cross told me he is in some concentration camp,' she said, dabbing her mouth with a serviette, 'somewhere in Germany. Sadly, we had no children. Ethel's told me your wife passed away and you have a twelve-year-old son.'

'Yes.' Paddy took a deep gulp of beer then said, 'Patrick's a fine boy, so he is. Unfortunately, I haven't seen him for some time, but in his letters, he tells me he's doing well at school.'

Just before nine o'clock they finished their meal, and carrying cups of tea, returned to the front room. Before entering, Ethel drew the blackout curtains. Harry then switched on the light then the wireless. For the next half an hour they then sat down and laughed while listening to Tommy Handley's jokes on *ITMA*. (It's That Man Again.)

A few minutes after ten o'clock, Joyce glanced apprehensively at the mantelpiece clock and said to Ethel, 'I'd like to stay and help you wash up, love, but I'd best be off, just in case there's an air raid.'

Before Ethel had a chance to reply, Paddy stood up and said eagerly, 'And I'll be walking you home, just in case, like.'

'Thank you, Paddy,' Joyce replied, smiling, 'that's very nice of you.'

Ethel left the room and returned holding Joyce's coat. 'Thank you for a lovely evening, Ethel,' Joyce said as Paddy helped her on with her coat, 'I've really enjoyed myself.'

'And you'd better take this,' said Harry, handing Paddy a small Yale key. 'In case we're in bed when you come back,' he added with a sly grin.

Outside the house, the rays of a full moon were partially obliterated by grey clouds. The curtains of the houses were drawn and the road was quiet and deserted.

'I expect you miss your husband,' said Paddy as they walked down the road. 'How long were you married?'

'Ten years,' Joyce replied, turning up the collar of her coat to guard against the chilly westerly breeze, 'and I know this may sound terrible, but I don't miss him. When he was home, he spent most of the time with his cronies in the White Hart. And besides…' She paused and glanced warily at Paddy, then added, 'He had a vicious temper.'

'You mean he hit you?' Paddy asked as they reached the top of the road.

'Yes,' Joyce muttered, nodding her head slightly.

'But why, was he jealous or something?'

'He had no cause for that,' Joyce answered calmly. 'He was always like that when he drank.'

'And when he was sober?' Paddy asked, as they turned down the next road.

'For the first few years, everything was all right. Then he started to drink heavily. I'm ashamed to say I was glad when he was called up. At least I didn't have to use makeup to cover the bruises on my face.'

They walked down the next street and stopped outside Ethel's terraced house. 'How any man could treat a woman like you, is beyond me, so it is.'

'Thank you, Paddy,' Joyce replied, opening her hand bag and bringing out a key. 'I've really enjoyed meeting you.'

'Maybe I can see you again?' Paddy asked, looking into her eyes.

'Yes, I'd like that,' she replied. 'Give me a ring. Gosport seven, two, one, four, can you remember that?'

'To be sure, it's ingrained in me mind, so it is,' Paddy answered smiling broadly.

'Then I'll say goodnight,' she said, then kissed him warmly on the cheek.

'I'm going on a few days leave to see my son,' said Paddy, 'but I'll ring you when I get back.'

'Don't forget,' she said, then opened the door, and with a parting smile, went inside.

After Paddy and Joyce had left, Ethel turned to Harry, and with an all-knowing grin, said, 'I think they've clicked, love.'

'I think you're right,' Harry replied. Then, after giving her a quick kiss on the lips, added, 'now, let's forget about the washing up and go to bed.'

CHAPTER FIVE

At 0700, on Friday 19th May, *Helix* left the dry dock and tied up alongside Fountian Lake Jetty. Lying aft of her were the two hunt-class destroyers, *Dulverton* and *Eridge.* "Colours" had just ended. The white ensign fluttered lazily from the stern and a chilly breeze blew downriver, while high above, a cluster of grey cirrocumulus clouds partially hid an anaemic sun.

Manley and Penrose stood on *Helix*'s quarterdeck. The portly figure of Duty PO Podge Hardman, and QM Leading Seaman Sammy Smith stood nearby talking quietly.

'There's no getting away from it,' Hardman remarked glancing warily at several clouds of black smoke hovering over the city. 'While we've been away, poor old Portsmouth has certainly taken a pounding.'

'Not 'arf,' Smith solemnly replied. 'According to the BBC, last night three ratings were killed and two frigates in the harbour were damaged. The city's Guildhall was set on fire with incendiaries and several houses in South Sea were destroyed.'

By 1942, Germany's "Blitz Kreig" (Lightning War), had swept through Europe. The Wehrmacht had occupied every country from Norway to the Pyrenees; Hitler had broken the Pact of Steel with Stalin and invaded Russia. The previous year, the Royal Navy had lost several capital warships including the *Prince of Wales, Repulse,* and the mighty *Hood.* Singapore had fallen and Rommel's Africa Corps threatened Egypt.

The losses during the Battle of the Atlantic reached its zenith when, between 1941 and 1942, two thousand, nine hundred and sixty-one tons of merchant shipping were sunk. In December 1941, the bombing of Pearl Harbour brought America into the war. This meant that Britain no longer stood alone against the Axis powers that now included Italy.

In late September, 1940, Hitler changed the tactics of the German Air Force. He ordered the Luftwaffe to switch from bombing airfields and concentrate on Britain's major cities. Hitler's decision to do this was in retaliation for the RAF bombing Berlin. It was to be a costly mistake as it enabled the RAF to increase their attacks on the incoming enemy bombers. This resulted in the RAF winning the Battle of Britain, that effectively ended Hitler's invasion plans. However, on 7 September 1940, the Blitz began. London was incessantly bombed; attacks on Liverpool, Coventry, Bristol and Plymouth quickly followed. On January 10th, 1941, Portsmouth was devastated along with Gosport and South Sea.

'Everyone back off leave, Number One?' Penrose asked, feeling the warmth of the coffee he had had recently drunk gradually filter through his insides. 'Everyone except Sub Lieutenant Baker, sir,' Manley replied. 'I believe he was travelling down from Merseyside, so I expect his train was late.'

At that moment OOD Sub Lieutenant Milton arrived. 'This telegram for you just arrived, sir, it's marked urgent,' he said, handing Penrose a buff-coloured envelope.

A look of concern immediately became etched on the captain's face. Telegrams were invariably harbingers of bad news. And so it proved to be. Penrose ripped open the envelope, and as he read its contents, a deep furrow creased his brow. 'Great Scott, Number One,' he gasped. 'It's from the chief constable of Wallasey, apparently, Baker's been arrested for grievous bodily harm. He's being sent back to us and will be required to return at a later date to face a civil court.'

'Good Lord, sir,' pondered Manley, slowly shaking his head. 'I wonder what happened.'

With an expression of shock in his eyes, Penrose looked at Manley, and in a hoarse voice, said, 'We'll soon know, an official letter is being sent to me.'

Sub Lieutenant Milton, who had remained nearby, gave a strained cough. 'There's something else, sir,' he said. 'A signal arrived from the Movements Office in barracks. Captain Carter wants to see you in his office at 1400. The signal was repeated to the commanding officers of *Eridge* and *Dulverton*.'

'With a weary sigh, Penrose, looked at Baker and said, 'That's all I need. Let me know when Baker arrives, I'll be in my cabin.' He turned away and went through an open hatchway into the citadel.

Thanks mainly to Hardman and Smith, during "stand easy", the news of Lieutenant Baker arrest quickly spread around the ship. In the senior ratings mess, Chief Bosun's Mate, Charlie Jackson, took a good swig of tea, then, looking at Chief Coxswain Barnes, a small, sticky man with a shock of grey hair, said, 'GBH is pretty serious, isn't that right, Digger?'

'It certainly is,' Digger replied in a thick, Yorkshire accent. 'I wonder what happened.'

'I'll bet you a pound to a penny some bloody female is involved,' interrupted Chief GI Bob Shilling, a tall, dark haired man with a ram-rod stance. He and the Chief Coxswain were the ship's "policemen" and responsible for discipline. 'He could be for the high jump when he returns,' Shilling went on as he finished his drink.

'You mean a court-martial and dismissed from the ship,' chimed in Len Mills.

'Wouldn't surprise me in the least,' Shilling grunted and left the mess.

'I bet he caught his missus in bed with a Yank,' Dutch Holland said to Shiner Bamford. He and several other junior ratings were in the mess, smoking and drinking tea.

'Don't be daft, Doc,' Tansey Lee replied. 'I overhead him telling Lieutenant Millton he had some party at home, so he can't be married.'

'GBH, eh,' Bud Abbot remarked while stubbing out a dog-end in a tin lid. 'Sub Lieutenant Baker doesn't strike me as being someone who would fill anyone in, so he must have had a good reason.'

In the wardroom, the reaction to Baker's plight was more sanguine. 'Most unusual,' remarked Jock Jewitt, after taking a sip of tea. 'Probably had too much to drink and got into some sort of argument, what do you think, Derek?'

Remembering Baker's demeanour when he received a letter from home, Lieutenant Logan, gave Jewitt a cautious look, and said, 'In my opinion, there's a little more to it than that.'

Shortly before 1345, Penrose left the ship, climbed into a tilly and left the dockyard.

Two hours later, OOD, Lieutenant Milton and Manley were pacing around the quarterdeck. Manley had been in his cabin, finishing a letter to his parents. After glancing at his wristwatch he quickly left his cabin, and like Milton, was anxiously awaiting the return of the captain.

'He should have been here by now, its1530, Manley said, glancing furtively at his wristwatch. 'The meeting must be very important to have taken this long.'

'Yes, I think you're right, sir,' Milton answered ruefully. 'I wonder what the old man's got cooked up for us.'

PO Podge Hardman overheard Milton's remark and gave QM Sammy Smith a suspicious glance. 'Mark my words, Smudge,' he said in a thick Yorkshire accent, 'I bet the next time we sail it'll be on one of those fuckin' Russian runs.'

'More than likely,' Smith sullenly replied, 'just think, two weeks ago we were freezing our bollocks off in the Atlantic, now, if it gets any warmer, we'll all get dhobi rash.'

No sooner had he spoken, than the ship's telephone, situated on the bulkhead near the main entrance into the ship, rang. Smith strolled over and unhooked the phone. 'HMS *Helix,* duty QM.' A few seconds later, he glanced at the first lieutenant and said, 'It's for you, sir.' He handed the receiver to Manley.

'Lieutenant Commander Manley,' he said, wondering who could be telephoning him.

'Hello, Hugh, you old devil, I bet you'll never guess who this is?' The voice, slightly posh and plummy, sounded vaguely familiar.

'If you're the manager of Gieves, the cheque is in the post,' Manley replied, frivolously.

'Gieves be damned,' the voice answered, 'this is FP, Basil Foster-Price, if you remember we were at Oxford.'

'Err… of course I do,' Manley answered, remembering a tall, fair haired young man with beady brown eyes and a propensity for drinking too much.

'As I recall, you gained your two-two in geography and graduated a year before me then joined the navy,' FP replied. A year later, I managed a first in history, and despite Papa wanting me to be a civil servant, I joined the dear old Andrew.'

Manley suddenly recalled that he and FP were never close friends. He always considered him to be arrogant and too aware of his privileged background. The smug bugger, Manley thought, trust him to mention of the difference in their respective degrees. Manley smiled ruefully, remembering that "Papa", was Lord Harold Foster-Price, chairman of a large business conglomerate in "The City", who had amassed great wealth dealing in stocks and shares. Along with Prudence, his wife, they lived in an elegant Victorian mansion set in acres of lush countryside, a few miles outside Winchester. When introduced to company, Basil always insisted on being referred to as "The Right Honourable" Basil Foster-Pike, especially if the company included a pretty girl. As Basil was an only child, on the demise of his father, he would inherit the family title and fortune.

'What on earth are you doing in Portsmouth?' Manley asked, feeling as if the eyes of the OOD and the duty watch were watching and listening.

'At present, I'm attached to the movements office in barracks,' FP replied smugly. 'That's how I knew *Helix* had returned from the Atlantic and been in dry dock for repairs.'

'But how did you know I was on board?'

'Simple, dear boy,' FP replied, 'your name and all officers in HM ships are on secret lists to which I am privy.'

'I see,' Manley answered slowly, 'so what can I do for you?'

'Well, as it's my birthday today, I thought I could entice you to the mess for a few drinks and also catch up on things,' said FP, adding quickly, 'that is, if you can spare the time.'

With his free hand, Manley cautiously stroked his chin. 'At present we are replenishing stores, but I think I could come, what time do you suggest?'

'2230, old boy,' FP responded with a throaty laugh. 'Meet you in the wardroom bar, cheerio for now.' He put the receiver down.

Manley replaced the receiver, and for a moment, stood wondering if he had made the right decision, after all, he and FP had little in common and came from vastly different backgrounds.

The sharp voice of Sub Lieutenant Milton, interrupted his thoughts. 'Are you all right, sir,' he said. 'You look a little perplexed. Don't tell me she's ditched you?' he added with a playful grin.

'Nothing like that, Ray,' Manley replied tentatively, 'just an old acquaintance from college.

As Manley finished speaking, Able Seaman Sammy Smith, the duty QM, piped, 'Secure. Duty watch fall in outside the coxswain's office. Leave. Leave to the first and second part of Starboard and first part of port watch from 0400to0600.' No sooner had he done so than a tilly stopped at the bottom of the brow. The passenger door drew open, allowing Penrose to climb out.

Using his silver bosun's call, Smith bent close to the tannoy and piped, 'Attention on the upper deck. Captain coming on board.'

'Man the side,' Manley ordered. Straight away, Manley, Milton and Hardman formed a line at the top of the brow.

With agility betraying his thirty-four years, Penrose strove up the gangway. 'Morning everyone,' he snapped, returning the salutes of both officers and PO Hardman. His Devonian accent was clear and resonant. 'Ammunitioning all in hand, Number One?' As he spoke, he bayoneted Manley with a pair of intense pale blue eyes that seemed to look through the recipient.

'Yes, sir,' replied Manley. 'The chief bosun and the duty watch will rig up hoist on the starboard waist and the first and second part of port watch will muster there at twelve forty-five. Err… How was the meeting, sir?' He ventured nervously.

'Very interesting,' Penrose replied cagily. 'Report to me in my cabin in ten minutes and all will be revealed.' He then turned away, and after unhooking the clips on a hatchway, disappeared into the citadel.

'I wonder what's in the air, sir,' Milton pondered, furrowing his brow.

'Your guess is as good as mine,' Manley answered, 'but I think we'll soon find out.'

Penrose's cabin was situated directly below the bridge. Manley knocked on the door, removed his cap and was told to enter. Manley had been here before and was always struck by how sparsely furnished the room was. The deck was covered in brown, shiny cortisone and the bulkheads were painted a pleasant light green. A solitary shaded electric light hung from the middle of low-slung deck head, studded with electric wiring and pipes. A side door led into a cramped but adequately fitted galley.

Penrose was sat behind a wide mahogany desk on which rested a telephone and a small stack of fawn-coloured files. On the bulkhead behind his desk was framed photograph of King George V and Queen Elizabeth and a coloured map of the world.

'Ah, Number One,' said Penrose, 'come in and sit down.' He indicated to an uncomfortable looking hard-backed wooden chair. 'And I'd be grateful if you didn't smoke. These damn punkah louvres,' he went on, glancing warily up at the overhead trunking, 'are not very efficient. I must have a word with the engineer officer about them.' (Punkah louvres are adjustable openings fitted to the ventilation fan trunking and can provide different angles of air flow.)

Manley sat down, crossed legs and waited. Penrose sat forward and placed both hands palm down on the desk, noticing the curious expression on Manley's handsome features.

'I expect you're wondering why I've asked to see you,' he said, 'so I'll come straight to the point. As I'm sure you've heard the war in North Africa and the Med isn't going very well. Tobruck has been under constant siege since December last year and Malta is dangerously short of food and oil to work her water pumps.'

'Yes, sir,' Manley replied. 'This morning the BBC reported that Malta was considered to be the most bombed place on earth.'

'I'm not at all surprised to hear it,' reiterated Penrose, sitting back in his chair. 'And if Hitler does capture Malta, and Tobruk falls, convoys from Italy and Crete can keep his Afrika korps supplied with material. Rommel will then be able to take Egypt and cut off our oil supplies from Iran.'

'Surely our ships stationed at Alexandria can intercept convoys coming from Italy,' said Manley.

'Admiral Cunningham has ordered them to do so, and bombard the Germans from the sea, but he is short of ships, especially as he has to protect convoys to Malta.'

'Yes, I see,' Manley answered warily, 'but I believe Tobruk is well garrisoned by the Aussies, Poles the Free French and ourselves.'

'It was until two weeks ago, while we were at sea,' Penrose sighed. 'Winston ordered most of the Western Desert Group to leave the Tobruk area and sail to Greece to reinforce the Greek Army against the German invasion, leaving Tobruk under General O'Connor.'

'That was a bit rash, wasn't it?'

'Yes indeed,' said Penrose, slightly shaking his head, 'but apparently we have a treaty with Greece that states we will come to her aid if invaded by an enemy.'

'Just how far away is Rommel from Tobruk, sir?' Manley asked.

Penrose stood up and faced the map. 'The signal says his tanks and infantry are at Derna, about a hundred land miles from Tobruk,' Penrose said, indicating a spot on the Libyan coast. 'And as the vast expanse of the Quattara Depression lies to the south, here,' he added. 'Rommel can only be supplied from the sea. As you know, Tobruk is the only deep sea port on the coast that can accommodate large ships, other than Benghazi, which is too far away west on the Gulf of Sirte, so the blighter has to take Tobruk to continue his invasion of Egypt.'

'Does the signal say when Rommel is expected to attack Tobruk, sir?'

'Yes indeed,' Penrose replied as he sat down. 'After consolidating his position in Derna, he attacked Tobruk last month.'

'So Tobruk must be held and supplied by sea,' Manley replied, realising why Penrose had sent for him.

'Correct,' replied Penrose. 'Unfortunately *Dainty, Grimsby* and supply ships were sunk off the coast of Tobruk early last month. This has left the inshore squadron, ferrying urgently needed stores from Alexandria to Tobruk, somewhat short.'

'I see,' Manley answered warily, 'and how many ships are in the inshore squadron, sir?' Manley asked uncrossing his legs.

'Not many,' replied Penrose, 'four Australian destroyers, the gunboats, *Gnat, Ladybird,* and *Diamond.* This is the tenth destroyer squadron under the command of Commodore Walter.'

'So where does that leave *Helix* and the other two Hunts, sir?' enquired Manley, uncrossing his legs while looking expectantly at the captain.

'That's what the meeting between myself and the other two captains was about. As senior officer, earlier today I received a top-secret signal from Captain Nick Carter, head of movements section in barracks.'

Penrose's mention of the words "top secret" immediately made Manley feel uneasy. A few seconds later, the galley door opened and in came Steward Morris, carrying two mugs of steaming hot tea. 'Thought youse could do with a cuppa, ser,' said Morris.

'Err… Thank you,' said Penrose, 'just leave them on my desk, then close the door and make sure we're not disturbed.'

By this time Manley was more than anxious to hear what Penrose would say. Doing his best to calm his nerves, he reached across the desk, picked up a mug and carefully took a good sip of tea.

Ignoring his drink, Penrose sat forward and took out a folded sheet of paper from his inside jacket pocket, opened it and placed it before him. In a quiet, concerned voice he read, 'On Monday, 13th May, a convoy of four merchant ships together with five hunt-class destroyers and the cruiser *Carlisle,* will leave Liverpool. At 0800 the next day, *Helix, Dulverton,* and *Eridge* are to sail from Portsmouth and rendezvous with the convoy at latitude forty nine degrees south, longitude seven degrees north. Captain Neame in *Carlisle* will be in command.'

Penrose stopped reading and folded the paper, then took a deep, thirst-quenching gulp of tea, and sat back in his chair.

'And our destination, sir?' Manley asked, leaning forward, an eager expression on his face.

'Gibraltar,' Penrose replied. 'We take on extra fuel then then proceed into the Med and rendezvous with Admiral Vian's 15th Cruiser Squadron at latitude thirty-five, longitude ten. That's approximately a thousand miles east of Sicily. Then continue to Malta. As Tobruk is in urgent need of ammunition and food, I expect *Helix* and others will be needed to supply the army. In that case, I expect *Carlisle* to accompany the three Hunts and work with the inshore squadron. At the moment the details haven't been worked out, but you will be sent these in due course. Top-secret, of course. Any questions?'

'Yes sir, about the convoy?' Asked Manley, giving Penrose a questioning look. 'It seems a very large escort for four merchant ships.'

'I agree,' replied Penrose, 'but there it is. Now, is there anything else?' he added, sitting forward, and placing both hands flat on his desk.

'May I ask what you intend to do about Sub Lieutenant Baker?'

'At the moment, I'm not sure,' Penrose answered, 'I'll wait until the letter from the chief constable arrives and also hear what Baker has to say.'

'Can we send those men who are due their ten days on leave, sir?' asked Manley.

'Yes, when we've finished storing and ammunitioning,' Penrose replied. 'That's when I'll be taking four days leave, and I suggest you take five when I return.'

'Incidentally, sir,' said Manley, slowly uncrossing his legs, 'I'll be going ashore at 2000to see an old friend in the barracks wardroom, I'll be back about 2300.'

With a sly grin, Penrose stood up and said, 'Relatively sober, I hope.' He added, 'I'll meet all officers in the wardroom tomorrow at 0900 to put them in the picture, and please tell the officer of the day to let me know when Baker arrives.'

CHAPTER SIX

Shortly before 2015, Manley left his cabin and made his way to the quarterdeck. Here, he was met by officer of the day, Jewitt, who had earlier relived Milton. Close by stood Nutty Slack, a small, thickset petty officer and the stout figure of duty quartermaster Able Seaman Dinga Bell. Each man carried a steel helmet hooked over a khaki canvas satchel, containing a gas mask.

'Good evening, Jock,' Manley said, returning their salutes. 'All quiet?'

'Yes, sir,' Jewitt answered, 'I don't think Jerry will pay us visit tonight.' 'He glanced cautiously up at the mass of low lying, densely black cumulonimbus clouds, blotting out the weak rays of the full moon. 'Visibility too poor for the buggers.'

'I hope you're right,' Manley answered, then walked down the gangway, slid open the passenger door of a tilly and climbed inside.

The journey through the dockyard and up Queens Street to the barrack wardroom took ten minutes. This large, imposing red-bricked, Edwardian building lay opposite the main gate of the naval barracks. Even though Manley had been here on several occasions, he was nevertheless, always impressed by the lavish Baroque façade, with its mullioned windows, multi-fluted chimneys, decorative cornices and ashlar centre bock, crowned by an iconic cupola and ship's finial.

'Thank you, driver,' Manley said, as he left the tilly. 'Please pick me up at 2300.'

'Very good, sir,' the driver replied in a thick Hampshire accent, 'I'm off duty in an hour, but I'll pass on the message at the garage.'

Manley unhinged a tall, wrought iron gate and walked up a wide gravelled path, up two flights of stone steps. Guarding the arched oaken door stood a tall, stocky matelot wearing a white belt and gaiters. Upon seeing Manley he snapped to attention and saluted. Manley immediately returned the salute and showed his pay book containing his photograph and details. 'Thank you, sir,' said the guard, opening the door.

A glittering glass chandelier hanging from a cream-coloured stuccoed ceiling, bathed the entrance hall in a clear white light. Directly ahead, a highly polished oaken staircase, carpeted in royal blue, led up to the officer's quarters. Obeying the words on a red sign resting on a small, highly polished table, he signed the visitors' book. Making sure his tie was in place, he walked past two naval lieutenants engrossed in a heated conversation with an attractive Wren officer. He then made his way across the shiny black and white marbled floor, down an oak-panelled corridor on which hung oil paintings of famous admirals and equally famous battles, and arrived at the wardroom door, above which was a frieze depicting galleons in full sail.

After passing the dining area, flanked on either side by oak-panelled wainscoting, on which hung paintings of the Glorious First of June, Copenhagen and Trafalgar, he arrived at the wardroom. From inside the room, which he knew from previous visits housed the bar, came the melodic sound of Vera Lynn singing the nostalgic strains of *White Cliffs of Dover*. He removed his greatcoat, cap, gas mask and steel helmet and hung them up on a hook, alongside a row of other service accoutrements, and opened the door.

The spacious room, warm and smoky, was decorated in pale green. Several more paintings of naval battles hung on the walls and royal blue carpeting, studded with tiny gold anchors covered the floor. From a ceiling, identical to that in the dining room, three electric lights surrounded by round yellow lampshades provided perfect lighting. Several brown leather armchairs and mahogany tables were occupied by officers and their female guests.

Manley immediately saw the tall, fair-haired figure of FP. FP and three officers, all of whom were from the other two hunt-class destroyers. They were stood in front of the bar, engaging a third officer Wren in animated conversation. Manley inwardly smiled, thinking FP hadn't changed much since there university days — still using his forceful personality to impress the girls.

It was only when one of the officers moved away that Manley was able to obtain a clearer view of a third officer Wren. Manley guessed she was in her early twenties. She stood about five feet three, and even though she had her back to him, he could see that her uniform failed to hide the slight seductive curve of her buttocks and trim waist. Her auburn hair, worn as a chignon, was half hidden under her blue tricorn cap. She held an empty glass in her left hand while the other hand rested on her black leather service shoulder bag. Upon seeing her glass, FP turned and asked a white-coated steward behind the bar for a refill. In doing so, he saw Manley looking directly at him.

'Hugh, old boy,' cried Manley, pushing his way forward, 'so good to see you. Do come and join us, Horse's Neck?' As he spoke Manley noticed FPs beady brown eyes creasing into welcoming smile.

'Sorry to be a bit late, FP,' Manley replied as they shook hands, 'but tell me, FP, what the devil have you been doing since you left uni?'

'Like you, I joined the navy,' FP answered, 'against my father's wishes, he wanted me to go into politics. After obtaining my commission as a lieutenant, I served on a minesweeper.' He paused and took a good gulp of his drink. 'Then a year as a deck officer on board HMS *Duncan*, after which I took a gunnery course at Whale Island then was appointed to *Glasgow* as assistant gunnery officer. On the way back from Mumansk, I slipped on the deck and suffered concussion and was admitted to Haslar. And when I was discharged, I was given a desk job on Captain Storey's staff in the movements office. It's as boring as hell, so I'm going to put in for a seagoing job.'

'Good Lord,' Manley replied, 'you have been busy.'

'Just like you,' FP answered, slapping Manley playfully on the back, 'now, come and join the happy throng.'

While FP was ordering the drinks, the Wren suddenly turned and saw Manley staring directly at her. For a few seconds Manley took in her pear-shaped face; high cheek bones, straight nose and beguiling, violet eyes that held his gaze. Then, with half a smile playing around her full lips, she quickly looked away.

'*My God*,' Manley thought, feeling slight tingle of excitement run through him. '*She's absolutely lovely, no wonder those blighters are all over her.*'

'Come on, Hugh,' FP said, handing Manley his Horse's Neck. 'Let me introduce you to Laura, Captain Carter's gorgeous secretary,' he added, grinning at the four officers standing close to Laura. 'I suspect they're all hoping to get her knickers off.'

Laura overheard FP's sarcastic remark and turned around.

'Don't be crude, FP,' she said, accepting her drink, while looking past him at Manley, 'and introduce me to your handsome friend.' Her West Country accent was distinct and clear, and as she spoke, her captivating eyes creased into a wistful smile.

'This, my darling, is Hugh Manley,' said FP somewhat haughtily. 'We were at Oxford together, now he's the first lieutenant of His Majesty's ship, *Helix.*'

'Laura Trevethick,' she answered, extending her right hand, 'how very nice to meet you.'

'And you also,' Manley answered, feeling the soft warmth of her palm in his. As he smiled, Laura couldn't help but notice the dimple appearing in his chin that added to his heavily tanned, good looks. For a few seconds they looked at each other, before releasing hands.

'Trevethick, that sounds Devonian,' Manley remarked.

'*Cornish,* if you don't mind,' Laura answered frowning slightly.

'I do beg your pardon,' Manley pleaded. Then, with a smile, said, 'Tell me, how long have you been Captain Carter's secretary?'

'Just a month,' Laura answered, while refusing a cigarette from one of the officers, all of whom were becoming increasing annoyed at the way Laura was suddenly ignoring them. 'There are two of us,' she added, 'Susan and I work twelve-hour shifts.'

'And a jolly good job they do,' interrupted FP. 'Now let me introduce you to her admirers,' he added, grinning at the other officers.

'No need, we've met before we sailed on convoy duty,' Manley replied. 'Nice to meet you again, gentlemen,' he added, shaking their hands.

'Good to see you again, Hugh,' said one of them, a tall, dark haired lieutenant commander, 'it seems we might be returning their sooner than we think.'

'You could be right, Geoffrey,' Manley replied. As he spoke, he noticed Laura discretely remove FPs arm from arounds her waist.

'Do you mind, sir,' Laura said, 'you're spilling my G and T.'

'Sorry about that,' FP replied. Then, in an effort to cover his embarrassment, he grinned sheepishly then added, 'Come on you lot, drink up, the next round's on me.'

Just then, from behind the bar came the soothing sound of a record playing Glen Miller's *Moonlight Serenade.* As if programmed, several officers stood up and moved chairs and tables back. In a matter of minutes, the space was filled by couples dancing to the steady beat of the music.

'Come along, old girl,' FP said, taking hold of Laura's hand, 'let's trip the light fantastic.'

With a bored sigh Laura replied, 'If we must.' She handed her half-full glass to Manley and with a wistful look in her eyes, said, 'Be kind enough to hold this for me, I'll be back shortly to claim it.'

'Of course,' Manley answered, 'providing I can have the next dance.' Laura didn't reply. Instead, as FP lead her away, she turned and gave him a quick coquettish smile.

'You know, I think she rather fancies you, old boy,' Geoffrey remarked. 'What do you think, chaps?' he added, grinning at the other officers.

'Lucky bounder,' replied a tall sub lieutenant with an envious sigh, 'I wish it were me.'

'Not on your pay, David,' said a small, bleary-eyed lieutenant, 'I hear her family are well-to-do and live somewhere in Devon.'

'I wouldn't let that put me off,' said a stocky lieutenant with brown curly hair and tired looking brown eyes. 'You know what they say, "the Lord helps them that helps themselves".'

'Oh, don't be an ass, Harry,' said Geoffrey, toying with his empty glass. 'I do believe it's your shout.'

While only half listening to their facetious banter, Manley was watching FP and Laura. The dance area was crowded but he noticed Laura moved her head away whenever FP tried to place his cheek against hers. Manley gave a gratuitous smile as he saw Laura quickly remove FPs hand as it slowly slid from her waist onto her shapely backside. A few minutes later the tempo quickened to the rhythmic beat of *Chattanooga Choo Choo,* at which point, FP and Laura returned.

'Damn jitterbug music,' gasped FP, moping his sweaty face with a handkerchief. 'Bloody uncivilised, if you ask me.'

'Don't be such a bore, FP,' said Laura, who, despite her efforts on the dance floor, looked amazingly cool. 'Now that the Americans are in the war,' she added, accepting her drink from Manley, 'you'll have to get used to it, what do you think, Hugh?'

With a sly grin playing around his mouth, Manley replied, 'I agree, and I'm sure the girls will appreciate their nylons as well as the music.' As he finished speaking the melodic strains of *At Last,* filtered into the air.

'Our dance, I believe, Hugh,' said Laura, handing her empty glass to FP, 'or is it too fast?'

'If you insist,' Manley answered, downing his drink then placing the glass on the bar. 'But Fred Astaire, I'm not.'

Laura took his hand and seconds later their bodies were pressed together while moving to the slow tempo of a foxtrot. In doing so Laura could smell the faint aroma of his aftershave and feel the warmth of his cheek against hers.

As they moved around the floor, Manley became aware of the softness of her body pressing against his, and felt his penis stiffen. He immediately attempted to move away from her. However, Laura grasped his waist, looked up and smiled coyly. 'Don't be a spoil sport, Hugh,' she said, seeing a look of embarrassment on Manley's face. 'I bet that doesn't happen to Fred when he dances with Ginger.'

Taken aback by Laura's suggestive remark Manley was very relieved to feel his erection subside. 'I, er… whereabouts in Cornwall are you from?' Manley asked, feeling a trickle of warm sweat run down the side of his face.

'Helston,' Laura answered, 'my father is a retired major and local JP.

'And your mother?'

'She caught flu during that terrible epidemic in 1920, and died,' said Laura, 'I was two at the time, Father never married again…' Her voice trailed away.

'I'm sorry,' Manley replied. 'Any boyfriends?'

'Yes, there was one, now stop fishing,' she replied, squeezing his sweaty palm. 'And what about you, I'm sure there must be a pretty girl somewhere.'

Manley was about to reply when the music ended. As they turned to join FP and others, she looked up at him, and lowering her voice, said, 'If you get time, phone me at the barracks at extension four five. If I'm off duty, leave a message or call again.'

'You two looked as if you were enjoying yourselves,' FP said, handing Laura a large gin and tonic. 'My turn again?'

'I'm afraid not,' said Laura, dabbing her face with a small, lace handkerchief, while glancing at her wrist-watch. 'It's nearly 2200and I'm tired, so I'll have to love you and leave you.'

'I don't suppose I could come and tuck you in?' burbled FP, leaning against the bar and leering lecherously at Laura.

Making light of his suggestive remark, Laura threw back her head and gave a solid laugh. 'I don't think you'd make it up the stairs, goodnight gentlemen,' she added, 'I've enjoyed myself immensely.' As she spoke her eyes lingered slightly longer on Manley. Flashing him a coquettish smile, she turned and left the room.

'Now that's what I call real good looking popsie!' exclaimed one of the officers, lighting a cigarette, 'you really are a lucky bounder, Manley.'

'Yes, he certainly is,' FP replied with more than a hint of jealousy, 'now drink up' he added, waving his empty glass in the air, 'the night is young.'

For the next half hour, the drinks flowed freely. Red-faced and sweating profusely, FP proceeded to bore his guest by reminiscing about university days and past friends. He didn't notice one of the officers give a sly wink to the others, and nod his head slightly towards the door.

'You'll have to excuse us, FP,' said Geoffrey, placing his empty glass on the bar, 'but we've all got a busy day ahead of us tomorrow.'

'Storing ship, and all that,' added Henry, 'isn't that right, David, Harry?'

'Yes indeed,' Harry replied, 'and I'm duty officer in the morning.'

'So, cheerio, FP, and from all of us, a very happy birthday,' said Geoffrey, as he and the others took it in turns to shake FP's hand.

A glance at his wristwatch showed Manley it was2030. Remembering his transport back to the ship was at 2300, he wondered how he too could diplomatically extract himself away.

No sooner had the four officers left than FP downed his drink and said, 'I wonder what happened to old Binky Brown, do you know, he still owes me a fiver.' By this time FP was slurring his words and his shouting was attracting the attention of the other officers and their guests.

'I'm afraid he'll never pay you back,' Manley answered solemnly.

'Why is that, old boy?' FP asked, swaying slightly while holding his glass in one hand, and a lighted cigarette in the other one.

'He joined the army and was killed at Dunkirk,' Manley answered solemnly, 'along with Johnny Jackson, who I believe, was in your year.'

'Damn, bad show,' slurred FP. 'I liked old Johnny, even though he once stole a popsie I had my eye on. Let's have another Horse's Neck,' he added, 'and give a toast old Johnny.' As he finished talking, he stumbled forward and dropped his glass on the floor which shattered into several pieces.

'Come on, old boy,' said Manley, taking hold of FP's arm. 'I think you've had enough, and besides, I too have to be on duty early tomorrow.'

'Just one for the road, old boy,' FP insisted, stumbling against Manley.

'If you have any more to drink you'll fall onto the road,' Manley replied.

Manley placed his arm around FPs waist and under the gaze of an amused audience, gently ushered FP out of the room. After making their way along the corridor they arrived at the entrance hall. Ignoring the grins of two officers, they reached the lift.

'Which floor are you one, FP?' Manley asked as he drew back the gated entrance.

'Two, cabin six, key's in my left jacket pocket,' FP muttered, 'and do hurry, old boy, as I think I'm going to be sick.'

A few minutes later they arrived outside FP's cabin door. Manley found the key and opened the door in time for FP to stagger inside the darkened room and disappear into the bathroom. Making sure the blackout curtains were drawn across the small window, Manley switched on the lights.

'Are you all right?' he shouted, looking into the bathroom and seeing FP kneeling in front of the toilet, vomiting violently.

'I am now,' groaned FP, resting his sweaty head on the toilet brim. 'Help me up will you?'

Ten minutes later Manley managed to remove most of FP's clothes and help him into a small bed.

'Sorry to be such an ass, old boy,' mumbled FP, before he fell asleep.

Manley left the light on and quietly left the room. The time was 2345. He hurried down the corridor and took the lift to the ground floor. A few minutes later climbed into the tilly and returned to *Helix*. It was only when he was safely ensconced in his bunk that he remembered Laura asking him to telephone her and felt his penis stiffening again.

CHAPTER SEVEN

By 0845 the next morning, under the supervision of PO Steward Sandy Powel, his stewards had cleared away the breakfast accoutrements in the wardroom, leaving the long oak table shiny and bare. Powel, a tall, pasty-faced man with deep set, dark eyes, was in charge of the ship's first aid team. The rest of his team, included Leading Writer Jack Jones, a small, thin, ex-shipping clerk, Stores Assistant Terry Benson, a curly haired, well-built youth, who before the war, was brickie's labour, and Leading Steward Dick Turpin, a tall, muscular, six feet plus ex-scrum half for London Welsh.

The nervous anticipation that permeated the wardroom air was palpable. A few officers stood around, holding cups of tea, others sat in leather armchairs, reading newspapers or talking in subdued voices.

'I wonder what the old man wants,' Midshipman Morgan muttered to Electrical Officer Tim Sherwood, standing close by, sipping tea. 'My guess it's the Atlantic again. What do you think, sir?'

'You're probably right,' Sherwood replied. He finished his drink, and was about to place the cup and saucer on a table, when the door suddenly opened. All faces turned and watched as Penrose strode in followed by Manley. Those officers sat down immediately stood up. The remainder stopped whatever they were doing and waited pensively. Penrose stood in front of them, his hands firmly on his hips. Glancing at PO Powel, he said, 'Close the door and make sure we're not disturbed, PO, and if you hear anything, remember, it's top secret.'

'Very good, sir,' Powell answered, doing his best to hide a sly grin.

Penrose turned, and looking at the faces he had come to recognise as well as his own, said, 'Please relax and smoke if you must.' A few officers remained standing and lit up while others sat down and finished their tea. A few seconds later Penrose continued speaking. 'The reason I have asked to see you is as follows.' For the next twenty minutes he explained the details of their next mission. He then paused and said, 'Any questions so far?'

Gunnery Officer Lieutenant Ted Powers raised a hand, and asked, 'What's the latest news from Tobruk, sir?' Powers was a twenty-three-year-old, RNVR officer, whose pale features and clear blue eyes gave him a perpetually youthful look.

'Good question, Guns,' Penrose replied. 'Reports from Ultra say British, and Australian forces, in conjunction with the Free French and South African and Polish brigades, are defending the Gazala Line, just outside Tobruk. If that is breached, then your guess is as good as mine.'

'You mean Rommel will be able to take Tobruk, sir?' added Sub Lieutenant Jewitt, a tall, fair-haired, gangly RNR deck officer from Dundee.

'It would seem so,' Penrose answered calmly.

Engineer Lieutenant Derek Logan raised a hand. 'From what I've heard, Admiral Vian's 15th Squadron is pretty big, surely this is too big an escort for four merchant ships.'

'I agree with you, Derek,' said Penrose. 'It does seem rather odd.'

'Och, if you'll excuse my pessimism, sir,' added Lieutenant Jewitt, 'the whole thing seems like using a hammer to crack an egg.'

'And, as Vian's squadron has passed though the Straits, I bet the enemy spies across in Algeciras will have alerted every U-boat in the area,' added Sub Lieutenant Ray Milton, a small, broad-shouldered RNVR deck officer. 'As well as the Luftwaffe.'

'Quite so, gentlemen,' Penrose replied guardedly, 'so we'll have to be on our toes. Meanwhile, when storing ship is finished, officers not needed and the ship's company will be given seven days leave. Now I suggest we have some coffee.'

The news of leave was received with feelings of relief and the tension in the atmosphere suddenly disappeared. Conversation over coffee became more animated and louder than usual.

'Och, it's all right for the Sassenachs,' grunted Jock Jewitt, looking guardedly first at fellow Scott, Surgeon Lieutenant Latta, and then at Lieutenant Logan. 'It'll take us the best part of a day to get to Scotland, and another to get back. It hardly seems worthwhile going.'

'Talking about leave, I wonder when young Baker will be back,' said Lieutenant Logan.

'One thing's for sure,' Latta added, finishing his drink, 'the poor chap won't be going on leave again for some time.'

'Secure. Hands to tea. Shift into night clothing,' had just been piped at 1600, when a taxi arrived at the bottom of the ship's gangway and Lieutenant Baker climbed out. Over his uniform he wore a naval Burberry and carried a gas mask satchel and canvas holdall. For a few seconds he stood still, then glanced nervously up at OOD Sub Lieutenant Milton and PO Sharky Ward, waiting at the top of the brow. Baker took a deep, weary breath, and with a sinking feeling in the pit of his stomach, slowly walked up the gangway.

'Hello, David,' Milton said, returning Baker's salute. In doing so he noticed a dark bruise under Baker's left cheek. 'How are you?'

'Tired and pissed off,' Baker replied. 'I suppose the old man wants to see me?'

'Yes, he does,' said Milton, 'but first, I suggest you stow your gear and have a wash and brush up.'

Oblivious to the curious glances of the duty QM and a small working party, Baker made his way down a stairway to his cabin. On his way he met Manley. 'What the devil happened, David?' Manley asked. 'You look terrible. Where did you get that bruise on your face?'

'It's a long story, Number One,' Baker answered, carefully touching the side of his cheek. 'I'll tell you later when I've seen the captain. I expect he's none too pleased.'

'Yes, you could say that,' Manley replied with a wry smile.

'Any idea when we'll be sailing?' Baker asked.

'I'm sure he'll tell you when he sees you,' said Manley, 'now I'd better get along. Defaulters in half an hour.'

Ten minutes later, Baker, feeling his throat suddenly go dry, he knocked on the captain's door and was told to enter.

'And about bloody time, too,' grunted Penrose, looking up from behind his desk. Before him lay a buff-coloured letter. 'You look terrible,' Penrose added, noticing Baker's pale features and bruised cheekbone, 'I think you should sit down. Coffee?'

'Thank you, sir,' Baker replied and sat down in an armchair.

Penrose pressed a small red button his desk and a few five minutes later, Steward Morris, having listened to their conversation from behind the galley door, duly arrived, carrying two mugs of steaming hot coffee. He placed one on Penrose's desk and handed the other one to Baker.

'Kindly leave, Morris,' said Penrose. 'Close the door and make sure we're not disturbed.'

'Now,' said Penrose, 'I have received an official letter from Chief Constable Smithers of Wallasey, giving me the details of what happened, but I'd like to hear your version.'

Baker took a nervous sip of coffee, then, holding the mug, sat forward and began by telling Penrose about receiving Susan's "Dear John" letter. As he spoke, Penrose noticed the painful expression in Baker's eyes, and the slight catch in his voice. Raising a sympathetic hand, Penrose said, 'Now, take your time and try and relax.'

Baker took a good gulp of coffee then placed the mug on Penrose's desk and continued. 'I travelled to Wallasey and booked in at the Victoria Hotel in New Brighton, not far from the road where she lived. By that time, it was just after 1900. At first, I thought of confronting her. Instead, I went to the hotel bar. The place was half empty but I saw her and this chap sitting at a table, holding hands.' Baker stopped talking and feeling his hand shake, picked up the mug and finished his drink, then went on. 'When she saw me, she let go of his hand and asked me what I was doing here. I must have said something rude as the fellow she was with stood up. He was over six feet and well built. He pushed me in the chest and told me to bugger off. That was when I lost my temper and hit him on the nose. Blood poured down his face. He retaliated by punching me on the face, hence the bruise on my cheekbone. I remember hearing Susan and a few other women screaming. We grappled with one another. That was when we both fell on the floor and he hit his head.'

For a few seconds Baker stopped talking then staring at the desk, went on. 'The manager must have called the police as two constables arrived. The fellow, whose name I later learned was Geoffrey Wainwright, lay on the floor unconscious. I was taken away and spent the night in a cell. In the morning I was charged with inflicting grievous bodily harm and that a letter would be sent to you saying when I would be sent before the judge to be tried. He also said a solicitor would be appointed to defend me.'

'Did you see your young lady again?' Penrose asked.

With a tired sigh, Baker replied, 'No, sir, I didn't.'

'Were you in uniform?

'Yes, sir, I was,' Baker answered lowering his eyes.

'Hmm… pity,' said Penrose, sitting back and folding his arms. 'What you've told me fits in with what the letter says, except to say Mr Wainwright is in hospital, suffering from concussion, and the date for your trial is on Wednesday 10th June, that's in just over three weeks' time.'

'I see, sir,' Baker answered. With an air of contrition Baker added, 'I'm so sorry about that, sir, I suppose I'll have to face a court-martial also?'

'Not so fast,' Penrose said, leaning forward and placing both hands flat on his leather-bound blotting pad. 'You see, by that time we'll be at sea, and as you have carried out your duties with great competence, I intend that you will sail with us.'

'But how, sir?' Baker hastily replied, 'surely you'll be breaking the law?'

With a hint of a smile playing around his mouth, Penrose replied, 'Maybe so, but without going into go details, I'll point in my reply to the chief constable, the ship will be sailing soon and the contingencies of war must take priority over the law.'

'Thank you, sir,' Baker answered, 'I imagined I'd be dismissed from the ship, or worse.'

Penrose stood up, and noticing the relieved expression on Baker's face, said, 'Now, I suggest you report to the first lieutenant for duty.'

Shortly after 1700, Manley decided to telephone Laura and left the ship. From the quarterdeck, Duty PO Jack Frost and QM Jock Forbes, watched as Manley entered a telephone booth situated some distance along the cobbled jetty.

With a curious expression in his eyes, Frost glanced at Forbes, and said, 'I wonder why he didn't use the ship to shore line.'

'Phoning some party, I expect,' Forbes replied, 'and wanted a bit of privacy.'

'And a bit of the other,' Frost replied with a mischievous grin.

Inside, the telephone booth was warm and damp. Hoping Laura was off duty, Manley got through to barracks and asked for extension five. A few seconds later Laura answered. 'Third Officer Trevethic speaking, who is this?'

Manley immediately recognised her slight Cornish burr and smiled. 'It's Hugh Manley,' he replied. 'If you remember, you did ask me to phone you.'

'Hugh,' she cried, 'of course I remember. I was wondering when or if you would ring. How are you?'

'Fine,' he quickly replied, 'I could meet you this evening, if that's convenient'

'Yes,' Laura answered quickly, 'I'm off duty so I'll meet you, say, 1930 outside the dockyard. Look for a dark green MG. Will you be able to make it?'

'Yes, that'll be fine,' Manley answered. Just then, the pips went, followed by the tinkling sound of the pennies dropping intro the phone box, then the line went dead. Manley left the phone booth and walked jauntily along the jetty. 'Lovely evening, isn't it', he said, smiling as he returned the salutes of PO Frost and QM Forbes, before making his way his to his cabin.

'If you ask me, PO,' Forbes remarked, giving Frost a meaningful look. 'Our esteemed first lieutenant is on a promise.'

CHAPTER EIGHT

A little after 1915, Manley returned the salutes of the duty PO and QM, then walked down the gangway and made his way through the dock yard. A warm wind blew in from the Solent and the evening was dry and balmy.

It was still daylight and the masts of Nelson's flagship, HMS *Victory*, could be seen poking into the clear blue sky some distance away in her permanent dry dock. Returning the salutes of several ratings, he showed his pay book to a keen-eyed policeman and walked through the gate into Queen Street. Traffic was sparse. He stopped on the pavement, hoping to see a dark green MG. Upon seeing no sign of one, he gave an impatient sigh and looked around.

Away to his right, a row of stalls on The Hard, a wide road running parallel to the harbour front, sold pasties and mugs of tea to a crowd of sailors. On the opposite side, next to the Keppel's Head was Gieves, Naval Tailors, with its heavily taped windows was, despite the lateness of the hour, still open for business. Close by, lines of pale green double-decker buses waited to take eager sailors into the city centre and its environs. Further along a cobbled road led to the station and a covered slipway, leading onto the ferry terminus. Across the bay, the rooftops of houses and church spires of Gosport were silhouetted against the evening skyline; while lying in the dark green waters of the harbour, a row of four sleek destroyers lay serenely at anchor, dwarfed by the close proximity of an air craft carrier.

Manley's attention was drawn to the grating sound of a car pulling up close to the pavement. He quickly turned and saw Laura sitting behind the wheel of the MG. The four-seater was covered with a black hood with a long, shiny, green bonnet.

'Sorry if I'm late, Hugh,' she said, smiling. 'Better not stand there too long or people will think you're on guard duty,' she added. Keeping the engine running, she reached across and opened the small passenger door. She was in uniform and her auburn hair was tied in a bun under a smart, tricorn cap.

'Actually, you're spot on time,' Manley replied casually, glancing at his wristwatch before climbing in the car. 'It's lovely to see you again,' he added. As he sank into the soft leather seat, he noticed her skirt had slid up, showing a good length of two well-shaped thighs encased in black stockings. She was well aware of his gaze, and still smiling, replied, 'And you, Hugh. Now close the door and put your tin hat and gas mask on the back seat before your eyes drop out.'

'Nice car, is it yours?' Manley said noticing the oak-panelled dashboard, 'I like the smell of your perfume.'

'Chanel No 5 is courtesy of my friend, Susan,' she replied, flashing Manley a radiant smile. After glancing casually into her rear-view mirror, she gunned the engine, and a few seconds later, drove off.

Turning and noticing her slightly flushed, high cheek bones and aquiline nose, Manley asked, 'As a matter of interest, where are we going?'

'To a rather quaint old pub and restaurant some of the girls and myself once visited,' Laura replied, her eyes focused intently on the road.

'And whereabouts is this quaint old pub?'

'Havant,' Laura replied, 'as I recall it's on South Street, near the town centre.'

A wide grin spread across Manley's face. 'Tell me, do you always go around hijacking men?' he asked, sitting back in his seat.

'Only the good-looking ones with dimples in their chin,' Laura answered, coyly.

After heading south east, they left Portsmouth and drove onto the A27. The traffic was sparse and twenty minutes later they entered Havant, a small coastal town approximately half way between Portsmouth and Chichester. After driving through a busy town centre, Laura slowed the car and looked to her left and saw a narrow, cobbled street. 'Ah here it is,' she cried, seeing a long, two-storey Tudor style cottage, painted white. A small, black wooden overhanging jetty, lay attached to the outside of one of the four taped windows on the upper floor. On the grounds floor there were two bay-windows, complete with colourful box flowers. A gravelled path, flanked by beds of beautiful red and yellow roses, led from the pavement to an imposing arched oak door. Above this, hanging outwards from a metal strut, a sign, painted in bright gold old English, and waving slightly in the breeze, read, "Ye Old House At Home".

'My goodness!' Manley exclaimed. 'Compared with those modern bungalows close by, it looks positively Shakespearean.' He added ponderously, 'I wonder what the beer is like.'

'You'll soon find out,' Laura replied, driving down a gravelled lane into a spacious concrete car park behind the pub. 'I've booked a table for eight thirty. The time is now eight o'clock,' she added, glancing quickly at her wristwatch, 'that'll give us time for a quick drink.'

'You seem to have everything well organised,' Manley remarked, feeling slightly guilty. 'What would you have done if I'd said I couldn't see you?' he added with a grin.

'Shoot myself,' she replied, gunning the engine slightly. '

Laura stopped the car next to a shiny black Humber Super Snipe, applied the handbrake then switched off the engine. After giving her make-up a quick examination in the small car mirror, she picked up her shoulder bag and opened the door. Leaving his gas mask and helmet on the back seat, Manley climbed out of the car and hurried around the bonnet, then helped Laura out. In doing so, his eyes were once again drawn to her shapely legs and thighs.

'Thank you, kind sir,' said Laura, while grasping his hand, 'I'm glad to see the age of chivalry is still alive and kicking.'

'My pleasure,' Manley answered, slightly bowing his head.

'I don't know about you, Hugh,' she said, running a hand down the back of her skirt, 'but my pleasure would be a large G and T.'

As they entered the car park, Manley couldn't help but notice a few vintage cars. Among them was a bright red Ford convertible. 'Looks like the clientele are well healed,' Manley remarked. 'I only hope my bank balance can stand it.'

As they walked up the gravelled path to the entrance, Laura took hold of Manley's left hand. She gave it a gentle squeeze,, and glancing up at him, said, 'I'm so glad you phoned, Hugh, I really have been looking forward to seeing you again.'

'Me too,' Manley replied, returning her smile and feeling the comforting warm of her hand in his.

Manley pushed open the door and they were met by a tall, middle-aged woman with short, well-groomed, grey hair. Her clear-cut swarthy features, full lips and slightly turned up nose, suggested that, in her younger days, she had been quite a beauty. She wore a dark skirt and white, long-sleeved blouse, opened at the neck, around which hung a small emerald Star of David, attached to a delicate silver chain. A receptionist with an open book stood on the side of narrow, oak-panelled lobby.

'Good evening to you both,' she said, glancing approvingly at their uniforms while proffering her hand to Manley. 'I am Mrs Jacobs, the proprietor. 'The Royal Navy is always welcome here. Can I help you?' Her accent sounded foreign, and as she spoke, the corners of her pale blue eyes creased into a welcoming smile.

'Good evening,' Manley replied, gently shacking her hand. 'I believe we have a reservation for two in the name of Kent.'

'That's me,' interrupted Laura. 'I made the reservation.'

Mrs Jacobs turned around and after consulting the book on the desk, said, 'Ah, yes, Miss Kent, eight thirty. This way.' She led them down a narrow, oak-panelled lobby into a small bar and lounge. A thickly piled, green patterned carpet covered the floor. In one corner, a log fire burned brightly in a stone fireplace and from the centre of low-slung ceiling, supported by stout oak beams, hung a glittering electric chandelier. On the walls, embossed in yellow and green, hung beautifully framed paintings of sixteenth century sea battles, along with a rusting set of crossed cutlasses. An open door next to the bar led into a restaurant. Suddenly, the mouth-watering smell of cooking attacked their olfactory nerves. To this was added the pungent aroma of mansion polish tobacco and alcohol, all of which gave the place a warm and relaxing atmosphere.

A well-stocked bar rested in a corner. Nearby an Army officer and a pretty, dark-haired woman stood holding glasses. Next to them, sitting on padded stools, a young RAF flight lieutenant and a WAAF officer stood talking quietly while staring lovingly into each other's eyes. Close by, an elderly, grey haired gentleman in a brown tweed suit and a stout woman, wearing a yellow woollen dress, occupied one of three tables.

Both of them casually glanced up as Mrs Jacobs, Manley and Laura entered.

'Would you care for a drink at the bar before dinner?' asked Mr Jacobs, glancing at Manley. 'Or would you prefer to have one brought to you in the restaurant?'

'What do you think?' Manley asked Laura, feeling her hand creep into his.

'A large gin and tonic in the restaurant, please,' Laura answered, gently tickling the palm of his hand with a finger.

'As you wish,' Mrs Jacobs reverently replied.

The restaurant was quite small. Except for the floor which was covered in highly polished brown linoleum, the stout oak-beamed ceiling décor and lighting were similar to the lounge. There were three tables covered in red and white chequered tablecloths. One was occupied by men and women in civilian clothes, the other by an army officer and an attractive blonde. Only the army officer glanced up and smiled as Mr Jacobs showed Laura and Manley to the third table.

'I must say, Mr Jacobs,' Manley said, looking around as he held Laura's chair allowing her to sit down, 'I'm very impressed. How long have you owned it?'

'My husband, Arron, and my daughter, Helen, left Germany in 1938 as it was not safe,' said Mr Jacobs. 'With the valuables we managed to smuggle out, we bought the pub.' She paused, then frowning slightly, went on, 'Sadly, my Arron died last year. The young lady you see standing by the kitchen door is Helen.'

'So sorry about your husband,' said Laura. 'From what we've heard, you and your daughter got out of Germany in time to avoid being taken in to custody.'

'Yes indeed,' Mrs Jacobs quietly replied while lowering her gaze, 'unfortunately our parents weren't so fortunate. The Red Cross have told me they're now in a concentration camp called Belsen.'

For a few seconds the acute pain in Mrs Jacob's eyes told its own story. Mrs Jacobs finally gave a slight cough, then regaining her pose, continued. 'The whole place used to be two sixteenth century cottages,' she said, 'and was joined together after the First World War, then became a pub and restaurant in the late twenties. And incidentally, I'm told, some of those oak beams you see came from one of the ships in the Spanish Armada.'

Laura gave a small cry, and sitting back in her chair, said, 'There, Hugh, I told you it was quaint, didn't I, now what about those gin and tonics?'

'Of course,' she replied, 'my daughter will take your order while I make sure the blackout curtains are drawn. Meanwhile, may I recommend the steak and kidney pie, I made it myself.'

'Sound delightful, doesn't it, Hugh?' Laura said, eagerly rubbing her hands together.

'Yes, indeed,' Manley replied, 'and a nice bottle of whatever you have in stock to go with it.'

A few minutes later Helen arrived with the drinks. 'I hope I haven't put too much tonic in them,' she said. 'My mother has given me your order,' she added, glancing quickly at her pad, 'it won't be too long.' Then, flashing Manley a lovely smile, she turned, and went into the kitchen.

Just as Helen left, the dulcet tones of Geraldo's Palm Court Orchestra, playing Cole Porter's *Night and Day,* came from a gramophone behind the bar.

'How appropriate,' Laura said quietly, then humming the tune, she reached across the table and covered her hand over his.

Manley raised his glass and looking into Laura's beguiling violet eyes, said, 'Yes. it is, and God willing, there'll be many more evenings like this.'

As she predicted, Mrs Jacob's steak and kidney pie, washed down with a bottle of Médoc, was delicious.

'Tell me, Laura,' Manley said after taking a sip of coffee, 'you mentioned someone you met before me, was he in the forces?'

Lowering her eyes, she stared meaningfully into her coffee cup, then in a quiet, almost melancholy voice, replied, 'Yes, the RAF, his name was Clive.' Raising her voice slightly, she went on. 'But, that was in the past, now let's enjoy the rest of the evening.'

Sensing the reluctance to pursue the subject, Manley replied, 'Of course, forgive me, I didn't mean to be intrusive.' Then, in an effort to change the tone of the conversation, went on. 'Tell me, how long have you lived in Helston?'

'Except for three years at Exeter University, all my life,' Laura replied. 'Then, much against my father's wishes, I joined the navy. Incidentally,' Laura added, leaning forward and lowering her voice, 'perhaps I shouldn't say this, but as I told you, I work in the movements office and I'm aware that you'll soon be sailing, and where too.'

'In that case,' Manley said, smiling while reaching across and taking hold of Laura's hand, 'I think I'll send for the police and have you clapped in irons.'

'A shame, really, I was hoping we could spend more time together,' she replied, gently squeezing Manley's hand.

'We still can,' Manley said. 'We finish storing ship tomorrow. The captain is then taking five days leave and should return on the twenty-sixth. I'm due five days leave starting the next day, so you see, we can see each other again.'

Laura's face broke into a broad smile. 'I have a better idea,' she replied. 'I'm due a week's leave, so why don't we go down to Cornwall. I'm sure you'd like Father.'

Laura's suggestion took Manley completely aback. He sat back in his chair, and for several seconds, stared at her. Then, taking a deep breath, said, 'Er… yes, what a good idea. I'd love to meet him. How would we get there, by train?'

'No, we could drive down,' Laura answered noticing the surprised expression Manley eyes. 'I have a full tank and the car has only done five hundred miles. So if I met you outside the dockyard, at 0900 on the twenty-seventh, we could reach Helston that evening. How does that sound?'

'Splendid,' Manley replied. 'I only hope your father likes me.'

'Don't worry, Hugh,' Laura answered confidently, 'I'm sure he will.'

Just as Laura finished speaking, Mrs Jacobs arrived. 'How was your meal?' she asked, smiling politely.

'Most enjoyable, wasn't it?' Manley answered, glancing at Laura.

Especially your steak and kidney pie,' replied Laura.

'Good,' said Mrs Jacobs, 'would you like anything else, more coffee perhaps?'

'No thank you,' Manley replied, 'perhaps the bill…'

Ten minutes later, after leaving a handsome tip, they thanked Mrs Jacobs and left. The time was ten thirty. Hand in hand, they walked to the car park. Darkness had fallen, and high above, clusters of dark clouds partially hid a full moon.

'That wind is quite chilly,' Laura said as she opened the car door. 'I hope the heater is working.'

'To hell with the heater,' Manley replied, gently pulling her against him and giving her a long, passionate kiss. Finally, they broke their embrace.

'I've been longing for you to do that all evening,' she said, catching her breath while staring longingly into his eyes.

'Me too,' Manley replied. 'Now let's get inside and do it again.'

Laura turned and demurely lowered herself into her seat. In doing so, Manley noticed her skirt had, once again, ridden tantalisingly, up her thighs. She noticed this, and feeling the sexual juices rise, smiled coyly and put the car in gear. She then watched as Manley climbed into the car. The growing sense of eroticism between them suddenly made her feel lightheaded. She switched on the engine and with her dimmed lights making a blue blur in the darkness, drove carefully through the town.

'For God's sake, find somewhere,' Manley said hoarsely, while resting a hand on one of her soft warm thighs.

As if anticipating Manley's plea, she turned into a narrow lane, stopped the car and abruptly switched off the engine. Without speaking their arms went around one another. Their kiss, warm and hard, lasted for over a minute, each of them conscious of their hearts pounding a cadence in their chests. They broke away, then kissed again. At the same time Laura parted her legs, allowing Manley's warm hand to probe under her silk panties. As his fingers parted the wetness of her vagina, she let out a guttural cry of ecstasy as he found her magic spot. She, in turn, quickly felt his erection pushing up under his trousers. He gave a throaty gasp as her hand gave it a firm squeeze. 'God,' he gasped trying to draw her panties down her legs, 'I want you so.'

Perhaps it was the cramped conditions in the car, she wasn't sure. But, despite the almost uncontrollable sexual arousal running through her body, she suddenly felt ill at ease. 'I want you also, darling,' she cried, 'but not here. Somehow, it doesn't feel right.'

'Why?' Manley asked, feeling trickles of warm perspiration run down the sides of his face.

'I don't know,' she said, 'but please…'

'All right,' Manley answered, slowly withdrawing his hand from between her legs. 'But I don't think I'll be able to sleep tonight.'

Feeling his erection subside, she replied, 'Me neither, but there'll be other times, especially when we go away.'

It was a little before midnight when they arrived a few yards from the dockyard gate. Even at that late hour, a small crowd of ratings could be seen standing outside the dimly lit stalls, ordering mugs of tea and pies.

'Thank you for a lovely evening, Hugh,' Laura said, turning in her seat and looking deeply into Manley's eyes. 'And I'm sorry about…' her voice quickly trailed away.

Manley lent forward and kissed her warmly on the lips. Then, gently touching the side of her face with his hand, said, 'As you say, there'll be other times.'

'And they can't come quick enough,' Laura replied wistfully, then added, 'I'm on duty till 2000tomorrow, so phone me any time after that. Now, you'd better go as I'm missing you already.'

After giver Laura a quick kiss, Manley opened the door, and with a parting smile, walked down the road, flashed his pay book to the policeman and went into the dockyard.

CHAPTER NINE

Throughout the morning of Sunday 21st May, the crew were kept busy storing ship. In the afternoon, a lighter came alongside. Smoking throughout the ship was forbidden. Rum issue was postponed till 1400. Under the watchful eyes of Chief Coxswain Digger Barnes and CGI Bob Shilling, a hoist was rigged. Boxes of 4.7 shells and smaller ammunition was then brought onboard and lowered into the magazines. By 1600, replenishment was completed, and much to the relief of a tired crew, rum was issued. Leave was granted and those ratings living locally soon left the ship.

During the next week Paddy visited Joyce every evening. Up till now, their relationship had been warm, friendly and platonic, although Paddy's ardour when they kissed aroused a sexual desire in her that, with great willpower and pangs of conscience, she managed to subdue. Once or twice, Joyce allowed him to stay overnight and sleep on the settee. Paddy didn't mind as he looked forward to a well-cooked breakfast of bacon and eggs. Sometimes they would go to the local cinema, hold hands and enjoy a bar of Cadbury's milk chocolate, Paddy had bought from the ship's NAFFI. Occasionally they accompanied Harry and Ethel and had a drink and sing-song at the White Hart. The evening before the ship was due to sail, they were sitting in the front room. The time was a little after nine o'clock. On a nearby table, several empty bottles of ale and a small bottle of Gordon's gin lay alongside two glasses.

'Y'know, darlin',' said Paddy, 'I think I love you, and if things were different, I'd ask you to marry me.'

'Oh, Paddy,' Joyce replied, looking longingly into his eyes. 'If it wasn't for Jack, I'd marry you in an instant, but what can we do? You're going soon, and…' Her voice trailed away.

'But, to be sure,' Paddy muttered as he kissed her forehead, 'I'll be thinkin' of you all the time 'til I come back, so I will.' That night Paddy didn't sleep on the settee.

At 0900 on Monday 22nd May, Penrose left the ship. With the shrill sound of the bosun's pipe ringing in his ears, he climbed into a tilly and was driven through the dockyard. A cool breeze blew downriver and a cerulean, sunny sky, dotted with barrage balloons, promised a warm day. He wore his best uniform and carried a brown canvas holdall in his left hand. A gas mask satchel, with a steel helmet attached, was slung over his left shoulder.

A few minutes later they arrived at Portsmouth Harbour station. A tall, elderly driver with wiry grey hair climbed out and slid open a side door, allowing Penrose to climb out.

'Safe journey, sir,' said the driver, 'and have a good leave.'

'Thank you,' Penrose replied, then returning the salute of two passing sailors, hurried up a flight of steps, flashed his travel warrant to an attendant and made his way onto the platform in time to catch the 0945 train to London. Two hours later he arrived at Waterloo and took a taxi ride, northwards, across the city to St Pancras. With fifteen minutes to spare before his train left at twelve thirty, he telephoned Jean.

'Henry, darling,' Jean cried, 'what a wonderful surprise. It's so lovely to hear you. Are you all right?'

'Yes, dear, I'm fine,' Penrose replied. 'I have a few days leave, and as I recall, the journey to St Albans takes about an hour, so I should arrive, say…' he glanced at his wristwatch, then said, 'About two thirty.'

'Splendid,' Jean hastily replied. 'Luckily Janet is on half term till Monday, so we'll both meet you at the station.'

He was sharing a first-class compartment with an elderly, stout vicar, who, after smiling benignly, proceeded to bury himself behind a copy of *The Methodist Church Times*. Minutes later, the train left the station, and after a brief stop at Watford, arrived at St Albans shortly after half past two. The vicar stood up, yawned and folded his newspaper. Penrose opened the compartment door, allowing the vicar, who, after a polite nod, stepped carefully onto the platform. Penrose collected his steel helmet and gas mask and left the compartment and saw his wife, Jean, and daughter, Janet, standing behind the ticket collector at the end of the platform. He grinned and immediately gave a quick wave and hurried towards them. Upon seeing him, both women broke into broad smiles and waved back. The low-heeled brogues Jean wore made her look slightly smaller than Janet, whose broad-brimmed yellow straw school cap and scarlet school jacket contrasted sharply with her mother's fawn coat and green Robin Hood hat, only partially covering her short, fair hair.

The ticket collector, a small, stout, middle aged man, glanced casually at Penrose's uniform and travel warrant, then, touching the peak of his small, round cap, smiled respectfully and said, 'Afternoon, sir, I was in your lot in the last war, so good luck to you.'

Penrose was about to thank him when Janet, wide-eyed and grinning, threw her arms around Penrose's waist and cried, 'Oh Daddy, I've missed you so.' Then, standing tip-toe, kissed him warmly on the cheek.

'And that goes for me, dear,' said Jean, kissing his other cheek. In doing so she noticed the dark rungs under his eyes and how tired and drawn he looked. 'The car's outside,' she added, linking his arm.

'Mummy tells me you've only got five days leave,' gushed Janet, taking Penrose's holdall from him. As she spoke her dark blue eyes, matching those of her mother, creased into a broad welcoming grin. 'Is that right, Daddy?'

'I'm afraid so, chicken,' Penrose replied. 'And I'm lucky to have that,' he added, as they left the concourse. At the bottom of two flights of wide steps, a black Morris Eight was parked on the road next to a delivery van.

'Still running well?' Penrose asked as Jean opened the driver's door and climbed in.

'Yes, darling, but the engine needs a good overhaul,' Jean answered as Penrose sat next to her.

'Daddy will fix it, won't you,' cried Janet from the passenger's seat behind them.

Jean gave a loud laugh. 'Your father knows as much about car engines as I do.' Then, pulling the choke half way out, she turned on the engine.

The city of St Albans, or Verulamium, as it was known in medieval times, lies twenty miles north-west of London. Its name is derived from Alban, Britain's first saint who is buried in the beautiful Romanesque-Gothic Cathedral whose central tower dominates the city.

'How's work?' Penrose asked as Jean pulled away from the curb and drove down Victoria Street, a wide, busy shopping area in the centre of the city.

'Other than a few divorces and accident claims, things are quiet,' Jean replied, as she turned the car into Bricket Road, a wide, cobbled-stoned cul-de-sac, lined on either side by bungalows built before the war. Jean drove down the road and stopped the car opposite a fairly large red-bricked bungalow. Two squat chimneys poked up from the middle of a slightly sloping blue slated roof. A wooden fence, painted bright yellow surrounded a slightly overgrown lawn through which a narrow, gravelled path led up to a small, overhanging porch and varnished oak door. On either side of the door, a taped window with its blackout curtains drawn to one side to protect against the dangers of the bombing, which, so far, had not affected the city.

'Here we are, darling, home is the sailor,' said Jean switching off the engine, and opening her door.

'And the hunter home from the hill,' added Janet, grabbing Penrose's gas mask and helmet and climbing out of the back seat onto the narrow pavement. 'I told that to Mummy, it's by Robert Louis Stevenson. We learnt that at school.'

'And if I may say so, very appropriate,' Penrose remarked, opening the passenger door and leaving the car.

Janet insisted on carrying Penrose's gas mask, steel helmet and grip and followed her parents up the path.

'I expect you're dying for a cup of tea, dear,' Jean said, using a small silver Yale key to open the door.

'With a drop of Scotch, if you have any,' Penrose replied, following Jean inside.

'Indeed, I have, courtesy of my boss,' Jean replied, 'and by the looks of you, darling, you also need a good night's sleep.'

On one side of the hallway, carpeted in dark green, was an umbrella stand, coat hooks and small table. Penrose placed his holdall on top of the table and hung up his gas mask and steel helmet. He then followed Janet and his wife down the hallway, passed a small but well-furnished dining room into a tiled kitchen complete with a modern ice box and gas stove. Penrose entered a surprisingly spacious lounge, followed by Janet.

Smiling broadly, she cried, 'Oh Daddy, Mummy and me have missed you so, it's so good to have you home, even if it's only for a few days.' She flopped down into a large, brown settee.

Feeling his shoes sink into the soft pile of floral-patterned carpet, Penrose took off his cap and eased himself comfortably into one of the two armchairs. A quick glance around showed the familiar sights; the shiny sandalwood table, complete with a Waterford sherry decanter, matching glasses and telephone; the stout oak sideboard, family photographs and the same yellow and green striped wallpaper and paintings of local scenes he and Jean had hung a year ago. On a tiled hearth lay a brass coal scuttle, set of iron tongs and poker in a round metal container. Next to this, in a three barred fire grate, lumps of coal lay over pieces of firewood and crinkled newspaper, all of which were protected by a wire mesh shield. Above the white marble surround was a mantelpiece. In the middle rested an ornate, emerald green ormolu clock, flanked on either side with framed family photographs. Next to this was a tall lamp stand topped up with a tasselled lampshade, and close by, on a well-polished table, a bunch of red roses poked out of a glass vase next to a brown Bakelite wireless. With a satisfied sigh, Penrose murmured, 'My goodness, it's feels good to be home.'

Jean came in carrying a silver tray containing three cups and saucers and a teapot covered by a woollen tea cosy. She had taken off her coat, revealing a dark brown pleated skirt, a fawn twin set and a delicate row of pearls around her slender neck. Janet followed on behind holding a folded copy of *The Times* and handed it to Penrose.

'Thank you, chicken,' said Penrose, accepting the newspaper and placing it by his side. 'I'll read it later.'

'Milk and sugar in all the cups,' Jean said, placing the tray on a table'

'Ah, I detect that spot of whiskey,' said Penrose, sniffing the air, 'thank you darling.'

The time was five o'clock. For the next hour, Penrose and Jean sat and discussed the war and friends, while Janet reluctantly retreated to her room and did her homework.

'It said on the BBC this morning that the Americans have lost an aircraft carrier, called the *Lexington*, along with a destroyer sunk in the Coral Sea.'

'Yes, dear, I heard it before I left the ship,' Penrose answered dryly, 'and sixty of the American planes were lost also.'

'What about the Japanese losses?' Jean asked. 'Any news about them?'

'Yes, I'm glad to say,' Penrose answered, with a wry smile. 'One aircraft carrier, several cruisers, a destroyer and over eighty planes.'

'How splendid,' Jean said, placing both hands on her knee, 'I think that deserves a small sherry each, dear.'

'A large one, I should say,' Penrose replied, 'don't you think, darling?'

A few minutes later, Janet came into the lounge. She had discarded her jacket, her tie was undone and hung loosely down the front of her open-necked white shirt. 'Can anyone help me with these lousy quadratic equations?' she asked, frowning while brandishing an exercise book in her hand. 'They're a mystery to me.'

'Your father's the mathematician, aren't you, dear?' Jean said, picking up the decanter and pouring out two glasses of sherry.

Sensing this was an excuse by Janet to join him and Jean, Penrose gave a loud laugh and said, 'Come over here, you duffer.' And for the next half hour, with Janet cuddling close to him on the settee, he instructed his daughter in the intricacies of O level algebra.

After listening to the six o'clock news, they sat down in the kitchen and enjoyed a roast beef dinner. By the time they finished it was a little after eight o'clock. Penrose had taken off his uniform and now wore a cream shirt, maroon tie, and grey slacks. Jean did likewise and was dressed in a long-sleeved dark brown button-down dress while Janet, doing her best to look older, looked smart in a pleated green skirt and yellow blouse.

'I suggest we take our coffee into the lounge,' said Jean, standing up and picking up her cup, 'and perhaps you can light the fire, dear, while Janet draws the blackout curtains.'

In the lounge the warmth from the fire added to the cosy, relaxed family atmosphere. Jean sat in an armchair, knitting, while on the settee, Penrose asked Janet about school, then played snakes and ladders.

At nine o'clock everyone sat on the settee, listening to the deep-seated voice of Valentine Dyall, narrating the BBC's horror series, *The Man in Black.*

'Now, brush your teeth and off to bed with you, dear,' Jean said, then with a cautious smile, added, 'and remember, we're going to church tomorrow.'

'Oh, all right,' Janet replied. With a sigh of mock anguish, she stood up, and after kissing both parents on their cheeks, said 'goodnight,' and left the room.

After Janet had gone, Jean put down her knitting, and looking at the tired expression etched on her husband's face, said, 'I didn't want to discuss this in front of Janet, dear, but you look so tired, are you sure you're feeling well?

'Of course, darling,' Penrose replied, doing his best to sound convincing, 'never felt better, so don't worry.'

'Well,' she answered, leaving her chair and sitting beside him on the settee. 'You know I do,' she mockingly chiding him before putting her arms around him and kissing him warmly on the lips.

St Alban's Cathedral with its large rose window flanked on either side by tall Gothic towers, stood in the centre of the town, surrounded by lush parkland. Penrose parked the car alongside several others and joined a crowd walking up a gravelled path leading to the stout oak twelfth century arched entrance. Jean wore her pale green Robin Hood hat and a dark blue dress under a belted fawn cashmere coat, while Janet, looking every inch a teenager in a pink dress, proudly linked the arm of her father whose brass buttons on his uniform glinted in the mid-morning sunshine. Among the crowd, Penrose noticed the unmistakable, round, pale face and partially bald head of Doctor Peter Smyth, standing next to the cathedral's open door. The dark blue suit he wore contrasted sharply with the pristine white cassock worn by Reverend Horace Willloughby, the tall, grey-haired Bishop of St Albans, with whom he was engaged in subdued conversation.

'Excuse me, dear, go straight inside,' said Penrose. 'I've just seen Peter Smyth, so pardon me while I say hello to him.'

If you must, darling,' Jean replied, glancing around, 'but don't be long, there looks like being a large congregation.'

'Don't worry, Dad,' chimed in Janet, squeezing his hand, 'I'll save you a place next to me.'

'Thank you, chicken,' Penrose replied. Making his way through the crowd, he arrived next to the doctor. The bishop left the doctor, and still smiling benignly, greeted an elderly couple. The doctor turned and saw Pentose standing next to him.

'Henry, old boy,' said the doctor as they shook hands. In doing so, he cast his medical eyes on Penrose's haggard features. 'Wonderful to see you, old boy. I thought you were still at sea. How is the ticker?' he added, lowering his voice.

'That's why I want to see you,' Penrose replied, smiling weakly at Jean and Janet as they walked past them into the church. 'While we were at sea, I've had a few bad turns and now, I've almost run out of tablets, and we sail again shortly.'

'Hmm... I see, 'Peter replied, furrowing his brow. 'Then you'd better come and see me tomorrow at ten o'clock. Now I think we should go inside before the ceremony starts.'

The church was quite crowded but Penrose spotted Jean and Janet sitting on the end of a line of padded benches.

'You took a long time to say hello,' whispered Jean, as he sat down, 'we thought you'd deserted us, didn't we, Janet?'

'Yes, and...' The strident voice of Bishop Willloughby asking the congregation to stand, interrupted her.

The service lasted over an hour. After several hymns, led by the church choir, and the bishop's long sermon, everyone stood up and sung the national anthem.

'Thank heavens for that, Mummy,' Janet murmured as they filed out the church, 'I thought the bishop would never stop.'

'Don't be so irreverent,' Jean replied, taking hold of Janet's hand. 'If Adolf gets his way, we'll need all the prayers we know. Isn't that right, dear?' she said, glancing up at Penrose.

'More than a few prayers, I'd say,' Penrose answered dryly, as they reached the car.

After lunch, Janet asked her parents if they would take her to Verulamium Park to see the remains of the city's Roman walls. 'I haven't been there since I was little and can't remember much about it. You see, we're doing local history at school and I'd like to do a few drawings.'

'What do think, dear?' Janet asked Penrose. 'It's such a lovely day. We could have a picnic.'

'What a good idea, darling,' Penrose replied, picking up his cup and taking a good sip.

They left the bungalow at two o'clock. The sun was shining and the sky an eye-smarting cerulean blue. Jean wore a pair of dark slacks, a white blouse and sandals. Janet had discarded her school uniform and wore a pale blue dress, while Penrose was dressed country fashion in brown corduroy trousers and an open neck white shirt and a pair of thick-soled shoes.

After a short journey through the town, Jean drove the car into a gravelled car park and stopped next to a Ford. They climbed out the car and made their way to a high, red-bricked wall surrounding the park entrance. 'It's a pity that lovely wrought iron gate and the railings were taken away last year, it makes the park look so open and bare, doesn't it, dear?' Jean asked Penrose.

'Desperate times require desperate measures,' Penrose replied. 'As Mr Howe told the nation on the wireless, every bit of iron and steel is urgently needed to make weapons and ships.'

After exploring the Roman walls, during which time Janet made several sketches for use at school, they settled down on a grassy verge. During the next hour they relaxed in the sunshine and enjoyed the apple pie and tarts. A few minutes later, Janet lay back on the grass next to her parents and fell asleep. With her head resting on Penrose's chest, Jean closed her eyes and murmured, 'My goodness, dear, you'd hardly believe there's war on, it's so peaceful.'

'Yes, darling, peace, perfect peace, but what will tomorrow bring,' Penrose solemnly replied.

That night in bed Penrose held Jean close, and feeling himself becoming aroused, murmured, 'Darling, what was that you said earlier about me being too tired?'

Shortly after eight thirty the next morning, after a few hugs and kisses, Jean drove Janet to school then carried on to the office of Barnet and Cross on the high street. Before leaving Jean said, 'I'll be back at one thirty, darling, so put the kettle on.'

'And please, Daddy, will you help me with my algebra again tonight?' Janet added, before climbing into the car.

'Of course, chicken,' Penrose replied, giving the tip of her nose a gentle tap, 'and I'll even let you beat me at snakes and ladders, now off you go.'

After a quick wave, Penrose watched the car disappear down the road then, with a nostalgic sigh, went inside the bungalow, sat down in the kitchen and made a cup of tea. An hour later, wearing an old brown Harris Tweed jacket, white shirt, service tie and fawn trousers, Penrose left the house. The blue sky, littered with a few fluffy clouds, promised another fine June day. A few minutes after ten o'clock, after a short walk through the city centre he was sat with Doctor Smyth in his surgery, one of several red-bricked houses situated on Beachwood Drive, a wide thoroughfare, lined with laburnum and ash.

Ten minutes later, after examining Penrose, the doctor, wearing his usual dark blue suit, sat down, and after placing arms over his ample girth, said, 'You're blood pressure is sky-high and your pulse is still jumping around like a rubber ball.' As he spoke a worried frown appeared on his pale features. 'You really should see your naval doctor. If it were up to me, old boy,' he added, his intelligent brown eyes fixed intently on Penrose, 'I'd have you in hospital for a thorough going over.'

'With great respect, Peter,' Penrose replied after rolling down his sleeve and putting on his jacket, 'it's not up to you, and as I expect we'll be at sea for some time, I really would be grateful for those pills. And by the way, Jean doesn't know about this, so keep it to ourselves.'

'Hippocratic oath, and all that, Henry,' the doctor answered with a wry smile.

Ten minutes later, with a box containing an ample supply of Digoxin in his jacket pocket, Penrose left the surgery and walked home.

That evening the atmosphere over dinner was strained. Even though Jean and Janet had experienced the comings and goings of Penrose over the years, this was wartime, and the realisation that he would be leaving the next morning to face unknown dangers hung in the air like a heavy shroud. It was a situation, families of servicemen throughout the country, had to often contend with. But with each goodbye, the pain and worry increased.

Jean allowed Janet to stay up late and play snakes and ladders with her father, while she did her best to concentrate on knitting. After listening to the ten o'clock news, Jean put down her knitting, switched off the wireless, then with an air of stoicism, looked around and said, 'Time for bed everyone, and Janet, don't forget to brush your teeth.'

Ten minutes later, Penrose quietly opened Janet's door. Her bedside light was on and she was lying on one side, facing him with her eyes open.

Upon seeing him she turned and sat up. 'Oh, Daddy,' she cried, reaching out for him, 'I'm going to miss you so.'

Penrose sat down on the side of the bed and placed his arms arounds her warm pyjama-clad body, kissed her on the cheek, and in a tender voice, said, 'And I you, chicken. I know things are difficult.' Using a finger to wipe away a tear from the corner of an eye. 'But we've all got to be brave, so promise me you'll work hard at school and look after your mother till I return. Understand?'

'I'll do my best, Daddy,' Janet whispered, while nodding head.

'Good girl,' Penrose replied, smiling, 'now lie down and try to sleep.'

Janet lay down and Penrose gently tucked her in. He then bent and kissed her tenderly on the forehead, and in a quiet, fatherly voice, said, 'Good night and God bless, and always remember, I love you very much.'

He stood up and for a few seconds he looked nostalgically at the huddled figure he had, between commissions, witnessed growing up into a lovely young girl. He then switched off the light and left. No sooner had he done so than Janet buried her head in a pillow and cried herself to sleep.

Five minutes later, Penrose and Jean lay cuddled up to one another in bed. The curtains were drawn and the rays from the full moon flickering between dark clouds, occasionally lit up the room. 'I know I shouldn't ask, darling,' she said, her voice quietly strained, 'but where will it be this time, the Med, the Atlantic or Russia?'

'I can't say, dear,' he whispered into her warm ear, 'but I expect to have a good tan when I return.'

Next morning, at eight thirty, breakfast was eaten in uneasy silence. Aware that the journey to Portsmouth would take about six hours, Jean made Penrose some egg and watercress sandwiches, wrapped them up in paper then filled a flask with tea and took them to Penrose in his room.

After packing his grip, Penrose, wearing his uniform, managed to get through to *Helix* and speak to Manley. 'If the train's on time, I should arrive at Portsmouth about1630,' he said, glancing quickly at his wristwatch. 'Please arrange transport to meet me at the harbour station. How is everything on board?'

'Other than two defaulters for fighting ashore, and a stoker sick onshore, everything's fine. Hope you've had a good break, sir.'

'Thank you, Number One, I have,' said Penrose, and put the telephone down.

That evening, Manley telephoned Laura. 'The captain is arriving later today. I'm officer of the watch till after colours tomorrow, so what time and where shall we meet?'

'How does 0930sound? I'll park the car a few yards up Queens Street, outside the dockyard gate. How does that sound?'

'Splendid,' Manley answered, feeling a sharp, thrill of excitement run through him. He went on, 'Shall I bring my mess undress with me?'

'Oh, my goodness, no,' she laughingly cried, 'we dress quite informally in the country. Just pack something you're comfortable in.' She paused momentarily then added, 'And Hugh, I can't wait to see you.'

Penrose's train to London was due to leave St Albans at ten thirty. At nine thirty, with Janet, clutching her school satchel, sat huddled next to Penrose in the back seat, Jean drove the car away. Even though it would make Janet late for school, Jean had decided Janet should come with her to the station. A few minutes later, they arrived outside the station. Along with a few passengers, they made their way onto the platform. Janet, unable to fight back the tears, kept her arms tight around Penrose's waist.

'Better go, my love,' said Jean glancing at her wristwatch, 'your train leaves in five minutes.' Fighting back the tears, she removed an arm and took out a small brown paper parcel from her handbag. 'It's a silk scarf. It'll keep you warm at sea.' She then reached up and kissed him warmly on the lips. Feeling an egg-sized lump in his throat, he gently removed Janet's arms, and after kissing her on the cheek, said hoarsely, 'Bye-bye chicken, with a bit of luck I'll be a four-ring captain when I return.'

'Never mind that, darling,' Jean replied, fighting back tears, 'just come back to us safe and sound.'

Minutes later he was sat in an empty first-class compartment returning their tearful waves, as the train, billowing steam, gradually pulled away from the platform. By the time he arrived at Portsmouth, the early morning blue sky had disappeared and dark clouds promised rain. Along with several sailors who had joined the train at London, he left the station. The tilly he had ordered earlier was parked at the bottom of the station steps. The same civilian driver who had collected him from the ship five days ago, slid open the passenger door, and with a toothy smile, asked, 'Good leave, sir?'

'Yes, thank you,' Penrose replied. Minutes later he walked up *Helix*'s gangway onto the quarterdeck and returned the smart salutes from Manley, OOD Sub Lieutenant Baker and PO Len Mills.

'Enjoyed your break, sir?' Manley asked, noticing the dark smudges under his captain's eyes had disappeared.

'Yes, thank you, Number One,' Penrose replied while glancing wistfully around, and remembering Janet's words, muttered, 'Home is the sailor, indeed.'

CHAPTER TEN

At nine thirty on Thursday evening Manley, PO Hardman and QM Knocker White had just finished night rounds and were standing outside the stairway leading to the officer's quarters.

'Thank you, PO,' Manley said, 'I'll be in my cabin if you want me.'

'Very good, sir,' Hardman replied, then with a smile added, 'I hear you're away on leave tomorrow, sir.'

'Yes, five glorious days,' Manley answered with smile.

'Well, enjoy it, sir,' Hardman replied, 'as I expect we'll be away for some time.'

'You could be right,' Manley said, smiling pensively. Even though the date for sailing was supposed to be top secret, on board small ships like *Helix,* the tom-toms ensured such information soon became known to the ship's company.

Manley went to his cabin, and as he packed his holdall, the thought of having Laura to himself for the next five days sent a surge of excitement running through him.

At that moment, Laura was in her quarters, sitting on the side of her narrow bed in her cabin. A towel was wrapped tightly around her body, and she was busy using another one to dry her hair. Susan, he closest friend, occupied a chair opposite a small dressing table, cluttered with a few toilet accessories.

'I hope you know what you're doing, Laura,' said Susan, toying with a nail brush. 'I should hate you to get hurt, I mean, you've only known him for a short time and after… Her voice trailed away.' Susan was a tall, striking blonde with baby blue eyes and a figure that attracted attention of every officer, including FP, in the wardroom.

'Don't worry,' Laura replied, turning to her slightly and smiling, 'I know what I'm doing, now, please pass me that hair brush in front of you.'

'But surely you're not in love with him?' asked Susan, noticing a faraway expression in in her friend's eyes.

'I know it sounds crazy,' said Laura, turning and looking at her friend, 'but I do believe I am.'

Half an hour after "colours" the next morning, Manley, wearing his best uniform, handed over his duties to Sub Lieutenant Milton and left the ship carrying his gas mask and steel helmet over his left shoulder. With his Burberry slung over the crook of his left arm that held his holdall, he made his way through the dockyard. The sky was an anaemic blue, forcing Manley to lower his eyes from the glare of the early morning sun that promised another warm day.

After showing his pay book to the policeman at the main gate, he saw Laura's dark green MG parked a few yards away on Queen Street. The canvas hood was down, and as she saw him, her face, half hidden by a shiny scarlet headscarf, lit up into a broad, welcoming smile. 'Right on time,' Laura said, as he threw his holdall and accoutrements on the back seat.

'Punctuality is the sign of princes and kings,' he replied as, without opening the small door, he climbed into the car.

'Then give your princess a kiss and let's get cracking,' she laughingly replied while reaching across to him.

Traffic was sparse, the sun was shining, and the atmosphere happy and relaxed. Twenty minutes later they had left Portsmouth behind. Laura unbuttoned her jacket, and loosened her tie. Then, with a quick twist of her hand, she removed her headscarf, allowing the warm, southerly wind to play havoc with her auburn hair. Manley, also bareheaded, followed suit, feeling a sense of exhilaration run through him as the car sped through Hampshire's verdant countryside. With Portsdown Hill away on the right, where, four years later on 5th June 1944 in Southwick House, General Eisenhower would order the D-Day landings to take place. They bypassed Fareham and headed west, passing through Lymington and continued along a wide, dusty coastal road, studded with concrete pill-boxes and fields of barbed wire.

'My goodness,' Laura cried, glancing left, 'see how the sunshine on the water makes the channel looks all silvery and serine, isn't it lovely?'

'It certainly is,' Manley thoughtfully replied, 'but I'm afraid looks can be deceiving.'

'What do you mean?' Laura asked, using a finger to brush away a strand of hair from her face.

'Just over the horizon is a string of coastal gun batteries and U-boat pens, stretching from Calais to St Nazaire.' As if to emphasize his remark, a small convoy of tankers, escorted by destroyers, gradually appeared out of the heat haze heading south. Suddenly, the sound of gunfire broke the stillness of the morning. Plumes of white water exploded around the vessels, shrouding some in clouds of spray. Then, one by one, the merchantmen broke the line and took evasive action.

'Why don't the destroyers return fire, Hugh?' Laura shouted.

'The batteries are out of there range,' Manley replied dryly.

The convoy, seemingly undaunted by the enemy's barrage, continued on their way. Manley watched, sensing the fear the ship's companies were experiencing. Then, as if the barrage had been a warning to the vessels not to come too close, the gunfire stopped. Fortunately, none of the vessels were hit. Next time, Manley thought, they might not be so lucky.

'So much for serenity,' Manley quietly muttered.

With the lush, green Dorset Downs sweeping away on there right, they drove through Bournemouth. The time was just after one o'clock when they arrived at the historic market town of Dorchester. They adjusted their uniform, and while enjoying a late lunch a small café, Laura looked out of the window at the cobbled stoned street, and said, 'Did you know that Thomas Hardy used Dorchester as a setting for the *Mayor of Casterbridge*? We read it at school. And Lawrence of Arabia is buried not far away at Moreton.'

'No, I didn't,' Manley replied while chewing a chicken sandwich, 'any other pearls of information?'

'Yes, darling,' she laughingly replied, 'it's your turn to drive.'

Bathed in glorious sunshine, and with the warm breeze fanning their faces, they drove through Dorchester. Then, still keeping to the coast road, they skirted around the dark blue waters of Lyme Bay and entered Devon. On Laura's advice, Hugh left the coastal road and drove inland. They bypassed Exeter and carried on through Ashburton and by five o'clock, arrived in Plymouth and stopped outside a café for a quick tea break.

'I think I'd better drive, now,' Laura said, wiping a blob of cream cake from her upper lip. 'Father told me the city centre is still in ruins after the bombing, so I'll have to drive around it and go through Milehouse and take the ferry across the Tamar to Cornwall.'

Numerous bombed buildings, evidence of the Blitz, could be seen as Laura drove through Devonport to the ferry. After paying a sixpenny toll, she, and a few cars and a delivery van, drove up a wide ramp and parked close to the other cars in an area below decks, ready to leave. Shortly after, the rumble of the chains operating the ferryboat vibrated, as the vessel slowly edged its way from the sloping landing stage.

'It only takes about ten minutes, so we'd better stay in the car,' said Laura, turning around and smiling at him. 'However, that gives me plenty of time to give you a kiss,' she added, pulling him close and kissing him passionately on the lips. The warmth of her body and lips sent a tingle of excitement running through Manley. Laura became aware of the bulge in his trousers pressing against her thigh and broke away from him.

'The sooner we get to Helston, the better,' gasped Laura, giving his erection a teasing pat.

'But your father, won't he…' he muttered.

'Love laughs at locksmiths,' Laura replied, giving him a quick kiss.

'Where did you learn that?' Manley asked, staring into Laura's beguiling violet eyes.

'At school. *Venus and Adonis,* a poem by Shakespeare,' she replied as the ferry began to slow down.

'That sounds like some school,' Manley replied, grinning while shaking his head slightly.

Five minutes later, the ferry had crossed the River Tamar and arrived at Saltash, a small hillside town opposite Plymouth. The door of the carpark opened then a ramp was lowered, allowing the cars to leave.

'Ah, dear old Cornwall,' Laura said, taking a deep breath, as she followed the delivery van onto a wide concrete slipway.

'Where to now?' asked Manley, looking at the rows of quaint grey stone cottages on either side of a narrow, winding road leading into town.

'Liskeard then Lostwithiel,' Laura replied, turning left down a wide, gravelled road.

Manley gave a Laura a searching look and said, 'What odd names.'

Keeping her eyes firmly fixed on the road, Laura replied, 'Don't be so condescending, Hugh. For your information, Lostwithiel in Cornish means "tail of wooded area" and likewise, Liskeard simply means "court". Happy now?'

'Thank you, darling,' Manley answered, gently squeezing her thigh, 'you really are a hive of information.'

'Seeing as how I lived in Cornwall for twenty years,' she replied, 'I ought to be, and please keep your hand where it is, it feels rather lovely.'

'How far away is Helston?' Manley enquired.

'Not far,' Laura answered, giving him a sideways smile, 'just sit back and enjoy the scenery.'

Half an hour after passing through Lostwithiel, they drove through St Austell. They then drove through Truro and continued down a dusty secondary road to Redruth. 'Not long now,' said Laura, turning off the road into a narrow driveway. 'You can see our house on the left.'

'That's quite a house,' retorted Manley, staring at a large grey-stoned, two-storey building, surrounded by a high, uneven, drystone rock wall, used throughout Devon and Cornwall. 'It looks more like a mansion.'

'Actually, it's called Trevethick House,' said Laura, stopping the car outside a tall, wrought iron gate. 'It's been in the family for generations. Now be an angel and open the gate, then I suggest we tidy ourselves up before we meet Father.'

The time was a little after seven o'clock as Laura drove up a wide gravelled drive, dissected by well-kept lawns and beds of bougainvillea in full bloom, and parked near the foot of two flights of stone steps. A thin trail of smoke eddied from two tall chimneys set on top of a slightly slopping red, tiled roof. Green leafed creepers swarmed around each corner of the ashlar façade. In the front, white lace curtains adorned the four tall, six-panelled windows on the top floor. Two smaller windows with floral curtains lay either side of highly polished oak door, flanked on either side by tall, white fluted pillars. Above this a fanlight, a triangular glass pediment, added to the building's symmetrical appearance, typical of the Georgian period.

'I must say, Laura,' Manley remarked, glancing up at the front of the building, 'It looks like one of houses described in a Jane Austen novel.'

'That's nothing, darling,' Laura replied, laughing heartily, 'wait till you see the ghost.'

No sooner had she spoke than the door was opened by a tall middle-aged man, whose upright bearing, well-trimmed brown moustache strongly suggested a military background. He had a firm jawline and the slight bend in his otherwise straight nose, a legacy from an old rugby injury, added a touch of toughness to his healthy, ruddy complexion. His thick, wiry, dark hair was streaked with grey, and he wore an open necked, checked shirt and the rounded tips of two highly polished, brown shoes peeked out under the end of a pair of baggy, black, corduroy trousers.

'How lovely to see you,' he cried, raising both arms, 'do come in. I've asked Aida to prepare a nice piece of roast lamb for supper.' He spoke with a distinctive Cornish accent, and in doing so, the corners of his pale blue eyes creased into a welcoming smile. 'And you must be Hugh,' he added, proffering his hand. 'Laura told me she was bringing you down.'

'A pleasure to meet you, sir,' Manley nervously replied, feeling the firmness of her father handshake.

'You also, my boy,' Laura's father answered jovially, displaying a row of slightly tobacco-stained even teeth. 'And you can forget the "sir" and call me Jonathan.'

A small, stout, elderly, grey-haired woman appeared behind them. Her fleshy, pale face was round and rimless glasses, were perched on the bridge of a snub nose. Over a plain, long-sleeved, dark dress, a red and white striped apron was tied around her ample waist. Her strong, muscular legs were bare and she wore a pair of well-worn brown leather slippers.

'Och now, stop your blethering,' she said, hands on her hips while smiling benignly. 'If you stand there any longer, all my lovely cooking will go cold.'

'Ah, this is Aida, my house keeper,' said Johnathan, 'we'd better do as she says. As you can tell, she's from Scotland and is the real boss of the house.'

'And dina forget I'm chief cook, maid and bottle washer,' Aida said. With a broad, toothy grin, she looked at Manley and added, 'Welcome to Trevethick House, sir.'

'I expect you'll want to unpack,' said Johnathan, 'and when Aida has shown you to your rooms, I'll meet you in the study for a drink. Dinner in half an hour.'

They walked through a small lobby onto a floor tiled in black and white. In doing so, Manley noticed Jonathan walked with a slight, left-sided limp. Portraits of austere looking gentlemen and equally stern ladies hung on shiny oak walls, and lying close to the foot of a winding staircase, stood a suit of gleaming silver armour.

'One of your ancestors?' Manley jokingly asked Laura.

'Yes,' she replied, 'and protection against my honour.'

'You'll be in your usual room, Miss Laura,' Aida said leading them upstairs, 'and yours,' she added, looking sternly at Manley, 'is the guest room at the end of the hall. The door hinges need oiling so give it a wee push.'

'Thank you, Aida,' said Laura, then, giving Manley a doleful look, she opened her door and went inside.

For a few seconds Laura stood and was amazed to see that her room hadn't changed since she was here six months ago. The round coloured lampshade hanging from the cream-coloured ceiling and small window and floral curtains was exactly as she remembered it. The yellow and pink walls with her favourite country scenes, the single bed, shiny emerald coverlet and bedside light, even the small dressing table and toilet accessories and wardrobe, were the same. A glance through an open door showed the bathroom, with its gleaming white tiles looking as pristine as ever. With a nostalgic sigh she placed her small suitcase on the side of her bed, feeling her shoes sink into the pile of the familiar dark green carpet and began to unpack, while at the same time, thinking about Manley.

At that moment, Manley was also sitting on a bed much larger than Laura's, admiring the wallpaper embossed in rich Burgundy. Floral curtains were drawn across a wide panelled window and oil paintings of Helston and other towns hung on the walls. His gaze switched to a small, but delicate glass chandelier hanging from a high, white stuccoed ceiling and the floor was covered in a dark brown, thickly piled, Axminster carpet, a tall, highly polished oak wardrobe resting in one corner, near a dressing table and chair, and a half open door leading into a bathroom tiled in light green.

After unpacking, he had a quick shower, and wearing a light grey, singled breasted suit, white shirt and naval tie, left the room and walking along the floor, detected the strong smell of tobacco. Having ignored them when he arrived, Manley paused momentarily and looked at the portraits of men and women wearing clothes dating back to the reign of Charles II on the walls. Suddenly, Jonathan's distinctive Cornish burr, coming from below, interrupted him. He turned and saw him standing at the bottom of the stairs. He held a meerschaum pipe in one hand with the other resting on the top of the bannister knob.

'Christian Trevethic, one of my ancestors,' Johnathan said, smiling, 'fought for the Royalists in the Civil War and was knighted. He was granted land and built this house. His ghost is supposed to haunt the premises.'

'Have you ever seen it?' Manley asked.

'No, my boy, but Laura says she has,' Jonathan laughingly replied.

As he spoke, a door opened and Laura arrived. She wore a short-sleeved, button down, yellow dress. Her auburn hair, usually worn in a chignon, hung loosely down her back and a string of pearls adorned her swanlike neck. Her make-up, carefully applied, added to the beauty of her high cheekbones, which, along with the dark red lipstick, accentuated the delicate glow of her porcelain skin. 'I see you're still using that horrible tobacco, Father, it smells disgusting,' she said, slightly shaking her head.

'You sound just like your mother,' Johnathan replied. 'Besides,' he added, holding the pipe up, 'it's one of the few of life's pleasures I have left.

'Poppycock,' she laughed. Then, looking at Manley, she raised her eyebrows, and smiling, said, 'My goodness, Hugh, why are you staring at me like that?'

'Sorry, Laura,' he muttered incongruously, 'it's just that this is the first time I've seen you out of uniform. You look absolutely gorgeous.'

'Thank you, kind sir,' she replied, giving him a mock curtsey. 'Flattery will get you everywhere. Now let's go down to dinner before Aida gets on to us.'

Dinner, consisting of roast beef and Yorkshire pudding was taken in a small, but intimate dining room, lined with shiny oak panels and eaten on a long mahogany table, covered with an Irish linen tablecloth, and decorated in the centre by a vase of red and yellow roses. Three courses eaten off elegantly designed crockery with silver cutlery, added a touch grandeur to what was a memorable occasion.

After toasting the king and queen, they adjourned to the lounge, situated at the rear of the house. This was a spacious, well-lit room with a black leather Chesterfield and two matching armchairs, facing an unlit fire with a marble surround. A small coffee table stood next to a Chippendale wine cabinet and a handsome, mahogany sideboard, lined with family photographs. Above this was an ornately framed portrait of a vivacious, auburn haired woman, whose beguiling violet eyes and daring, low cut scarlet costume, complimented her milk white shoulders and creamy complexion.

'I miss her every day,' sighed Johnathan, staring nostalgically up at the painting.

'I'm sure you do,' said Manley, who was standing next to him and Laura, looking up at the painting.

'She died far too young,' sighed Johnathan. Then turning to Laura, he added solemnly, 'But at least I have you, my dear, to remind me how beautiful she was.'

Laura didn't speak. Instead, she quickly turned away and sat down on the settee. Manley joined her and gave one of her hands an understanding squeeze.

Half an hour later, after enjoying coffee and brandy, Johnathan pushed himself up from his chair and stood up. 'Do excuse me,' he said, holding his unlit pipe, 'I have some papers to sign in my study.' Then, bending down, he kissed Laura tenderly on the cheek and added softly, 'It's so good to have you home, dear, even it's only for a few days. Goodnight, I'll see you both at breakfast.' Limping slightly, he left the room.

'Papers my eye,' said Laura, after kissing Manley warmly on the lips. 'He's going into his study for a quiet smoke. Anyway,' she went on, glancing at the clock on the mantelpiece, 'it's nine thirty, so I suggest we, err… retire.'

They walked hand in hand up the stairs and stopped outside her door. 'Goodnight, darling,' she said, opening the door, and with a mischievous twinkle in her eyes, kissed him on the lips and went on. 'Sleep tight, and sweet dreams.'

'If I do dream, they'll be of you, darling,' he whispered, after returning her kiss. Then, with a frustrated sigh, he watched her close the door.

Twenty minutes later he lay in bed on two large pillows. His hands were behind his neck and he was staring up into the darkness, thinking of Laura, imagining her all warm and cosy, lying naked in bed. Suddenly, he heard an eerie creaking noise as the door slowly opened. He sat up and saw, silhouetted against the hall light, a white-faced figure wearing a long black cloak. A plume of feathers fluttered gently from the top of a wide brimmed hat and a gloved hand held a long silver sword pointing onto the floor. The other hand was hidden in the folds of the cloak.

For a few seconds he was too startled to speak. However, it was only when he heard the figure give a quiet, girlish giggle, he realised what was happening. 'I have a gun and I'll shoot if you don't clear off,' he cried, feigning fear.

'Ha! I had you going for a moment,' Laura cried, closing the door and switching on the light. 'Didn't I, darling. The sword belongs to Father,' she added, carefully laying it across the arms of a chair, 'but the cloak and hat are mine, relics of my student days.' From under folds of the cloak she brought out a hand holding two glasses and a small bottle of brandy. 'What do you say we have a nightcap before we… er, sleep,' she added with a sly smile. She placed the glasses and bottle on a bedside table. Seconds later, after removing her cloak, she stood in a flimsy white ankle length nightgown, which, aided by the bedside light, showed her nakedness. She sat on the bed and poured out the brandy and handed a glass to Manley.

'Here's to locksmiths,' said Manley, raising his glass and draining the glass.

'And long may they laugh,' Laura replied. After finishing her drink, she stood up, and with a flourish of arms, quickly removed he nightgown and climbed into bed.

At first their lovemaking was fast with a depth of animal passion that left them weak and speechless. Afterwards, bathed in warm perspiration they lay, arms around each other, gasping for breath.

'My God, darling,' Manley murmured, while listening to his heartbeat gradually subsiding. 'I've never felt like this before. That was incredible.'

'Yes,' Laura answered, burrowing her head in his chest, 'I know exactly what you mean.' Ten minutes later, feeling his penis stiffen against her stomach, she slid her hand down and gently cupped his testicles and whispered, 'For goodness sake, darling, do it again before I go crazy.'

Throughout the night when they made love, each mutual caress, kiss and bodily movement, ensured they gave one another total sexual satisfaction; and as dawn crept through the window, they lay, bedclothes askew, entangled in each other's arms.

During the next two days they visited the ruins of King Arthur's castle at Tintagel. Staring over the battlements, they followed the local custom and made a silent wish then kissed. They visited the White Hart in Helston where Manley sampled "scrumpy" a local drink made from apples, then walked up Wendron Street and read the blue plaque over the door of the cottage where world heavyweight boxing champion, Bob Fitzsimmons was born.

On Sunday morning they left Helston and after passing through Penzance, drove to Land's End. With a stiff westerly wind attacking their faces and ruffling their hair, they stood, arms around one another, on a gorse covered verge and gazed at the jagged, rocky outcrops and the vastness of the silvery seas stretching in all directions.

'It looks so… so peaceful, darling,' Laura said, hugging Manley. 'It's hard to believe there's war on.'

Manley was about to reply when, suddenly the serenity of the scene was disturbed by the faint rattle of machine gun fire. Shielding their eyes from the sun's glare, they looked up and saw circular patterns of thin, white vapour trails and black dots, barely visible against the blueness of the cloudless sky.

'It's looks as if the RAF are doing their stuff,' Manley said, tightening his hand around Laura's waist.

'My God,' she gasped as they saw a one of the dots vanish in a ball of yellow flames. 'One of them has been hit.' This was quickly followed by a stream of black smoke coming from another dot, as it hurtled downwards and splashed into the sea. 'I only hope it's not one of ours,' Manley said solemnly.

A few minutes later the aerial battle was over. The dots disappeared over the horizon, leaving the vapour trails fading in the sky like wisps of dead men's shrouds.

The atmosphere during dinner was strained. Manley and Laura ate very little and avoided looking at one another, toying with their food, knowing that that tomorrow they would leave for Portsmouth and dreading the farewells. Johnathan sensed this and did his best to be cheerful by recounting anecdotes from his army days. After dinner, Johnathan and Manley adjourned to the study while Laura, sensing her father wanted to talk privately to Manley, helped Aida to prepare coffee in the kitchen.

Laura was right. Having lit his pipe, Jonathan, sitting in his armchair opposite Manley, took a good puff, then, wafting away a cloud of blue smoke, said, 'You know, Hugh, I've never seen Laura so happy since Clive...'

'Yes, I know,' Manley said, leaning forward in his chair, 'Laura told me.'

'And it's all down to you, my boy,' Johnathan replied, 'the light in her eyes when she looks at you, reminds me of the way my dear wife used to look at me. Laura is clearly in love with you.'

'And let me assure you, sir,' Manley answered, looking directly intro Johnathan's eyes, 'I am with her.'

At that moment, Laura came in, carrying a tray of coffee. 'My ears were burning,' she said, placing the tray on a table. 'I hope Father hasn't been telling you tales about when I was little,' she added, handing a cup and saucer to Manley.

'Of course,' Manley replied, grinning, 'but only the nice ones.'

That night they made love with such tenderness, that when it when it was over, they clung together desperately, wishing the night would never end. But, sadly it did. Shortly before six o'clock, Laura woke up, and after kissing Manley, sneaked back to her room. An hour later, looking pale and tired, and wearing their uniforms, they sat down and did their best to do justice to Aida's bacon and eggs.

'Now, I've put a small hamper of beef sandwiches and a flask of coffee in the boot of your car along with your luggage, Miss Laura,' said Aida, pouring out tea, 'so be sure and eat it, as you've both hardly touched your breakfast.'

'And, Laura, I've put your car top up, just in case it rains,' said Johnathan, giving her a warm hug.

By nine o'clock, Laura said a tearful goodbye to her father and Aida. Johnathan then gave Manley a warm handshake and feeling a lump in his throat, said, 'Godspeed to you and your crew, and come back safely for Laura and myself.'

Five minutes later they drove down the pathway and turned into the Redruth road then headed east. A stiff northerly wind beat against the windscreen while the sun's rays did their best to peak through the umbrella of grey, cirrostratus clouds. After pass-ing through Lyme Regis, they stopped at a lay-by and enjoyed Aida's beef sandwiches and coffee. Manley took the wheel, and on the way to Dorchester, the heavens opened and it poured down. The time was now two o'clock and with each passing mile, they became acutely aware that time was running out; in just over four hours they would say goodbye.

With the windscreen wipers swishing angrily, Manley drove through Dorchester and continued to Bournemouth, arriving there shortly after four o'clock. Traffic was sparse, but the rain had stopped. After passing Portsdown Hill, they entered Portsmouth. It was five o'clock when Manley pulled up on Queen Street, a little distance from the dockyard gate.

'Better change seats and I'll drive you to the ship,' Laura said quietly.

They did so, and after flashing their pay books at the policeman, Laura drove through the gate into the dockyard. As it was still day, in order to avoid prying eyes, she parked the car a good distance from *Dulverton* and *Eridge,* both of whom were tied up behind *Helix.*

For a nearly a minute they sat in silence, knowing the moment they had both dreaded had arrived. Suddenly, Laura turned and doing her best to fight back tears, said, 'Darling, as I've told you I work in the movements office and so I am privy to Ultra decrypts.'

'Yes, I do, so…' Manley slowly replied.

'I know about the convoy you're going on,' she muttered cagily, 'I can't go into details, but there's… there's something unusual about it.'

Somewhat taken aback by Laura's strained remark, Manley said, 'Something unusual, darling, what exactly do you mean?'

'I'm not sure, my love,' cried Laura, 'so do be careful. Now, for pity's sake, Hugh, kiss me and go before I go crazy.'

Manley pulled her fiercely against him; their kiss was so hard their teeth pushed through their lips. Afterwards, with his heart beating a cadence in his chest, he reached over his seat and grabbed his grip. After another passionate kiss, he opened the door and climbed outside.

Still doing her best not to cry, Laura looked up and in hushed tones, said, 'Darling, remember, I'll all ways love you. God bless you and your crew and please, please, come back safe.'

Feeling his throat contract, Manley replied hoarsely, 'don't worry, darling, I will.' He quickly turned away. But as he walked down the wharf towards his ship, Laura's words concerning the convoy rankled in his head. What could she possibly have meant, he asked himself, as he turned and gave her a final wave before making his way up the gangway.

PART TWO
CHAPTER ELEVEN

By 0700, on Tuesday 31 May, *Helix*'s engines were flashed up in readiness to leave harbour. Two hours earlier, after breakfast, everything throughout the ship had been stowed correctly; the steering gear, sea communications and compasses had been checked and tested. While in dry dock, the new ten-centimetre radar equipment had been installed. As this gave detections of surface submarines at a range of four miles or more, it greatly improves the ship's fighting capability.

At exactly 0730, Manley knocked on the captain's door and was told to enter. 'Ship ready for sea, wind strong, nor-nor-west, sir.'

'Thank you, Number One, carry on,' replied Penrose, standing up from behind his desk. 'I'll be up straight away. As senior officer, I'll be Captain D, so *Helix* will leave first.'

Five minutes later, the pipe. 'Close all screen doors and scuttles. Special seamen report for duty. Hands fall in for leaving harbour.'

On the port starboard side of the fo'c'sle and quarterdeck, gusts of warm wind attacked the collars of sailors, waiting to release the heavy hemp ropes from the bollards. After looking up and down from the starboard wing, Manley gave an affirmative nod to Penrose who was sat in his chair. 'Let go aft,' snapped Penrose. Seconds later, he added, 'Let go for'd. Slow ahead, revolutions five.'

'Slow ahead, revolutions, five,' sir,' reported Chief Coxswain Digger Barnes from the wheelhouse.

With the gentle vibrations of the engines purring, the ship, rolling slightly at first, moved imperceptibly away from the jetty.

'Half ahead.'

'Midships.'

'Midships... Wheels amidships, sir.'

'Steady.'

'Steady, sir.'

'Starboard five, revolutions ten.'

Helix gradually increased speed, and by 1030, the small flotilla passed Fort Blockhouse and entered the Solent. By 1100 they had sailed past the lighthouse situated at the end of the Needles, a row of jagged pillars of chalk, lying off the extremity of the Isle of Wight, and entered the choppy grey waters of the English Channel.

'Stand down special sea duty men and revert to cruising stations, Number One,' said Penrose, surveying the horizon with his binoculars. 'Anything on radar?'

'No reports as yet, sir,' replied Manley.

'Thank you, Number One,' Penrose replied, reaching for the ship's intercom. 'I think I'd better tell the ship's company where we're going.' For the next ten minutes, Penrose explained the ship's schedule and mission, ending with, 'We will not be stopping at Gib. I will keep you informed of any future developments. That is all.'

Just as he finished speaking, the voice of Buster Brown in the crow's nest came over the bridge intercom. 'Two unidentified aircraft approaching roughly two thousand feet on the starboard bow.'

Immediately everyone looked up and saw two aircraft, their black shapes barely clear against the greyness of the sky.

'Better sound action stations, Number One,' snapped Penrose, 'just to be on the safe side.'

This was the first time the crew had heard the harsh sound of the claxon echoing around since the ship had returned from convoy duty two months ago. However, as everyone hurried to their stations, Manley's voice announced, 'False alarm, aircraft were ours. Up spirits and revert to cruising stations.'

In the seamen's mess, ratings came in, sweating and breathing heavily. 'Thank fuck for that,' cried Dinga Bell, a tall, fair-haired lanky HO able seaman. 'I've got make and mend and a juicy French book to read in my mick,' he added, hurriedly dragging off his anti-flash gloves and hood.'

'Since when can you read French?' enquired Bob Rose, a small, stocky, able seaman, from Barrow, who, before the war played left back for Manchester City.

'You don't have to, Bob,' Dinga replied smugly. 'All you need to know are the dirty words.'

'And what may they be?' asked Tug Wilson, a tall, dark-haired, leading radar operator from Barnsley.

'Well, "putain" roughly means fuck and 'salope' means slut,' said Dinga, giving Rose a licentious grin.

'What about "cunt"?' enquired Bud Abbot.

'No translation. A cunt is a cunt in any language,' Dinga answered promptly.

'And if you ask me,' said Dutch Holland, 'you are as well. After you with the book.'

In the senior ratings mess, Harry Johnson had just removed his anti-flash gear and was enjoying a mug of steaming hot tea. Standing nearby, Paddy O'Malley stood quietly smoking a cigarette.

'How are things between you and Joyce?' he asked Paddy, while blowing over the top of his mug.

Paddy took a deep drag of his cigarette, then turning his head slightly, exhaled a thick trail of smoke, and said, 'To be sure, Harry, they'd be much better if she wasn't married.'

'And if she wasn't?' Johnson asked, looking over the brim of his mug.

'I'd ask her to marry me, so I would,' he firmly replied, then left the mess.

On the bridge, Penrose was sat in his chair, thinking about his wife and daughter and the pleasant Sunday they had spent together. The warm sun caressed his face. The sea was relatively calm, and high above, the fluffy white cumulus clouds promised the continuation of good weather.

Manley stood nearby, listening to the steady throb of the engines and wondering what Laura was doing. Meanwhile, OOW Sub Lieutenant Baker was busy using his binoculars, surveying the horizon.

Just then, Steward Johnny Morris arrived holding a tray of sandwiches and a mug of tea and stood next to Penrose.

'As it's now sixteen hundred and youse 'ave missed yer lunch, ser,' he said in his distinctive Scouse accent, 'I thought youse would be hungry.'

It suddenly occurred to Penrose that he had been on the bridge since the ship left Portsmouth and he hadn't eaten.

'Thank you, Morris,' Penrose replied, placing the mug on the small table attached to arm of his chair, then accepting the sandwiches. 'They're just what I could do with, chicken, I take it?'

Flashing Penrose a toothy smile, Morris replied, 'Of course, ser.' He then left the bridge.

'Anything on asdic or radar, Number One?' Penrose asked, wiping a piece of bread from the corner of his mouth, 'And our position?'

Manley was about to say there was nothing to report, when as if anticipating his captain's request, OOW Sub Lieutenant Baker interrupted him. 'Land's End, away to port, sir, about fifty miles.'

'Thank you, Pilot,' Penrose replied. Glancing at Manley, he added, somewhat nostalgically, 'I suppose that'll be our last sight of dear old England for some considerable time, eh, Number One?'

Using his binoculars, he looked to his left and was too engrossed to reply. Instead, he stood remembering the wind blowing in their hair as he and Laura stood on a grassy verge looking at the jagged rocky outcrops, and wondered when or if he would see her again.

'Did you hear me, Number One? Penrose asked.

'Sorry, sir, I was err… just thinking the same thing,' Manley hurriedly replied.

By 0600 the next morning, the stars and moon had finally disappeared, leaving the sun to rise imperceptibly from the east to change the grey, choppy Atlantic waters into a carpet of shimmering silver.

On the bridge, OOW Sub Lieutenant Baker was slumped in the captain's chair. Having checked the ship's position, he was now deep in thought, thinking about Janet and wishing things hadn't changed between them.

Suddenly the gruff Lancastrian voice of PO Hardman interrupted his thoughts. 'You never get used to it, do you, sir?'

'Err… what was that you said, PO?' Baker replied, unconsciously fastening the top toggle of his duffel coat.

'The sunrise, sir,' Baker said, nodding away to his left. 'Lovely, ain't it?'

'Yes, it is,' Baker replied, sitting upright and staring at bright white haze spreading across the horizon.

'Another dawn, another day,' muttered QM Knocker White, stifling a yawn.

'Och, it's a poet you are,' said Jock Weir, a small, thick-set, duty leading signalman from Dundee. Just as he finished speaking, Buster Brown's voice, up in the crow's nest crackled over the bridge intercom. 'Nine ships, roughly ten miles on the starboard beam, sir.'

'Thank you,' Baker replied, then, glancing at Hardman, said, 'anything on asdic?'

'No, sir,' Hardman replied.

Baker was about to inform Penrose, when the captain arrived on the bridge. Even though it was June, a chilly wind blew from the east, and like those on duty, he wore a duffel coat.

'I overheard what came over the intercom,' Penrose said, tucking the silk scarf Jean had given him, around his neck. 'It must be the convoy, what's our position?'

'Ninety miles, or so, from Brest, sir,' Baker answered confidently.

'Good, right on time,' Penrose replied. Focussing his binoculars to his right, he was able to make the outlines of the four merchantmen, the escorts and the two tall funnels and superstructure of HMS *Carlisle*. With a quick smile, he looked at Baker, and said, 'Now, kindly give me back my chair.' Looking at Leading Signalman Jock Weir, he said, 'Signal *Eridge* and *Dulverton,* and say, *"remain on station. Intend asking instructions. Will keep you informed".'*

Placing his Aldis lamp in the crook of his arm, Weir did this. A few minutes later, both ships flashed back in acknowledgement.

'The four merchantmen are… *Breconshire, Clan Campbell, Pampas* and *Talbot,* sir,' said Manley, peering through his binoculars. 'They're all low in the water so they must be carrying heavy cargo and have a destroyer on either side of them. *Carlisle* is in the van and is flanked by a destroyer. The remaining two destroyers are on each side of the convoy.'

'Thank you, Number One,' replied Penrose, 'I expect Captain Neame will want just to protect the convoy's rear. Signal *Carlisle,* say, *'"Nice to see you. Request instructions".'*

Minutes later, a signal repeated to *Eridge and Dulverton,* arrived. *'"Flotilla take station one mile in rear".'*

Twenty minutes later, the convoy turned ten degrees to port and headed due south. Throughout the morning, the dark green, undulating sea was calm; a slight breeze blew from the south and high above, in an almost cloudless blue sky, the strong rays of the sun bathed the convoy in warm sunshine.

'Just think, Terry,' Leading Writer Jack Jones said to stores assistant Bensen, 'Before the war, my boss in the shipping office used to go on cruises in the Med.' They were standing on the quarterdeck, leaning against the guard rails admiring the clarity of sparkling blue sea.

'Aye,' Bensen replied curtly, 'but he didn't have to keep watches and be closed up at action stations all hours of the day and night.'

'Or be attacked by fuckin' dive bombers,' added Dinga Bell, idly flicking a cigarette dog-end overboard.

'But if that happens, 'said Dutch Holland, looking ahead of the convoy at the frothy wake of *Carlisle,* 'at least we've got those high angled four inchers of the cruiser to protect us.'

'Be that as it may,' said Jack Jones, grinning at Holland, 'but my boss had gorgeous girls in bathing suits to ogle instead of a load of ugly buggers like you.'

By evening rounds, darkness had fallen. From a clear sky, a full moon bathed the heavy rolling sea into a mass of sparkling diamonds. Almost immediately, the ships began to roll heavily as they encountered the undulating swell of the Atlantic Ocean. On the bridge, Sub Lieutenant Baker glanced warily at the barometer.

'Temperature's dropping, sir,' he said to Penrose. 'Looks like we're in for a drop of roughers as we enter the Bay during the night.'

Penrose was sat in his chair. His binoculars were clamped to his eyes and he was glad to see none of the merchant ships had strayed out of position. 'That doesn't surprise me, Pilot,' he replied, 'the Bay of Biscay is invariably unkind to shipping at this time of year.'

'*Carlisle* signalling, sir,' said Jack Tate, a tall, three badge PO Signalman. '"*Convoy and escorts alter course five degree to port".'

'Acknowledge' Penrose answered, lowering his binoculars. 'This will allow the convoy to head into this strong south easterly wind. Better pipe for the Buffer, Number One, to report to the bridge.'

A minute or so later, Chief Bosun's mate, Charlie Jackson, came onto the bridge. The overalls he wore over his stocky figure were once dark blue, but due to constant washing, they were now almost white. 'You sent for me, sir,' he said, taking out an off-white handkerchief and wiping his brow.

'Yes, chief,' said Penrose, 'during the night we'll be entering the Bay, and you know what that'll mean.'

'Aye, that I do, sir,' Jackson replied, stuffing the handkerchief into a pocket. 'And I've already had the duty watch secure the sea boats and Carley floats.'

With a wry smile, Penrose replied, 'Thank you, Chief, please carry on.' Penrose leaned forward and unhooked the ship's tannoy and informed the ship's company to be ready for rough seas,' adding, 'It'll take the convoy two days to pass through the bay. We will then go through the Straits, and with luck, meet up with Admiral Vian's battle group the next day.' He paused to allow his words to sink in, then went on. 'I expect the enemy's spies in Algeciras will have alerted the Italians of our presence, so be prepared to go to action stations at any time. The ship is about to turn to port. That is all.'

Out of earshot of Manley and Penrose, QM Knocker White looked at PO Podge Hardman and muttered, 'Here we go again, corn dog and kye.'

'Just be bloody glad we're not on the Russian run,' said Podge, 'or we'd be lucky to get that, and if you did, you'd be too cold to eat it.'

Everyone on the bridge felt the deck cant, as the ship turned left. 'I must say, sir, I'm very impressed,' remarked Sub Lieutenant Baker, watching a splurge of white waves burst over the fo'c'sles of the merchant ships and escorts as they turned almost in unison. 'It's almost as if some puppeteer was pulling strings to make us move together.'

'It's called expert seamanship,' Manley replied, grinning.

Throughout the night, the convoy was buffeted by strong winds and high waves. On the open bridges of the escorts, everyone held on to anything at hand as the wind whipped against their faces and tore into their duffel coats. In the mess decks, the incessant *thud, thud* of the sea beating against the bulkheads, made sleep virtually impossible. Men were almost flung out of their hammocks as their ship reared up then, quivering violently on the crest of a wave, was sent crashing down, bow first, on into a trough. This deadly movement was repeated so often, men simply closed their eyes and prayed for the dawn.

On board *Helix*'s bridge, the strong winds had thrown back the duffel coat hoods of ghostly figures on watch. With his woollen mittens, a cold, soggy mess, using one hand, PO Telegraphist, Jack Frost, clung desperately to the binnacle. For the umpteenth time, using the back of his other hand, he wiped water from away from his eyes and noticed OOW Sub Lieutenant Milton's hunched figure holding onto the conning intercom.

'This is worse than the bloody Atlantic, eh, sir?' shouted Frost, his words barely audible above the howling wind.

'I expect it'll get worse before it gets better,' Milton replied stoically.

As if on cue, a sudden crash of thunder was quickly followed by jagged bolts of lightning, momentarily lighting up the sky, and for the first time since coming on watch at 0400, Milton caught a momentarily glimpse of the wet, pale faces around him.

During the next two hours, the storm clouds faded, leaving the sky a deep blue. The force of the wind dropped and the barometer readings started to rise. However, a tanker and cargo ship had broken formation and were escorted back by a destroyer.

On board *Helix,* at exactly 0600, the pipe. ''Eavo, 'eavo, 'eavo. Lash up and stow. Cooks to the galley,' echoed around the ship. In the mess decks, weary men tumbled out of their hammocks onto a wet, slippery deck.

'Thank fuck for that,' groaned Chats Harris, securing the last of the six turns around his hammock. 'I thought the ship was going to capsize.'

'That's now't,' said Dutch Holland, emptying seawater out of his boot, 'all my bedding is soaked.'

At 0900 on Saturday 4th June, Able Seaman Tug Wilson reported sighting Gibraltar, together with the Spanish mainland, on his green radar screen. By 1000, the jaw-like mass of the rock could be seen, jutting up into the clear blue sky. Seconds later, Buster Brown in the crow's nest reported an unidentified aircraft approaching from the west.

'It looks like a Junkers 88, sir,' Buster said, 'about ten thousand feet.'

'Thank you, Brown,' said Penrose. Then, giving Manley a cautious look, said, 'It's probably a spotter.'

'I agree, sir,' replied Manley, who, like everyone on the bridge was using their binoculars to search the sky. 'I expect we'll have company soon.'

CHAPTER TWELVE

Throughout the morning, the convoy passed through the Straits of Gibraltar and entered the Mediterranean Sea. Away to port, the rugged Cordillera Baetica Mountains could be seen a few miles inland from Spain's coast. While, on the opposite side, lay the white, sandy beaches of Morocco. High above, in a dazzling blue sky, clusters of fluffy cirrocumulus clouds shared the heavens with an eye-smarting sun.

'So this is what Mussolini calls his *Mare Nostrum,* eh, sir?' Midshipman Morgan asked Sub Lieutenant Jewitt, watching Morgan using a sextant to take a midday fix. Jewitt had just relieved Sub Lieutenant Milton and was now OOW. Like the rest of the ship's company, he now wore tropical white shorts and shirts. (*Mare Nostrum* is Latin meaning 'Our Sea.' In 1942 Mussolini wanted to dominate the Mediterranean Sea and used the term to promote his Fascist programme.)

'If I were you, Mid,' Jewitt grunted while making note of the ship's speed and position in relation to the other escorts and convoy, 'I'd stop using fancy Latin words and concentrate on getting your measurements right, or you'll never get your watch-keepers ticket.' He then contacted radar operator Dolly Gray, a tall, dark-haired slightly built, leading seaman. 'Anything to report, Gray?'

'Nothing on the screen except the convoy and escorts, sir,' replied Gray.

After taking requestmen and defaulters earlier, at 1100, Penrose came onto the bridge, followed by Manley and Sub Lieutenant Baker.

'What's the speed of the convoy, Number One?'

'Fifteen knots, sir,' Manley replied.

'Let's see now,' Penrose said, pursing his lips, 'at that speed we should be off the coast of Algeria tomorrow. What do you think, Pilot?'

Baker quickly consulted his chart, and after using a pair of dividers, replied, 'That's about right, sir, about a hundred miles.'

'Good,' Penrose said, while easing himself into his chair. 'By then we should sight Vian's battle group, so keep a sharp lookout.'

Steward Morris came onto the bridge holding a mug of steaming tea. 'Thought youse would like this, seein' as 'ow youse missed stand easy.'

'Thank you, Morris,' said Penrose, 'it may be a long night.'

Morris gave Penrose a toothy grin, and added, 'An' don't forget your dinner as youse missed it last night.' He then turned and hurried away.

'He looks after me like a mother hen,' Penrose said to Manley, 'only, at times, I don't quite understand what he's saying.'

Baker's prediction was fairly accurate. Shortly after midday, the next day, Radar Operator Slinger Wood reported a large group of ships, roughly ten miles directly ahead of the convoy. 'There's three big ones and about ten smaller ones, sir. Speed roughly fifteen knots.'

'I expect the big ones will be the cruisers,' said Penrose.

'Would one of them be a carrier, sir?' asked Manley, giving his captain a searching look.

'I'm not sure, but I doubt it,' Penrose replied pensively, 'I expect the rest are destroyers.'

Half an hour later Vian's battle group hove into view.

'You were right, sir,' said Manley surveying the small armada of warships. 'There's no carrier, only three cruisers surrounded by ten destroyers.'

After studying the battle group, Baker went into his small chart room and looked the cruisers up in *Jane's Fighting Ships*. 'They're Dido Class light cruisers, sir, armament, five sets of five point two, and one set of four-inch plus heavy and light machine guns.'

'As well as two triple torpedoes and pom-poms, sir,' added PO Signalman Jack Tate. 'One of those cruisers is my old ship, *Euryalus*. I served aboard her in '38.'

'Thank you both for that valuable piece of information,' Penrose said, giving Baker and Frost a reassuring smile.

Frost was about to say something when he saw one of the cruisers flashing a signal to *Carlisle*.

'Better read it, PO,' said Penrose.

Using his binoculars to read the flashes, Tate carefully replied, *"'Glad to see you. . . Admiral… Ichino… Left Taranto… with Littorio… and three heavy cruisers… none have radar… remain with convoy. I will take station twenty miles… on your port beam, Vian, Cleopatra"*.'

'*Carlisle* is flashing to all escorts and merchantmen, sir,' Tate reported. 'Signal is repeating Vian's message, sir.'

'Thank you, PO,' said Penrose, 'acknowledge.'

'Great Scott, sir,' cried Baker, 'the *Littorio* has nine fifteen-inch guns, twelve six-inchers as well as…'

'Yes, thank you, Baker,' Penrose said, quickly interrupting him, then calmly added, 'tell me, Pilot, how far away are we from Taranto?'

'Just over five hundred miles, sir,' Baker replied, 'it's on the southern tip of Sicily.'

Penrose pensively stroked his chin and muttered, 'Let me see now, that will place the convoy closer to Taranto than the battle group. I wonder what Vian's up to.'

Penrose's remarks reminded Manley of Laura suggesting there was something unusual about the convoy. Could it be, he asked himself, that Vian was using the convoy to act as bait. The thought that Vian would risk the lives of men, and a precious cargo badly needed in Malta, to attack the Italian fleet was too dangerous to contemplate, or was it?

The concern of Penrose and Manley was well founded. Unknown to them and everyone in the convoy, Vian had received a secret Ultra signal, intercepted by a submarine, informing him that Admiral Ichino knew the position of the convoy and intended to launch an attack.

Shortly after "stand easy" on the morning of Monday 6th June, Tug Wilson reported to Penrose the presence of a large group of dots on his screen. 'Roughly ten miles away on our starboard quarter, sir.'

Seconds later, Taff Williams, a tall, dark HO able seaman in the crow's nest confirmed this by seeing thin trails of smoke and several mast heads on the starboard horizon.

The thought that a salvo from one of *Littorio*'s sixteen-inch guns hitting *Helix* suddenly increased Penrose's heartrate. Reaching into his jacket pocket, he nervously undid the top of the small box of Digital tablets. Then, avoiding the eyes of those around him, quickly placed a tablet in his mouth and swallowed it. A few minutes later, he felt the beating of his heart slowly decrease in volume. 'Better sound action stations, Number One,' he said

Seconds later, QM Knocker White's distinctive Yorkshire accent came over the tannoy. 'Hands to action stations. Close all screen doors and scuttles.'

In the seamen's mess, Sammy Smith glanced warily at Able Seaman Murphy. 'Here we go, Spud,' he said, grabbing hold of his anti-flash gear. 'Here's hoping the Ities have eaten too much spaghetti and have indigestion.'

'If they haven't then you'd better rattle your rosary, and say a few words for us,' added Dutch Holland as they and the other ratings hurried up the stairs.

In a matter of minutes all departments were closed up. In the boiler and engine rooms, stokers struggled into their ant-flash hoods and gloves. 'It's hot enough without havin' to wear these itchy things,' growled a tall, pale-faced stoker.

'If a shell hits us you might be glad you wore it,' Johnson replied. 'Now, shit in it and check those heat gauges.'

Meanwhile, PO Steward Sandy Powel and the first aid party had mustered in the canteen flat. 'Check your first aid kits,' he said, looking sternly first at the tired face of NAFFI manager, Ted Grainger, then at the other three men. 'And make sure the pom-pom crews have shell dressings in their bags, and after you've done that, check the straps on the Neil Robertson stretchers.'

'Is all this really necessary, Sandy? grunted Grainger, running fingers through his sparse, grey hair. 'It's interfering with my invoice checking.'

'As they say in the Russian navy, Ted, toughskie- shitskie,' Sandy sarcastically replied, 'now get on with it.'

Shortly after 1300, the Italian battle fleet was sighted.

'*Cleopatra* flashing, sir,' shouted Jack Tate. '"*To convoy and escorts. Turn ten degree south, Will place myself between you and the enemy. Carlisle, Avon Vale, make smoke to protect convoy. Enemy aware of our position.*" Signal by wireless, sir.'

'Acknowledge by wireless,' Penrose replied.

Laura's words, saying she thought there was something about the convoy, sprung into Manley's head. 'So he is using the convoy as bait to draw the Italians out,' he said to Penrose.

'I think you're right, Number One,' Penrose replied pensively. 'Thank God the Italians haven't got radar or we'd be in deep trouble.

'But, sir,' pleaded Manley, 'is sacrificing the lives of the men ships and cargo worth Vian taking on the Italians, after all, they have a stronger fleet than us.'

'Ours is not to reason why,' Penrose nervously replied, taking out a Digital tablet from a pocket in trousers.

'Are you all right, sir?' asked Manley, watching as Penrose quickly put the tablet in his mouth.

'A headache, just an aspirin,' Penrose tentatively answered.

In the crow's nest, Pony Moore, a thick-set able seaman from York, suddenly felt his small compartment and main mast sway uncomfortably as *Helix, Eridge, Dulverton* and *Carlisle,* together with the convoy, turned to port.

On *Helix*'s bridge, everyone turned and using their binoculars, saw the destroyer, *Avon Vale*, break away from the battle group and lay a thick smoke screen between Vian's warships and the Italian fleet. The time was shortly after 1430.

'Great Scott!' exploded Penrose. '*Cleopatra, Dido* and *Euryalus* are going through the smoke screen. I do believe they're going to attack the Italians.'

Seconds later, the booming sound of gunfire could be heard beyond the denseness of the smoke screen. Yellow gun flashes, barely discernible through the smoke, accompanied the detonations as more exchanges of loud gunfire rent the air.

'I wish we knew what was going on, Number One,' Penrose said, peering through his binoculars hoping to catch a glimpse of the action.

'I can see our cruisers coming out of the smoke screen, sir,' yelled the port lookout.

'Yes, we can see that,' Penrose replied, 'they're taking evasive action against the enemy's heavy guns.'

'But where the hell is the Italian fleet?' said Manley.

'Radar reports part of the Italian fleet is about twenty miles away,' said Penrose. 'Our cruisers must be on their way to engage them.'

'By the sound of the gunfire,' Penrose said, 'there's more than two enemy cruisers beside the *Littorio*.'

'You could be right, sir,' said Manley, watching the three British cruisers turn back into the smoke screen. This was quickly followed by exchanges of gunfire. Suddenly, the gunfire stopped. Everyone on the bridge watched the British cruisers coming out of the smoke screen, seemingly unscathed. By this time the convoy was only ten miles away from the battle. However, with the use of radar and high-powered Barr and Stroud binoculars, the men on the escorts were able to establish a rough idea of what was happening.

'What the blazes is Vian up to, I wonder?' puzzled Penrose. 'He seems to have ordered the cruisers to play cat and mouse with the Italians.'

'In that case, sir,' Manley replied, 'maybe he's trying to lure them further ahead into a trap. After all, sir, you thought there is three enemy cruisers giving fire, and remember, according to the radar, the main Italian fleet is only twenty miles away.' (The three Italian cruisers were the *Gorizo, Trento* and *Giovanni Della Bande Nere*.)

'And as that north westerly is increasing,' Penrose replied, feeling a gust of wind attack his face. 'it's blowing the smoke screen to the south. That should help the Italian gunners, but without radar, they're at a distinct disadvantage.'

'I agree, sir,' Manley replied, 'and the wind should help the smoke screen protect the convoy.'

'Excuse me, sir,' interrupted Baker, 'radar reports large group of enemy warships joining the two enemy cruisers.'

'That'll be the *Lottorio* and her escorts,' said Penrose. 'If they manage to break through Vian's group, Admiral Iachino will be after the convoy.'

The time was 1500. For the next hour, Penrose and everyone watched anxiously, as once again, the British warships, including the cruisers, darted in and out of the smoke screen, returning the enemy fire.

'It looks like Vian's trying to confuse Iachino and entice him to come closer,' said Penrose, nervously biting his lower lip.

Manley gave Penrose a searching look, and said, 'Dangerous tactics, sir, seeing as how he's outgunned.'

'Yes indeed, Number One,' Penrose replied, 'and if he fails, Iachino will be after the convoy. Better hoist battle ensign just in case.'

Manley gave a quick nod to Tate, who along with an assistant "bunting tosser", Dixie Dean, a tall, ginger-headed leading signalman, obeyed Manley's order. With a slight mixture of pride and trepidation, everyone watched as a large white ensign was quickly hoisted to the yardarm.

Suddenly, the sound of gunfire, more ferocious than earlier, could be heard. High above in the crow's nest, Pony Moore wiped the lens of his binoculars, and straining his eyes, managed to have a reasonably good view of the battle.

'*Cleopatra*'s been hit and she's on fire,' he shouted down the intercom, 'but her guns are still firing.'

(Part of *Cleopatra*'s bridge was destroyed and sixteen men were killed.)

Seconds later, Brown's voice, now slightly hoarse, reported two more British cruisers and two destroyers were on fire. 'Hard to say who they are as there's too much bloody smoke,' he added, slightly out of breath, 'but one of the destroyers has stopped, looks like she's dead in the water.' (This was the destroyer *Havcock* who had suffered a direct hit. Her engine and boiler rooms were hit and flooded, plus her searchlights, torpedo tubes were badly damaged, killing fifteen of her crew. Vian subsequently ordered her to leave the battle group and make for Malta for repairs.)

'A destroyer coming through the smoke screen, sir,' shouted Moore, 'and she's heading towards the convoy.'

On the bridge, everyone turned and trained their binoculars aft and saw the foamy bow waves of a destroyer a mile away.

'It's *Kingston*, sir,' said Manley, 'and it looks as if she's lost her after gun turret and pom-poms.'

A few minutes later, Taff Taylor, a short, stocky leading telegraphist arrived on the bridge. 'Message from *Cleopatra* to *Kingston*, sir.'

'Yes, yes, what does it say?' Penrose asked impatiently.

'"*Take position port side of Carlisle for passage to Malta. Neame*".'

'Thank you,' Penrose answered, 'make to *Kingston*. "*Do you need assistance?*"'

Taff Taylor hurried away, and returning a few minutes later, said, 'Message from Kingston, sir, it reads, "*No thank you. Can make fourteen knots*".'

The time was 1800. A bright moon cast a silver sheen over a calm sea and a warm wind blew lazily from the east. 'Darken ship,' was piped. Throughout the ship, dead lights were secured and canvas covers drawn across hatchways. On the bridge, everyone managed to see *Kingston* arrive two hundred yards on *Carlisle*'s port beam. By this time, the convoy was some twenty miles from the battle, too far for Moore to see through the darkness at the smoke screen.

'Vian appears to be sending his destroyers to engage the enemy, sir,' reported Radar Operator Dolly Gray, peering at a series of black dots on his green screen leaving the battle group.

'Against the cruisers,' said Penrose, frowning, 'surely not. They'd get blown out of the water.'

'The destroyers are firing their torpedoes, then going in and out the smoke screen, sir,' Gray reported somewhat exuberantly.

For the next ten minutes, everyone strained their ears to hear the noise of the torpedoes hitting home. But none came.

A perplexed expression slowly spread over Manley's heavily tanned features. 'I wonder what's happened, sir,' he said, looking at Penrose.

'God only knows,' Penrose muttered solemnly.

Unknown to Penrose, even though the convoy lay within range of *Littorio*'s broadsides, the feinted attacks by Vian's destroyers had kept the battleship at bay.

'I say, the Italians are buggering off, sir,' Moore reported excitedly.

'Great Scott!' yelled Penrose, slapping a thigh. 'The blighters have had enough!'

Manley was right. Vian had ordered a torpedo attack, but unfortunately, none of the torpedoes hit home. Nevertheless, as the Italian ships were short of fuel. Iachino, whose fleet had suffered little or no damage, ordered his ships to return to Taranto. But to the onlookers on board, the merchantmen and escorts, it looked like the Italians had given up and were running away.

Taylor hurried onto the bridge. 'Message from *Cleopatra*, sir,' he said breathing heavily. '"*Enemy repairing to the north west. Destroyers,*

Sikha and Legion, badly damaged and leaving for Tobruk. Remaining battle group making for Alexandria along with Euryalus. *Penelope, slightly damaged, to join convoy and continue to Malta. God Speed and good luck. Vian".'*

A look of relief appeared on Penrose's tanned features. 'Thank you, Taylor,' he said. Then, reaching for the ship's tannoy, he looked at Manley and added, 'I think the ship's company will be more than glad to hear that, Number One. Stand down from action stations and lower the battle ensign.'

Penrose was right. The news that the Italians broken off the battle was greeted with wild cheering.

'I expect the Ities have run out of vino,' Bud Abbott, the captain of A gun, said to his team of gunners.

'Maybe now we can have a decent meal,' said Able Seaman Wacker Payne, taking off his anti-flash hood. 'Those corn beef sarnies are giving me wind.'

'So that's what the noise was, eh, boyo?' replied Able Seaman Dai Morgan. 'And all the time I thought it was the sound of gunfire.'

On the bridge, Penrose eased himself from his chair. 'Take over, Number One,' he said, stifling a yawn. 'I'll be in my cabin. Looks like Vian has achieved his aim and beaten the Ities.'

'But, sir,' Manley replied, giving Penrose a dubious look, 'the damage caused by the enemy on our ships outweighs that inflicted by us on them. Is it possible that Vian really did use the convoy to tempt the Italians into battle?'

'Only Vian knows that,' Penrose answered dryly. 'But even though the convoy has been slowed down, thank goodness it's safe.'

'For the time being, at least,' Manley answered laconically.

CHAPTER THIRTEEN

On the morning of Wednesday 8th June, the convoy was steaming due west when the weather began to deteriorate. By 1100, the barometer had dropped and the wind was now blowing a wild force five. The sky, hitherto a clear, eye-catching blue, had become a vast concave of darkness while the sun, disappeared behind a vast canopy of black clouds.

On board *Helix*, the fierce wind had torn away the canvas awning protecting the bridge from the elements. The upper deck was awash and out of bounds to all hands as strong winds sent huge angry waves crashing against the ship, tossing her about like a cork. As in previous bouts of stormy weather, all loose gear was stowed away. Those ratings off duty took to their hammocks as once again, cooks valiantly prepared the usual corn beef sandwiches. In the engine and boiler rooms, stokers held onto anything at hand to prevent them slipping on the steel gratings. Sixty plus miles an hour gusts of wind prevented lookouts climbing up the rattling rigging to the crow's nest, while directly under the bridge, Chief Coxswain Digger Barnes kept both hands firmly on the wheel as he obeyed the erratic movements on the steering repeater.

On the bridge, Penrose held on tightly to the arms of his chair watching the ghostly superstructures of *Penelope, Kingston, Eridge* and *Dulverton* regularly plunge, bow first, into troughs of heaving black sea, only to reappear in clouds of white foam. Like Manley and the others on duty, Penrose wore a black sou'wester and oilskin with a towel tucked in around his neck.

'How long will this bloody weather keep up, Pilot?' Penrose shouted to Baker, while using his leather-gloved hand to wipe water from his eyes.

'Hard to say, sir,' Baker cried, 'in these waters at this time of year, usually about twenty-four hours.' Their voices were barely audible over the sickening whine of the wind.

Due to the rough weather, rum issue had been postponed until evening and duty cooks were told to collect soup and corned beef sandwiches from the galley. The intermittent booming, as each angry wave bounced against the bulkheads, vibrated throughout the ship causing the electric lighting to flicker on and off. In the mess decks, tobacco smoke hung in the damp atmosphere like a blue cloud. The pale-yellow lighting cast an eerie glow over everything, while hammocks, some occupied and sagging, others empty and loose, swayed in perfect unison with each roll of the ship. Those ratings off duty were sitting at the wooden table doing their best to play uckers. Nobody noticed the thin frame of Hamish MacBride, a tall, gangly, junior seaman from Dundee doing his best to climb out of his hammock to visit the heads. Then, wearing only a pair of underpants and vest, he slipped on the wet linoleum deck. The sudden, loud cry as he hit a leg on the edge of the table immediately interrupted Tug Wilson, who was about to try and shoot a six. Dolly Gray and Dusty Miller immediately stood up then went beside Hamish who was half bent holding his left leg.

'What's the matter, Hamish?' asked Gray, 'got cramp or summat?'

'Och, it's me fuckin' leg,' Hamish cried, 'I've hurt me fuckin' leg, you daft bugger.'

'Take it easy and lie still, Jock,' said Dusty Miller, noticing the awkward angle of Hamish's leg. 'And I'll phone the sick bay.'

Five minutes later SBA Bamford arrived, breathing heavily and carrying a first aid bag.

'What's up, Jock?' Bamford asked, taking off his spectacles and wiping them with a handkerchief while noticing someone had covered Hamish with a blanket.

'It's me leg, Doc,' Hamish replied. His voice sounded weak and as he spoke, beads of perspiration ran down the sides of his face.

Bamford carefully pulled back the lower part of the blanket and saw Hamish's hand covering an ugly looking, anaemic, white lump protruding from the left middle-edge of his tibia.

'Lie still and don't move your leg,' said Bamford. With an expression of grave concern, he looked up at Gray. 'Phone the bridge. Tell the officer of the watch to pipe for the MO to come to the mess, chop chop.'

Meanwhile, several members of the mess, hanging onto anything to avoid falling over, crowded around Hamish.

'What's he done, Doc?' asked a rating. 'Is it serious?'

'Has he bust anything?' another rating said, glancing anxiously at Bamford.

'Someone, get a pillow and blanket,' snapped Bamford, ignoring the questions.

'You'll be all right, mate,' said Bungy Williams, kneeling down and supporting Hamish's head, allowing Bamford to put the pillow under it. At the same time, Dusty Miller came, and said, 'd'you want a fag, Jock?'

'No ta, Dusty,' Hamish said, grimacing with pain, 'I don't feel too good.' The paleness of Hamish's face and the beads of sweat on his brow told Bamford, Hamish was going into shock. Just then, the pipe requesting the medical officer to go to the seaman's mess, came over the tannoy. Shortly afterwards, the tall figure of Surgeon Lieutenant Latta arrived. He wore a duffel coat over his uniform and carried a brown leather Gladstone medical case. Bamford quickly explained what had happened.

'How are you feeling, laddie?' he asked Hamish, kneeling down and placing a finger over Hamish's wrist and finding his pulse, weak and rapid. He carefully pulled back the blankets. A glance at the swelling on Hamish's tibia immediately showed the doctor that the swelling was the end of broken bone, pushing up through Hamish's skin, a sure sign of a compound fracture.

'A wee bit sick, sir,' Hamish answered faintly, 'and the pain is bloody bad. Any chance of a drink?'

The doctor nodded to Bamford, and said, 'Just a drop or two. We might have to…'

'Yes, sir, I understand,' Bamford quickly replied, realising the doctor implied that he would have to try and reduce the fracture under whatever anaesthetic they had.

'You've done yersell a nasty injury,' said the doctor, replacing the blanket. 'I'm going to give you two injections, one to ease the pain, the other to prevent infection. Then, when you're feeling better, we're going lift you off the deck and put you on a stretcher, and make you comfortable.'

Bamford immediately left the mess, returning a few minutes later carrying a folded army type stretcher. With the help of Dusty Miller, they unhooked the metal supports under the stretcher, opened it out then placed it alongside Hamish.

By this time, Latta had opened his bag and taken out a wooden box containing small glass ampoules of morphine sulphate and a glass syringe and needle. Waiting for the ship to pause before dipping into a trough, and being careful not to touch the needle, he attached it to the end of the syringe. After gently tapping the ampoule to clear any air, he used a tiny metal saw to remove the top of the ampoule, and using the needle, drew the morphia into the syringe, waited for the next shudder of the bulkhead to subside then quickly changed the needle. Bamford handed the doctor a large piece of cotton wool he had manged to soak in surgical spirit. Using the cotton wool, Latta cleaned an area in the outer aspect one of Hamish's upper arms, then expertly inserted the needle. After a quick withdrawal to ensure the needle wasn't in a blood vessel, he injected 1/6 grain of morphia into Hamish.

Latta placed the used syringe in his bag and brought out a glass vial containing 4,000 units of gas gangrene antitoxin. He changed the syringe and gave Hamish another injection.

'There, then,' the doctor said, giving Hamish's arm a good rub, 'that should help.'

'Is… is it bad, sir?' muttered Hamish. 'Is me leg really bad?'

'I'm afraid it's broken, laddie,' Latta quietly replied. 'But we'll soon fix you up,' he added, giving Hamish's shoulder a reassuring squeeze. 'Now try and relax.'

The doctor stood up with a worried expression on his face, and said, 'The captain has told me the weather should improve during the next twenty-four hours.' He paused, momentarily in thought, then making sure Hamish couldn't hear him, went on, 'We'll have to have to keep him here as it'll be too dangerous to move him to the sick bay.' As if to prove his point, a wave thundered against the bulkhead, momentarily rocking the ship. 'Let's get him off this wet deck onto a canvas stretcher.'

With Bamford's help they opened it out and after ensuring the steel struts were locked, they opened it out. Bamford spread a blanket inside the stretcher, then, with the assistance of the doctor, Gray and White, they lifted Hamish onto the stretcher and covered him in another blanket.

'Better raise the end of the stretcher on some pillows as he's in shock,' said the doctor. 'And when the weather improves, we'll transfer him to the sick bay in a Neil Robertson stretcher. Meanwhile, I'll give him an injection of Pethidine, that'll sedate him for a few hours, during which time I'll straighten his leg out and then we'll splint him up. Now, I'll stay with him while you go and get the splints and the Neil Robertson.'

Bamford gave a quick nod then left the mess. After Bamford had left, the doctor looked down at Hamish. The morphia was beginning to take effect and Hamish was groggy. Nevertheless, the doctor told him what was going happen. Hamish merely nodded and closed his eyes.

Minutes later, Bamford arrived and managed to pass the stretcher and splints to Dolly Gray before climbing down the stairs into the mess. By this time, Hamish was asleep. They waited until the ships came out of a trough, then lifted the stretcher onto the mess table. Bamford left the mess and returned, red-faced and panting, holding small wooden box containing a sphygmomanometer (a device for taking blood pressure), and a stethoscope.

After accepting the box from Bamford, the doctor opened the lid containing a mercury pressure gauge. He attached a small rubber tube to the rubber cuff and wrapped the cuff around Hamish's upper arm. Using a small rubber bulb, he inflated the cuff. He then placed the drum of the stethoscope over an artery in the crook of Hamish's arm, noting when the pressure faded then returned. This gives two blood pressure readings. The first is called the 'systolic', the second the 'diastolic. In a healthy adult this is recorded, 20 diastolic/80 Systolic.

It's a hundred and ten over sixty-five, too damn low,' said the doctor, giving Bamford a worrying look while removing the stethoscope from his ears. 'Which means he is still in shock. We'd better check it every quarter of an hour. When he wakes up, give him two tablets of sulphanilamide, along with the anti-gangrene injection I've given him, it should prevent any infection. Now I'd better go and see the captain,' he added, standing up.

The doctor managed to make his way to the bridge and inform Penrose about Hamish's injury. 'Hamish has a compound fracture and will need urgent hospitalisation. How soon will the convoy reach Malta, sir?'

Penrose pensively stroked the bristles on his chin, then, with a weary sigh, replied, 'This damn weather has slowed the convoy down, so I don't expect us to reach Malta for two days, isn't that right, Pilot,' he shouted to Baker, who was holding onto an arm of Penrose's chair.

'Yes, sir,' Baker answered, grimacing as a cold watery spray hit him in the face. 'Friday, sometime in the morning.'

'Just over forty-eight hours,' the doctor muttered to himself, silently praying the gas gangrene antitoxin injection he gave Hamish would work.

Throughout the evening and night, Bamford and the doctor kept four hourly watches over Hamish. Just after 0230, Hamish woke up. The erratic movements of the ship had lessened. The mess lights were on and the movements of the hammocks of those ratings off duty had reduced, giving a clear indication that the weather was improving.

Beads of sweat ran down the sides of Hamish's pale face and he was grimacing with pain. 'It's me leg, sir,' he muttered staring up at the doctor. 'It's killin' me, so it is.'

'Steady on, old boy,' the doctor quietly replied, noting with relief that Hamish's BP had fallen and his pulse was stronger. He gave Hamish a shot of morphia, then said quietly, 'That should help, now try and get some sleep.'

A few minutes later the doctor looked up and saw the tall figure of Penrose climbing down the stairs. His weather-beaten face looked drawn and haggard; his cap was soaked and the black oilskin he wore glistened with rainwater. The doctor began to stand up, but Penrose, motioned him to remain seated. 'How's our man?' Penrose quietly asked, looking at Hamish, who appeared to be sleeping.

'Holding his own, sir,' whispered the doctor. 'But he has a compound fracture so the sooner we get him to Malta, the better.'

'The wind has dropped and the sea's calmer, so we should sight the coast soon,' Penrose replied. 'The admiral has given us permission to steam on ahead of the convoy into Grand Harbour. Now I'd better return to the bridge. Let me know if you need anything.'

The doctor suddenly felt the ship wasn't rolling as much as before and the table upon which Hamish lay on the stretcher seemed to be stable. The ear-splitting booming of the sea was now a gentle thud and the hammocks were swaying less, a sure sign that the sea was calmer.

At that moment, Knocker White, his black oilskin glistening with rain, came down the stairs carrying a white enamel mug of kye.

'Thought you could do with this, sir,' he said, handing it to the doctor, 'but mind, it's hot.'

'Thank you,' the doctor replied, giving White a grateful grin, 'that's just what the doctor ordered.'

'How's Hamish, sir?' asked Bamford, looking at Hamish's pale face.

'He's doing fine,' replied the doctor, blowing across the top of his mug. 'But you'd better check his temperature and pulse.'

Bamford took out a thin, silver, metal tube from his first aid bag, screwed off the top then took out a glass thermometer. After a few quick wrist shakes, ensuring the mercury in the thermometer had fallen, he gently eased Hamish's vest to one side and slid the thermometer under his arm. Bamford then took Hamish's radial pulse. 'Eighty-eight, sir,' said Bamford. 'And his temperature,' he added, removing the thermometer, and reading the mercury level, 'is ninety-nine.'

The doctor gave a satisfied nod. 'Good,' he replied. 'The gangrene antitoxin seems to be working, thank God.'

Just before 0400, Bamford, who had been doing his best to sleep, fully clothed, in a spare hammock, heaved himself onto the deck, yawned, and asked how Hamish was.

'He's sleeping,' the doctor replied, 'but as you can no doubt feel, the weather has improved so I'll give him another shot of Pethidine, then we'll splint his leg.'

'Very good, sir,' said Bamford, who immediately padded each splint with cotton wool and undid some bandages.

After the Pethidine had taken effect, the doctor turned back the end of the blanket, exposing Hamish's injured tibia. 'Hold onto his lower thigh firmly,' the doctor said to Bamford who, after wiping his glasses, knelt down and feeling his hands shake slightly, gripped Hamish's thigh. He watched as the doctor carefully exerted a gentle downward pull on the lower aspect of Hamish's tibia until the bony lump appeared to be smaller. 'Quickly, Bamford,' said the doctor who was still holding the leg, 'put the splints firmly on either side of his leg and tie a bandage over and below where the leg is injured.'

Without speaking, Bamford did this, then secured another bandage around Hamish's ankle and upper thigh.

'Well done, Bamford,' said the doctor. 'You did a damn good job. Now let's get him into the Neil Robertson and take him to the sick bay.'

Latta supported Hamish's injured leg head while Bamford and the first aiders, carefully lifted Hamish onto the Neil Robertson stretcher and strapped him inside. After checking to see if Hamish was still sleeping, Latta, using a strap, secured Hamish's head to stretcher. Even though the weather had abated, the ship was still rolling precariously. 'OK, now, lads,' said Bamford, 'each of you take hold of one of those rope handles you see on the side of the stretcher. We'll wait until each roll of the ship settles down, then we'll him to the bottom of the stairs. I will take hold of the head rope and go aloft. We'll wait again, then I'll help to pull him up. Understood?'

Dusty Miller and the other first aid team gave a quick nod. Five minutes later, after pulling Hamish up, they arrived outside the sick bay in time to hear, "hands to action stations, hands to action stations, close all screen doors and scuttles", being piped over the tannoy.

CHAPTER FOURTEEN

'Enemy aircraft, red, roughly ten thousand feet,' Taff Williams reported from the crow's nest. The time was 0600. The sun was well up into the pale morning sky and the blueness of the sky almost obliterated by foggy heat haze. "Call the hands", had just been piped and those ratings off duty were climbing out of their hammocks.

Tansey Lee, who was fully clothed except for his boots, climbed out of his hammock and grabbed his anti-flash gear. While shaking his head, he gave Bud Abbott a disgruntled look, and said, 'Always at fuckin' breakfast time. You'd think the Ities would have more consideration.'

'Next time I see old Musso, I'll mention it to him,' Abbott replied sarcastically, grabbing his steel helmet and life jacket. 'Now, let's get to B gun before the bastards nail us.'

On *Helix*'s bridge, everyone watched apprehensively as a dozen twin engine fighter bombers from Mussolini's *Regia Aeronautica*, moving in a tight, V formation, approached the convoy.

'They're twin engine, Savoia-Marchettis, sir,' cried Baker, using his high-powered binoculars to identify the three black lines on white roundels on the underside of their mustard-coloured wings. 'And they each carry six five-hundred-kilogramme bombs, sir,' Baker added, almost as an afterthought.

'Thank you, Pilot,' Penrose replied, impressed yet again, by Baker's knowledge and quick thinking. His voice was almost lost in the sudden roar of gunfire from the high angle guns of *Carlisle* and *Penelope*. Almost immediately the sky was peppered with puffs of black smoke as shells exploded around the bombers.

'They're coming down, sir,' yelled the port lookout, watching, as one by one, the bombers broke formation and angled down towards the convoy.

'Enemy in range, sir,' Lieutenant Ted Powers reported from the gunnery direction platform.

Everyone on the bridge strained upwards and saw the dive bombers swooping down from the sky. 'There's one of 'em heading right for us,' yelled Able Seaman Wacker Payne, the starboard lookout.

'Starboard five!' yelled Penrose.

But it was no use. On and on it came, yellow sparks flickering from the 20mm cannons on each wing. With agility betraying his age, Penrose left his chair and joined the others taking cover on the deck, hearing the deadly tinkle as shells tore into the ship's superstructure.

'*All guns open fire!*' snapped Penrose, climbing back into his chair. The ship suddenly heeled over to the right, sending a huge frothy wave crashing over the fo'c'sle. At the same time, the deck shuddered violently as the 4.7 guns of A, B and X guns belched smoke. Leading Seaman Darby Allan, manning the starboard pom-pom, pressed his eye against the spidery gunsight, and angling the gun's quadruple barrels upwards, pressed the trigger. Straight away, pulsating streams of deadly cannonade poured towards one of the bombers, who immediately turned away unscathed.

The guns of the cruisers, together with the escorts, produced and ear-splitting cacophony. In seconds, the blueness of the sky was almost obliterated by a plethora of black shell bursts. For a few seconds, the acrid cordite in the air stung eyes before being carried away on the wind.

'Port five,' shouted Penrose. Peering through their binoculars, everyone on the bridge watched as a Savoia, bravely ignoring the barrage, hurtled downwards before unleashing a stick of bombs onto the transport, *Clan Campbell,* lying roughly a hundred yards astern of *Breconshire*. The bomber then banked sharply before darting safely into the sky. Seconds later, a huge pall of yellow and red flames shot into the air as the missiles hit *Clan Campbell* amidships. Two more tremendous explosions rippled along her deck. In a matter of minutes, the stricken vessel was enveloped in a massive cloud of dense black smoke and flames. Two more eruptions sent daggers of scarlet and yellow flames shooting into the air. Suddenly, the sea was a mass of flotsam and men swimming away from the doomed vessel.

The ear-splitting dissonance from the attack was so loud, people could hardly hear themselves think. Penrose trained his binoculars astern of *Clan Campbell* and recognised Captain Hutchinson, the convoy commodore, standing on the bridge. He had removed his cap, displaying a shock of white hair. Next to him stood two officers. They watched calmly as the last of the crew dived overboard. The officers appeared to shake the commodore's hand then left the bridge.

'For God's sake, man,' Penrose cried, 'get away while you…'

'She's starting to go down, sir,' cried Baker, watching the stern on the stricken vessel tilt ominously low in the water. '*Eridge* and *Dulverton* have their scrambling nets out and are moving in to pick up survivors, sir.'

With a sigh of relief, Penrose saw the commodore leave the bridge, knowing that, as captain, he would be the last to leave his ship before it went under.

'Port ten. X gun cease fire. A and B continue firing. Revolutions five.'

'Ten a port wheel on. Revolutions five,' came the distinct Yorkshire voice of Chief Barnes below in the wheelhouse.

'Steady as you go,' Penrose said as the ship turned and slowly cut through the sea towards the men struggling in the water.

From the port wing, Manley watched as Chief Bosun's Mate, Charlie Jackson and several seamen removed the guard rails on the quarterdeck and lowered a large scrambling net over the side.

'Stop engines,' Penrose shouted, his voice barely audible over the continued booming of gunfire. He then unhooked the tannoy. 'This is the captain speaking. *Clan Campbell* has been badly damaged and is sinking. All hands muster on the quarterdeck to help survivors. Chief Cook to prepare hot drinks and sandwiches. Medical Officer and first aid party stand by.' Turning to Manley, he added, 'Please go and ask the survivors if any of them saw the commodore being picked up.'

Manley nodded and left the bridge. A few minutes later he returned, and slightly out of breath, said, 'No, sir, none of them remembers seeing the commodore'

'Pity,' Penrose replied, furrowing his brow. Just then everyone ducked as a Savoia-Marchetti soared over the ship, unloading a bomb which exploded twenty yards away from *Helix*'s port beam, sending a deluge of water over the bridge. 'Start engines, port ten, revolutions twenty, X gun open fire,' shouted Penrose, glancing warily up, as despite the continued barrage from the cruisers and escorts, the bombers pressed home their attack.

'One of the bastards has been hit!' shouted Able Seaman Dixie Dean, the port lookout.

All eyes watched anxiously as a stream of black smoke poured from one of the bomber's twin engines. Seconds later, the aircraft burst into flames then splashed into the sea.

'That's one less for a spaghetti supper, eh, sir?' quipped Bud Abbott.

'Quite so,' Manley quickly answered, 'but we'd better duck 'cos here comes another one.'

In the sick bay, Bamford and Latta placed Hamish, who was asleep, onto the leather examination couch. Daly and the other first aiders had left to go to their respective action stations. Bamford and the doctor had begun unstrapping Hamish from the Neil Robertson, when the pipe telling them to stand by to receive survivors, came over the tannoy.

'You'd better go and see what's going on,' said the doctor, undoing the last strap of the stretcher.

Bamford nodded and grabbed a medical bag and arrived on the quarterdeck in time to see PO Steward Sandy Powel and members of the first aid party helping soaking wet men onto the quarterdeck and covering them with blankets. Some of the survivors wore only a shirt; others wore overalls that clung to their bodies like a wrinkled skin; all of them were pale-faced and shivering.

'Look lively and get them below into the seamen's mess deck,' Chief Bosun's Mate, Jackson, shouted to a group of ratings.

'And tell the stores assistant to issue them with number eights and overalls,' said Lieutenant Milton.

'Any of them injured, sir?' Bamford asked.

'As you can see,' Milton replied, nodding towards PO Powel who was in the process of putting a shell dressing around a man's bloody head, 'one of 'em is hurt. The rest seem all right.'

One by one, the survivors were helped down into the seamen's mess and each given a mug of steaming hot kye. The injured man was a small, sturdily built Scot with dark, matted hair.

'You're lucky,' said Bamford after removing the shell dressing, 'it's only a bad graze. No need for stiches, but were you knocked out?'

'Och, no, laddie,' the man answered after taking a welcome sip of kye. 'It takes more than a fuckin' Itie bomb to do that.'

'Good for you, Jock,' Bamford replied, while cleaning the injured area and applying a fresh dressing. Bamford checked to ensure none of the other survivors were injured then left.

In the sick bay, Doctor Latta had just checked the splints on Hamish's leg when Bamford entered. 'Anything serious below?' he asked very quietly while removing his stethoscope earpieces.

'No, sir,' Bamford replied. 'How is Hamish?' he whispered, looking at Hamish's face poking over the bedclothes and the bulge of the protective cradle Bamford had earlier placed under the bed coverlet.

'He was in pain, so I've given him another shot of morphia,' the doctor replied.

'Any signs of…' Bamford muttered, ominously sniffing the air for the tell-tale smell of gangrene.

'No, thank goodness, but we'll have to keep a careful watch on him,' the doctor answered warily.

The time was shortly after 1000. Most of survivors appeared to have been rescued, when, suddenly, *Clan Campbell* exploded. An ugly mushroom of dense, black smoke billowed into the air like a volcanic explosion. Everyone on *Helix*'s bridge flinched as a warm shock wave fanned their faces. In a matter of minutes, the ship had vanished beneath the sea, leaving behind a swirling mass of detritus and the grisly remains of her crew.

For the next hour, there was a welcome lull in the action as, one by one, the bombers regrouped some five thousand metres above the convoy. The guns on the escorts and cruisers ceased firing.

Penrose looked guardedly at Manley, and using a handkerchief to wipe his sweat stained face, said, 'Better remain at action stations, Number One, I don't think they're finished with us yet.'

'I agree, sir, look at them,' Manley replied, shielding his eyes with hand while gazing upwards. 'The bastards are circling around like vultures ready to swoop on their prey and…' Sub Lieutenant Baker who was standing nearby interrupted him.

'Not for long, sir,' Baker cried, 'they're peeling off and diving down.'

'*All guns open fire!*' Penrose shouted.

Once again, pandemonium broke out as the blueness of the sky became a pastiche of black explosions. 'Starboard five,' cried Penrose, watching one of the bombers approaching the ship a mere hundred yards above the sea. His order came just in time to avoid two bombs. The vibrant underwater percussions caused by them exploding fifty yards away violently rocked the ship. Once more all officers and ratings on the bridge were subjected to a watery deluge. Men closed up at the guns, clung onto anyone and anything to avoid falling over. Curses rang out as stokers in the engine and boiler rooms slipped over on the metal grating sustaining bruised heads and twisted ankles, while in the sick bay, Bamford almost fell off his chair while preventing Hamish from being flung out of his cot.

On the bridge, Penrose and the others became aware that the enemy bombers had switched tactics and were concentrating on the three merchant ships. During what seemed an eternity, but was only a mere ten minutes, the bombers circled above the convoy. Then, one by one, broke formation and dived onto the ships, dropping their deadly cargos, before darting up through a maelstrom of gunfire and unleashing their bombs. This was quickly followed by palls of water shooting into the air as bombs burst harmlessly around *Pampas* and *Talbot*. The bombers banked away, then, after turning slowly, dived towards *Breconshire* and unloaded a stick of bombs onto the tanker.

The explosive impact of the bombs caused massive walls of white water to completely obliterate the vessel. For what seemed like an age, a thick curtain of water hung in the air like a shimmering white shroud, before slowly collapsing into the sea.

'Bloody hell, sir, it's a bloody miracle,' shouted Manley, who, like everyone else, watched in awe as the tanker, apparently unscathed, gradually appear out of the watery mist. 'She's still afloat!'

'Yes, but she's not moving,' said Penrose, 'she's obviously badly damaged.'

'The bombers have left, sir,' Baker shouted looking up into the sky, now empty, except for the black shell bursts slowly fading away.

'I expect they've run out of bombs,' Manley muttered, 'and we're probably down on ammunition, so I hope the buggers stay away.'

'Cease firing, Number One,' said Penrose, 'and send a signal to *Breconshire,* and ask, *"How badly are you damaged? Can we help?"'*

Anticipating his captain's order, PO Signalman Spud Tate, using his Aldis lamp, flashed the message to the tanker.

For several minutes, everyone waited anxiously for a reply. Just after 1200, a series of white flashes appeared from the port side of *Breconshire's* bridge. The reply read, *All engines out of action. Cannot make steam. Will require a tow. Tonnage of m y ship too much for a destroyer. Have asked Carlisle for help.'*

'Signal being flashed from *Carlisle,* sir,' said Tate, training his binoculars ahead of the convoy. '"*Carlisle, Eridge, Dulverton to escort Pampas and Talbot to Malta. Penelope to take Breconshire in tow. Helix to proceed to Malta ahead and land injured man. Good Luck, Neame".'*

'Reply, *"Wilco, God's speed, Penrose".'* Giving Baker an enquiring glance, he went on, 'What's our ETA Malta?'

'Let's see, sir,' muttered Baker as he consulted his chart, 'the air attack has slowed us down so I'm afraid it'll take us four days to arrive in Malta.'

'Thank you, Pilot. Increase speed five knots. Number One, phone the doc then tell the chief bosun's mate to pack Hamish's kit ready for when we transfer him to Bighi.'

Manley gave a quick nod of acknowledgement, then telephoned the sick bay. 'How is Hamish bearing up, Doc?' he asked Latta.

'At the moment he's asleep,' the doctor quietly replied, 'but he's still running a temperature. Could you send a signal to the C-in-C informing him of the injury and requesting an ambulance to meet us on arrival?'

'Of course, Doc,' Manley replied, and replaced the handset. However, what the doctor didn't say was the area around Hamish's fracture was slightly discoloured and despite the ant-gas gangrene injection, he feared the worst.

Shortly after 0600 on Sunday 12th June, radar reported the coastline of Malta fifty miles on port bow. Everyone on *Helix's* bridge watched as *Penelope* took up a position fifty yards in front of *Breconshire* and took the merchantman in tow.

'The barometer beginning to drop, sir,' Baker reported to Penrose, 'and the wind is increasing.'

'Looks like a storm is brewing,' said Penrose, watching as *Penelope* began to move. In doing so, the tow ropes that had hung into the sea suddenly became taught, shedding clouds of water. 'Well, they'd better get a move on,' Penrose remarked, glancing cautiously up at the ugly black clouds approaching from the east.'

'With a bit of luck, we'll be safely in Valletta before the storm breaks,' said Manley.

However, by 1300, the wind had become bitterly cold, bringing tears to the eyes of everyone on *Helix*'s open bridge. Ten minutes later, the heavens opened. Thick lines of rain slanted down, turning the relatively calm sea into a vast carpet of tiny fountains. Shortly after 1500, the pipe, "Special sea duty men fall in. Wet weather routine", echoed around the ship.

On the bridge, Sub Lieutenant Baker glanced at Penrose, who was sat in his customary chair, and said, 'Radar, report minefield a hundred yards dead ahead, sir, it's marked two hundred wide on my chart.'

'Thank you, Pilot,' Penrose sighed. 'That's all we bloody need, rough weather, a crippled tanker in tow and the danger of another air attack. Reduce speed to ten knots, port five.'

With the use of radar and expert seamanship, Penrose managed to navigate *Helix* through the minefield, and after passing through the breakwater, everyone gave a sigh of relief as *Helix* entered Grand Harbour. From the port side of the rain swept bridge, the sturdy walls of St Angelo could be seen angling downwards into the sea.

Using the local, durable, yellow sandstone, this mighty, four-storey bastion was built by the Order of Saint John in the sixteenth century. Since then, it had stood like a mighty sentinel, guarding the entrance to the harbour. By the outbreak of war, the fort has housed five batteries, manned by Royal Marines and the Royal Artillery. In 1942 it was now the headquarters of Admiral Sir Browne Cunningham, C-in-C Mediterranean.

"Attention on the upper deck. Face the port", came the pipe.

'Just think,' Dutch Holland said to Knocker White, who along with those ratings off duty, were fallen in on the port side of the fo'c'sle, 'tonight we'll be havin' vicious run ashore down the Gut.'

'Canteen leave, more's the likely, what with these fuckin' air raids', Knocker replied, feeling a cold finger of rain trickle down his neck.

'St Angelo flashing, sir,' said PO Tate. 'Signal says, "*Berth port side, French Creek. Ambulance and doctor to meet. Cunningham*"'.' (French Creek is so called after Napoleon landed here in 1768 in an effort to capture the island.)

'Good Lord,' exploded Penrose, 'I though ABC was still in Alexandria. Reply, "*Wilco. Many thanks, sir. Penrose, Helix*".' (Admiral Brown Cunningham was affectionately known as ABC.)

Giving Manley an appreciative look, Penrose, said, 'French Creek is the first one on the left past the fort. With luck we'll be alongside in about twenty minutes. Better inform the doc.'

"Hands fall in for entering harbour", came over the tannoy.

In the sick bay, Hamish had just woken up. Doctor Latta who was standing by his cot, looked at him, smiled and said, 'How are you feeling, old boy?'

'Not too bad, sir,' Hamish replied, lazily blinking his eyes, 'but me leg hurts like hell.'

An earlier examination showed the slight discolouration around Hamish's fracture remained the same and his blood pressure was raised.

'We'll be alongside shortly,' said the doctor, bending down and feeling Hamish's radial pulse and finding it full and bounding.'

'Theres's an ambulance waiting to take you to the hospital, but before that, we're going to put you in a Neil Robertson stretcher and carry you up to the quarterdeck. Do you feel up to it?'

'I suppose so,' Hamish replied, smiling weakly.

'Good,' said Bamford, placing the stretcher on the deck alongside Hamish's cot and laying a blanket inside. 'I've packed the gear you came in, in a grip. The rest of your kit will go with you to hospital.' He paused, and giving Hamish a reassuring grin, added, 'Just think, in a little while you'll be surrounded by gorgeous nurses.'

'Fat lot of use I'll be to 'em,' Hamish murmured disconcertedly.

As he finished speaking, the door opened and in came PO Sandy Powel. Behind him, the other three members of the first aid party.

'Ready when you are, sir,' Powel said, smiling confidently at the doctor. The doctor supported Hamish's head as Powel and Bamford carefully lifted Hamish up and lowered him into the stretcher.

'Keep both arms outside,' Bamford said to Hamish as he tucked the blanket firmly around him. Then, with a cheerful grin, he added, 'And don't worry, matey, we'll have you up top in a jiffy.'

Twenty minutes later, with the rain pelting down, and the yellow stoned buildings and churches of the three cities, Vittoriosa, Senglea and Cospicua, on their right, *Helix* berthed starboard too, alongside French Creek. Waiting on the wharf was a dark blue ambulance with "Royal Navy'" painted on its side. No sooner had the guardrail on the quarterdeck been partially removed and the wooden gangway lowered into place, than the ambulance door opened and out stepped a tall surgeon lieutenant, and a rating, wearing shiny black oilskins. The driver, an elderly man with grey hair, remained inside. With the officer leading, they walked up the gangway, saluted and were met by OOD Lieutenant Ted Powers.

'Clive Bartram,' said the officer. 'I believe you have an injured man on board?'

'Ted Powers, Gunner Officer,' replied the OOD. Then, with a wry smile added, 'Yes, he's in the sick bay. My QM will show you to where it is.'

'Thank you,' the doctor replied, using a finger to wipe away drops of rain off his nose.

'This way, sir,' said QM Sammy Smith, leading them though the after deck house. Smith stopped outside the sick bay, and after knocking on the door, was told to enter. They did so and immediately saw Hamish being secured by Bamford into the Neil Robertson stretcher. Doctor Latta, who had just finished writing up Hamish's medical notes, stood up from his desk. After a brief introduction, and an equally brief resume of Hamish's injury, Bartram strongly suggested they get Hamish off the ship and into hospital forthwith.

'I'll support his head,' said Surgeon Lieutenant Latta, 'Bamford and Bensen, take the rope handle on one side of the stretcher, Jones and

Turpin, grasp the ones on the other side. You,' Latta added glancing up at the SBA covering Hamish with his Burberry, 'steady the end of the stretcher, and PO Powel, can carry Hamish's grip. Ready?' The five men gave a quick nod. 'Two six, lift,' said Latta.

Surgeon Lieutenant Bartram, holding an envelope containing Hamish's medical history, slid open the door. A few minutes later, the first aid party carrying Hamish, arrived on the quarterdeck. Braving the harsh wind and vain, Dutch Holland, Bud Abbot and the rest of Hamish's mess mates waited, and said a hurried farewell to Hamish. Manley, Hamish's divisional officer, standing nearby, did the same.

'The lads have packed a few cartons of fags in your kit,' said Dutch. 'Along with a medicine bottle of neaters from the senior rates. See you in Pompey,' he added, giving Hamish a confident grin.

'Good luck, old, boy,' said Surgeon Lieutenant Latta, 'and get well soon. Now let's get you out of this filthy weather.'

'Thanks a lot, sir,' Hamish muttered, feeling the rain belting down onto the Burberry.

As the first aid party carried the stretcher down the gangway, Hamish pushed a hand out of the Burberry and gave a weak wave. The driver had left his seat and had opened the two back doors of the ambulance. The stretcher was quickly slid inside and was followed by Bartram and his SBA. The doors were then closed.

The time was 1600. Except for the duty QM and PO, the quarterdeck was empty. The QM's voice came over the tannoy. 'Hands to tea, duty watch, fall in outside the coxswain's office. Canteen leave in the dockyard to the port watch and second part of starboard 1600 to 2359.'

'What did I tell yer,' Knocker White grumbled to Dutch Holland as they entered the mess. 'Fuckin' canteen leave and warm beer.'

CHAPTER FIFTEEN

The next morning at 0900, the pipe everyone had been waiting for echoed around the ship. "Mail, Mail is now ready for collection and will close at 2300."

Twenty minutes later, throughout the ship, letters, small bundles of newspapers and parcels were being ripped open.

In the senior ratings mess, Paddy O'Malley was sat down at the table, eagerly reading the first of two letters from Joyce. Harry Johnson, sitting opposite Paddy, was busy opening a small brown paper parcel. 'It feel heavy, so I bet it's a few pots of jam,' he said, quickly glancing up and noticing the huge smile on Paddy's face. 'You look happy enough, mate,' Harry said, removing the cardboard wrapping and taking out a large jar of blackcurrant jam. 'Who's it from, as if I didn't know?'

'It's from Joyce,' Paddy replied. 'To be sure, I shouldn't be smiling, as she says she's received a telegram from the Red Cross telling her that Jack has died of pneumonia.'

'So what will you do, now?' Harry asked, unfolding a letter that accompanied his parcel.

'Be Jezzus,' Paddy replied, his pale blue eyes twinkling merrily. 'I shall ask her to marry me, that's what I'll do.' He paused momentarily then went on. 'Now, tell me, how's Ethel?'

'Ethel's fine, and sends her best,' Harry answered, then carried on reading his letter.

In the wardroom Manley, feeling his heart rate quicken, picked out two white envelopes from the cubby hole in the mail rack, hoping to find one from Laura. However, as he recognised his mother's neat handwriting on each envelope, he felt his stomach sink. Holding the unopened letters, he slumped into an armchair, wondering why Laura hadn't written. His parents' letters were dated ten days ago – surely, she must have known he was at sea and couldn't write. Suddenly, a voice interrupted his thoughts. He looked up and saw Lieutenant Ted Power looking down at him. 'What's the matter, Number One,' Powers said, giving Manley an inquiring look. 'Bad news?'

Manley quickly composed himself, and replied, 'Err... No, I was just expecting a letter from a friend.'

'If I were you, I shouldn't worry,' Powers said, noticing the disappointment etched in Manley's eyes, 'I was expecting a letter from my wife, but it's probably been held up. Now how about a quick Horse's Neck. You look as if you could use one?'

Despite his altercation with Linda, Baker was half hoping to hear from her, but he was disappointed. However, as he left the wardroom, he was relieved to discover there wasn't a letter from Wallasey's chief constable.

Everyone in the seamen's mess received a letter except Pusser Hill, a tall, dark-haired HO able seaman from Hackney, an area in London's East End he knew had been badly bombed.

'Before we sailed,' Hill muttered, to Dutch Holland, who had finished reading a letter from his wife, 'I told my missus to take the kids to her mother's house in Morden, but she wouldn't have it. "I don't like Morden",' she said, '"they're all snobs out there".'

'I shouldn't worry, mate,' said Dutch, 'remember the old saying, no news is good news.'

But it wasn't. Half an hour later, Hill was piped for and told to report to the captain. Shortly afterwards he returned to the mess. His face was ashen and he was accompanied by Sub Lieutenant Baker, his divisional officer. Everyone stopped what they were doing and looked up as Hill slumped heavily onto the bench alongside the table. Suddenly, a feeling of unease could be seen on the faces of Hill's messmates.

'What's up with Pusser, sir?' Dutch Holland asked Sub Lieutenant Baker.

Baker responded by slowly shaking his head, then in a quiet voice said, 'Look after him, he's had some, er... terrible news.'

Covering his face with both hands, Hill muttered, 'They've all been killed, a direct hit...' His voice faded as he broke down and with his shoulders moving violently, he sobbed uncontrollably. At that moment, the tall, imposing figure of Chief GI Bob Shilling came into the mess. 'Better help him pack his gear,' Shilling said, looking gravely at Bud

Abbot who was the leading hand of the mess. 'He's being transferred to the *Manxman*[3]. She's the one that brought us the mail and is anchored in Silema.' He paused for a few seconds, then, furrowing his weather-beaten brow, went on. 'And you'd better chop-chop. After refuelling, *Manxman* is sailing.' He then gave Hill a sympathetic pat on the shoulder, and said, 'I expect she'll be stopping at Gib then you'll be flown home.'

'To what?' muttered Hill, who was now sat staring blankly, 'there's now't to go home to.'

An hour later, after sombre farewells, everyone watched as Hill, along with his kit bag and holdall, left in the ship's launch and headed towards *Manxman*, lying sedately at anchor opposite Custom House Steps, with smoke trailing from each of her three tall funnels.

Situated at the end of French Creek, the canteen consisted of a simple building with wooden walls, a long bar, an old record player which played equally old records, and a flat tin roof that sounded like thunder whenever it rained. Shortly after 2300, Bud Abbot, Dutch Holland, Tansey Lee and several other ratings off *Helix* and another destroyer, having drank the last of the beer, burbled a lecherous goodnight to the two busty barmaids and left the canteen.

'So that's what they call a bomber's moon, eh, Tansey?' Dutch Holland said to Lee, glancing charily up at the large yellow orb in a cloudless sky.

'Fuckin' Job's comforter,' Tansey replied, giving Dutch a look of distain, 'the bastards will be here soon enough without you tempting providence.'

Even though darkness had fallen five hours ago, a full moon cast a silver sheen on the calm harbour waters, highlighting the presence of the cruisers *Carlisle* and *Penelope*. *Eridge* and *Dulverton* lay opposite one another in Kalkara Creek, receiving oil from the tenders. *Pampas* and *Talbot* were tied up alongside Dockyard Creek.

---

[3] HMS *Manxman* and her sister ship, *Welshman* were two Abdiel Class minelayers. Their speed of over 39knots made them too fast for enemy warships, but ideal for ferrying important personnel, mail and vital stores from England to ports in the Mediterranean.

Tansey Lee's prediction proved to be correct. At precisely 0530, the next morning, the ear-splitting rattle of the action stations alarm bell woke everyone up. Men, some yawning, others cursing, tumbled out of their hammocks and hurriedly dressed.

'No fuckin' breakfast,' Knocker White moaned to nobody in particular as he grabbed his anti-flash gear. 'I could eat a horse.'

'Never mind,' said Tansey Lee, grinning as they left the mess, 'you're too fat anyway. If you don't stop eating, you'll soon look like a horse.'

On *Helix*'s bridge, Penrose stood by the binnacle, and along with OOD Sub Lieutenant Baker, Manley and PO Mills, looked up in the sky and saw a formation of Italian twin engine Fiat CR.25 heavy bombers, roughly five thousand feet, was approaching Malta from the west.

'Here they come,' yelled Baker, 'thank goodness they're low enough for our guns to fire at them.'

No sooner had Lieutenant Powers reported the bombers were in range, than Penrose, his binoculars pinned to his eyes, shouted, 'All guns, open fire!'

Penrose's order was almost drowned out as the armament from the AA batteries surrounding Valetta joined in with the guns of *Carlisle, Penelope,* Fort St Angelo and St Elmo. The barrage was deafening. The ground seemed to shake as a myriad of tiny black explosions dotted the pale blue sky. Lines of bombs fell from the underside of the bombers, wavering slightly, before continuing their deadly decent. Jets of white water sprung up like geysers around the two cruisers, the escorts and the two merchant ships. Everyone on *Helix*'s bridge ducked as a bomb exploded nearby, sending a shower of watery spray over the fo'c'sle. When n everyone looked up, Valetta's skyline had virtually disappeared under a thick mass of billowing grey smoke.

'*Great Scott*,' cried Sub Lieutenant Baker. 'The three cities are taking a helluva pounding[4]!'

'So are the two merchant ships…' shouted QM Sammy Lee. His strained voice was suddenly drowned out by a series of tremendous

---

[4] During 1942, 15,000 tonnes of bombs were dropped 0n Malta, making it the most bombed place on earth.

detonations erupting from the two oil tankers, *Pampas* and *Talbot*. Suddenly, as if lit by a torch, the waters surrounding the two tankers became a flickering inferno as oil spewed from the ships' ruptured tanks, spreading outwards towards the middle of the harbour. Some men, in various states of dress, ran down the gangways onto the wharf.

Other men, stripped to the waist, some, wearing shorts or overalls, dived overboard. Ignoring the blistering heat, small craft arrived and dragged men on board while others, using heavy rubber hoses, sprayed arches of foam onto the stricken vessels.

Adding to the chaos, the sonorous wail of ambulance sirens, echoing from the three cities, could be barely heard above the bombs exploding on and around French Creek.

Shielding their eyes from the hot glare of the flames, everyone on *Helix*'s bridge looked on as the sickening crackle of yellow and red flames spread ominously across the decks of both merchant ships.

Five minutes later, the enemy, minus one bomber, shot down, slowly turned away. Doing his best to appear calm, Penrose, sitting in his chair, felt his heart pounding against his ribs and managed to pop a digoxin tablet into his mouth and watched as the bombers headed towards the Italian coast, two hundred miles away, leaving both merchantmen blazing hulks.

'Pipe "Cease fire", Number One, and revert to defence stations,' said Penrose, feeling his heart rate slow down. Then added, 'and make sure the crew have a good breakfast, just in case the buggers come back.'

'So much for our precious convoy,' quipped Leading Seaman Tansey Lee, listening to the pipe echoing around the ship. 'None of the four ships left we were supposed to protect,' he added, angrily throwing his anti-flash hood onto the deck.

'Makes you wonder if it was all worthwhile, dunnit?' replied Tommy Tucker, a small ginger headed able seaman, standing next to Tansey. 'All those lives lost on the other two merchant ships, as well as our lads killed on the escorts, for what?'

On the bridge, everyone stood in silence, watching the last of the flames on the tankers being gradually subdued by the firefighters.

'I wonder how much oil they got off, sir,' Manley said to Penrose, while taking off his steel helmet and wiping the sweat from his brow with a handkerchief.

'Not a great deal, judging by the size of the flames,' Penrose solemnly replied. As he eased himself from his chair, Leading Signalman Weir arrived holding a sheet of paper. 'Yes, what is it?' Penrose asked, removing his steel helmet.

'Signal from *Carlisle,* sir,' Weir solemnly replied. It reads, "*Tobruk desperate for ammunition. Commanding officers of Helix, Eridge, and Dulverton, to report to me at 1000.* Neame".'

CHAPTER SIXTEEN

'Good morning, gentlemen,' said Captain Neame, pushing his stocky, six-foot-plus frame up from behind a large mahogany desk. 'Thank you for coming at such short notice,' he added, shaking the hands of the three officers standing in front of him.

David Marmaduke Neame, was forty-three and spoke in a well-modulated, clear voice. His strikingly clear grey eyes, well-groomed straight silver hair and heavily tanned features made him look the epitome of a Royal Naval officer. The four silver bars on each epaulette on the shoulders of his short-sleeved pristine white shirt; the mauve medal ribbon of a DSO, set among a row of other campaign ribbons, all contributed to give the impression of someone who was used to being in command and having his orders obeyed.

'Do sit down,' he added, indicating to three, brown, leather armchairs. 'Coffee?' Without waiting for a reply, he pressed a small red button on his desk. Almost immediately a side door opened an in came a small, pale faced PO Steward, wearing white jacket.

'Coffee for four, please, Jenkins,' said the captain, 'and a few of your precious digestives.'

'Very good, sir,' the PO replied in an artificial "posh" accent. 'Chocolate or plain,' he added, before hurrying away.

'Cheeky bugger, before the war he was head steward on the Queen Mary,' the captain remarked. 'At times, he thinks he still is.'

The captain's remark produced smiles from the three officers, which helped them to relax.

'I must say, sir,' remarked *Erdge*'s commanding officer, glancing around, 'you do live rather well.' Lieutenant-Commander William Gregory-Smith was a tall, well-built officer, whose naturally tanned complexion and dark brown eyes betrayed his Latin antecedents.

'The comforts of command,' replied the captain smiling smugly.

'I have to agree with Bill, sir,' remarked Lieutenant-Commander Walter Petch, *Dulverton*'s captain, a strikingly handsome, six-foot-plus man with clear-cut, weather-beaten features. He was about to say the room made his cabin look like a rabbit hutch, but thought better of it.

Penrose didn't offer a comment. Instead, he sat back in his chair and quickly took in what, compared with his cabin, was nothing short of palatial. The deck was covered with a dark blue carpet, inlaid with tiny gold anchors. Twin sets of neon lighting from a low-slung cream-coloured deckhead provided clear, all-round lighting. Shelves of leather-bound books, secured by wooded barriers, lined two of the bulkheads painted pale-green. Behind the captain's desk was an ornately framed, coloured photograph of King George VI and Queen Elizabeth and a large map of the world. An expensive looking wine cabinet occupied one corner and close by, rested a large globe of the world. Penrose inwardly smiled, thinking the room looked more like a gentlemen's club than the quarters belonging to a senior naval officer.

'Now, I'm sure you're all very busy,' said the captain, 'so smoke if you must, and let's get on.'

None of the three officers accepted his offer. The side door opened and Jenkins came in, holding a silver tray and four small cups of coffee.

'No biscuits, sir,' said Jenkins, giving the captain a supercilious glance, while placing a cup and saucer on the captain's leather-bound blotting pad, 'you ate the last one yesterday.'

'Never mind,' replied the captain, 'just make sure we're not disturbed for the next half hour.'

'As you wish, sir,' the PO answered tardily, then left the cabin.

As soon as the galley door was shut, Neame opened a desk drawer and drew out a buff-coloured envelope marked "TOP SECRET". He took out a sheet of white paper and placed it before him. Bayonetting the three officers with a steely glare, he said, 'I received this signal from the C-in-C two hours ago. The Gazala Line, that ring of defences surrounding Tobruk, has in part, been breached by Rommel.' The captain took good sip of coffee, then continued. 'Auchinleck is desperately short of medical stores and ammunition and the Desert Air Force is badly depleted. He has asked for help, and that, gentlemen, is where *Carlisle* and your ships come in.'

'You mean we're going to supply them with shells and anything else they need, sir?' Penrose asked, after taking a sip of his drink.

'Yes, Henry, and that will include *Carlisle*,' Neame replied, draining his cup. 'Our high-angled guns with give covering fire against an air attack, and also bombard the enemy positions.'

'Just so I understand, sir,' Lieutenant Commander Gregory-Smith, said, furrowing his brow, 'we are to load up with ammunition, most of which will be boxes of shells and small arms ammunition, and sail into a port that is under siege. Am I right, sir?'

'More or less,' Neame replied, casually pushing his cup and saucer to one side.

'But what about the inshore squadron at Alexandria, sir? asked Lieutenant Commander Petch, 'Alex is closer to Tobruk than Malta, surely they'll be involved.'

'And what about Admiral Vian's battle group, sir,' Penrose added, 'will they help?'

'In answer to your question, Henry,' Neame said, looking at the anxious expression on the face of *Dulverton*'s commanding officer, 'even though Alex is, as you say, closer to Malta, *Diamond* and *Ladybird* were badly damaged during a previous attempt to supply Tobruk and are out of action, and *Gnat* is in dry dock undergoing a refit.' He paused, sat back, folded his arms, and continued to answer your question, Hugh,' he said, staring keenly at Penrose, 'earlier, *Cleopatra* suffered too much damage and is undergoing repairs. Vian will sail in *Warspite,* and along with *Dido* and a group of destroyers, he will patrol a few hundred miles off the coast of Taranto to prevent Ichiano from coming to attack us.'

'And what if Ichiano does decide to come out and make a fight of it, sir?' asked Petch. 'After all, his ships were virtually undamaged during their previous meeting.'

'He won't,' Neame replied flatly. 'Ultra, intercepted a signal from Mussolini instructing Ichiano not to risk his capital ships[5]. You see, the Italian ships don't have radar, and Ichiano can't be sure how strong our fleet is. That's why he ordered his fleet to return to Taranto when they met recently.' The captain stopped speaking and sat forward. Clenching both hands, he went on. 'Each of you will take on fuel and replenish

---

[5] Ultra was the British Intelligence Service used to break high-level enemy radio teleprinter communications at Bletchley Park.

stores this afternoon. Tomorrow at 0800, boxes of artillery shells, ammunition for Vickers machine guns, mortar bombs, plus medical stores will be delivered to your ship.'

'When do we leave, sir?' Penrose asked cautiously.

'At 2200 on Friday 17th, under cover of darkness. ETA Tobruk, early on Sunday.' He paused momentarily, allowing his words to sink in, then went on. 'Now, as you will see on your charts, Tobruk is on a peninsula, showing two harbours. You will enter the western harbour, which is the deepest. *Carlisle* will enter the harbour first, unload the ammunition and take on wounded, then leave and wait outside the harbour. *Helix, Eridge* and *Dulverton* to follow. Unload ammunition and take on injured. Leave and rendezvous with *Carlisle* and proceed to Alexandria. Any questions?'

'How badly has the Gazala line been breached, sir?' asked Gregory-Smith.

Neame pursed his lips then replied, 'the C-in-C's signal doesn't say, but the port and Allied defensive positions are being constantly shelled by 21st Panzer Division west of Tobruk.

'Just to recap, sir,' said Penrose, leaning forward, 'we're being ordered to sail,loaded with high explosives, into a port that is under constant bombardment, am I right, sir?'

'That's about the gist of it, Hugh,' Neame answered dryly, 'but don't sound so dramatic. The ships will be protected from air attack by my guns and also by the heavy ack-ack the defenders will put up when you arrive.'

'But no air cover?' Gregory-Smith commented sombrely.

'I'm afraid we'll have to wait and see,' Neame said, standing up. 'Now, gentlemen, as the sun is over the yardarm, may I suggest large gin and tonics all around?'

Half an hour later, sitting in the stern sheets of *Helix*'s motor launch, Penrose suddenly realised, if the mission was successful, his chances of promotion would be greatly enhanced. With this on his mind, he arrived back onboard *Helix* and was met on the quarterdeck by Manley.

'Better come with me, Number One,' Penrose said, grinning, while returning Manley's salute, 'I have some interesting news for you.'

'Not another convoy, I hope, sir?' Manley asked as they left the quarterdeck.

Penrose didn't reply. A few minutes later they entered his cabin and were met by Steward Morris. 'Good afternoon, ser,' he said cheerily, 'can I get youse anything?'

'No,' grunted Penrose, 'just leave and make sure we're not disturbed.'

'Very good, ser,' Morris replied, and left the cabin, surprised at Penrose's unusual curt manner.

'Better take a seat, Number One,' Penrose said, walking behind his desk and wearily sitting down. 'Perhaps I should have told Morris to bring you a Horse's Neck, you may need one after what I've got to tell you.'

For twenty minutes, Manley sat in silence and listened as Penrose told him about the forthcoming mission to Tobruk. Afterwards, Manley sat back in his chair, and slowly shaking his head, said, 'I don't want to sound defeatist, sir, but it seems very dodgy. I mean, each ship will be carrying tons of high explosive. One bomb and whoosh!' He added, raising both hands, 'And we'll all be goners, lock, stock and barrel.'

'Quite so, Number One,' Penrose replied stoically. 'But keep everything I've said to yourself, officers only to be informed. I'll address the ship's company after we leave Malta. Loading ammunition will be enough to spark off rumours. Oh, and have a word with the doc as I'm sure he'll need to order extra medical stores.'

'Yes, sir, I understand, sir,' Manley answered, feeling his pulse rate increase.

However, Manley knew Morris would be standing outside the cabin door, listening to everything that was said. Within the next hour, details of the ship's next mission spread around the ship like wildfire.

'Are you quite sure you heard right, Scouse?' Cook Murphy asked Moran. It was "tot time", and they were in the Supply and Secretariat mess. 'If we don't have any air cover we'll be sitting ducks.'

'And I bet the Jerries will be waiting for us,' said Leading Steward, Powers, taking a good gulp of his rum. 'They're not stupid. They know the army's been holed up in Tobruk for over a year and must be short of ammo.'

'Better make sure we've all made out our wills, then,' Leading Writer Jack Jones, remarked before finishing his "tot".

A similar air of trepidation prevailed in the seamen's mess. 'Full of ammo and no air cover,' muttered Dusty Miller, using the back of his hand to wipe his mouth after downing his rum. 'Sheer fuckin' madness, that's what I calls it, sheer fuckin' madness.'

'And, according to what Scouse heard, we'll be the first ship to enter the harbour,' said Dolly Gray, sipping his tot.

'That's if we get that far,' came Slinger Woods' pessimistic reply.

'Ah, stop worrying and think about Alex,' Tug Wilson remarked, finishing off his tot. 'I was there on board the *Warspite* in '39, those belly dancers will give you a hard-on for weeks.'

'Not to mention a knap hand, I bet,' he added with a salacious grin. (A knap hand is slang for a dose of VD and pubic lice.)

'Scouse also mentioned old Vian would be stopping the Ities from attacking us,' Dusty Miller casually remarked, 'so relax and enjoy your dinner.'

'To me, that's just like this fuckin' chicken,' replied Bob Rose, 'too hard to swallow.'

Shortly after 1330, Dusty and a few others left the mess. Walking along the passageway, Dusty met the tall, imposing figure of Chief GI Barnes. 'Excuse me, Chief,' said Dusty, 'what do you and the other senior ratings think of us going to Tobruk, topped up with ammo?'

'The buffer and the coxswain think it's a bit dicey, to say the least,' Barnes replied. Then as he walked away, he turned and with a wry smile, added, 'But don't tell them I told you.'

Upon overhearing one of the stewards talking about going to Tobruk, the reaction of some officers was somewhat more sanguine. 'I'm sure the admiral knows what he's doing, David,' Lieutenant Powers remarked to Sub Lieutenant Baker as they sipped their tea.

'You're probably right, Ted,' Baker replied, 'as I'm sure the Italians won't fancy facing Vian's battle group again.'

At 1400 the fuel lighter came alongside the ship. Manley and Engineer Officer Logan stood on the port waist and watched the chief stoker and his team attach pipelines from the lighter onto couplings on *Helix*'s deck.

'This Tobruk business is obviously very important, even though we might lose ships and men, but do you think it's wise, Number One?' Logan asked Manley as they listened to the hissing sound of fuel from the lighter being transferred via pipe lines into *Helix*'s tanks.

'Apparently Admiral Vian thinks the risk is worth it,' Manley replied, 'because, as you know, if Tobruk is captured, Rommel will have a free run into Egypt.'

'I agree,' Logan answered. 'But it strikes me as being very dodgy, and I'm sure Rommel will be aware of what's happening and will give us a warm welcome.'

At that moment, Penrose was standing on the port wing. By sheer coincidence he was thinking the same thing. Feeling his hand shake slightly, he reached into a trouser pocket, and after fiddling with the lid of the small box, took out a Digoxin tablet and quickly put it in his mouth.

CHAPTER SEVENTEEN

At 0900 the next morning, a convoy of trucks arrived alongside *Helix* and the other two warships. On each vessel, lower deck was cleared. All ratings not on duty, formed a chain from the quarterdeck's gangway onto the wharf. The warmth of the early morning sun began to take effect and soon each man, although stripped to the waist, began to sweat profusely as they passed the heavy boxes to one another. At the top of the gangway the boxes were handed to another group who began stacking them up.

'If I drop one of these fuckin' boxes on my foot,' grunted Knocker White as he accepted a box from Dolly Gray, 'do you think I'd end up in Bighi and get my ticket home?'

'Probably,' Gray replied, sweating profusely while grasping hold of the handles. 'But remember, you don't get your tot in hospital, and they stick needles in your arse.'

'Bollocks to that,' Knocker said, turning and passing the box to Bud Abbot, 'I don't mind the needles, but going without my tot wouldn't be worth it, even if I did get my ticket.'

Standing on *Helix*'s quarterdeck, Manley looked at the weather-beaten face of Chief Bosun's Mate Charlie Jackson, and said, 'Some of the boxes can be stored in the after deck and main passageways.'

'Aye, aye, sir,' Jackson replied. Then, giving Manley a thoughtful look, added, 'If you don't mind me saying, sir, wouldn't it be better to secure the heavier boxes either side of the port and starboard waist, it would help trim the ship in case to we have to dodge a few bombs.'

'I agree, Buffer,' Manley answered feeling slightly embarrassed having not considered how the weight of the cargo could dangerously affect the ship's trim.

By 1130, loading was finished. "Up spirits, cooks to the galley," was piped. After ensuring the boxes were safely stowed, Manley went to the captain's cabin and reported this to Penrose.

'Thank you, Number One,' said Penrose who was sitting at his desk writing up the ship's log. 'We leave at 2200, by which time the minesweepers will have cleared a path through the minefield outside the harbour.'

'Very good, sir,' Manley replied, adding cautiously, 'canteen leave for those off watch?'

'No,' Penrose answered, shaking his head, 'I've already ordered Derek to flash up the boilers, and special sea duty men will be required for leaving harbour. Besides,' he added with a sly grin, 'I want clear heads in case we have to go to action stations.'

On his way back to his cabin, a pipe over the tannoy telling the crew that mail would close at 1600, reminded Manley to write to Laura.

In the sick bay, Bamford was checking the contents of two large cardboard box of medical stores that had arrived from Bighi.

'Everything you asked for seems to be here, sir,' said Bamford, picking up a small bottle of anti-gas green serum.

'No medicinal brandy, I suppose?' the doctor asked, giving Bamford a sarcastic grin.

'I'm afraid not, sir,' replied Bamford, 'but they have sent two dozen boxes of condoms.'

'Here's hoping they'll use them,' the doctor answered. 'I've read that gonorrhoea is rife in Alex.'

'Thanks for the warning, sir,' Bamford said ruefully, as he stowed everything away in a cupboard. As an afterthought, he added, 'Do they have a hospital in Alex?'

'Yes,' the doctor replied. 'The medical officer on board *Eridge* told me. It's called the Queen Alexandria Hospital and is manned by army medical staff.'

'Just as well,' said Bamford as he stowed the stores away in a cupboard, 'as I expect we'll have plenty of patients for them.'

Shortly after 2100 on Friday 17th July, *Helix* slipped her moorings and moved slowly from the wharf. *Eridge* and *Dulverton* followed on, and with *Carlisle* in the van, the small flotilla slowly approached the breakwater guarding the entrance to Grand Harbour. On *Helix*'s bridge, Penrose, who was sitting in his chair, glanced apprehensively up at the sky. Like everyone else on the bridge, he wore a duffel coat and muffler to protect against the chilly night air. Turning to Manley, he said, 'So much for secrecy, Number One, the damn moonlight is showing up every ship.'

'I see what you mean, sir,' Manley answered, glancing at Fort St Angelo's yellow sloping walls and towers, 'but so far, there's nothing on radar or asdic.'

'Thank you, Number One,' Penrose replied, 'I think I'd better tell the ship's company where we're going.'

Just then, Steward Morris arrived. 'Yousef left most of your breakfast, sir,' he said. 'So I thought you'd like this,' he added, handing Penrose a steaming hot mug.

'Very considerate of you, Morris, thank you,' said Penrose, accepting the mug with his free hand.

Morris grinned, and as he turned to walk away, Manley gave him a searching look, and said, 'I have a strong suspicion the ships already know where we're going, sir.'

Ignoring Manley's caustic remark, Penrose lent slightly forward, and using his free hand, unhooked the ship's annoy. 'D'you hear there,' he said, 'this is the captain speaking.' Throughout the ship, everyone stopped what they were doing and listened.

'No prizes for guessing what he's going to tell us,' Dutch Holland said to Bud Abbott while taking a good gulp of tea from his mug. "Stand Easy" had not long been piped and they were in the mess.

'Well, you never know,' Bud replied, as he lit a cigarette, 'he might have changed his mind and say we're going home.'

'Aye,' chimed in Dingo Bell, 'and pigs might fuckin' fly.'

After Penrose had finished speaking, Knocker White shook his head, and giving Tansey Lee suspicious look, said, 'Sounds like a fuckin' suicide mission to me.'

'So what,' Tansey replied, nonchalantly shrugging his shoulders, 'nobody lives forever.

Meanwhile, on the bridge, PO Signalman Spud Tate reported. 'St Angelo flashing, sir.' Using his binoculars, he went on. 'Signal reads, *"Good luck and God's Speed. Vain"*.'

'Thank you, Yeoman,' Penrose replied, muttering warily, 'I think we'll need all the luck we can get.'

No sooner had they passed the breakwater than everyone felt the deck rise and fall as the flotilla was met by a pronounced swell from the Mediterranean Sea.

'Fall out special sea duty men, Number One,' said Penrose, 'and revert to defence stations.'

Minutes later, a signal was received from *Carlisle*, ordering the three destroyers to increase speed to twenty knots, then ten degrees to port and continue due south. Penrose gave Manley an all-knowing glance, and said, 'Neame isn't wasting any time, eh, Number One?'

'Can't say I blame him, sir,' Manley replied, feeling a cold breeze fan his face, 'the quicker we deliver this ammunition the safer we'll all feel.'

The time was 0100. The ship was darkened and all dead lights were down. Canvas awnings covered the inside of all entrances from the citadel into the ship. On the bridge, all was quiet. Penrose was sat in his usual chair, watching *Carlisle*'s frothy wake churning the sea, a hundred yards in front of *Helix*. The dim blue lights from the various dials on the ship's board cast an eerie glow on his face and on the figures around him. The only sound to disturb their thoughts was the hissing of the sea and the dull throbbing of the ship's engines.

OOW Sub Lieutenant Milton stood a few feet away, looking through the prism on the compass repeater, checking the distance between *Helix* and *Carlisle*. He was about to report his findings to Penrose, when Asdic Operator Dusty Miller's strident voice came over the intercom. 'Contact bearing green four hundred, depth two hundred feet, sir.'

Using their binoculars, everyone immediately turned to the right and peered into the darkness, hoping to see the tell-tale wash of a periscope. Seconds later, a signal to the three destroyers confirmed this, adding, "Ships take evasive action. Do not attack, repeat, do not attack".'

'Reply, "Wilco",' snapped Penrose. 'Hard a starboard, evolutions one five.'

QM Knocker White, in the wheel house, repeated the order. Seconds later, as the ship heeled precariously to the right, everyone on the bridge held onto anything at hand to avoid falling over. Stokers, taken aback by the ship's sudden movement, almost slipped on the shiny metal grating, and in the mess decks, men, cocooned in the warmth of their hammocks, swayed in gentle unison as if touched by an unseen hand.

'Shall I sound action stations, sir?'

'No, not yet, Number One,' Penrose calmly replied. 'Where is the sub now?'

'Asdic reports it is has changed course and is roughly three hundred yards on *Carlisle*'s port quarter, sir.'

'You know what I think, Number One?' Penrose said to Manley. 'I think the bastard's planning to attack *Carlisle*. Sound action stations. Starboard ten, increase revolutions ten.'

'But, sir,' Manley replied, giving Penrose a searching look, 'we were only ordered not to attack but to take evasive action, surely…'

Penrose gave a sly grin, and said, 'And so we are, Number One. And in doing so, if we just happen to meet the bloody U-boat, we'll have no choice but to prevent the blighter from attacking. What say you to that?'

'I say you're taking a helluva risk, sir,' Manley answered bluntly. 'What if we're…'

Penrose quickly interrupted Manley. 'Flash a signal to *Carlisle*, Number One, and say, "*U-boat closing on your port quarter I intend attacking her*".' And you'd better tell the TAS officer to stand by to fire a pattern of four, set at three hundred feet.' He then unhooked the tannoy. 'This is the captain speaking.' As he spoke, the thought that they would soon be in action increased his heartrate. 'We have detected a U-boat that is about to attack the cruiser. I intend dropping depth charges, hoping to scare the blighter off or sink her. That is all.'

'Reply from *Carlisle*, sir,' said Manley. '"*Am aware of danger. Will take evasive action. Eridge to assist attack. Good luck*".'

Penrose's announcement immediately spread alarm throughout the ship. Tension became palpable.

With fear etched in his eyes, one of the stokers in the engine room looked at CERA Paddy O'Malley, and said, 'The old man must be crazy. One torpedo and we'll all be fish bate.' His loud, north country accent carried over the steady throb of the engines, and was overheard by the stokers on duty.

'Well, if that happens,' said a tall, ginger-headed stoker, wiping his sweaty brow with a piece of cotton waste, 'at least it'll be quick.'

'To be sure, that's a wise piece of philosophy,' O'Malley replied. 'Now,' he added, looking around at the anxious expressions on the faces surrounding him, 'I suggest you all keep a level head. I'm sure the captain knows what he's doing.' But he suspected his words had fallen on deaf ears.

On the quarterdeck, Lieutenant Barry Goldsmith unhooked the telephone. 'TAS officer,' he said, gripping hold of a stanchion as the ship heeled to starboard. Seconds later he said, 'Very good, sir.' He passed Penrose's order to Nick Carter and his team of TAS ratings, manning the four depth charge throwers. Carter was a tall, dark-haired, three badge petty officer, who didn't suffer fool gladly.

'Fat lot of use the three hundred pounds of TNT in each of these beauties will do if the fuckin' U-boat puts a tin fish in us first,' muttered Leading Seaman Smudge Smith, as he set the depth charge adjuster to the appropriate level.

'Pipe down,' snapped Carter, 'and get on with it.'

However, Smith's remark wasn't lost on the rest of the TAS ratings who gave one another a series of anxious looks.

On the bridge, Penrose glanced warily at Manley and asked, 'What's the position of the sub, now, Number One?'

'It's altered course and is now some thee hundred yards on our...'

At that moment, Buster Brown's thick Yorkshire voice, reporting from the crow's nest, interrupted him. 'Torpedo track two hundred yards on starboard bow!'

Straight away, all heads turned to the right and saw a white line, deep in the dark waters, heading directly towards the ship.

'*Full speed ahead, hard a port!*' yelled Penrose.

Below, in the wheelhouse, Chief Coxswain Digger Barnes repeated the order while giving his QM, Knocker White, an anxious look. 'Looks like we're in a bit of trouble.'

'You mean the U-boat has spotted us,' Knocker replied.

'I hope not,' Digger answered, feeling his mouth suddenly go dry.

As the ship was carrying a heavy load it took longer than usual to gain speed and turn sharply to the left. On the quarterdeck, it was Lieutenant Goldsmith who first spotted the torpedo's bubbly white line cutting deeply through the sea towards the ship. In a matter of seconds, Nick Carter and the other TAS ratings saw it.

'*Holy Mother of God*!' one of them screamed. '*Now we're for it. What'll we do if the bastard hits us, jump overboard?*'

'No,' Goldsmith replied, doing his best to sound calm. 'Hold on to anything, wait and…'

'And pray like fuck, sir,' said Carter, clutching hold of a nearby stanchion.

Like the ratings on the quarterdeck, everyone on the bridge knew only too well what would happen if the ship was torpedoed. Abject fear was written on everyone's faces as they watched the torpedo track darting towards them.

'*Christ almighty!*' shouted Gunnery Officer Ted Powers. '*We'll never make it!*'

'*Good Lord, sir,*' cried Manley, grabbing hold of Penrose's arm, 'he's right, I think we should abandon ship.'

'Too damn late,' Penrose replied, doing his best to sound calm, 'I'm afraid we won't turn in time.'

'*Oh, God, oh God!*' screamed Leading Signalman Jock Weir. '*We've fuckin' had it!*'

Numb with fear, Manley rushed past Weir and hit his head on the port side of the bridge. The last thing he saw before fainting was Laura's face and the path of the torpedo disappearing under the ship…

CHAPTER EIGHTEEN

The first thing Manley saw when he opened his eyes was the yellow orb of the moon, partially blocked by a thin layer of grey clouds. He was covered with a blanket and his head, resting on a pillow, ached terribly. For a few seconds he lay, confused, unable to believe he was still alive.

'Are you all right, sir?' Manley blinked a few times and through the dull blue lighting and saw the weather-beaten face of Leading Signalman Jock Weir looking down at him.

'Wha… what happened?' Manley muttered, 'The torpedo…'

'It passed under us, sir, thank God,' Weir replied.

'How long have I been out?'

'About ten minutes, sir. You collapsed onto the port wing deck. Lieutenant Milton and PO Tate brought you inside. The doc told us not to move you.'

'And the captain, how is he?' Manley asked, using the palm of a hand to feel a painful lump on the back of his head.

'Like the rest of us, he's a badly shaken,' Weir replied. 'He's in his cabin, the doc says he's gunna be all right.'

Sub Lieutenant Baker arrived and knelt down beside Manley. 'The doc'll be up shortly, how are you feeling, sir?'

'Very grateful to be alive,' Manley sighed, 'but I wonder what exactly happened. Was the torpedo a dud or what?'

'I'm not sure, but we were damn lucky, sir,' Baker replied, covering Manley's shoulders with another blanket. As he finished speaking the dull rumble of underwater explosions could be heard about a mile away to starboard.

'That'll be *Eridge*'s depth charges,' said Baker, 'we received a signal telling us she was attacking the U-boat.'

'Good luck to her,' gasped Manley, as PO Spud Tate and Lieutenant Baker helped him up. 'Here's hoping she sinks the blighter.'

Just then Penrose arrived. His face, normally well-tanned, looked tired and drawn. Behind him stood Surgeon Lieutenant Latta. 'How are you feeling, Number One?' Asked Penrose, heaving himself into his chair. 'I believe you had a fall?'

'Yes, indeed, sir,' Penrose replied, 'apparently, the torpedo passed right under us.'

'That's right,' Penrose said, 'it must have been one of those type G7es. I received a secret memo about them, a year ago *Nelson* was hit by three of them. Two failed to explode and the third passed underneath her.'

Manley was about to ask Penrose how he was, when PO Tate arrived. 'Signal from *Carlisle*, sir,' said Tate, '"*Eridge reports U-boat sunk. Resume stations. Well done everybody*".'

'Thank the Lord for that,' said Penrose, 'fall out from action stations. Number One, I suggest you let the doc have a look at you, then pass on the "well done" to the crew. Alter course three-five, revolutions ten, and fall out from action stations.' He carefully lowered himself from his chair, and glancing at Sub Lieutenant Baker, who was OOW, added, 'I'll be in my cabin, call me if you want me.' And with a tired sigh, he slowly left the bridge.

The pipe ordering hands to secure from action stations was welcomed by everyone. On the quarterdeck, PO Nick Carter looked around at the relief on the faces of his TAS ratings, and sniffing the air, said, 'Has someone shit himself?'

'Yes, PO,' replied Lieutenant Goldsmith, 'I'm afraid it's me.' Feeling very embarrassed, hurried away.

Shortly after 0500, everyone on *Helix*'s bridge watched the sun rise. In the blink of an eye, the sky changed from an umbrella of darkness into a canopy of burnished gold, while at the same time, the sun's rays turned the sea into an undulating carpet of glowing amber.

'Beautiful, isn't it, sir?' Carter muttered to Sub Lieutenant Milton who had taken over the watch from Lieutenant Goldsmith.

'Yes, indeed, PO,' Milton replied, placing his binoculars around his neck. At that moment the temperature was ten degrees centigrade. 'It's hard to believe there's war raging just over the horizon.' As if to confirm his words, the dull thud of gunfire could be heard directly ahead of the flotilla. Flashes of yellow and red appeared on the horizon, a clear indication that a barrage was in progress. 'Sounds like Tobruk is taking a pasting,' Milton remarked, noticing *Carlisle, Eridge* and *Dulverton* had kept good station during the night. As he finished checking the ship's position, speed and course, Penrose arrived followed by Manley.

'How far are we from Tobruk?' Penrose asked Milton.

'Fifty miles, sir,' replied Milton, 'the flotilla's doing twenty –five knots, so we should sight the coastline in about an hour.'

'Thank you,' said Penrose, 'better call the hands straight away and go to action stations at 0700. Oh, and ask the doctor to come and see me.

Five minutes later, looking tired and pale, Surgeon Lieutenant Latta arrived. Over his tropical whites he wore a duffel coat. 'You sent for me, sir,' he said, stifling a yawn.

'Yes, good morning, Doc, if the sick bay becomes full of wounded, you can use the wardroom, so tell the PO steward to remove the chairs and tables, just in case.'

'Very good, sir,' Latta replied, 'but where will the officers eat?'

'With the senior ratings,' Penrose answered, giving Manley a warning glance. 'Now, please carry on,' he added, dismissively.

The time was 0600. Having had less than four hours sleep the ship's company stumbled wearily from there hammocks. In the seaman's mess, Knocker White rubbed his eyes and groping for his shorts, looked at Able Seaman Bell and said, 'No fuckin' peace for the wicked, eh, Dinga?'

'Just think of the poor buggers ashore,' said Bell, hearing the gunfire, 'so be grateful for small mercies.'

After breakfast, the pipe, "hands to action stations, close all screen doors and scuttles", echoed around the ship.

By 0700, the dark brown coastline of North Africa stood out against the pale blue of the early morning sky. A soft warm breeze blew from the east and the calm sea was a beautiful shade of indigo. Using his binoculars, Penrose noticed Tobruk was situated on a rocky peninsula. The harbour was wide and horseshoe shaped. On the south side of the port, an escarpment and tall cliffs swept gently into the sea. This, he concluded, formed a natural barrier to an advancing enemy, and was probably the main reason Rommel's Panzers were laying siege to the port from north.

Palls of black smoke hung over the port which was proving a stubborn, stumbling block to the Axis advance into Cyrenaica. As the flotilla came closer, a scene of devastation could be seen. The barrels of Allied gun emplacements poked defiantly up from the town which was now mass of yellow rubble. Looking like a watery graveyard, remnants of masts and yardarms, funnels and ships, littered the harbour.

'Signal from *Carlisle*, sir,' said Manley. '"*As previously planned. Carlisle will enter harbour first. Helix, Eridge and Dulverton to follow. Rendezvous as arranged. Good luck*".'

'Acknowledge,' Penrose said, then added, 'anything on asdic?'

'No, sir,' Manley replied, 'but lookout reports unidentified aircraft approaching green five thousand.'

'Good Lord, that's all we need,' grunted Penrose, who, like Manley, was shading their eyes against the early morning sun's glare and peering up into the sky.

'They're Savoia-Marchettis, sir,' Sub Lieutenant Baker shouted, 'six of them and they're losing height and peeling off.'

'I can see that, Pilot,' Penrose tartly replied, 'but where exactly are they heading to.'

No sooner had he spoke than the blueness of the sky was distorted by balls of black smoke as *Carlisle*'s 3-inch anti-aircraft guns opened up. 'Hopefully that should keep the bastards away from us,' Manley said, feeling his heart rate increase.

Ignoring *Carlisle's* barrage, the bombers continued towards the port. 'They're levelling off and appear to be attacking the ports perimeter defences,' Baker shouted.

With relief etched on their faces, everyone watched anxiously as, one by one, the bombers dived down and released a stick of bombs, before turning and swopping upwards. On *Helix*'s bridge, everyone cheered as a Marchetti was hit by gunfire and burst into a bright ball of yellow flames.

'I think the buggers have had enough, sir,' shouted PO Signalman Jock Weir. '*Carlisle* has ceased firing and planes are buggering off.'

'Thank God for that,' Penrose muttered, as he watched the five Marchettis turn away, leaving the outer limits of the port shrouded in clouds of swirling black smoke. The attack lasted five minutes, by which time the flotilla had reached the mouth of the harbour.

'*Carlisle* flashing, sir,' reported Weir. '"*All ships berth south side on the wharf behind me*".'

'Acknowledge, steer one five, speed ten knots,' Penrose replied, watching *Carlisle* turning slightly to starboard and head towards the dock. With tension etched on the faces of everyone on *Helix*'s bridge, the three ships followed the cruiser. The time was just after 0730.

'I see there's quite a welcoming committee on the wharf, sir,' said Manley, looking at groups of soldiers, wearing shorts and stripped to the waist, standing near lorries, ambulances, and several small cranes.

'Quite so, Number One,' Penrose replied, 'muster all hands and tell Derek to keep his engines flashed up as I'll want to get under way as quickly as possible.'

Carlisle was the first warship to tie up alongside the wharf. *Helix, Eridge* and *Dulverton* hove into position and were quickly secured alongside the wharf.

A small contingent of soldiers quickly placed a wooden gangway onto the quarterdeck of each ship. Cranes then lowered a large net on board. Under the guidance of the chief bosun's mate, the nets were loaded with heavy boxes, then lifted onto the wharf and transferred into the lorries. Soldiers and ratings, their bodies gleaming with sweat, carried the lighter boxes ashore and placed them into the transport. When each vehicle was fully loaded, the driver quickly drove the heavily loaded vehicles away.

While this was happening, wounded soldiers were being helped on board each ship. As arranged, those soldiers who needed operative treatment were taken on board *Carlisle*. The lesser injured were helped into the sick bays and mess decks.

Earlier, on board *Helix,* SBA Bamford and the first aid party had turned the wardroom into an emergency hospital. The furniture had been removed and the carpet rolled up to reveal a steel deck. Sections of the long mess table had been reduced in size, enabling it to be used for minor surgical procedures. Directly above the table, panels in the deck head had been taken away, revealing emergency lighting in the form of a series of electric bulbs set into a wooden ring. Three sheets strung across the room divided the room into two sections; one to allow surgical treatment to be carried out, the other to provide privacy for injured. This space was soon taken up with soldiers with severe injuries. A soldier with dirty, blood-stained bandages around his abdomen was helped onto the table. His uniform was torn and his face, tired and unshaven. Surgeon Lieutenant Latta and SBA Bamford immediately removed his clothing and re-dressed a deep wound in the soldier's left side.

'What's your name, laddie?' asked Latta.

'Corporal Peterson, sir,' murmured the soldier.

'Well, Peterson,' Latta said, looking warily into the soldier's blood-shot eyes, 'I'm afraid you've got a bullet in your gut, and it'll have ta stay there until we get you ashore to hospital, but try not ta worry.' He gave the corporal's shoulder a reassuring pat, 'We'll give yer some morphia and make yer as comfortable as possible.'

'Thanks, sir,' the corporal muttered, and fell asleep.

Several injured soldiers were helped below into a mess and given hot drinks of tea, laced with a welcome shot of rum. Like all the casualties being brought on board, their unshaven faces looked tired and their khaki shirts and shorts were torn and blood-stained.

After taking a good sniff then a gulp of tea, one of them, whose left upper arm was partially covered with a dirty, blood-stained bandage, looked at one of the sailors and said, 'Stone the crows, if I knew the tea was like this, I should 'ave joined the bloody navy.'

'They wouldn't 'ave taken you, mate, as you told me your ancestors were convicts,' chimed a soldier whose right ankle, despite being heavily bandaged, was oozing blood.

'Fuckin' rubbish,' said a soldier with tightly bandaged head wound, 'so were mine, and my brother went to England and he's in the RAF.'

Meanwhile, PO Powel and the first aid party helped three soldiers down a flight of stairs into the sick bay. 'Boy are we glad to see you lot,' said one of them, a tall, fair-haired Australian whose blood-soaked shell dressing hid half of his heavily tanned, face. 'Most of our own doctors and medics are all goners, ain't that right, Shorty?' His question was directed to a small, dark-haired, stocky soldier with his left arm in a sling.

'Too bloody true, mate,' he replied, as Powel helped him into a chair. 'The bastards seemed to know exactly where our first aid posts were.'

The third soldier, a thick-set man with a heavily bandaged, right lower leg, who was being supported by SA Terry Bensen and Steward Dick Turpin, gave him sideways glance and muttered, 'Poor buggers, my pal, Chalky White, who was best man at my wedding, was one of them.'

The time was 1000. The sky was now a clear, deeper blue and the temperature a sweltering twenty-nine degrees centigrade. On the quarterdeck, Penrose watched as *Carlisle* slowly pulled away from the wharf. Next to him stood a tall, dark-haired colonel, in Australia's 29th Brigade.

'You lot have done a damn fine job,' he said, scratching the hairs on his unshaven chin. 'The ambulances have left, so the sooner you get out of here the safer you'll be.' As he spoke, the black rings around his deep-set, bloodshot eyes were clear indications of fatigue and lack of sleep. No sooner had he spoke than Manley arrived.

'That's about it, sir,' Manley said to Penrose, while giving the colonel a quick nod. '*Eridge* and *Dulverton* are ready to leave and the doc tells me we're full, so I suggest we get under way.'

'Very good, Number One,' said Penrose, 'all hands stand by to leave harbour.' He then looked at the colonel and added, 'I only hope the stuff we've brought helps you to hold out longer.'

'I can assure you we'll give it a bloody good try,' the colonel answered, giving Penrose a confident smile.

'Incidentally,' Penrose added, 'according to Lord Haw Haw on the wireless, you lot have become rats of the desert.'

The colonel's heavily tanned face broke into a wide grin. 'I don't know about that,' he said as they firmly shook hands, 'but if we stay here any longer, we'll certainly smell like them.'

No sooner had the colonel left than the gangway was taken away. *Helix* gradually moved away from the wharf and increased speed. *Eridge* and *Dulverton* quickly followed on, and as they met up with *Carlisle,* the sound of gunfire could be heard coming from the ports perimeter. Plumes of smoke shot up close to the wharf and around the remnants of the port.

Manley shot Penrose a relieved look, and said, 'Looks like we left just in time, sir.'

'Yes indeed, Number One,' Penrose answered, seeing a black umbrella of smoke settling over the port. He gave a worried sigh and said, 'I wonder how long the poor blighters can hold out?'

'*Carlisle* flashing, sir,' cried PO Signalman Spud Tate, '"*Well done. All ships alter course, green ten degrees. Increase speed twenty-eight knots*".'

'Acknowledge,' snapped Penrose, and repeated the order to Digger Barnes in the wheelhouse. He then glanced at Baker and said, 'At this speed, what's our ETA at Alex, Pilot?'

Baker quickly consulted his chart and after using his dividers, replied, 'Alex is some four hundred miles away, sir. I'd say, early on Monday the 20th, sir. There are two main entrances, Great Harbour and a smaller one in the old port.'

'Yes, thank you, Pilot, I am aware of that,' said Penrose. 'Anything on asdic, Number One?'

'No, sir,' Manley answered. He was about to use a handkerchief to wipe beads of perspiration from around his neck, when Buster Brown's thick Yorkshire accent in the crow's nest reported, 'Aircraft approaching, sir, red fifteen, roughly four thousand feet!'

'Action stations, Number One,' said Penrose, 'I thought things were going to be smooth.'

'They're those bloody Marchettis again, sir,' yelled Baker, 'eight of em.'

'And they're just about in too high for our guns to bare, sir,' Manley added. At that moment, *Carlisle*'s armament opened up, and once again, the blueness of the sky became a panoply of black puffs of smoke.

'Four of 'em are peeling off and making for the cruiser, sir,' shouted Baker. 'The rest are heading inland.'

'They're well in range, sir,' reported Gunnery Officer, Ted Powers, from the gunnery platform.

'Very good, all guns open fire,' snapped Penrose.

Everyone watched as the four Italian bombers dived through *Carlisle*'s intensive maelstrom before unloading their deadly cargo. Despite taking evasive action, a bomb hit home and a pall of flames and smoke shot into the air, aft of the cruisers bridge. This disappeared as the cruiser emerged from a wall of white water, her guns still defiantly blazing away.

'The Ities are turning away, sir,' said Manley, 'they appear to be heading inland to join the others.'

'Signal *Carlisle*,' Penrose said calmly. '"*How badly are you damaged? Can we help?*"'

'*Eridge* and *Dulverton* are also signalling, sir,' Tate said, 'they're asking the same as you.' A few minutes later, Tate reported, '*Carlisle* replying, sir, "*No help required. Damage amidships to searchlights and pom-poms. Continue on present course and speed*".'

By this time, Tobruk was shrouded in a vast cloud of smoke as the bombers, having completed their mission, turned away, apparently unscathed, and disappeared westwards.

CHAPTER NINETEEN

Shortly after 0900 on Sunday, 19th July, Able Seaman Slinger Wood reported sighting the rugged coast of Libya on his radar screen.

'Thank you,' replied Penrose, 'what's our position, Pilot?'

Sub Lieutenant Baker bent down, and after looking through the small square glass panel on the compass repeater, replied, 'Coast bearing zero four five degrees, sir.'

The previous evening, just before evening rounds, Penrose had addressed the ship's company, telling them that the flotilla would arrive in Alexandria the next day. After a brief introduction, he went to say, 'As you may know, Admiral Cunningham moved the fleet from Malta to Alexandria for safety reasons. Although having been badly bombed last year, Alex is now relatively safe as the Luftwaffe and Italians are concentrating on Tobruck. Tropical routine is to be observed and leave granted, and hopefully the mail will have caught up with us. There are a hundred piasters to the pound and money changing can be obtained from the pay office at 1100 tomorrow. That is all.' After replacing the handset, he glanced at Manley and said, 'What's our speed, Number One?'

For a few seconds Manley didn't answer. The mention of mail made him hope there would be a letter from Laura. 'Er… twenty-five knots, sir,' he stuttered.

Manley wasn't the only officer concerned about the mail. Sub Lieutenant Baker's immediate thoughts centred on the captain receiving news from the chief constable in Wallasey. Suddenly, he wondered why he was so worried; if a U-boat torpedoed the ship or they were hit by a bomb, his worries would be over, so to hell with it.

Throughout the ship, Penrose's words were greeted with alacrity. In the senior ratings mess, Petty Officer "Podge" Hardman's face lit up. 'Alexandria,' he said, looking at "Chippy" Tug Wilson, 'I served on board the *Barham* in '38. It was one of the best runs ashore I ever had.'

'What's the beer like?' Tug asked.

'It's called Stella and it's served in cans, ice cold,' Podge replied, lighting a cigarette. 'Cheap too, as I recall, just a few piasters a can.'

'Pay no attention to him, Tug,' Chief GI Bob Shilling chimed in. 'I was there a year ago in *Belfast* and some fuckin' Arab picked my pocket. Stole my pay book and wallet, so he did, and to make things worse, I caught the boat up.'

'So the morale of your story is,' grinned Chief Bosun's Mate Charlie Jackson, 'stay on board, save your money and I'll lend me one of my Jippo AFOs to read.' (JIPPO AFO's meant Egyptian Admiralty Fleet Orders, ie. Pornographic booklets obtained in Malta and other ports in the Mediterranean.)

In the seamen's mess, the reaction was the same. 'Dear old Alex,' said Leading Asdic Operator Dusty Miller, as he climbed into his hammock. 'I was there before the war. It's a great run ashore.'

'I say, Dusty,' asked Sammy Smith, who, like a few others, had finished cleaning the mess, ready for rounds. 'What's the best place for a bit of the other?'

'I expect the red-light district will be out of bounds,' Dusty replied, 'but as I remember, there's plenty of partys in the clubs and pubs in Sister Street.' (Party is a naval nickname for women.)

'Then that's where we'll be headed, eh, Slinger?' he said to Leading Radar Operator Wood as he lit a cigarette.

'OK by me,' Slinger replied, 'but I only hope the French letters I've had since we left Pompey haven't rotted away.'

At that moment, the shrill sound of the duty QM's bosun's call heralded the approach of the OOW and night rounds.

Sunday dawned warm and clear. A light breeze blew from the south, and high above, in a pale blue sky, a myriad of twinkling stars, together with anaemic moon, gradually faded away over the horizon. A little after 0600, the outline of Alexandria appeared on Dolly Gray's radar screen. This sighting was confirmed by Buster Brown, in the crow's nest, looking through his high-powered binoculars at the tops of the numerous minarets and cranes dotting Alexandria's skyline.

By 0700, everyone on the bridge could clearly see the two entrances to the harbour, the dockyard and the various yellow sandstone buildings and mosques.

'Signal from *Carlisle,* sir,' said Leading Signalman Jock Weir. '"*Helix, Eridge and Dulverton berth south wharf Great Harbour. Medical assistance will meet. Carlisle will berth wharf eight to effect repairs and land injured*".'

'Port five, Number One,' ordered Penrose, 'and reduce revolutions, two zero, special sea duty men fall in.'

'Ah, the ancient city Alexandria, sir,' Baker sighed, watching as *Helix* slowly turned left and followed *Carlisle.* 'It was founded by Alexander the Great in 331 BC, and was once the greatest city in the Hellenistic world and it was here that Cleopatra dallied with Julius Caesar.'

'Och, y'mean he shagged her, sir,' said Weir, with a grin.

'It's hard to believe that eight months ago, two Italian midget submarines managed to evade the boom and place limpet mines against the battleships, *Queen Elizabeth* and *Valiant,* eh, sir?' Manley remarked, as the small flotilla approached the port.

'Yes, indeed,' Penrose replied, 'eight sailors were killed on board the *Queen* and Mussolini awarded the officers and men involved the Italian Medal of Honour, the equivalent of our Victoria Cross.'

'Signal from Captain Neame, in *Carlisle,* sir, "*All commanding officers report to me immediately when secure in Alex*".'

'Now I wonder what he wants, eh, Number One?' Penrose asked Manley, creasing his brow.

'Your guess is as good as mine, sir' Manley answered, as the flotilla slowly nosed its way towards the harbour entrance. 'But I don't like it. Luckily wharf eight is close by, so you can leave as soon as the gangway is in place.'

Cranes, looking like black praying mantis', poked up in the air from a dockyard, while yellow and white sandstone buildings of the city stretched inland from a wide, horseshoe shaped harbour. On one side, guarding the port entrance stood an imposing, castle, its turrets and crenelated walls shining in the morning sun. Two tankers were tied up alongside a wharf, while some distance away, a large group of fishing boats and motor launches nestled against one another, rolling gently against the incoming tide.

The boom defending the harbour was opened, and by 1000, the three destroyers were tied up alongside the long wharf that led directly into port. Waiting on the wharf was a small convoy of army ambulances. Each one was white with large red cross painted on both sides and on the roof. Gangways were hurriedly put into place, allowing contingents of army medics to board the ships where they quickly began helping the wounded ashore into the ambulances. At the same time, Penrose left *Helix* and went on board *Carlisle,* berthed in front of the three destroyers.

Penrose and the other two commanding officers were familiar with Captain Neame's cabin, and therefore gave it scant attention.

'Good morning, gentlemen,' said the captain, who was sat behind a mahogany desk, cluttered with an assortment of official papers and folders. He wore tropical shorts and his bronzed face and muscular arms were in sharp contrast to the pristine white of his short-sleeved blouse. 'Please be seated,' he added, indicating to three armchairs. 'Two hours ago,' the captain said sternly, 'I received a top-secret communication from the First Sea Lord, Sir Dudley Pound. In it, he informs me that there is an extremely important operation being planned in England for which every available destroyer will be required.' He paused, and leaning slightly forward, he looked gravely at the three officers, and continued. 'The details of the operation were not given, but as you may be aware, up to the beginning of this month, we have lost one thousand, six hundred and sixty-four merchant ships in the Atlantic. Therefore, I suspect it'll be for convoy duty.' For a few seconds he stopped talking, then, furrowing his brow, slowly went on. 'Now, you can guess what I'm going to say next.'

'Yes, sir,' replied Gregory-Smith, *Eridge*'s captain, staring hopefully at Neame. 'We're being sent home.'

'You're quite right, Bill,' said Neame.

'When, sir?' Penrose asked, picking up a glass of water from a nearby table and taking good sip.

'In two days, you'll be glad to hear,' Neame answered calmly.

'Indeed, it is, sir,' replied Penrose, giving the two other officers a quick welcoming smile.

'Absolutely, sir,' added Gregory-Smith.

'Then, gentlemen,' Neame replied, standing up and warmly shaking each officer's hands, 'that's settled, you'll sail at 0800 in two days. That's the twenty-second. Make a quick refuelling stop at Malta. Then make all haste. If you meet any enemy convoys, you must use your judgement. Is that clear?'

'Yes, sir, 'Penrose answered, suddenly feeling uneasy.

'Good, any questions?'

'If this operation that's being planned is so important,' Peters asked, giving Neame a searching look, 'will any destroyers from Admiral Vian's battlegroup be sent back to England also?'

'I very much doubt it,' Neame replied. 'Vian's already lost *Havlock* and *Kingston.* He'll therefore need every ship in order to deal with Iachino's fleet should they leave Taranto. Also, his battlegroup, will be needed to intercept convoys bringing re-enforcements to Rommel from Italy.'

'Is there any more information about why we're being recalled, sir?' asked Penrose.

'None whatsoever, Henry,' Neame flatly replied. 'Nevertheless, it must be extremely important. Now, do carry on, I'm sure your ship's companies will be glad to hear the news.'

'Well, that came out of the blue,' Penrose remarked to Gregory-Smith as they walked down *Carlisle*'s metal gangway.

'It's certainly not what I expected,' Gregory-Smith replied.

'I couldn't agree more,' chimed in Peters, 'but what will you decide if we do meet a convoy, as I expect it'll have an escort?'

'Let's wait and see,' Penrose replied, as they stepped onto the wharf.

CHAPTER TWENTY

No sooner had Penrose left for *Carlisle*, than Surgeon Lieutenant Latta greeted a tall, fair-haired, army doctor as he stepped on board *Helix*.

'Good to see you, John Latta,' the doctor said, proffering his hand.'

'Peter Harris,' the army doctor replied, as they warmly shook hands.

As he spoke SBA Bamford, Petty Officer Powel and the first aid party came through a hatchway, carrying the soldier with an abdominal wound, on a stretcher. His head rested on a pillow, his eyes were closed and he was covered with a brown blanket.

'He has a bullet lodged in the left side of his abdomen,' Latta told Harris, using a handkerchief to wipe the sweat from his brow. 'I've done what I can, but he'll need operative treatment.'

'Then the quicker we get him ashore the better,' replied Harris. 'Is there anything we can do for you?' Latta noticed how pronounced Harris' Australian accent was.

'Yes, my sick berth attendant tells me we're short of morphia,' Latta replied.

'Then you'd better come with me and I'll give you what you need,' Harris said.

A white-coated army medic helped Powel and SA Bensen to pick up the soldier and slide the stretcher into the back of the ambulance, then climbed inside.

Latta turned to Bamford, and said, 'You'd better remain here and help Powel to put the wardroom back together, and thank the first aid party. They did damn good job.' After telling the officer of the day where he was going, Latta and Harris walked down the gangway and climbed into the ambulance next to the driver.

The journey to the military hospital took the small convoy of ambulances twenty minutes. During that time, they passed along dusty roads, crowded with buses, plying for space with gharrys, and maniacs riding bicycles. Colourful bazaars, heavily populated cafes, shops selling everything from beautiful silks to opium, added to what was a hive of bustling activity. There were women wearing niqābs, a black dress that covered everything except the eyes. Others were dressed in the more traditional hijab, a large headscarf, enveloping the shoulders. Some women preferred deeply religious burqa, a full body garment, while there were those who were clothed in the Abaya, an attire that enveloped everything including the arms and legs.

In contrast to all this mixture of religious and European garb, men wore the dishdasha, a modest garb consisting of a long, ankle-length robe, usually white and tailored. Added to this polyglot of humanity, were swarthy men in white suits; heavily tanned women wearing colourful headscarves and western style clothing; service men in tropical gear and ragged beggars crying desperately for baksheesh.

The hospital, surrounded by a high, red-bricked wall, consisted of a central, three-storey, yellow sand stoned building. Flanked on either side were two, much longer, flat-roofed, two-storey structures, built like a square with one end missing. After each driver showed his identification to an armed soldier, they drove through the main gate, along a wide gravel road edged on either side by a large, well-kept beds of red poppies and purple-headed thistles.

The ambulances stopped in line, near the main entrance situated in the rear of hospital. As the rear doors of the ambulance were opened, they were met by teams of medical orderlies and nurses pushing metal framed trollies.

The rear door of *Helix*'s ambulance opened, allowing PO Powel and Bensen to get out and slide the corporal's stretcher out onto a trolley. The time now was a little after 1100. With Latta and Harris close behind, the trolley was taken up a concrete ramp and met by a tall, white-coated doctor. Behind them came groups of walking wounded from *Eridge* and *Dulverton.* The serious cases were helped into wheelchairs, and along with the wounded, were taken through a wide, oaken door into the hospital. Here, they were met by teams of nurses then taken to the wards.

Latta and Harris were standing by the corporal's trolley when they were approached by a small, nursing sister, wearing a grey skirt and scarlet shoulder cape. This distinguished her from the white uniform worn the male and female nurses. Turning her head away so the corporal couldn't hear her, the sister asked Harris, 'How serious is he, Doctor?'

As she spoke, the dark rings under her brown eyes told of long, busy days and nights on duty.

'Bullet wound, lower abdomen, Sister,' Harris quietly replied. 'He'll need immediate surgery. This is Doctor Latta,' he added, 'the ship's surgeon.

'Nice to meet you, Doctor, we'll take it from here' she replied. In a business-like manner, she looked at two nurses and added, 'Ward five, clean him up. I'll be along shortly.'

'Good luck, old boy,' Latta said to the corporal, giving him a reassuring smile, 'you're in good hands now.'

'Thank you, sir,' the corporal murmured weakly, as the nurses wheeled him away.

'Now about that morphia,' said Harris, 'I'll give you some from one of my wards. It'll save a long trip to the store room and paper work.'

They left the reception area and walked down a long corridor, tiled in white. On their way nurses and patients being wheeled on trolleys, passed them. After passing a door with "Radiology", painted in red, Harris stopped at an oak door marked "Surgical One", and pushed it open. From a high, cream-coloured ceiling, a cool breeze from three metal fans helped to reduce the warmth of the morning sun. Almost every bed on either side of a long, wide, white-tiled ward was occupied by soldiers, recovering from various injuries. Some lay quietly, their heads, arms and hands bandaged. Others lay flat out, the bedclothes covering full body plaster casts. Several patients sat up reading old newspapers, a metal cage under their bedclothes protecting badly wounded legs. A pair of patients wearing blue dressing gowns and clearly on the mend, sat on armchairs glancing at one of the pretty nurses, and after making a slightly risqué remark, received a look of mock disgust. A few nurses stood by patient's bedsides, sharing a joke with them. White screen surrounded some beds, allowing patients to be treated in privacy, some of whom gave out an occasional painful cry.

'Och, are you always this busy?' Latta asked.

'Always, this is one of my wards and it's full of wounded from Tobruk,' Harris replied stoically, 'thanks to the navy, I expect the casualties will keep on coming. As long as Tobruk hold out, that is.'

At that moment, a tall, pale-faced sister approached them.

'Good morning, Doctor Harris.' Her Scottish accent was soft and distinct. As she spoke the corners of her tired-looking blue eyes, creased into a smile.

'Good morning, Sister,' Harris replied, 'this is John Latta, one of the destroyer's doctors.'

'Pleased to meet you,' the sister replied, 'Heather Johnson.'

'Och, now,' Latta said as they shook hands, 'do I detect a touch of eastern Scotland in yer accent?'

'Edinburgh born and bred,' Heather proudly replied. 'Did my training in Edinburgh General.'

'Well, well, so did I,' Latta answered with a smile.

'Then, we're both a long way from home, aren't we?' she said, still smiling.

'What will happen if, God forbid, Alex become in danger of falling?' Latta asked. 'Where will you and your staff evacuate to?'

Her smile slowly faced. Glancing ruefully around, she replied, 'Nowhere very far, I can assure you.' Then, looking at Harris, added, 'Will you be doing your morning round, Doctor?'

'Five minutes, Sister,' Harris replied.

'Nice meeting you,' she said to Latta, 'now if you'll excuse me, I must get on. Give my love to Edinburgh when you get home.'

With a solemn smile, Latta answered, 'Aye, that I will, and I'll raise a wee dram for you.'

'Make it a good malt,' she replied, and walked to a nurse and began talking.

'Now, if you come this way, I'll give you the morphia. Then I'll see if I can get you transport back to your ship.'

CHAPTER TWENTY-ONE

Shortly after 1200, Latta arrived on board *Helix*. Waiting for him at the top of the brow, was the tall, gangly figure of OOD Sub Lieutenant Jock Jewitt. As he walked up the gangway, he heard the duty QM pipe, "Secure. Hands to dinner. Mail. Mail is now ready for collection and will close at 1600. Leave to the first and second part of port and first part of starboard watch from 1300 to 0600".'

'You'd better hurry, Doc,' he said, as Latta saluted while stepping on board. 'The captain has just returned from *Carlisle* and wants to see all officers in the wardroom right away, so you'd better chop-chop.'

Latta did as Jewitt said, and by the time he reached the wardroom, he was breathing heavily. Every officer was present, and as Latta opened the door and went inside, all heads turned and looked at him.

'Sorry to be late, sir,' Latta quietly replied as he took his place next to next to Sub Lieutenant Baker.

'Right, then,' Penrose said, pursing his lips before looking around at the faces he had come to know as good as his own, 'I'll come straight to the point as I know you're all dying for a Horse's Neck before lunch.' Of course, this brought more smiles and an occasional burst of laughter. 'Gentlemen,' Penrose said, placing both hands behind his back, 'you'll be pleased to hear that we are going home.' His words were immediately received with wide grins and widespread murmurs of approval.

'When, sir?' asked Sub Lieutenant Baker, raising a hand.

'This Wednesday,' Penrose replied.

'That great news, sir,' said Lieutenant Powel, 'but why so soon?'

For the next ten minutes Penrose reiterated the admiral's reasons for their early departure, adding, 'So your guess is as good as mine, Ted. Now, how about that Horse's Neck?'

Ten minutes later, Baker came in to the wardroom carrying a handful of letters. He had checked them and was relieved to find there was no correspondence from Wallasey's chief constable, and was half-hoping to hear from Linda, but was disappointed. Everyone watched, as, instead of placing them individually in the mail rack, Baker left them on a table.

Being aware that the ship's company hadn't received mail for over three weeks, Penrose said, 'I suggest we take a ten-minute break.'

The officers broke away and crowded around the mail table. Some picked up letters and began ripping them open. Others turned, and along with Manley, walked sullenly away, empty handed.

'Don't look so downhearted, Number One,' Penrose said, seeing the look of disappointment on Manley's face. 'The only mail I received was a large bill my wife sent me was for new curtains. Anyway,' he added, finishing his drink and placing the glass on a table, 'as you know, the mail is very erratic, so cheer up.'

'Er… excuse me sir,' Baker ventured, 'do you know if we'll be receiving anymore mail before we sail?'

Penrose was well aware for the reason behind Baker's question. He shook his head and replied, 'I'm not sure, Pilot, it was *Manxman* that brought the mail, and she is returning to England this evening.'

Baker nervously cleared his throat, then replied, 'Thank you, sir.' He left the room.

'Will you be informing the ship's company that we'll be leaving for England, sir? asked Electrical Officer Lieutenant Sherwood.

'Yes, indeed,' Penrose replied, glancing at Manley. 'Number One will do that as soon as he's finished his drink.

In the senior ratings mess, Paddy O'Malley eagerly ripped open his letter. 'It's from Joyce, so it is,' he said excitedly to Harry Johnson, 'She's keeping well, and sends her best to you, Harry,' he added. After finishing reading the letter, he went on. 'The bombing has stopped but, so far, Portsmouth hasn't been hit by any doodlebugs. How is Ethel?'

'She's OK,' Harry replied, 'and sends you her best,, and bless her, she says she made some more blackcurrant jam.'

CHAPTER TWENTY-TWO

The news that the ship would be returning to England was naturally greeted by the ship's company with peels of cheering and back-slapping. In the seamen's mess, everyone stood in line as Bud Abbot, the killick of the mess, watched as everyone dipped the Bakelite measuring beaker into the "fanny" and poured out the correct measure of rum into a rating's mug or glass tumbler. Slinger Wood carefully tilted his "tot" into a badly scratched enamel mug, and was about to take a gulp when he looked at the tall figure of Leading Asdic Operator Miller, and said, 'How about showing us where Sister Street is, Dusty?'

With a sly grin, Miller replied, 'All right, but it'll cost you gulpers.'

'You're on,' Bud answered, reluctantly handing Dusty his mug.

At 1400, the pipe, "Liberty men fall in on the quarterdeck", echoed around the ship. A few minutes later, Dusty Miller, Slinger Woods, Bud Abbot and Bob Rose, and several other ratings, were fallen in on the quarterdeck. The supply and secretariat ratings wore white short sleeved shirts and peaked caps. The seamen were dressed in white shorts, white fronts. All branches wore blue stockings and shoes.

Duty PO Len Mills glared at them, and in a thick, Devonian accent, snapped, 'Liberty men are warned leave expires at 0600 and that the red-light district is out of bounds.' This order immediately brought a ripple of muted laughter from several ratings. 'Pipe down,' shouted Mills. 'Liberty men are reminded that they are only allowed to take twenty cigarettes or an ounce of tobacco ashore.' He paused, again, then shouted, 'Liberty men shun.' He did a quick about turn, and standing frigidly to attention, he gave OOD Lieutenant Goldsmith a parade ground salute, and grunted, 'Liberty men ready for inspection, sir.'

'Thank you, PO,' Goldsmith answered quietly while returning Len's salute.

'Fuck me,' Dusty muttered to Bud Abbot who was standing next to him, 'you'd think we were on parade in Jagos[6].'

'Keep quiet, there,' shouted Mills, as Goldsmith quickly walked between the two ranks of ratings, giving a cursory inspectorial glance at one or two, before stopping at the end of the last line.

After returning Mill's salute, he gave a quick nod, and said, 'Thank you, PO, carry on.'

Mills turned, and facing the men, said, 'Liberty men carry on.' Then with a wide grin, added, 'And keep yer hands on yer pay books and yer dicks in yer shorts.'

Upon hearing Len's remarks, Goldsmith, grinned, then disappeared through a hatchway and made his way to the wardroom.

Dusty and the others made their way through the cobbled dockyard and were immediately surrounded by groups of swarthy, bearded beggars, rolling their bloodshot eyes upwards, cupping their hands in supplication, and crying, '*Baksheesh, effendi, baksheesh!*'

Having been to Alexandria before, Dusty Miller took out a couple of piasters from his money belt and threw them a few yards away from where the beggars were gathered. This prompted them to turn, and with eager cries, grapple with one another in an attempt to pick up the coins.

'It's the only way to get rid of them,' said Dusty, giving Bob Rose and the others an all-knowing glance.

'Where to now?' Slinger asked Dusty, looking down a street full of cars, old and new, gharry horse-drawn cabs and stalls slanted with colourful shades.

Dusty grinned, and waving at a passing gharry, said, 'Relax, oppo, and leave that to me, our transport has arrived. How much to Sister Street?' he asked, looking up into the driver who was wearing an off-white disdasha, a red fez and a face resembling an overripe walnut.

'Ten piasters, effendi,' cried the driver, displaying a wide gap between a set of yellow, uneven teeth.

---

[6] Jagos was the nickname for HMS *Drake,* R.N Barracks, Devonport. The name was derived from Jago Alphonso (1876-1928) who was responsible for having General Messing installed in the barracks.

'No way,' cried Dusty, shaking his head. 'Five,' he shouted, showing five fingers, 'five piasters.'

'Six, six, effendi,' he said, clasping his hands and pleading vigorously, 'big family, many children.'

'Bloody 'ell,' retorted Bob Rose, in his sharp Lancastrian accent, 'the bugger speaks better English than me.'

'Let's face it, Bob,' said Bud, giving Rose a friendly dig in the ribs, 'everybody speaks better English than you.'

The three of them laughed as they listened to Dusty continued to haggle with the driver. 'OK,' Dusty replied, nodding his head, 'six it is.'

'Bless you, effendi,' said the driver, 'we go Sister Street, I know very good bar, dancing girls.'

'Sound good, eh, lads?' said Dusty, as they climbed up into a fairly wide canvas covered compartment with a long, well-worn leather seat. With a slight flick of the driver's whip, the elderly horse broke into a slow, steady gallop.

During the next fifteen minutes they made an uncomfortable journey through wide, dusty, streets, teeming with all types of humanity, passed ancient minarets, modern buildings and colourful bizaars. With a tug of the reins, the driver then turned the gharry down a narrow, cobbled street. On their way, the melodic beat of Arabic music could be heard coming from behind closed doorways.

'Where exactly is the red-light district, Dusty?' asked Bud Abbot, hearing Arabs standing outside darkened doorways shouting, and gesticulating wildly, 'Come in, Ingleesh sailors, dancing girls, young and clean.'

'I can't rightly remember,' Dusty replied, 'but I think we're there.'

'Then we'd better bugger off,' said Bob Rose, cautiously glancing up and down the street, 'before the red caps arrive and see us.'

As he finished speaking, a door opened and out stepped a small, beautiful, raven-haired girl. She wore a long pleated black dress and a short, scarlet blouse, displaying a well-tanned midriff and a tantalisingly low neckline and the swell of a pair of well-formed breasts. In one hand she grasped a round tambourine; the other held a set of shiny, silver castanets. With a quick toss of her head, she gave a wicked smile, and at the same time, raised the tambourine above her head, rattled it, then, speaking in surprisingly good English, no doubt picked up from countless servicemen, said enticingly, 'My name is Fatima. Come inside and I will dance for you, and do other sexy things…' Then, with a swish of her dress, quickly turned and leaving the door open, disappeared.

'There don't seem to be any red caps around,' said Bud Abbot, grinning salaciously at Dusty, 'so maybe we could give it a go. What say you, Slinger?'

'OK by me,' replied Wood, nervously licking his lips. 'Just for a few minutes, like.'

'All right,' said Dusty, 'but don't blame me if you 'catch the boat up,' and you three are married.'

Dusty paid the driver, and as they left the gharry, the doorman, smiled benignly and displaying a row of uneven, yellow-stained teeth, opened the door. Straight away, the indigenous sound of Arabic music, coming from lower down in the building, filled the air.

'Navy very welcome,' said the doorman. A small, fat, swarthy-faced man wearing a white dishdasha. 'My name is Mohammed, follow me.' He led them down a flight of narrow stairs and opened a door that led into a dimly lit room. Dusty and the three others blinked several times to accustom their eyes to the gloomy darkness. The heavy smell of tobacco smoke, together with the pungent aroma of hasheesh, hung in the air. With the exception of two men in white suits, accompanied by girls wearing off the shoulder blouses and tight-fitting skirts, sitting in darkened alcoves, the place was empty.

In the middle of a white-tiled floor stood the same girl they had met earlier. She was smiling seductively at her audience while swaying her hips to the rhythmic beat of the tambourine and the melodious clink of the castanets.

Dusty and Slinger occupied one alcove, while Bud and Bob sat in the one next to them. Upon seeing them, Fatima gave them a bedazzling smile and continued dancing, allowing her dress swirl around her long, shapely legs.

The four ratings found a table and sat down. Straight away each of them was joined by a pretty, dark-haired girl, who sat on their laps and put their arms around them.

'And what ees your name?' one of them asked Bud, slowly sliding her warm hand up his thigh onto his crotch.

'My er... mates call me Bud,' he replied, feeling her hand press down on his erection.

'My name is Zara,' she answered, nibbling his ear. 'You buy Zara a drink, yes?'

'Yeah, sure,' Bud replied. Glancing around at the other three, he saw they were similarly engaged with girls, kissing his mates while watching their hands slide up onto their legs.

Using her free hand, she looked up at tall swarthy waiter, and snapped, 'Champagne, and hurry up.' She allowed her skirt to ride up her thighs.

'*Champagne!*' yelled Bud. 'Who d'yer think I am. Rockfeller? You can piss off,' he added angrily, pushing the girl onto the floor.

'Tight arse Engleesh bastard,' she shouted, pulling her skirt down.

The girls that Bob, Dusty and Slinger were with had also requested champagne. They also realised they were about to be to be fleeced and reacted accordingly.

'Come on, lads,' shouted Dusty, 'let's bugger off out of here, it's a fuckin' clip joint.'

'Too bloody true,' cried Bob and Slinger, standing up and pushing the girls ceremoniously off their laps. One of the girls gave a shrill scream, and tumbled onto the floor. The other one stood defiantly with her hands on her hips, and glaring at the three husky waiters, shouted angrily, 'Throw them out.'

One of the waiters grabbed one of Bob's arms and forced it up his back and began to frog march him towards the door. Bob reacted by using the heel of his shoe against the waiter's leg, who immediately yelled, and let go of Bob's arms. Bob then turned around and punched the waiter in the nose. The waiter yelled and covered his nose as blood dripped through his fingers onto his grubby white shirt. At the same time, the other three were involved in a scuffle with the other waiters. Tables fell over, glasses crashed onto the floor and girls screamed. Suddenly, the ear splitting wail of the air raid siren rent the air.

'*Jesus Christ!*' Dusty yelled, as he was about to hit one of the waiters. '*It's a bloody air raid!*'

'No, no, effendi, it can't be,' a waiter cried. 'We haven't been bombed since last year!' His voice was drowned out by a violent, explosion that shook the building.

'Well, you fuckin' well have, now,' shouted Dusty, as bits of dirt fell down from the ceiling. 'Come on, lads,' he shouted, while grabbing his cap, 'let's get the fuck out of here and leg it back to the ship.'

Dusty and the other three stopped fighting and pushing the girls and a waiter out of the way, made their way through the gloom, opened the door and ran into the street. After blinking their eyes to accustom their eyes to the sun's glare, they saw people scurrying around, seeking shelter, as the sharp retort of ack-ack guns and explosions rent the air. As the four ratings ran up the street, shielding their eyes, they glanced up and saw the pale blue sky dotted with grey blobs of smoke and a group of Marchetti bombers, some distance away from the city. 'It's the fuckin' ities,' he yelled, 'they're turning away, looks like they're leaving.'

'Thank fuck for that,' said Slinger, feeling lines of sweat running down his face. 'I don't know about you three, but I'm parched.'

'Me too,' added Dusty, 'maybe now we can find somewhere and have a few wets.'

'Hey, 'old on a minute,' cried Bud, noticing the flap of his purse in his belt was open. 'All me money's gone. That fuckin' bitch in the club must 'ave robbed me.'

'Mine's gone as well,' shouted Dusty. 'What about you two?' he added, looking at Slinger and Bob.

'The bitch I was with has dipped me also,' replied Slinger, angrily shaking his head.

Just then, the monotonous drone of the "All Clear" sounded.

'Well, my money's safe, thank fuck,' said Bob, tapping the purse in his belt. 'So let's go back and sort them party's out,' said Dusty, clenching his fists.

'Good idea,' Bob replied, glancing apprehensively down the cobbled street they had just left, 'but maybe those two red caps walking towards us might have to disagree with you, matey.'

'Then, I suggest we scarpa,' said, Bob. 'Come on, lads, the first round's on me.'

'And the rest,' muttered Dusty as they hurried down the main road and into the nearest bar.

CHAPTER TWENTY-THREE

Shortly after 1400, a sharp knock on his cabin door momentarily distracted Penrose from the letter he was writing to Jean. 'Come,' he sighed putting down his fountain pen and sitting back in his chair. Naturally he couldn't say the ship was homeward-bound, but he did write, *we were about to head westward*, hoping she would understand. The door opened and in came the tall, stocky figure of Radio Communications Officer, Sub Lieutenant Brownlow RNVR who had joined the ship earlier that day and hadn't met the captain. This was his first ship. He was twenty-three with a first in mathematics and a fiancée called Fiona who was a nurse and lived in his home town of Whitby.

'Ah, Brownlow,' said Penrose, looking up, 'Daniel, isn't it?'

Brownlow blinked his pale blue eyes and replied, 'Yes, sir.' As he spoke, he took off his cap, revealing well-groomed dark brown hair, parted neatly on the left side.

Noticing Brownlow's pale features and obvious nervousness, Penrose gave him a fatherly smile and said, 'Relax, dear boy, I'm not going to eat you, now, what is that you've got for me?'

'A signal marked, "top secret", signal sir,' Brownlow answered, feeling his mouth go dry.

'Top secret, eh,' muttered Penrose, pensively stroking his chin, 'then you'd better tell me what is says.'

'Er… with respect, sir,' he said, feeling his hand shake as he handed the signal to Penrose, 'It's very important. I think you'd better read it yourself.'

'Very well,' sighed Penrose, accepting the signal. '*Great Scott!*' he exclaimed, as he read it. 'Tobruk has fallen and thirty-five thousand men have been captured. How many others besides yourself know about this?'

'Only me, sir,' Brownlow replied.

'Good, keep it that way until I've informed the officers,' Penrose answered wearily. 'Also, inform the commanding officers of *Dulverton* and *Eridge*e, by signal. Mark them "secret" and say, "Tobruk fallen, keep a sharp lookout for enemy shipping when we sail". And pipe for all officers to muster in the wardroom immediately. Now carry on, and be quick about it,' Penrose added, standing up and making for the door. However, neither officers realised Scouse Morris was listening behind the galley door.

A few minutes later, "All officers muster in the wardroom straight away", echoed over the tannoy.

On the way to the wardroom, Logan met the Surgeon Lieutenant Latta. 'Any idea what the old man wants, Doc?

'No, I havna,' retorted Latta angrily. 'It's just as well as I finished putting in a few stiches in a seamen's head, or he would have ta wait for me.'

Every officer, including Sub Lieutenant Milton, who was OOD, was in the wardroom. A few sat around on armchairs, talking quietly. Some sipped coffee, courtesy of PO Steward Sandy Powel, while other officers stood around, quietly smoking.

A few minutes after 1430, Penrose came in, followed closely Manley. Those officers who were sitting down immediately stood up and joined the others who were quietly standing to attention.

'Stand at ease, gentlemen.' Then, nodding to PO Powel, he said, 'Kindly leave enough coffee in the urn for everybody then leave us, and close the door.'

As soon as Powel left, Penrose furrowed his brow and looked at the anxious face staring at him. 'Gentlemen,' he said, gravely, 'I'm sure you want to know why I've asked to see you, so I'll come straight to the point. I regret to tell you, Tobruk has fallen.' Immediately, his last three words were met by an all- round murmur and concerned glances.

'Excuse me, sir,' said Lieutenant Powers, 'how will that affect us?'

Placing both hands behind his back, Penrose replied, 'Now that Tobruk is in enemy hands, it means that Rommel will seriously threaten Egypt, including the Suez Canal and the trade route to the east. Now, to do that he will need to be supplied from the sea…'

'Which means convoys from Italy, sir,' interrupted Lieutenant Goldsmith.'

'Correct, Barry,' Penrose curtly replied.

'That's if they manage to break through Admiral Vian's blockade, sir,' added Lieutenant Sherwood.

'Quite so, Tim,' Penrose said, smiling ruefully, 'but Vian will have to contend with the Italian and German air force, as well as submarines, so our small group of three destroyers will have to be extra vigilant at all times.'

Will you inform the ship's company, sir?' asked Lieutenant Logan.

'Knowing how the tom-toms work on board,' Penrose replied with a wry smile, 'they'll already know. Any questions?'

'Just one, sir,' piped up, Latta, grinning, 'how about some coffee afore the urn goes cold.'

'Splendid idea, Doc,' Penrose replied, rubbing his hands together, 'but as the sun is well over the yardarm, I'd prefer it if we could all have something stronger.'

PART THREE
CHAPTER TWENTY-FOUR

Shortly after 0900 on Wednesday, 22nd July, the boom protecting the entrance to Alexandria's widest harbour was removed, to allow *Helix, Eridge* and *Dulverton* to begin their journey back to England. High above, in the eye-smarting, cerulean sky, the early morning sun made the calm sea twinkle like a million tiny stars.

With *Helix* in the van, the three destroyers formed up line abreast. Penrose was on the bridge, sitting comfortably in his chair. With an approving smile, he watched as each of the two destroyers sent spumescent bow waves curling over their fo'c'sles as they cut through the sea.

'A wonderful sight, eh, sir,' remarked Manley, taking off his cap and wiping his brow with a handkerchief. He had seen a similar sight many times before, but he couldn't help but admire the way the destroyers dipped in unison in out of the sea as if controlled by a puppeteer.

'It is indeed, Number One,' Penrose replied, 'and I suggest, you fall out special sea duty men. Anything on radar or asdic?'

'No, sir,' Manley answered.

The morning passed quietly. At 1130, "Up spirits, cooks to the galley", was piped. Half an hour later, Lieutenant Tim Sherwood took over the afternoon watch from Sub Lieutenant Baker. The lookouts were changed, Leading Signalman Weir relived PO Signalman Spud Tate and Able Seaman Jock Forbes exchanged duties with QM Able Seaman Brum Appleby. Manley was about to leave the bridge when he looked at Penrose, who was using his binoculars to survey the surrounding sea, and said, 'Excuse me, sir, are you not going to lunch?'

Without lowering his binoculars, Penrose replied, 'No, I don't feel hungry. But maybe you could ask Morris to bring me a cup of coffee?'

'Very good, sir,' Manley, replied, 'but Morris told me you missed breakfast. Are you sure you're feeling well?'

Penrose lowered his binoculars, and giving Manley a stern look, said, 'Of course I am, Morris is a bloody fuss pot.'

Manley left the bridge and met Morris on the wardroom flat, carrying a large mug of steaming hot vegetable soup and said, 'He only wants a cup of coffee.'

'He'll 'ave this soup if I 'ave to pour it down 'im mesef,' Morris firmly replied.

Manley gave Morris a searching look, and said, 'He's not in a very good mood, so on your head, be it.'

Lieutenant Sherwood later told Manley that Morris had refused to leave the bridge until Penrose ate the soup. With a rueful smile, he added, 'So the captain eventually capitulated.'

By 1800, the sun, now a great round orb, bathed the sea in a vast patina of dazzling orange before sinking into the east. Visibility was clear and a balmy breeze blew from the east. The small flotilla was roughly three hundred miles west of Crete when Asdic Operator Dusty Miller reported a small blip on his radar screen. 'Looks like a submarine, sir,' he cautiously added, 'twenty miles on *Dulverton*'s port quarter.'

'*Dulverton* and *Eridge* have reported sighting it on radar also, sir,' Manley said to Penrose.

'Sound action stations,' snapped Penrose. He bent foreword and unhooked the ship's tannoy. 'This is the captain speaking. Radar has reported sighting a submarine. It's probably a U-boat, I will keep you informed.' After replacing the tannoy, he looked at Manley, who, like everyone else, had donned anti-flash gear, and said, 'What's our speed?'

'Twenty-one knots, sir,' Manley quickly replied.

'Signal to both ships, "increase speed to twenty-five knots, and turn ten degrees to starboard". Let's see what the blighter will do.' As he spoke, Penrose felt his heart pound like a hammer. He felt beads of sweat break out on his brow and run down the sides of his face. He reached into a pocket in his shorts and managed to fumble with a small box and brought out a Digoxin tablet and quickly put it in his mouth and swallowed it.

'How are you, sir?' Manley asked, noticing tiny beads of sweat running down the sides of Penrose's heavily tanned face.

'Fine,' Penrose replied. 'Just a touch of indigestion, nothing to worry about,' he added, taking out a handkerchief and quickly wiping his face.

Digger Barnes's throaty reply, confirming Penrose's order, came from the wheelhouse. Almost immediately the ship increased speed and heeled precariously to right

'Torpedo track five miles away, heading towards *Dulverton,* sir,' shouted the port lookout.

With their binoculars pressed tightly to their eyes, all heads quickly turned to the left. 'Now we know what the sods are up to,' Penrose calmly remarked.

A minute later, Sub Lieutenant Baker shouted, 'Torpedo passed about fifteen yards from *Dulverton*'s stern, sir.'

'Luckily you ordered that turn to starboard, eh, sir,' Manley remarked, feeling a trickle of sweat run down the left side of his face.

'*Dulverton*'s attacking, sir, she's fired a spray of depth charges,' Able Seaman Wiggy Bennett reported from the crow's nest. (Each depth charge contained 200 tons of TNT.)

'Where's the bastard, now, Number One?' asked Penrose.

'A hundred yards on *Dulverton*'s port quarter, sir.'

No sooner had Manley spoke when everyone on the bridge, and those in exposed positions on the upper deck, heard a gigantic *whoosh,* as a thick wall of white water exploded some distance behind *Dulverton.* Another detonation, higher and just as loud, quickly followed. Gradually both huge jets of water settled in the sea in ever widening circles of swirling whirlpools. The night's clear visibility allowed all eyes to search for tell-tail oil stains, bits of wreckage or bodies, but none appeared.

'Signal *Eridge* to attack, Number One,' snapped Penrose. He contacted Lieutenant Logan in the engine, and said, 'Stand by to increase speed five knots, when I will order the depth charges to fire, I don't want the ship to be caught in the back draft of the explosions. Understand, Derek?'

'Yes, sir,' Logan replied, and replaced the hand set.

'Right, Number One,' Penrose said, sitting upright in his chair, 'let's give *Eridge* and *Dulverton* a hand.'

Helix gradually gained speed, until she was some hundred yards in front of *Eridge*. 'Where is the bugger, now, Number One?' asked Manley, feeling his heart beat a hurried cadence in his chest.

'About a hundred yards in front of us, sir, two hundred and fifty fathoms deep,' Manley answered, breathing heavily.

Using the intercom, Penrose quickly contacted Goldsmith and said, 'I want you to drop the first depth charge astern, set at two hundred feet, then, a few seconds later, as we move ahead, drop one to port and starboard set at two hundred and fifty feet; and finally, lay one astern at three hundred feet. Then stand by to fire. Understand?'

'Perfectly, sir,' Goldsmith answered firmly, 'a diamond formation.' Straight away, Goldsmith ordered his team of operators, to alter the Depth Adjuster on each depth charge to the required sea level.

Meanwhile, the tension on the bridge was palpable. Manley glanced apprehensively at Penrose and noticed his captain hunched up. He held the quarterdeck intercom in his hand and he was nervously biting his lip. Suddenly, Penrose seemed to spring to life. And sitting bolt upright, said in a loud voice, 'Increase speed five knots, fire all depth charges.' Penrose pushed himself off his chair, and followed by Manley, hurried to the port wing. Sub Lieutenant Baker and Sub Lieutenant Milton, who was now OOW, QM Jock Forbes and PO Pony Moore made for the starboard wing. With baited breath, everyone watched and waited, feeling every vibrant beat of the engines beneath the wooden deck. Then, after what seemed like minutes, but was in fact seconds, four loud eruptions of white seawater could be clearly seen two hundred yards away on the port quarter, before gradually settling in the sea. However, the tension in everyone faces remained as they hoped to see evidence of a kill. They didn't have long to wait.

Wiggy Bennett in the crow's nest was the first to report what everyone anxiously hoped for. 'Dark stains in the water, sir,' he yelled down the bridge intercom. Then, straining his eyes through his binoculars, added excitedly, 'Looks like oil, in fact I'm sure of it, about a hundred yards in our stern.'

However, the cheering and back-slapping on the bridge and throughout those on the upper deck, was somewhat muted when bodies, half naked and others mutilated, lying face down, were seen amongst the various pieces of wreckage and debris.

'A bloody awful way to die, eh, Chalky?' Leading Seaman Lee, captain of B gun, said solemnly to Knocker White, standing next to him on the gunnery platform.

'Aye, yer right there, Tansey,' White answered, noticing a headless corpse floating in sea. 'But,' he added while taking off his anti-flash hood, 'it was either them or us.' It was a sentiment shared by the rest of the crew.

'I say, sir,' Baker said to Penrose, 'I can see what looks like a cap floating in the sea a few yards away from the side of the ship, do you want it as evidence?'

'Yes,' Penrose replied quietly. 'Have it hooked on board, perhaps it'll help to identify the U-boat, and secure from action stations.'

Ten minutes later, the thick-set figure of PO Len Mills arrived, holding a soggy white cap. It was wrinkled with a row of silver oak leaves around the edge of the peak. 'Looks like it belonged to the skipper, eh, sir,' said Mills, handing the cap to Penrose.

Penrose took the cap and turned it inside out. The words in faded gold lettering, read, "*Heinri (*something or other), *Stern*". Penrose pursed his lips, then replied, 'Looks like *Heinrich Von Stern,* the "*Von*", indicates he was an aristocrat.' He paused momentarily, then, added, 'I think you could be right, PO. It did belong to the sub's captain. Take it to my cabin and tell Morris to put it somewhere safe to dry out.'

'Aye, aye, sir,' Mills replied, accepting the cap and leaving the bridge.

'Better send a signal to C-in-C Med, Number One, "U-boat sunk, give the position, and add, no survivors".' He then unhooked the ship's tannoy and said, 'Well done the TAS crew.'

Mills did as ordered, and took the cap to Penrose's cabin and gave it to Morris then told him what the captain said.

'Bloody 'ell! PO!' Mills exclaimed. 'A real Nazi captain's, lid, wait till I tell the lads in the mess about this,' he added, carefully running his fingers along the gold leafed peak.

'No, you won't, my 'andsome,' snorted Mills, 'you'll do as the old man says, and stow it somewhere, or I'll 'ave yer guts for garters.'

'Don't worry, PO,' Morris replied warily, 'I'll take good care of it.'

'You'd better,' grunted Mills, and left the cabin.

No sooner had Mills closed the cabin door, than Morris couldn't resist temptation. He went into the captain's bedroom, and ignoring how wet the cap was, carefully put it on his head. He looked into the large mirror situated on the front of the wardrobe. Standing frigidly to attention, he shot out his right arm and shouted, '*Heil! Hitler!*' With a satisfied grin, he took off the cap, then wiped his face with a handkerchief. He was about to go into the captain's bathroom and hang the cap up on a hook behind the door, when he paused, and had an idea. He carefully folded the cap up and tucked it down his white front, closed the door and left the cabin.

The time was shortly after 2000. In the S and S mess, the atmosphere was heavily tinged with tobacco smoke and the stale smell of sweat. Some ratings were sat at the long wooden table playing uckers and cribbage. A few sat writing letters while one or two lay, cocooned in their hammocks, doing their best to sleep before going on watch at midnight.

Suddenly, the tranquillity of everything was abruptly interrupted by Morris coming down the stars, holding the cap in one hand and shouting, 'Look what I've got, lads.'

Everyone stopped what they were doing and looked up at him, even Terry Bensen poked his head over his hammock to see what all the commotion was about.

'This,' said Morris, placing the cap on his head and walking haughtily into the mess, 'is the cap belonging to the skipper of the U-Boat. Len Mills had it fished outa the drink.'

Dick Turpin topped playing uckers and stood up. 'Here,' he said to Morris, reaching out with a hand, 'let's try it on.'

Morris handed the cup to him, and warned, 'Be careful, it's still a bit wet.'

For a few seconds, Turpin held the cap in his hand, and staring at it, said, 'Bugger me, to think this has been on Nazi captain's bonce.' He put the cap on, and did a quick, "*Heil! Hitler!*" However, with the exception of Leading Writer Jack Jones, everyone in the mess had a good look at the cap and tried it on.

'What's the matter, Scribes?' asked Morris, offering the cap to Jones. 'Don't tell me you're superstitious?'

'No, I'm not,' Jones flatly replied, 'but it belonged to a dead man.' He added, staring cautiously at their faces. 'Chuck it back in the sea or it'll bring bad luck, mark my words…'

CHAPTER TWENTY-FIVE

The next day dawned calm, warm and clear. The time was 1230. Afternoon watchmen were closed up and the ship was at cruising stations. As usual, Penrose was comfortably ensconced in his chair.

'What's our position, Pilot?' Penrose asked, noting how well the other two ships kept formation.

'Latitude thirty degrees west, longitude twenty-five degrees south, sir,' Baker replied, having plotted the ship's position when he took over the watch from Lieutenant Ted Powers.

'That would place us where, exactly?' Penrose asked, pensively stroking his chin.

'Two hundred and fifty miles west of Malta, sir.'

'What's our ETA, Malta?'

'1800 on the twenty-fifth, sir,' Baker replied, then quickly added, 'do you think there'll be any mail there, sir?'

'I very much doubt it,' Penrose replied, sensing Baker's anxiousness regarding news from the magistrate in Wallasey. 'We'll only be there for a quick refuelling stop. I'm afraid there won't be any in Gib which we should pass on the twenty-ninth.'

'I see, thank you, sir,' Baker muttered aimlessly, then turned away and looked down at his chart.

'Better send a signal to C-in-C, Malta,' Penrose said to Leading Signalman Jock Weir. Weir hurriedly picked up a pad from the bridge dashboard and took out a pencil from his pocket. 'Say, "Request refuelling and berthing instructions for *Helix, Eridge* and *Dulverton*", and give our ETA.'

Weir quickly wrote down his captain's words and left the bridge.

Ten minutes later, Weir arrived on the bridge holding a signal pad. 'Reply from C-in-C, Malta, sir.'

'Then, read it, man,' Penrose snapped, who, like Manley, Baker and the others, were busy watching a pod of dolphins bounding merrily in and out of the sea some fifty yards in front of the ship.

'"*Three ships berth Palarorio wharf. Oil tenders will meet. Cunningham*".'

'Thank you, Weir,' replied Penrose, 'kindly repeat it to *Eridge* and *Dulverton.*'

'Och, d'yer think those buggers know summat we don't, sir,' Jock Weir said to Baker, looking at the dolphins' perpetual smiles.

'Maybe they know where the hell our mail has got to,' Baker replied sourly.

Malta was quiet and peaceful as the three destroyers arrived, a welcome change from the incessant air raids the island had suffered recently. The cloudless sky was an umbrella of glittering stars and the moon cast a silver sheen onto the still waters of Grand Harbour.

On the flotilla's starboard beam, the spires of Valetta's many churches dominated the skyline, while away to port, the partial ruins of Vittorioso, Conspicua and Senglea, the victims of constant bombing, lay shrouded in darkness.

By 1900, the flotilla passed Senglea Point, and turned to port. Fifteen minutes later, all three vessels were berthed alongside Palatorio Wharf. Under the sharp eyes of Chief Stoker Harry Johnson and Lieutenant Logan, *Helix*'s fuel tanks were opened, pipes were passed from the ship to the lighters alongside. The same procedure was happening on board *Eridge* and *Dulverton,* and an hour later, refuelling was completed.

Shortly after 2100, the flotilla slipped quietly out of Grand Harbour, turned to starboard and were met by the steady swell of the sea.

'When will we pass Gib and enter the Bay of Biscay, Pilot?'

Baker knew Penrose would ask him this and had earlier worked this out. 'At our present speed, sir,' Baker confidently replied, 'early on the morning of the twenty-ninth, sir.'

'Four days, thank you, Baker,' Penrose replied with a wry smile. 'As usual, most efficient.'

The news that the ship was not stopping at Gib, soon spread throughout the ship like wildfire. The feeling that the next stop would be Portsmouth sent an air of excited anticipation running through the ship. However, in the seamen's mess, one person had slight misgivings. It was just after "pipe down" and several ratings were preparing to get turned in.

'In a way, it's a pity we're not stopping at Gib,' said Wiggy Bennett, as he reached up to the iron rail and pulled himself into his hammock. 'I was hoping to buy a few rabbits, for the missus and kids.' (Rabbits are a nickname for presents.) Gibraltar was usually the last port of call before England and was popular place to buy last minute presents before reaching England.

'What's up, Wiggy?' Dinga Bell remarked as he was about to get undressed. 'Is your conscience bothering you after shagging Manky Mary the last time we were down the Gut?'

'Rubbish,' retorted Bennett, squirming down in his hammock and picking up his dog-eared copy of *Health and Beauty* from under his pillow. 'I was very considerate, I wore a johnny, which is more than you did when you disappeared with Slack Alice.'

'Ah, maybe,' Dinga Bell, replied cautiously, 'but you forget, I'm separated from my missus.'

'Is that why I saw you in the heads, taking tablets, and why the doc has stopped your tot?' said Wiggy, oggling a photograph of two nude girls playing with a beach ball.

'Bad guts,' replied Bell, giving Bob Rose, who was standing across from him, a sly wink.

In then engine room, CERA O'Malley was wiping his hands on some cotton waste, when Chief Stoker Johnson came in. 'To be sure,' O'Malley said, throwing the cotton waste in the gash bin, 'good news, eh, Harry, next stop dear old Pompey.'

'I hope so, Paddy,' Harry replied, 'but at the speed we're going, I only hope my boilers don't burst.'

'Sweet Jesus,' said Paddy, grinning like a Cheshire cat. 'If we do, I'll fuckin swim home, so I will.'

'Are you going to propose to Joyce?' Harry asked, wiping his brow with a handkerchief.

Paddy's pale blue eyes lit up. 'Too bloody true,' he answered with a wide grin. 'And you'll be my best man, won't you?' he added, slapping Harry on the back.

'With pleasure, Paddy,' Harry replied, 'now how about a cuppa tea in the mess, to celebrate.'

'Better still, me boyo,' said Paddy, 'it just so happens, I've got one in the bottle.' (Meaning he had put some of his tot in a medicine bottle, to be drunk later, or offered as a favour.)

In the wardroom there was an air of relaxation. Night rounds were completed. Manley, stood, sipping a coffee and wondering why he hadn't had a letter from Laura. Was she too sick to write? Had she had an accident? Another man, perhaps. Why? Why? he asked himself, had she not written?

'Och, what's up, old boy?' asked Surgeon Lieutenant Latta. 'Are you all right, you look miles away?'

'Oh, just thinking about going home,' Manley replied. 'All things being equal, that is,' he added, with a wry smile. He finished his coffee and slowly walked out of the room.

During Sunday the 26th, the three warships continued peacefully westward. With the ships' company at cruising stations, many ratings off watch relaxed on the quarterdeck. They lay on towels wearing only their shorts, while others wore bathing costumes. In sharp contrast to their white backs and fronts, their arms and faces looked heavily tanned.

'This is the life, eh, Dutch,' mumbled Bud Abbot to Leading Seaman Holland who, like Abbot, was lying face down, resting on both folded arms. 'Bronzy, bronzy for leave. My old girl will think I look like Errol Flynn.'

'No chance,' Holland muttered. Even though they had only been lying there for ten minutes, with the warmth of the deck slowly penetrating the thickness of his towel, and the heat of the sun on his back, he was beginning to feel like being baked in an oven. 'You're so big and hairy you'll end up looking like King Kong.'

Abbot was about to say something when he heard the sharp voice of Chief GI, yelling, 'Right, you lot, remember the Jimmy's warning about self-inflicted wounds, now up you get and back to your messes, pronto.'

'Och, Chief,' Jock Forbes said, sitting up and shielding his eyes from the sun, 'in peacetime, toffs have ta spend a fortune ta do this.'

'In your dreams, Jock,' Shilling replied sarcastically, 'two minutes or you'll all be on report.'

The time was 1300. Except for the steady beat of the engines and the *thud, thud* of the ship dipping in and out of the sea, all was quiet. Penrose was below in his cabin. OOW Sub Lieutenant Jewitt was bent over the compass repeater, ensuring *Dulverton* was not too close. Using a sextant, Midshipman Morgan was checking a "fix" he had taken earlier. Manley was sat in the captain's chair watching the line of foam fizz down either side, as the ship cut through the dark blue sea. Leading Seaman Sammy Smith, was lent on the binnacle, sharing a joke with PO Signalman Spud Tate. QM Knocker White stood next to them, quietly farting, as PO Len Mills, using his binoculars, swept the never-ending curvature of the horizon. Suddenly, all heads turned as Scouse Morris burst onto the bridge. His round, podgy face was lighter shade of pale than usual and there was a look of panic in his eyes.

'Better come and 'ave a look at the captain, ser,' Morris gasped, breathing heavily. 'I think there's summat wrong with 'im. He's holding 'is arm and he seems to be in pain. He's says 'e wants 'is tablets.'

'I'd better go and see what the problem is, Jock,' Manley to said to Jewitt, 'and pipe for the MO to go to the captain's cabin.'

Manley followed Morris down the flight of metal stairs, onto the captain's flat. After knocking, he opened the captain's door. 'You'd better wait outside,' Manley said to Morris, 'I'll call you if needed.'

'But, ser,' Morris pleaded, 'maybe I can help.'

'Just do as I say,' Manley replied, and went inside. The sight that met his eyes alarmed him. Penrose was slumped in his chair. His sweat-stained, ashen face was grimacing with pain and he was clutching his left arm. 'What's the matter, sir?' Manley asked, hurrying behind Penrose's desk and gently touching him on the shoulder.

'Pain's in my chest,' he muttered, 'terrible pain… my tablets.' he added as his voice faded.

At that moment, a knock came at the door and Surgeon Lieutenant Latta came in. SBA Bamford followed behind. In one hand, Latta carried a bulky black leather Gladstone valise, and the other held a stethoscope. Latta immediately saw Penrose's face was grimacing with pain.

'Where exactly is the pain, sir?' Latta asked, taking Penrose's radial pulse and finding it weak and over a hundred.

'Here,' Penrose mumbled, using his right hand to indicate an area behind his breast bone.

'And when did it start?'

'It came... on suddenly... just after... call the... hands,' Penrose managed to say, 'but please, Doc, my tablets... they're in... the left pocket of... shorts.'

Latta put his hand into the captain's tropical shorts and found a small, white pill box. 'What are these?' Latta asked taking out the box and opening the lid.

'Digoxin,' Penrose muttered. 'I've been on them... for over... a month. My GP... gave them... to me.'

'Och, man, why didn't you tell me?' Latta asked, realising the captain was having a heart attack.

'You'd have... sent me,' Penrose muttered, 'to hospital and... I'd have missed... the ship... please... give me... two of... them.'

Latta was reluctant to do as Penrose asked, but fearing it would increase Penrose's anxiety if he refused, he took out two tablets and placed them in Penrose's open mouth. Bamford arrived, holding a tumbler half-filled with water. He allowed Penrose a good sip to swallow the tablets, then dabbed his mouth with a gauze swab. He then placed the box containing the tablets in a side pocket in his Gladstone Valise.

Latta gently lifted Penrose's shirt, and using his stethoscope, listened to the captain's heartbeat, and was not surprised to find it strong, fast and irregular. He then took Penrose's blood pressure and found it dangerously high.

'Try and relax, sir,' Latta said, removing the stethoscope from his ears and opening s Gladstone valise. 'I'm going to give you an injection, it'll help relieve the pain.' Feeling his own heart thumping, he took out a metal box containing two sterile 5cc syringes, needles and several small glass ampoules of morphine sulphate. He carefully picked out a needle and syringe. He attached a needle to the syringe. Using a tiny metal saw, he removed the top of the ampoule and withdrew its contents into the syringe. After carefully replacing the old needle with a new one, he expelled any air bubbles. Bamford passed him some cotton wool soaked in surgical spirit. Latta wiped the deltoid area on Penrose's upper arm and inserted the needle. After withdrawing the plunger slightly to ensure the needle wasn't in a vein, Latta injected the morphia.

'There, now, sir,' Latta said, gently rubbing the injected area. 'Sit back and in a little while you should feel a bit better.' Glancing at

Bamford, he added, 'Go to the sick bay and bring the Novox.' This was a resuscitation apparatus, weighing 60lbs. It consisted of a heavy wooden chest, a cylinder painted black with a white top containing two cubic feet of oxygen. Attached to the cylinder was a control valve, a length of corrugated tube, a special face mask and small glass dial.

A few minutes later, Bamford arrived, carrying the bulky Novox box. He lay it flat on the floor near Penrose's desk and unclipped the lid.

'I'm going to give you some oxygen,' said Latta, 'it'll help your breathing. Then, when you're feeling up to it, we'll get you into your sleeping quarters.'

Bamford removed the oxygen cylinder and held it, while Latta placed the mask over Penrose's nose and mouth and secured it around his ears with elastic straps. Careful not to turn on the oxygen too quickly and cause a sudden oxygen flow, he slowly turned on the valve and watched the hand on the dial move to the optimum level. 'Now, sir,' Latta said, 'I want you to try and relax and breathe slowly.'

Penrose did as Latta asked, and after about five minutes, his pallor and breathing began to improve.

'Och, well done, sir,' Latta said, 'you're doing just fine.'

Just then the bridge intercom on the bulkhead by the side of Penrose's desk rang out. Manley unhooked it from its holder. 'First Lieutenant,' he snapped.

'Jewitt, sir, how's the captain?'

'He's alright so far. I'll be up presently,' Manley replied, and replaced the handset.

'I'm returning to the bridge, Doc,' Manley, 'you seem to have everything under control, but keep me informed.'

'Just a minute, sir,' Latta said, handing the oxygen cylinder to Bamford. He turned, and in a church-like whisper, said, 'We'll have to land him at Gib, sir, I hear we'll be passing there on Wednesday, any chance of getting there sooner?'

''I'll speak to Derek, and let you know,' Manley answered calmly. Before leaving the cabin, Manley looked at the masked face of Penrose, and giving him an encouraging smile, said, 'Don't worry, sir, you're in good hands, you're going to be fine.'

However, what Manley didn't know, was Penrose's pulse and blood pressure remained perilously high and he could die any minute.

CHAPTER TWENTY- SIX

As Manley opened the captain's door, he met Leading Steward Morris. ''Ow is he, ser?' Morris asked, his eyes etched with concern. 'Is he all right, like?'

As Penrose's personal steward, Morris was close to the captain. Manley was well aware of this and quietly replied, 'The captain's in good hands, Morris, now, be a good chap and go below.'

'Ta, ser,' Morris meekly replied, then with a worried expression on his face walked down the stairway into the main passageway. The time was 1500. Secure was not for another hour and everyone was still turned too. The only men in the S and S mess were Steward Moran, a fellow Scouser from Toxteth, sitting at the table, writing as letter, and Terry Benson, lying in his hammock, reading a dog-eared copy of *Tit Bits*. Both men looked up as Morris came in and sat down at the table.

'What's up, Towns, 'as the old man sacked yer? Moran asked jokingly.

'Maybe he's caught you knocking back his gin,' Benson remarked.

'Why don't you two fuck off,' Morris retorted angrily, and stormed out the mess.

As Manley closed the captain's door he suddenly realised, that due to Penrose's indisposition, he was now in command of the ship. The thought sent a sudden wave of anxiety running through him. As he arrived on the bridge, he realised he would have to do some quick thinking.

'What's wrong with the captain, sir?' Jewitt asked.

Manley suddenly became aware that all eyes of those on duty were looking at him. 'The doc thinks he's had a heart attack,' he quickly replied. A look of alarm spread across the faces of everyone.

'A heart attack!' Jewitt exclaimed. 'My God! How is he?'

'He's very poorly,' Manley said. 'Now,' he added, 'please ask the engineer officer to come and see me immediately.'

A few minutes later, Lieutenant Logan came onto the bridge. Trickles of perspiration ran down the sides of his pale face and he was breathing heavily. His white overalls were stained with oil and he was busily wiping his hands on an old rag.

Manley quickly told him about Penrose's heart attack. 'I'm now in command of the ship and it's imperative the captain is landed at gib.' He paused momentarily, and staring intently at logan, went on. 'At present, we are doing twenty-five knots, I want to increase this to thirty,, and don't worry, Derek,' he added,' I'll take responsibility for your precious engines.'

Logan's face broke into a confident smile. 'I understand, sir,' Logan replied, 'I'll give you thirty and to hell with the engines.'

'Thank you, Derek, pleased carry on,' Manley replied. He looked at Jewitt and said, 'pipe for the gunnery officer and navigating officer to come to the bridge.'

A few minutes later Lieutenant Powers and Sub Lieutenant Baker came onto the bridge.

Manley, who was now sitting in the captain's chair, quickly told them about Penrose's heart attack. He looked anxiously at Baker, and said, 'If I increase speed to thirty knots, how soon could we arrive in Gib?'

Baker turned, and after a quick consultation on his chart, looked over his shoulder and replied, 'Tuesday, at roughly 1900, sir.'

'Thank you, Pilot,' Manley replied, 'kindly inform the doc, I'm sure he'll be pleased to her that. Now, Guns,' he went on, giving Powers a wry smile. 'As I am now in command of the ship, you are now my first lieutenant.'

Powers raised his eyebrows in surprise, and said, 'But sir, the engineer officer is senior to me, surely he…

Manley raised a hand and interrupted him. 'Derek will be too busy in the engine room. Do you, think you can do it?'

'Yes, sir,' Powers replied confidently.

'Good man,' Manley replied, 'now, keep close to me in case I need you.'

'Very good, sir,' Powers replied, wondering what his new duties would entail. 'Signalman, send the following signals to *Dulverton* and

Eridge.' Manley watched impatiently as Tate took out a pad and pencil. 'Say, "*Commander Penrose taken ill. Manley now in command. Intend stopping at Gib, on 28th. Both ships to lay off five miles while Commander Penrose is landed. Increase speed to thirty knots.*" Pipe for Sub Lieutenant Barlow to come to the bridge, please, QM.' he added, feeling slightly uncomfortable in the chair that was now his.

A few minutes later, the ship's radio communications officer arrived. 'Ah, Barlow,' Manley retorted, 'I have some important signals that have to go off immediately. The QM will write them down,' he added, glancing at Tate. 'The first is to the C-in-C. Portsmouth. "*Commander Penrose suffered heart attack, Sunday 26th July. Condition serious. Intend land him Gibraltar, ETA Tuesday 28th. Please inform next of kin. First Lieutenant, Lieutenant Commander Manley now in command*". Repeat this to Captain Storey, Movements Officer, RN Barracks, Portsmouth. Next, to, the medical officer in charge, BMH Gibraltar. "*Commander Penrose suffered heart attack today, Sunday 27th July. Intend landing him Gibraltar, ETA Tuesday 28th, 1900 approx. Request ambulance and doctor meet*". Last one, to, C-in C-Gibraltar. "*Commander Pentose taken ill. Intend landing him Gibraltar, ETA Tuesday 28th, 1600. First Lieutenant, Lieutenant Commander Manley now in command. Request berthing instructions*". Do you have all that, Tate?'

'Yes, sir,' Tate answered, tearing off a sheet of paper from his pad and handing it to Barlow.

Five minutes later, signals conveying best wishes to Penrose were received from *Dulverton* and *Eridge*. Shortly afterwards, Brownlow came on the bridge. 'Message from C-in-C Gibraltar, "*Wishing a speedy recovery to Commander Penrose. Berth South Mole*".'

'Thank you, Daniel,' Manley replied, then added, 'the time is now 1600, Number One, I want to meet all officers in the wardroom in half an hour, after which I'll address the ship's company.'

'Very good, sir,' Powers replied. As he left the bridge, the pipe, "Secure, hands shift into night clothing. Duty watch fall in on the quarter deck",' echoed over the tannoy.

After Power's departure, Manley sat in the captain's chair, staring out to sea. The events of the past hour had been so fast he hadn't really had time to think clearly. The thought being responsible for the safety of the ship and nearly two hundred people suddenly weighed heavily upon him. The gruff, Devonian voice of PO Len Mills brought him out of his reverie, unaware that news of Penrose's heart attack had provoked more than a few worried looks between those on duty.

'Beggin' your pardon, sur,' Mills said, 'just 'ow bad is the captain?'

'Not too good, PO,' Manley replied calmly, 'but I'm sure the doctor will make sure he's all right.'

'Thank, ee, sur,' Mills answered, who quietly added, 'only we're quite worried, like.'

'So am I,' Manley replied. He stared across at *Eridge* and *Dulverton,* who, like *Helix,* were speeding through the water, ending up a frothy bow waves curling over their bows. 'Keep her steady on course, Jock, I'll be in the wardroom if you need me' he said to Jewitt, then easing himself off his chair, he left the bridge.

In the wardroom the atmosphere, usually full of loud conversation, was subdued. A few officers were either sitting in the armchairs or standing about sipping tea, smoking and quietly talking. Thanks to Lieutenant Powers, they were all aware of the captain's heart attack.

'I say, sir,' Midshipman Morgan said to Sub Lieutenant Milton, who was standing next to the Lieutenant Logan, smoking a cigarette. 'Have you any idea how bad he is?'

'I really don't know, Mid,' Milton replied. 'But it must be serious for the doc to keep him in bed. What do you think, Derek?'

'I think we'd better wait and see what the first lieutenant has to say,' Logan quietly answered. As he spoke, the pipe, "Secure. Hands to tea. Shift into night clothing. Duty watch fall in on the quarterdeck", came over the tannoy.

At precisely 1630, everyone stopped what they were doing and looked as Manley, followed by Powers, came in to the wardroom. Those officers who were sitting in armchairs, placed their cups and saucers on a table and stood up. The rest stopped talking and remained standing.

'Stand easy, gentlemen, and carry on smoking,' Manley said, noticing the anxious expressions on some of their faces. 'Now, I know you are all busy, so I'll come straight to the point. Commander Penrose has suffered a heart attack and is confined to bed.' He then paused to allow the severity of his words to sink in. 'Consequently, the ship will be making a brief stop at Gibraltar, to transfer the captain ashore to the British Military Hospital. Our ETA at Gib will be approximately 1900 on Tuesday. In the meantime, I will be in command of the ship, and Lieutenant Powers will first lieutenant. Any questions?'

'Yes, sir,' said Sub Lieutenant Milton, 'who will be Captain D, now that Commander Penrose is ill?'

'Good question, Ray,' Manley replied. 'Lieutenant Commander Petch in *Dulverton* is the next senior officer, but under the circumstances, I expect he'll be guided by me until we leave Gib.'

'Do you think there'll be any chance of the mail catching up with us, sir?' Sub Lieutenant Baker asked, wondering why he hadn't heard from Wallasey's chief constable.

'I doubt if we'll be there long enough, Pilot, but you never know…' The events of the morning had overshadowed his worries about Laura, and Baker's question made him hope there'd be a letter from her in Gibraltar.

'Will the captain's clothing be taken ashore when we reach Gib, sir?' asked Lieutenant Goldsmith.

This was something else Manley hadn't thought about. 'Another good question, Barry,' he replied, 'I er… expect Morris and Bamford will handle that. Anything else?' he added, looking around. 'Right, I now intend to address the ship's company. Carry on.' With Lieutenant Powers in close attendance, Manley left the wardroom and went onto the bridge. Ignoring the inquisitive looks in the eyes of those on duty, Manley unhooked the tannoy from the console. 'This is the first lieutenant speaking,' he said, doing his best to sound calm. 'The captain has had a heart attack and is seriously ill. He is confined to his bed where he is being looked after by the surgeon lieutenant and SBA Bamford.' He went on to tell them the ETA at Gib, and ended by adding, 'In the meantime, anyone reporting sick are to see Chief Coxswain Barnes. That is all.' He then replaced the handset.

Thanks to Leading Steward Morris, who, having calmed down, had returned to the S and S mess, and told his mates that the captain was ill. The news of this soon spread around the ship. Nevertheless, Manley's announcement telling them that Penrose had actually suffered a heart attack, came as a shock not only to Morris, but everyone else.

'I 'ope the old man is OK,' said Bob Rose, to Morris, who, like the others, was sitting at the mess table enjoying a mug of tea.

'Me too,' Morris quietly replied. 'He was a gentleman, which is more than I can say for one or two of the other officers.'

'And he always got us 'ome safe and sound from those fuckin' Atlantic convoys,' Wiggy Bennett added, munching a piece of bread, spread judicially with plum jam.

'Not to mention that dash from Tobruck with all them pongoes on board,' added Knocker White.

'Too bloody true, Knocker,' muttered Dutch, as he pulled himself up on the overhead iron bar into his hammock, 'too bloody true.'

These remarks were repeated, not only by junior and senior ratings, but also the officers, and were indicative of the respect and affection they felt for Penrose.

In the sick bay, Latta was checking Penrose's blood pressure every fifteen minutes. At 1645 the systolic had risen from 160 to 180 and the diastolic had gone up from 100 to 120.

'It's this ache, Doc,' muttered Penrose, placing a hand over his breast bone, 'It seems to be getting worse.'

'Try not to be worried, sir,' Latta said, giving Penrose a reassuring smile. 'I'm going to give you another injection. Meanwhile, keep taking deep breaths of oxygen.' Ten minutes after giving Penrose the injection of morphia, Latta was relieved to find the pain in Penrose's chest had subsided. Half an hour later, Latta decided it was safe to move him. With the help of Bamford, who was holding the oxygen cylinder, they helped Penrose from his chair into his sleeping quarters and onto his bunk. They managed to remove Penrose's tropical clothing and had him sitting back, supported by pillows.

'It's the pain, Doc,' he added, sitting forward, 'it's come back, and I can feel my heart pounding like hell.' For a few seconds, Latta thought that Penrose might die. What the hell could he do to slow down Penrose's pulse and ease his pain, he asked himself; it was far too soon to give Penrose another shot of morphia, and to make matters worse, the oxygen level in the cylinder was low.

CHAPTER TWENTY-SEVEN

During the move from the chair into the sleeping quarters, Penrose's oxygen mask had slipped down and was now resting on his chin. Latta replaced this and said, 'Lie back and keep taking slow, steady, deep breaths.' It was then he remembered the Digoxin tablets.

'Quickly, Bamford,' Latta said. 'There's a small box in a side pocket of my bag, get it out and give it to me.' Detecting a touch of panic in the doctor's voice, Bamford quickly looked inside the bag and found the box. He passed it to Latta, who, feeling his hands tremble, opened the box and took out two white tablets.

'Open your mouth, sir,' urged Latta, 'and swallow these,' he added placing the tablets on Penrose's dry, white-coated tongue. With the help of a sip of water, he managed to swallow them and closed his eyes.

Feeling his own heart thumping, Latta checked Penrose's pulse every fifteen minutes. Bamford, who, like his boss, watched and waited anxiously for the Digoxin to take effect. Their vigil was rewarded when, just after 1900, Penrose's pulse began to drop from a hundred and twenty to a hundred, and the sharp pain in his chest was now a dull ache.

'Cup of tea, sir?' Bamford asked, watching Latta use a gauze swab to wipe away the beads of sweat from Penrose's brow.

'Good idea,' Latta replied, 'and give the captain a few sips as well.'

Shortly after 2000, a knock came at the door and Morris came in carrying a tray containing two plates of sandwiches.

'As youse missed supper I thought youse could do with a bite to eat,' Morris whispered. Placing the plates on a small, nearby table, he looked at Penrose, who appeared to be sleeping, then at Latta. ''Ow is the captain, sir,' he asked, 'we were all wondering, like?'

'All right,' Latta replied, while nodding his head in reverent acquiescence.

'Thanks for the sarnies, Scouse,' Bamford said, 'I could eat a horse.'

'Corn dog,' Morris replied quietly, 'the chief cook made 'em 'imself. I'll be in the mess if yer want me, ser.'

Shortly after night rounds, Manley gave a quiet tap on the door of the captain's cabin and entered. The main area was in darkness and Bamford was slumped in an armchair, gently snoring. Manley tip-toed across the room, and after a gentle knock, then went inside the captain's sleeping quarters.

Penrose lay back in a wall of pillows. A towel draping over Penrose's overhead light reduced the lighting to a minimum. An inflatable sleeve was wrapped around his upper left arm allowing his BP to be taken without disturbing him.

At first, Latta didn't see or hear him, as he was using his stethoscope to take Penrose's blood pressure. Wearing a worried expression, Latta removed the stethoscope and saw Manley.

'How is he, Doc? Manley whispered.

'He's holding up well, sir' Latta replied, hoping Penrose wasn't asleep and could hear what was being said.

'Good,' Manley replied, nodding his head. He gave Penrose a worried glance, then left the room.

Throughout the night, Latta and Bamford kept two-hourly watches. At 0400, Penrose opened his eyes and gave a loud moan. 'Please, Doc,' said Penrose reaching across and griping hold of Latta's hand. 'It's my chest, it feels on fire.' As he spoke, small beads of perspiration appeared on the brow of Penrose's ashen features, and trickled slowly down the sides of his face. Latta immediately gave Penrose another injection of morphia. Then, staring at his captain's flickering eyelids, silently prayed for the pain in Penrose's chest to subside. Latta's prayers were heard and by 0600, the morphia had taken effect.

'It feels a bit better, now, Doc,' murmured Penrose wearily. He raised a tired hand and grasped Latta's arm. 'If I die, promise me you'll write to my wife,' he muttered, looking desperately at Latta.

'Now, less of that, sir,' Latta replied, doing his best to sound confident. 'You're not going to die, so stop your blethering and I'll make you a nice cup of tea,' he added, patting Penrose's warm hand.

Shortly after 0900, the slightly built figure of PO Telegrapher Jack Frost came onto the bridge. 'This signal just arrived from the C-in-C Portsmouth, sir, it's good news,' he said, handing Manley a small sheet of paper. As he spoke, Manley noticed Frost's heavily tanned features were wreathed in smiles.

'Good news, be dammed,' Manley retorted as he read the signal, 'it's bloody great news.' With everyone staring at him, he hurriedly left the bridge.

'What on earth was in the signal, PO?' asked OOW Lieutenant Goldsmith.

'Just wait and see,' Frost cheerily replied, 'and all will be revealed.'

Manley arrived outside Penrose's cabin and went inside. Without knocking, he entered Penrose's sleeping quarters. Penrose was lying back in his bunk. Both arms were under the bedclothes and his eyes were closed. Latta had just removed a narrow glass thermometer from under Penrose's tongue and was disappointed to see the thin line of silver mercury had stopped at 100 degrees Fahrenheit (the normal reading is 98.4F).

'Sorry to interrupt you, Doc,' said Manley, panting slightly. 'You'd better read this,' he added, handing Latta the signal.

Latta passed the thermometer to Bamford, then, after reading the signal, he gently touched Penrose on the shoulder. Penrose gave a short, throaty cough and slowly opened his eyes.

'This just come for you, sir,' Latta said, grinning. 'It's from the C-in-C, Admiral Sir William James. Congratulations, you've been promoted to captain.'

Penrose immediately opened his eyes. 'Let me see that,' he said, blinking his eyes a few times. He read aloud, "*From Admiral Sir William James, C in C Portsmouth, to Captain Henry Penrose, Commanding Officer, H.M.S. Helix.*

On my recommendation, the Lords of the Admiralty have promoted to you to the rank of captain, with six months seniority starting from July 27th."

'Great Scott!' exclaimed Penrose, sitting forward, his eyes glued to the signal. For a few fleeting seconds he closed his eyes and imagined four gold rings on each sleeve. 'This is wonderful, my wife and daughter will be so proud.' As he spoke, he felt his chest tighten. Latta watched as Penrose's face suddenly became ashen. His captain's free hand shot to his chest, then giving a child-like whimper, he collapsed back into the pillows.

Realising the shock, albeit, of good news, looked like being too much for Penrose. He nodded to Bamford, who slowly turned on the oxygen cylinder. He then passed the mask attached to the rubber tubing to Latta who placed the mask over Penrose's face. 'Easy does it, sir,' said Latta, 'and take a few slow breaths.' Penrose closed his eyes and did as Latta suggested. A few minutes, later the oxygen took effect and Penrose's face regained its pallor and he began to breathe easier. Penrose turned his head, and raising a hand, beckoned Manley to come near. 'Drinks all round in the wardroom, Number One,' he whispered, 'tell the ship's company this reflects on them and splice the main brace.'

'Very good, sir,' Manley replied, gently squeezing Penrose's clammy hand, 'and many, many, congratulations.'

Everyone on the ship was aware that Penrose's heart condition was serious and that he might die. This knowledge was reflected in the behaviour of the crew. Anyone passing the captain's cabin did so almost on tiptoe. Instead of the usual lower deck banter, talk was muted; even conversations in the wardroom were conducted in respectful quietness - it was as if their raised voices might somehow disturb their captain's rest.

However, thanks to PO Jack Frost, the atmosphere was about to change. After delivering the signal to Manley, Frost hurried to the bridge, telling anyone he met that they now had a four ring captain.

Throughout the ship, the news of Penrose's promotion and the issuing of an extra "tot", was greeted with alacrity. In the seamen's mess, Tug Wilson slapped Knocker White on the back and said, 'Just think, Knocker, me old gash bucket, I'm rum bosun today, and as well me tot, I'll get sippers to toast the old man's health.' ('Sippers was any rum left in the 'fanny' after issue was claimed by the rating who collected and dished out the rum.)

'Aye, but don't forget you owe me gulpers,' Knocker replied with an impish grin.

'And you're relieving Dolly Gray in the radar room at twelve o'clock,' added Slinger Woods, 'so, seein' as how I've got the morning watch, I think you'd better give your extra tot to me and I'll drink his health as well.'

Chief Cook Dai Evans was in the senior ratings mess and was about to ease his portly frame into an armchair when Manley's announcement came over the tannoy. 'If you ask me, boyo,' he said, wiping beads of sweat from his round, fleshy face, 'his promotion's more than overdue, so it is.'

'And so is the extra shot of rum,' Chief 'Chippy' Tug Wilson, replied, taking a good gulp of tea from a cracked enamel mug.

'And proper job, too, my 'andsome,' added Len Mills, lighting a cigarette, then exhaling a steady stream of blue smoke, 'but I'm gunna bottle mine and 'ave it later as I've got the middle.'

Night rounds had just finished. Penrose appeared to be asleep. Manley, Latta and Bamford were standing a few yards away from Penrose's bunk, quietly discussing the best way to move Penrose to the quarterdeck when the ship arrived in Gib.

'We could then transfer him onto a normal stretcher and take him onto the quarterdeck,' Manley whispered.

'No,' Latta replied, scratching his unshaven chin, 'too much movement.'

Suddenly, Bamford, feeling very self-conscience, looked, at Latta, and said, 'Excuse me, sir, wouldn't it better if we carried the captain in a Neil Robertson stretcher to the quarterdeck, *then* transferred him to a stretcher then took him ashore.'

'Good idea, well done, young man,' Latta replied, giving Bamford an approving smile.

Just after 0400, Penrose, who appeared to be sleeping, opened his eyes and placed a hand on his chest. 'It's this bloody pain, Doc, it's come back and it feels worse. Are you sure I'm not going to die?'

CHAPTER TWENTY-EIGHT

Latta looked at the fearful expression in Penrose's tired, pale blue eyes and doing his best to sound convincing, replied, 'No, sir, you're not going to die. I'm going to give you another injection. Now lie back and try to relax,' he added, giving Penrose's hand a reassuring squeeze. Half an hour later, even though the morphia had slightly reduced the pain in Penrose's chest, his BP and pulse remained dangerously high.

At precisely 0600 the pipe "Eavo, eavo, Lash up and stow. Cooks to the galley. Hands to breakfast", came over the tannoy.

Dawn had broken and the coast of Algeria loomed, long and sandy, twenty miles on the flotilla's port beam. The cloudless sky was a clear, eye-catching blue and the warm, silky, easterly breeze, fanning the faces of everyone on *Helix*'s bridge was a welcome relief from usual cold night air.

'How long before we reach Gib, sir?' QM Sammy Smith asked OOW Sub Lieutenant Baker.

'We should sight the rock round about 1830,' Baker replied, as he opened his mouth and gave a tired yawn.

'Not that it'll do you much good,' PO Podge Hardman said to Smith. 'The only person that'll be going ashore will be the captain.'

As Hardman finished speaking Manley came onto the bridge. 'Anything go report, Pilot?' he asked Baker as he eased himself into the captain's chair.

'Speed steady at thirty knots,' Baker quickly replied. Then, lowering his voice, asked, 'How is the captain, sir?'

Before coming onto the bridge, Manley had gone to the captain's cabin to speak to Latta. Except for the somnolent hissing of the air conditioning and the steady throb of the engines, all was quiet. Bamford and Morris, who were busily packing Penrose's kit in his trunk, looked up as Manley entered, then, carried on working.

Manley gave a gentle knock on the door of the captain's sleeping quarters and went inside. 'How's is he?' Manley whispered, looking at Penrose who was lying back in bed, asleep.

'Och, he's bearing up,' Latta cautiously replied, 'what time are we due in Gib?'

'1900 approximately,' Manley answered, 'everything all in hand?'

Latta put his fountainpen down and stood up. 'A quiet word outside, sir,' he asked, trying hard to disguise the deep concern in his voice. Latta opened the door allowing Manley to leave first. Once outside, in the main section of the cabin, Manley gave Latta a worried look, then asked, 'What's the problem, Doc?'

'I'm very worried about the captain's blood pressure, sir,' Latta replied. 'It's still very high and carrying him in a Neil Robertson stretcher to the quarterdeck, as Bamford suggested, might be too much for him.'

'Good Lord,' Manley replied, lowering his voice as two ratings walked past. 'Is there any other way you can move him?'

'No, the army type stretcher would be too difficult to manoeuvre down the stairs,' Latta replied.

'So what do you want to do?' asked Manley.

'I suggest we wait until we reach Gib, and I'll ask the doctor from BMH when he comes on board,' Latta replied cautiously. 'Then we'll make a decision, after all, he's senior and more experienced than me.'

'And what will you do if he decides the captain is too ill to be moved?' said Manley, staring keenly at Latta. 'We can't very well remain in Gib until he's fit to be taken ashore as the ship is needed at home.'

Latta took a deep breath. 'I understand the difficulty, sir,' he replied. 'But I still think it would be prudent to wait and see what the army doctor says.'

'I hate to say this, Doc,' Manley said, raising his eyebrows slightly, 'but it sounds very much as if you're passing the buck?'

'Not at all,' Latta replied, feeling his cheeks redden. 'If I didn't tell the army doctor about the dangers of moving the captain and he were to die, I would have failed in my duty as a doctor.' He paused and took a deep breath, then went on. 'If you think I'm placing the responsibility for the captain's safety on the army, then, with respect, sir,' Latta stressed, 'you are quite wrong, because I am merely seeking a second opinion, something, under the circumstances, any doctor would do. And besides, supposing we were bombed or even torpedoed, and had to move him and he died, what then?'

'I'm sorry if I have offended you, Doc,' Manley said, 'but I hope you're…'

Still smarting from Manley's remark, Latta, opened the door, and curtly replied, 'Never mind that, now, if you'll excuse me, I'd better finish writing the captain's medical history.'

'Right, Doc,' Manley replied. Noticing the brusqueness evident in Latta's voice, he added, as a peace offering, 'If the army doctor agrees to have him moved, will you need any help moving the captain from the cabin to the quarterdeck?'

'No, Morris, Bamford myself and the first aid party will manage, thank you,' Latta answered briskly, and went inside the cabin.

Having overheard everything that was said outside, Bamford, noticing the exasperated expression in the doctor's face, and asked, 'Coffee, sir?'

'Yes, thank you,' Latta replied and with a tired sigh, sat down at his desk.

At 1830, Lofty Day, in the crow's nest reported seeing Gibraltar's giant monolithic rock, jutting in the sky like a prize fighter's jaw. The news of this soon spread throughout the ship. In the seamen's mess, the muggy smell of tobacco hung in the sticky, warm atmosphere. A few ratings sat around the table. Some were writing letters and smoking, while others played crib or uckers. A few ratings climbed in their hammocks, hoping to catch up with "Egyptian PT", before going on watch at midnight. (Egyptian PT is a colloquial expression for sleep.)

'Just think, Shiner,' Bud Abbot said to Shiner Wright, as he rattled his dice in a Bakelite beaker then rolled a six. 'In three days, I'll be in my local boozer then in bed with me missus.'

'That's if we 'ave any leave,' Shiner replied, stubbing his dog-end out in a tin dish. 'The buzz is we're needed for summat, that's why we've 'ad to 'urry 'ome.'

'Rubbish,' snorted Bud, rolling another six, 'we've got to take on stores and amo, and by the way, that's two fags you owe me.'

On the bridge, Manley was sitting on the captain's chair, staring out to sea, lost in thought. If Penrose's condition remained precarious, and couldn't be landed — what then? The thought of the captain dying before they reached England gave him food for thought. Should Penrose be buried at sea or taken home? Suddenly, the sound of someone coughing interrupted his torpidity. He turned and saw the burly figure of Morris standing in front of him. 'Yes,' Manley said, taking a deep breath, 'what is it?'

'Thought youse'd like this,' Morris replied, handing Manley a steaming hot mug of tea. 'I've, er… put a drop of whiskey in it, just to liven it up, like.'

Manley accepted the mug, smiled and said, 'Thank you, Morris, now I know why the captain thinks so highly of you.'

Shortly after 1830, the three warships passed through the Bay of Gibraltar. Darkness had fallen, leaving a full moon to cast a clear, silver patina over the sea.

'Pity about this bloody moon, sir,' Powers remarked to Manley, glancing warily away to starboard at the twinkling lights of Algeciras then across to the Gibraltar's houses and dockyard, all of which were clearly visible in the early evening moonshine. 'By now, every German spy in Algeciras will have reported our presence to Berlin.'

'And to one of Admiral Doenitz's WolfPack,' Manley added, who was bending over the compass repeater, checking the distance between *Helix* and the coast of Gibraltar.

'Anything on asdic, Number One?' he asked Powers.

'No, sir, all clear,' Powers replied.

'Thank you,' said Manley as he stood up. 'Special sea duty men close up. Then, make to *Eridge* and *Dulverton, "Intend turning five degrees to port towards Gibraltar. Remain on station and will re-join as arranged. Manley"*.' He unhooked the wheelhouse intercom and said, 'Turn five degrees to port. Speed twenty knots.'

'Chief Coxswain on the wheel, sir,' snapped Digger Barnes, then quickly repeated Manley's order. A few seconds later, *Helix* slowly turned away from the flotilla and headed towards Gibraltar. Gradually, the wide concrete South Mole, two hundred away to port, hove into view. On the quayside, a small crane and several dockyard workers waited to lower a wooden gangway in place. A few yards away, the letters "RN" could be seen on the side of the blue ambulance. A civilian driver stood next to the ambulance, smoking a cigarette. The army officer wore tropical khaki, the naval officer was dressed in white shorts and blouse. Next to them stood next to a white-coated orderly. All three looked up as the destroyer moved imperceptibly closer to the wharf.

'Reduce speed, to ten knots. Half ahead both engines.' This was the first time he had, as acting commanding officer, brought the ship alongside. He suspected those on the bridge knew this.

Using a small lever, Barnes moved the pointer on the Telegraph Order Receiver to "Half Ahead". Then replied, 'Speed ten knots, half ahead both.'

Manley unhooked the engine room telephone. Lieutenant Logan answered.

'Very shortly, the ship will be port side of the mole, Derek,' Manley replied, 'I'll want to leave quickly, so be prepared. All right?'

'Yes, sir,' Logan answered confidently, 'I'll keep the engines flashed up and ready.'

In the sick bay, Latta told Penrose what was about to happen. 'You may or may not be transferred ashore,' Latta said, trying his best not to sound alarmed, 'it depends on what the army doctor decides.'

'So you think there's a chance I might stay on board?' Penrose asked, a hopeful glint in his eyes.

'We'll just have to see,' Latta answered quietly, 'How is the pain now, sir?' he asked, checking Penrose's pulse and finding it full and racing.

Meanwhile, on the bridge, Manley went to the port wing and watched anxiously as the ship slowly moved towards the mole. It was now quite dark. A cool wind blew from the west and the pale moon had disappeared behind a mass of dark, altostratus clouds that promised rain.

'Stop both engines,' Manley said. Then, looking aft, saw seamen, under the watchful eyes of Sub Lieutenant Milton, accept heaving lines from the dockyard workers and secure them expertly around the ship's bollards. A similar exercise was carried out on the fo'c'sle, overseen by Midshipman Morgan. No sooner was this done than both officers, using a loud hailer, reported the ship was secure.

Glancing at Powers, he said, 'Better send the QM to the sick bay to tell the doctor the army medical officer will be with him shortly.'

Powers nodded to Knocker White, who, having overheard Manley, quickly left the bridge.

On the quarterdeck, guard rails were quickly removed and the wooden gangway was lowered in place. Ignoring the fact that the gangway was not properly secured, the army officer followed by his naval counterpart, hurried on board the ship and was met by Manley. 'Hugh Manley, First Lieutenant,' he said, proffering his hand.

'Major Rupert Andrews, RAMC,' replied the army officer. His Welsh accent, as they shook hands, was sharp and clear. The major was tall and slightly built with a heavily tanned face that exaggerated the pale blueness of his eyes.

'Peter Murray, Surgeon Lieutenant,' said the naval officer, a small, heavily set man with a sallow complexion.

'Right, gentlemen,' said Manley, 'our doctor is with the captain in his quarters, so if you'll come this way,' he added, indicating a hand. 'And mind your heads as we go through the hatchways.'

A few minutes later, they arrived outside the captain's cabin. Manley opened the door and led them across the main part of the cabin to the captain's sleeping quarters. On their way they saw Morris, who was sitting in an armchair. Nearby on the floor lay and open Neil Robertson stretcher. 'As you were,' Manley said, motioning to Morris as he was about to stand up. Manley knocked on the door, and with the two officers closely behind him, went inside.

Penrose lay on his bunk, wearing a pair of red silk pyjamas his wife had given to him before the ship sailed. He was awake and his breathing appeared shallow and slow. Latta had just finished taking Penrose's blood pressure, and stood up as Manley and other two officers came in.

'Looks like the doctors from BMH you mentioned,' muttered to Penrose, turning his head and looking at the two officers standing next to Manley.

'Yes, sir,' Latta replied, removing the stethoscope from around his neck. 'This is Major Andrews and Surgeon Lieutenant Murray. They will probably want to examine you.'

'Of course,' Penrose answered quietly, 'I understand.'

Latta drew the two officers to one side and said, 'I'd like a quick word, so I suggest we go into to the other room.' He then gave Penrose a warm smile and added, 'We're leaving you for a minute, sir, but in the meantime, I'm sure Bamford will make you a cup of tea.'

Penrose made no comment, instead he wearily nodded his head and closed his eyes. Latta looked at Manley and said, 'Would you pipe for the first aid party to come to the sick bay, please, sir.'

'Will do, Doc, so if you'll excuse me,' Manley replied, 'I'd better return to the bridge. Keep me informed.' Then left the cabin.

Latta and the two officers went into the next room. As he did so, the pipe came over the tannoy ordering the first aid party to report to the sick bay. Latta closed the door and told Morris to pick up the Neil Robertson stretcher and wait outside. Morris did this and was met by PO Steward Sandy Powell and the first aid party.

'What's happening, Scouse?' asked Sandy, who, like the three others, was staring intensely at Morris.

In a church-like whisper, Morris told them what they were to do. 'Youse 'ave all used the Neil Robertson stretcher, so wait here, and I'll tell youse when to come in.'

Meanwhile, inside the cabin, Latta looked at the major and lieutenant and said, 'I know you're busy so I'll come straight to the point.' He then quickly told them about Penrose's constant high blood pressure and pulse, adding, 'The morphia and digoxin I've given him has only had a limited effect.' He momentarily stopped talking, then went on. 'And his condition has deteriorated so much that, in my opinion, moving him could prove fatal. Alternatively.' Latta paused again. 'If I kept him on board, we could be attacked by U-boats or bombed. The quick movements of the ship and noise might also have an adverse effect on him.'

'And, of course, sir,' said the lieutenant, glancing pensively at the major, 'they could be sunk.'

'So what do you think, sir,' Latta asked edgily, 'should he be moved or not?'

'I understand what you are saying Doctor,' the major cautiously replied, 'but we do have a cardiac specialist who could treat him, should his condition worsen.

'Then what do you suggest, sir?' Latta asked.

'Judging by what you have told us I think he should be taken ashore right away. What do you think, Peter?' he added, giving Surgeon Lieutenant Murray a searching look.

'I agree with you, sir,' Murray replied, 'and the sooner the better.'

'Right, then,' Latta said, opened the door, allowing Andrews and Murray to return into the captain's sleeping quarters. Bamford, who was helping the captain to sip a cup of tea, looked at Latta, and said, 'Just finishing, sir.' Then he removed the cup and dabbed Penrose's mouth with a small piece of gauze.

'How are you feeling, sir?'Latta asked. 'How is the pain?'

'About the same,' Penrose quietly replied.

'Then, if you feel up to it, sir, we'd like to get you ready to go ashore,' Latta replied. After explaining how this was to be done, he added, 'It might be a little uncomfortable but we'll be as quickly as possible.'

'I understand,' Penrose murmured.

'Go outside the cabin and tell Morris to bring in the Neil Robertson,' Latta said to Bamford, 'then we'll get the captain ready to be taken to the quarterdeck.' Latta removed the bridge communication handset from the side of the captain's bunk. Seconds later Manley answered.

'In a little while we'll be bringing the captain to the quarterdeck,' Latta said, 'I thought you might like to tell the ship's company. And ask the buffer to make sure there's an army stretcher ready and open on the quarterdeck, then detail four ratings to collect the commander's trunk to take it ashore and put it in the tilly.'

'Thank you, Doc,' Manley replied. 'I'll do just that.'

A few minutes later, the metallic click of the tannoy echoed around the ship. 'This is Lieutenant Powers speaking. In a little while Captain Penrose will be taken ashore. Side party fall in, all officers muster on the quarterdeck. Clear lower deck.'

Morris brought the stretcher into sleeping quarters and laid it open near the captain's bunk. Bamford lay a blanket on it, with a pillow for Penrose to rest his head. Then, he and Latta carefully helped Penrose from his bunk onto the stretcher where Bamford quickly tucked the blanket around him.

'Just lie back and try to relax while you're being strapped in, sir,' said Latta.

When Bamford and Latta did this, Latta nodded to Powel and said, 'When you're ready, PO.'

'Very good, sir,' Powel replied. SA Bensen and Leading Writer Jack Jones took tight hold of the rope rings on one side. Steward Dick Turpin and PO Powel grasped the rings on the other side.

'Right, together, lift and launch,' snapped Powel. With Bamford supporting Penrose's head, the captain was then taken from the cabin and along the passageway to the open hatchway, leading onto the quarterdeck. Most of the ship's company occupied every space on X deck overlooking the quarterdeck. The rest were packed below on the lower port side of the ship. Officers and senior ratings were lined up facing the gangway. The side party, consisting of PO Len Mills, QM Leading Seaman Knocker White and three ratings, stood by the side of the brow. All eyes were focussed on the hatchway as everyone waited to see the captain. The first aid party emerged carrying Penrose in the NRS. Behind came Latta, Major Andrews and Surgeon Lieutenant Murray.

'Ship's company, *attention!*' cried Lieutenant Powel

High above, in a cloudless sky, the moon's rays bathed everything in a sheet of silver. The only sounds were the childlike crying of seagulls and the fresh south westerly wind, flapping the white ensign on the end of the stern. With palpable reverence, everyone watched the first aid party lower the NRS onto the deck next to the army stretcher on which was laid a blanket. Using the side hand grips the FA party gently lifted Penrose onto the stretcher.

Latta knelt down close to Penrose. 'How are you feeling, sir?'

'Not too bad,' Penrose quietly replied.

'That's the spirit, sir,' Latta said, gently touching Penrose's shoulder. 'I'll see you back in England.' Then, nodding at Powel, he stood up.

'Right, together lads, two-six, lift,' shouted Sandy Powel.

As they lifted up the stretcher, Manley cried, 'Ship's company, stand at ease. Three cheers for Captain Penrose.' He took off his cap and paused as every member of the crew, including the officers, removed their caps and joined in with a hearty, *'Hip, Hip, Hurray.'* The stretcher party stopped as Penrose raised a salutary hand. Suddenly, a rating in those crowding on top of the after deck, boomed out '*For he's a jolly good fellow, for he's a jolly good fellow.*' Everyone took up the song and continued singing as Sandy Powel and his fellow first aiders, carried the stretcher down the gangway. Latta, the major and surgeon lieutenant followed behind them. The driver opened the rear doors of the ambulance, and as they slid the stretcher inside, the singing gradually faded away.

The orderly climbed inside the ambulance, allowing the driver to close the doors. Latta handed a large envelope containing Penrose's medical history to the major. They shook hands and both officers climbed into the ambulance. From the top of the gangway, Manley saw Latta walking up the gangway. Behind him came the first party carrying the army and NR Robertson stretchers. Everyone watched in silence as the ambulance drove along the wharf and left the dockyard through the main gate. 'Not wishing to sound too disingenuous,' Latta said to Bamford as they reached the top of the top of the gangway, 'I do hope the captain makes a full recover, but thank goodness that's over.'

Manley walked to the side of the citadel and unhooked the tannoy. 'All hands turn to. Close all screen doors and scuttles. Special sea duty men fall in.'

Fifteen minutes later, the gangway had been removed and the guardrails were replaced. Using a loud hailer, Manley lent over the port wing of the bridge and shouted to Sub Lieutenant Jewitt on the quarterdeck, 'Let go, for'd.'

With expert ease, two burly seamen unravelled the heavy hemp ropes, allowing them to be dragged ashore by a couple of swarthy dockyard workers. Manley gave similar orders to Sub Lieutenant Milton on the fo'c'sle. Minutes later, the ship moved away from the wharf and rocked gently.

'Slow ahead,' snapped Manley who was now sitting on the chair.

'Engines, slow ahead, sir,' Digger Barnes replied from the wheelhouse.

'Starboard five, revolutions, five.'

No sooner had Barnes repeated the orders than *Helix* headed towards *Eridge* and *Dulverton,* lying at anchor, some five miles away.

'Next stop, dear old Pompey, eh, sir,' QM Knocker White said to Sub Lieutenant Baker, who was bent near the compass repeater taking a bearing on the other two warships.

Like the rest of the ship's company, he had been bitterly disappointed at not receiving mail. However, the thought of a policeman standing on the wharf when they arrived in Portsmouth sent a shiver running down his spine. 'Yes, White,' Baker replied half-heartedly, 'dear old Pompey.'

No such thoughts had entered Manley's mind. Since taking over the responsibility of running the ship, he had had no time worrying why he hadn't heard from Laura. And when he did manage to go to bed, he fell into a deep, dreamless sleep.

PART FOUR.
CHAPTER TWENTY-NINE

At 0200 on Thursday 30th July, the small flotilla passed through the Straits of Gibraltar. An umbrella of low-lying cirrostratus clouds hid an anaemic moon and a harsh, bluster of icy cold wind blew inform the Atlantic. Lieutenant Commander Petch, in *Eridge,* who was now Captain "D", ordered a ten degree turn to port. In doing so, the ships headed away from the violent waters of the Bay of Biscay into the Atlantic. Suddenly each vessel felt the intermittent hammering as the fierce ocean swell bounced against their bulkheads.

Manley stood on the bridge. Under his duffel coat he wore a warm, woollen sweater and uniform. One gloved hand gripped the arm of his chair while the other one used a handkerchief to wipe spots of icy spray from his face.

'A bit of a shock after the lovely warm Meddy, eh, sir,' OOW Lieutenant Goldsmith shouted as he held onto the binnacle. Unlike Manley, Goldsmith, PO Hardman and QM Buster Brown all wore heavy black oilskins over white service sweaters.

'At least it keeps the U-boats away,' Manley replied, watching as another white bow wave burst over the fo'c'sle before fizzing along the deck into the scuppers and disappearing over the side.

Throughout the night, the bitterly cold northerly wind whipped angry waves over the ship's side. With their oil skins shining like coal, some of the duty watch staggered along the port side of the upper deck, grasping the guard rail while securing a rope around the canvas of a life boat that the wind had torn loose. From the yardarms, the rigging rattled like the bones of skeletons as the ship bounded through the sea.

At 0800, the pipe, "Hands keep clear of the upper deck", echoed around the ship. The harsh wind produced ten-foot waves and ugly black clouds raced across the sky obliterating the remnants of the deathly pale sun. On the bridge, Manley sat, grasping the sides of his chair, as the ship shuddered violently before plunging into a trough before rising like an angry grey dragon. Glancing across at *Eridge* and *Dulverton,* he watched in awe as their behaviour mirrored those of his ship.

'*Eridge* flashing, sir,' yelled Leading signalman Weir, wiping water from his eyes. 'Message reads, "Reduce speed to twenty knots".'

'Acknowledge,' Manley shouted, then passed the order to the wheelhouse.

'Why are we doing that, sir?' enquired QM Knocker White, holding tightly onto the binnacle.

'In theory, it should help to reduce the strength of the waves hitting us,' shouted Manley.

'It might if we were a three-mast schooner, sir,' OOW Baker cried sarcastically.

'I'm inclined to agree, Pilot,' Manley replied, 'but anything's worth a try.' However, Lieutenant Commander Peche's order proved futile.

Throughout the day and night, men not on duty decided the safest place to be was cocooned in their hammocks. With the punka louvres in the fan trunking, the only source of ventilation available, the messes soon became cramped and sweaty. Hammocks swayed in unison. Every lurch and roll of the ship, sent anything not stowed away rolling back and forth on the deck, bouncing noisily against anything in their wake. At 0600, the shrill sound of the bosun's call forced bleary-eyed men to leave the warmth of their hammocks and face the dangers of another day.

Shortly after 0700, defying the laws of gravity, the cooks of the messes came down the stairs, balancing aluminium trays containing breakfast, and placed them, safe and sound on mess tables.

'Och, what is it the Yanks say, Dutch?' Jock Forbes said to Able Seaman Holland. 'Another day, another dollar.' Like Holland, Jock and a few other weary-looking ratings, were doing their best to prevent their plates of "train smash", (tinned tomatoes and fried eggs) from sliding off the table.

'Only they have hot coffee and thick steaks for breakfast, laddie,' Dutch replied, dobbing a piece of bread into his egg immediately burst open.

'And that's no yoke,' chimed in Dusty Miller, watching the remains of the egg run down Dutch's leg.

'Up yer pipe,' grunted Forbes, who wiped his plate then placed it into an aluminium basin lying nearby on the deck. As he stood up, the pipe, "Wet weather routine. Duty watch fall wearing life jackets, fall in on the canteen flat. Hands not on duty, keep clear of the upper deck", sounded.'

For the next five hours, the three ships continued to plough through the high, rolling sea. Then, the inky black cirrostratus clouds opened up. Sheets of rain reduced visibility to a hundred yards. The canvas covers on the open bridge gave scant protection against the icy wind and freezing spray. As far as the eye could see, minor explosions of rain covered the sea like a watery disease.

At 1300, a signal from Lieutenant Commander Petch ordered the flotilla to turn ten degrees to port.

'A good idea, eh, Number One?' Manley remarked to Powers, after he had given the order to PO Hardman in the wheelhouse. 'Even though it'll take us further into the Atlantic, at least we will avoid the German batteries along the French coast.

'And here's hoping this weather should keep the Luftwaffe away,' Powers replied, shivering slightly as a trickle of rain pierced his woollen scarf and ran down his neck.

But he spoke too soon. By noon next day, the rain had stopped and the pale sun began to periodically peak through the grey clouds. On the bridge, Sub Lieutenant Baker was in the process of relieving Sub Lieutenant Milton, when Radar Operator Able Seaman Slinger Wood reported, 'Two unidentified aircraft five miles on the port bow, sir.'

Straight away, Manley, using his binoculars, searched the sky away to his left. The others on the bridge did likewise.

'They're Stukas, sir,' said Baker,

'Signal from *Eridge,* sir,' yelled PO Tate. "*All ships take evasive action. Fire at will*".'

Manley cleared his throat and unhooked the tannoy. 'This is the captain speaking, we will shortly be under air attack. Hands to action stations,' he added, raising his voice. 'Enemy aircraft spotted, so be ready for sharp movements of the ship.' Turning to Powers, he went on, 'Tell the A and B guns's crews to man the Bofors, Number One, as our four point fives can't track the bombers fast enough.'

Over the past six months, the ship's company had wielded *Helix* into an efficient fighting machine. In a little under five minutes, each member of the ship's company, wearing anti-flash gear and steel helmets were closed up and ready for action.

In the crow's nest, Buster Brown looked up, and straining his eyes, cried excitedly, '*The bastards are breaking formation.*'

'*And they're beginning to dive, sir,*' Baker added, watching anxiously as the distinctive gull-winged bombers angled down towards them.

'*Hard a port, steady as you go,*' Manley shouted down the wheelhouse voice pipe.

Seconds later, a gigantic bow wave burst over the fo'c'sle as the ship heeled precariously to the right. Everyone on the bridge grabbed hold of anything at hand as the horizon and sea tilted before slowly becoming upright. That was when everyone heard the Stuka's spine-chilling, "Jericho wail."

'I remember that fuckin' noise from Dunkirk,' yelled Tansey Lee, pressing his right eye against the Bofor's gunsight, 'and it scared the shit out of me.'

'I wondered what that smell was,' shouted Knocker White, waiting to feed a band of 40mm ammunition into the gun.

Lee was about to reply when Manley's voice came over the tannoy, shouting, '*Fire at will.*'

All at once, the intermittent, ear-splitting *crump-crump,* echoed throughout the ship, as lines of grey gunfire streaked skywards. Like Bud Abbott manning the starboard Bofor, they ignored the cacophony and concentrated on firing at the Stuka as it slowly pulled out of its dive and levelled off.

What happened next seemed to take an age, but in fact, was over in seconds. With sparks flickering from each wing, the Stuka streaked towards them, firing their deadly 7.92mm cannon.

'*Jesus Christ!*' yelled Knocker White. '*The bugger's gunna ram us.*'

On the bridge, Manley and the others watched with bated breath as the Stuka, a mere hundred yards above *Helix*'s yardarm, released its bombs. For a fleeting moment, the black crosses on the underside of the cream-coloured wings flashed by as the bomber peeled away to the right.

'Full speed ahead, hard a port!' Yelled Manley.

The bombs exploding some ten yards away to starboard, sent ear-splitting shock waves reverberating throughout the ship. In the sick bay, SBA Bamford lay on the lower cot grasping the edges of the metal guards. Surgeon Lieutenant Latta sat on his chair, holding tightly onto the sides of the desk. Even though Bamford had stowed away books, trays and ink wells he couldn't prevent a few drawers, despite being locked, from flying open. At the same time, cupboard doors opened, threatening to send their contents leaping from their compartments onto the linoleum covered deck. Adding to the chaos, the loud gurgling made by the pipes under the sink sounded ominously like drowning men.

'I think we'll have a few customers after this, sir,' Bamford shouted.

'I'd say more than a few, laddie,' Latta warily replied.

Bamford's predictions were correct. On the bridge, the atmosphere was tense. Manley clung, white knuckled, onto the sides of his chair. Baker's cry as he fell against the compass repeater, and hit the side of his head, was lost by the sound of the wind. As he fell down, blood oozed through his anti-flash hood and ran down his neck. Powers suffered a badly bruised back, PO Mills collided with QM Jock Forbes and banged his head against the binnacle. In the mess decks, lockers flew open, scattering their contents everywhere. In the galley, aluminium pots and pans, jugs, cutlery and utensils littered the deck's non-slips surface. A stoker in the engine room slipped over and broke an arm. On the upper deck, except for the gun aimers who were strapped into their chairs, the gunnery ratings clung desperately onto the guard rails surrounding the gun platform.

As the ship gradually righted itself everyone staggered to their feet. Lieutenant Powers took out a shell dressing from the first aid box, and after tearing it open, applied it firmly around the gash on the left side of Baker's head. PO Mills rubbed his head and like Manley and QM Jock Forbes, he watched as both the Stukas, having bombed *Helix* and *Dulverton,* were about to attack *Eridge.*

At that moment Slinger Wood's strident voice came over the radar intercom. *'Two unidentified aircraft approaching, sir, five thousand feet on the starboard bow!'*

'*They're Spitfires,*' cried Baker, who, with the help of Mills, had managed to stand up and lean against the repeater to use his binoculars.

'The Stukas must have seen them, sir,' Baker shouted, 'as the blighters are turning away.'

'I do believe you're right, Pilot,' cried Manley, looking through his binoculars, 'and they're heading for France.' With an inward sigh of relief, Manley decided to slow the ship down. 'Port ten, speed twenty knots,' snapped Manley.

'The buggers better shift, sir,' interrupted PO Mills, 'cos the Spits 'ave seen them.'

With their camouflaged, elliptical wings glinting in the late afternoon sun, the spitfires turned and dived towards the enemy bombers who immediately broke formation. This was accompanied by the unmistakable *rat-tat-tat* of machine gun fire.

'One of the sods has been hit,' yelled Jock Forbes as one of the aircraft sprouted intermittent puffs of black smoke.

'Yes, but is it a Spit?' said Manley, who, like the others was using a hand to shield his eyes from the glare of the sun. They soon found out. Seconds later, a loud cheer emanated around the upper deck as the Stuka splashed into the sea. All eyes then turned skywards, half hoping to see a parachute, but there was none.

'Bugger me, sir,' PO Mills remarked, lowering his binoculars, 'the sky's clear. The Spits must 'ave chased the Jerries away.'

'So I see,' Manley replied. 'Revert to defence stations, Number One,' he said to Powers, 'and check for damage and casualties, then go and let the doc take a look at your head, Pilot.'

While Powers and Baker were away, Manley scanned around the sea but saw no signs of the other two warships. Just then, Powers returned. He was out of breath and sweating profusely. 'A stoker broke an arm and there's a few minor cuts and bruises. Nothing serious, sir,' he said, taking out a handkerchief and moping his brow. 'And, oh, yes,' he added with a grin, 'Baker's having a few stiches in his head.'

Suddenly, he felt a pang of guilt. During the attack he had been so determined to save *Helix,* he had forgotten about the safety of the other two warships, which were nowhere to be seen.

'Make to *Eridge* and *Dulverton*, Signalman. "*Helix undamaged. Have you been hit? If, can I help?*"'

A few minutes later, the reply came. "*Damage slight. No casualties. Will re-join*".'

'Two ships approaching, about ten miles on the port bow, sir,' reported the starboard lookout.

Manley trained his binoculars to the left and saw the frothy bow waves of *Eridge* and *Delverton* cutting through the sea. With a sigh of relief, he realised he had, as captain, managed to bring the ship and her crew, safely through his first encounter with the enemy. He unhooked the ship's intercom. 'First lieutenant speaking. Rum issue will take place at1700. Well done, everybody.'

CHAPTER THIRTY

At 0500, on Sunday 2nd August, the flotilla entered the English Channel. The bitter northerly wind had abated. This allowed the early morning sun to occasionally peak through the grey clouds and dapple the choppy sea in flickering sunlight. Two hours later, Dolly Gray reported seeing the rugged outline of Land's End flicker on his radar screen. 'Twenty miles off the port beam, sir,' he added, stifling a yawn.

On the bridge, Manley was sipping a mug of tea, hoping a letter from Laura would be waiting when they arrived in Portsmouth. He realised that the contingencies of war meant that mail reaching the armed forces was to say the least, erratic. No mail in Alexandria, nothing in Malta. Maybe she was sick, or met someone else and was reluctant to tell him. The thought made him feel physically ill. Whatever the reason, as soon as the ship docked, he decided to ring her in barracks. Suddenly, the quiet voice of Lieutenant Powers interrupted his thoughts.

'Excuse me, sir,' said Powers, 'as our ETA in Pompey is 1100, what time do you want special sea duty men to fall in?'

'Specials at 1000, hands fall in 1030,' Manley promptly replied.

'Signal from *Eridge,* sir,' shouted PO Spud Tate, '"*Eridge and Dulverton to enter harbour and dock at King's Wharf. Helix to follow last and secure alongside Fountain Lake Jetty*".'

'Quite a long way to walk to the dockyard, eh, sir,' Baker remarked, wondering once again, if a letter from Wallasey's chief constable awaited him.

At that moment, Sub Lieutenant Brownlow came onto the bridge. 'This signal has just arrived from the C-in-C, sir. It's marked "Top Secret", as he spoke, the corners of his pale-blue eyes creased into a warm smile.

'Great Scott!' exclaimed Manley, sitting forward in his chair. 'What on earth could he want?' Furrowing his brow, he accepted the signal. As he read its contents, a look of disbelief became etched on his face. To make sure he read it out aloud. '"*Due to the paucity of experienced officers, you have been promoted to Commander and are to remain in command of Helix, signed Admiral Sir William James".'*

Having read the signal, Brownlow grabbed hold of Manley's free hand, and shaking it wildly, said, 'Let me be the first to congratulate you, sir, and I'm sure everyone on board will be pleased to know you'll remain as our captain.'

Baker and Powers and everyone else on the bridge couldn't help but overhear what was said. As they offered their congratulations and shook his hand, Manley suddenly felt a lump in his throat. 'Thank you, gentlemen,' he managed to say, and left the bridge and went to his cabin.

The news of Manley's promotion and his remaining as their commanding officer spread around the ship like wildfire. As *Helix* prepared to enter harbour, ratings laughed and joked while they scrubbed the decks or mopped passage ways.

'Bloody great,' Bob Rose said to Dinga Bell. They were standing on the quarterdeck, polishing the ship's bell. 'He certainly knows how to handle the ship.'

'You're right there, mate,' Dinga replied, dabbing some Blue Bell cleaning fluid onto a piece of cotton waste, 'even though he once gave me a week's stoppage for being drunk.'

Chief Cook Dai Evans was busy making pastry for jam roly-poly, when PO Steward Sandy Powel came into the galley and told him about Manley's promotion. 'One thing's for sure,' said the chief, sprinkling flour onto the pastry, 'it's the best thing the navy's done since giving us our tot, so it is.'

'I wouldn't go that far, Taffy, my son,' Sandy replied, using a finger to remove a blob of strawberry jam from a large tin, and sucking it. 'He can be a bastard at times, especially if his tea isn't strong enough.'

Even Chief GI Bob Shilling, who was usually very strict and withdrawn, found time to give a guarded warning to a few ratings who were busy cleaning the breech of A gun. 'Good news though this is, remember, he knows everyone one of you, so I'd be careful if I were you.'

In the sick bay, Bamford was checking the crepe bandage around Stoker Ben Lyon's fractured wrist.

'Great about the Jimmy, eh, Doc,' said Lyons.

'Yes, it is,' Bamford replied, securing the bandage with a strip of plaster. 'But when we get alongside, you'll have to go into barracks for an X-ray.'

'Any chance of light duties, then, Doc?' Gray asked, grinning like a Cheshire cat.

With a cheeky grin, Bamford replied, 'Of course, Ben, me old china, but I'll have to stop your tot.'

Paddy O'Malley left the engine room, and opening the boiler room's hatchway, went inside to speak to his friend, Harry Johnson. Both wore old, dirty caps and well-worn, oil-stained, blue overalls. 'To be sure, Harry,' Paddy yelled over the constant noise of the engines, 'the Buffer's just told me the Jimmy's got a half stripe and is staying as our captain.'

'First I've heard,' Harry replied, wiping his sweaty brow with a piece of cotton waste. 'Maybe when we get into Pompey he'll chivvy up the engineer officer to get me a new repeater valve.'

'Anyway, in a few hours we'll be in Pompey,' Paddy said, excitedly rubbing his hands together and grinning, 'and I can't wait to surprise Joyce.'

'I doubt if it'll be a surprise, Paddy, me old son,' Harry replied, slapping Paddy on the back. 'The women in Pompey all have inborn radar. Anyway, as soon as we're alongside, I'll go ashore and phone Ethel.'

Meanwhile, Manley was sat in Penrose's cabin, thinking how his parents, in particular his father, who commanded a destroyer in the last war, would be proud of him. For a few seconds, he touched the two and a half gold rings around one of his sleeves and imagined how it would look with an extra thick stripe. At that moment, Morris came in hold a steaming hot mug of coffee. Immediately Manley detected the strong smell of alcohol.

'Congratulations, ser, thought youse'd like this,' he said handing Manley the mug. 'I've put a drop of summat to liven' it up, so ta speak.'

'Thank you, Morris,' Manley replied, blowing across the top of the mug and taking a sip, 'but you do know drinking alcohol off duty is against KR & AIs,' he added with a cheeky grin.

By 1000, with *Eridge* in the van, the welcome sight of Hampshire's misty green hills appeared on the port beam of the three warships. Shortly afterwards, the three ships passed the Isle of Wight and slowly turned left. Then came the pipe, "Special sea duty men fall in. Hands fall in for entering harbour at ten thirty. Rig, Number Twos."

In the seamen's mess, Dusty Miller was standing behind Dutch Holland straightening his mate's collar. 'Hail, rain or fuckin' snow,' moaned Dusty, 'I can never understand why we always 'ave to fall in when we enter a bloody harbour.'

'It dates back to Nelson's time, you ignorant bugger,' Dutch answered, feeling Dusty give a firm tug on his collar, 'to show the guns were not manned the visit was friendly.'

'You wait 'til I go ashore,' Dusty salaciously replied, 'I intend to be more than friendly with Big Bertha in the Sussex.'

'Och, I'd be fuckin' careful if I were you,' said Jock Forbes, balancing a small mirror on top of his locker and coming his hair, 'last I heard she poxed up half of *Reclaim*'s ship's company.'

'Not again,' laughed Dusty.

On the bridge, Manley stood next to the consul, watching *Dulverton*'s bubbly wash a hundred yards in front of *Helix*.

'Steady at fifteen knots, Coxswain, Revolutions ten.'

'Aye aye, sir,' snapped Digger Barnes and quickly repeated the order.

A line of ratings were standing at ease, either side of the fo'c's le. Nearby, stood the imposing figure of Chief GI Bob Shilling, and deck officer, Sub Lieutenant Milton. A smaller group, under the eagle eyes of PO Len Mills and Sub Lieutenant Jock Jewitt, were fallen on the fo'c'sle.

In a matter of minutes, the city and dockyard hove into view. The dockyard and many houses and official buildings bore the scars of the 1941 Blitz, when the city and its environs suffered eleven consecutive air raids.

After passing the imposing edifice of Fort Blockhouse and HMS *Dolphin,* the navy's biggest submarine base, the grey roofs of the naval hospital, Haslar, could be seen gleaming in the morning sun. Close by, the span of Pneumonia Bridge, leading from the MTB depot, HMS *Hornet,* into Gosport, wobbled slightly in the stiff breeze.

"Attention on the upper deck, face the port", was piped as the flotilla approached three destroyers, anchored on their port side. This ritual salute was repeated as the ships passed a light cruiser and two destroyers.

'Signal from Port Admiral, sir,' said PO Signalman Spud Tate. *"'Dulverton and Eridge will proceed to Fountain Lake Jetty. Helix berth King's Wharf. Commander Manley report room eight admin block, RNB 1400 today. Congratulations on your promotion".'*

'That's odd,' Manley remarked, pursing his lips, 'I wonder what he's cooking up for us now.'

'Sounds as if something's up, sir,' replied Tate.

'It wouldn't surprise me, acknowledge, and add, *"Thank you. Message received and understood".'*

With the Isle of Wight terminus and the Gosport Ferry landing stage, some two hundred yards on her starboard quarter, *Helix* slowly approached Kings Wharf. Manley was well aware that any error in ship handling or poor signalling would be noted by the naval base commander, Admiral Sir Harvey Rawlinson.

'Slow ahead, revolutions thirty.' Feeling his heart thumping in his chest, Manley watched anxiously as *Helix* moved imperceptibly towards the wharf. 'Ring off engines.'

This was quickly followed by a slight bump as the ship squeezed against a wall of huge rubber tyres protecting the wharf. With a mixture of pride and relief, Manley watched as lines from the burly dockyard workers were passed to ratings on the quarterdeck and fo'c'sle, and firmly secured around solid steel bollards. At the same time, a small section of the guard rails on the quarterdeck were removed, allowing a wooden gangway to be slide into place and secured.

Shortly afterwards, Lieutenant Powers arrived, red-faced and sweating. 'Ship secured, sir,' he said, panting slightly. The time was a little after 1130.

'Thank you, Number One, fall out special sea duty men, and well done,' Manley replied, then, with a sly smile, went on, 'when a new first lieutenant is appointed, I expect you'll be glad to revert to your normal duties.'

'Er... I expect I will, sir,' Powers replied diplomatically. 'If you'll excuse me, sir,' he added, 'I'd better go and do a round of the ship.'

"Up Spirits, Cooks to the galley", echoed around ship. Ten minutes later, Manley was sitting behind his desk, checking the watch bill, when the pipe, "Mail is ready for collection", made him drop his fountain pen and sit up. He was about hurry to the wardroom when a knock came at the door and in came Sub Lieutenant Brownlow, holding a small bundle of letters.

'These just arrived, sir,' Brownlow said, passing them to Manley.

Doing his best sound calm, he said, 'Thank you, David, that'll be all.'

By the time Brownlow had left, Manley had eagerly sifted through the mail, most of which were official. However, to his abject disappointment, he found there was none from Laura; only two from his parents and one whose scrawny handwriting he didn't recognise. 'Why! Why!' he exploded as he sat back and angrily threw the letters onto his desk. With a weary sigh, he lent forward and picked up the letter with the unfamiliar writing. After ripping it open, he glanced at the end and was surprised to see it was from Jonathan, Laura's father. It read:

Dear Hugh,

You will no doubt be worried why Laura hasn't written to you. I regret to tell you, the reason is, two weeks ago, the car Laura and Susan were travelling in was involved in an accident. Sadly, her left leg was badly damaged and had to be amputated just above her ankle. She has begged me not to tell you as she as she thinks, wrongly in my opinion, that you would not be interested in her now that she is crippled. However, I know how much you both love each other, and so I feel morally obligated to break my promise to her and write to you.

At present, she is in the Truro Infirmary. When she is fully recuperated, I intend making arrangements for her to see a prosthesis specialist in Harley Street. She won't tell me exactly what happened, other that she and her friend, Susan, were in a car driven by someone or other.

I hope this letter is not too distressing, and reaches you fit and well.

My very best wishes, to you and your crew.

Yours, Jonathan Trevethick.

Holding the letter, Manley slumped back into his chair. 'So that's why she hasn't written,' he muttered to himself. Suddenly he imagined

Laura sitting, in her room, staring out of a window in pain and worried about her future – the thought made him sick with worry. However, after reading the letter again, the details of the accident seemed vague and it was clear she was protecting someone. He took a deep breath and sat back in his chair, determined to find out who it was.

The sound of the galley door opening startled him. He looked up and saw Morris, holding a mug of steaming hot coffee. 'I've put a tot in it, ser,' he said, placing it onto the large leather-bound blotting pad on Manley's desk. 'Just to celebrate yer promotion, like, ser.'

'Thank you, Morris,' Manley answered, as the aromatic smell of alcohol suddenly played around his nostrils, 'I'll be leaving the ship at 1330, and I expect to be away most of the afternoon.'

'Right then, ser,' Morris replied, 'that'll give me time to take your best doeskin overcoat and cap to Gieves for that extra half stripe and scrambled egg.'

'As usual, Morris, your timing is perfect.' After taking a welcome sip of his drink, he picked up an official looking envelope lying on top of small pile of envelopes. 'Now what,' he muttered to himself as he tore it open and removed a solitary sheet of thick paper. As he finished reading its contents, a wry smile played around his mouth. Still holding the letter, he picked up the telephone and pressed the quarterdeck buzzer.

'Quarterdeck, Leading Seaman Sammy Smith.'

'First Lieutenant, kindly pipe for Sub Lieutenant Baker to come to my cabin.'

The pipe was made and seconds later Baker arrived. 'Ah, Pilot,' Manley said, 'do come in, you'll be pleased to hear I've some good news for you,' he added with a warm smile. 'I have received a letter from Chief Constable Smithers in Wallasey, apparently, this fellow, Wainwright, with whom you had this altercation, has dropped the charges.'

'That's wonderful, sir,' gushed Baker, 'maybe I can get back with my fiancée again. That's if she'll have me.'

'I'm sure she will,' Manley replied, placing both hands on his desk. 'In the meantime I suggest you go to Wallasey and find out. Kindly ask Brownlow to make out a travel warrant for you. Then ask Lieutenant Powers to come and see me.'

Not long after Baker left the cabin Lieutenant Powers knocked and came into the cabin. 'Do sit down, and relax, Number One,' said Manley indicating to one of the two brown, leather armchairs facing his desk. 'The C-in-C wants to see me at 1330, so please arrange for a tilly to pick me up at thirteen hundred.'

'Very good, sir,' Powers said, fiddling with the brim of his cap, he asked, 'what about leave, sir?'

'I'm coming to that,' Manley replied impatiently. 'Both watches from 0900 from Monday to Friday. Men living locally to take preference. Ask for volunteers, to form a skeleton crew.'

'And the officers, sir?'

'All except you and myself, I'm afraid,' Manley answered shaking his head, 'but, rest assured, I'll try and make it up to you. Now,' said Manley, sitting forward and interlacing his hands. 'I'll be leaving the ship directly after colours tomorrow morning. I'm going to Truro by rail and will be back early the next day. I will leave a telephone number where I can be reached with the officer of the watch. Kindly arrange for a tilly to take me to the station. Sorry about the leave.'

'That's all right, sir,' Powers sheepishly replied, 'I'm very friendly with a Wren in barracks.'

Manley gave a wry smile and said, 'Good for you, please carry on.'

CHAPTER THIRTY-ONE

Shortly after 1330, Manley left *Helix* and climbed into the tilly parked near the bottom of the gangway. The journey through the dockyard to the naval barracks took less than five minutes. After showing his pay book to an armed marine at the main gate, the driver, a middle-aged grey-haired civilian, drove passed the well-manicured quarterdeck and continued around a wide parade ground, on which groups of ratings were being drilled by stiff-backed instructors. The driver stopped the tilly outside administrative block, a squat, grey-bricked Victorian building on the far side of the barracks.

'I'm not sure how long I'll be,' Manley said to the driver, 'but I'm afraid you'll have to wait.'

'Looks like I won't be the only one,' the driver replied, glancing at several tillys parked nearby, 'but I've plenty of time as my missus is at the Bingo.'

Manley thanked the driver, and after sliding open the door left the tilly. He quickly climbed up the three flights of concrete steps where a three-badge matelot armed with a 303 rifle, stood at ease outside an arched mahogany door. Upon seeing Manley, he immediately snapped to attention.

After carefully examining Manley's pay book, he said, 'Room eight, sir, second floor, along the corridor on your right.'

The second floor was reached via two sets of winding staircase, encased in dark blue, thickly piled carpets. As he walked along the corridor, the *clickity–click* of typewriters echoed from behind several closed doors. Outside room eight, another matelot stood holding a check board. After glancing at Manleys pay book, he stifled a yawn, then said, 'I see you're the last to arrive, sir,' and with a quick movement, ticked Manley's name off his list. He then stepped to one side, allowing Manley to open the door.

The eyes of several officers, occupying rows of desks, turned as he entered. After giving a quick nod to one or two he recognised, he sat down next to Lieutenant Commander Wright, HMS *Bleasdale's* commanding officer.

'What's up, Bill?' Manley whispered, while removing his cap.

'Don't really know, dear boy,' replied Wright. 'But from what I can gather, it must be something rather big.'

The room reminded Manley of his old grammar school. The atmosphere was warm and stuffy. Rows of empty shelves, thick with dust-lined two sides of the room. Opposite three grimy windows, criss-crossed with brown tape, barely allowed the rays of the afternoon sun to penetrate. From a low-slung roof, supported by a series of cross beams, hung two white electric lights. The floor consisted of dusty bare boards. Two rows of wooden desks, separated by a centre aisle, were each occupied by a naval officer. On each desk, a round, a metal ashtray lay next to a small glass jug of water and a tumbler. At the end of the room was a wooden platform, on which rested a desk, a glass water jug and two tumblers. However, what drew Manley's attention was a large white sheet hanging over a blackboard, under which poked the edges of what was obviously a coloured map.

'Second front, maybe?' remarked Lieutenant Commander Peters, the captain of *Fernie,* who was sitting next to Gregory-Smith.

Another officer sitting in front of Manley, turned around, and giving a short laugh, said, 'Some bloody hope.'

Just then, a side door opened and in strode the sturdy figure of Captain Storey, the movements officer. Closely behind him strode the six-foot-plus frame of Admiral Sir William James, resplendent in an immaculately tailored doeskin uniform and gold braid. The grating of chairs on the wooden floor echoed around as everyone stood to attention. The admiral introduced himself and Captain Storey, sat down at a table and poured a glass of water.

'Stand easy, gentlemen, and do sit down,' said the admiral, placing both hands in his jacket pockets. He took a central position on the platform. 'And smoke if you must.' His voice was sharp and crisp, and as he spoke, his pale blue eyes set in a heavily tanned face, creased into a sly smile. 'Now, I bet you're all wondering what's behind the sheet,' he added, glancing at the blackboard. 'But before I enlighten you, I must stress that everything discussed in this is room is top secret.'

He paused momentarily, allowing a few officers to light cigarettes, then, pouring out a glass of water, continued. 'As you may have read in the newspapers or on the wireless, since Pearl Harbour last year, President Roosevelt decided that the invasion of Europe must take priority over events in the Pacific, especially after Italy's so called "Pact of Steel" with Germany. Now, it would appear that the president's promise, encouraged by Admiral King, who is a confirmed Anglophile, has come with a price. Roosevelt has insisted on an early European invasion. Stalin, despite receiving supplies via the Arctic, has been doing the same. Winston has constantly rebuffed these requests simply because of our commitments in North Africa and elsewhere, and stressing that any full-scale invasion could not take place until the U-boat war is won.' The admiral paused and took a good sip of water, then said, 'Any questions, so far?'

'I have one, sir,' said Lieutenant Commander York, the captain of HMS *Berkeley,* raising a hand. 'Surely after the losses we have sustained on the Arctic convoys is proof that we are doing our best to help Russia, and besides, sir, it wasn't all that long since Stalin broke off his pact with Hitler, so I think Old Joe has bloody nerve to ask for an invasion.'

'You're referring to Russia's non–aggression pact with Hitler in August 1939, that allowed him to invade Poland.'

'Yes, sir,' replied York.

'I agree with you, and I know Winston does also,' the admiral replied. 'By now,' he went on, 'I'm sure some of you have deduced why you are here.' A slight pause that served to raise the tension already prevalent in the room. 'On the morning of August19[th] ,' said the admiral, placing both hands on his hips, 'a force of six thousand men, British, Canadian plus a contingent of the First US Ranger Battalion, supported by a regiment of Calgary tanks will be ferried across the Channel by civilian transports, and land on the coast of France, code-named, "Operation Jubilee".

He turned around and with a dramatic gesture, loosened the sheet, allowing it to drop in a wrinkled heap on the floor. A murmur of surprise broke forth, as set before them, was a map of the southern England, part of the English Channel and the Normandy coast. The admiral picked up a wooden pointer and tapping the map, snapped, 'Here, at Dieppe.

Several officers gave each other searching looks as another murmur of surprise buzzed around the room.

'And as you can see, on either side of Dieppe, the landing beaches are colour-coded.' Using his pointer he said, 'Yellow Beach is on the eastern side of Dieppe, and Blue lies to the east of the town. Green Beach is east of Pourville. Orange Beach is here, nine kilometres west of Dieppe. Then comes Red and White Beaches directly in front of Dieppe. Any questions?'

Commander Wright raised a hand. 'I could understand it if it were Cherbourg, as it's a vital port, but why Dieppe, sir?'

'I wish I could give you a satisfactory answer,' said the admiral, looking slightly perplexed. 'But that decision was made by the chiefs of staff some months ago.'

Manley lent forward and raised a hand. 'What about support, sir,' he said, feeling the wooden seat pressing into his backside. 'I take it we'll have a cruiser or monitor to bombard enemy positions.'

'Er… I'm afraid not,' the admiral replied. 'Moutbatten did ask for a heavy cruiser. However, the First Sea Lord, Admiral Sir Dudley Pound, refused to allow any capital ships to be exposed to U-boat or air attack. The Polish destroyer, *Slazak*, will support the eastern flank. This will leave *Albrighton, Berkley, Brocklesby* and *Garth* to bombard the headlands prior to the main assault on Dieppe. *Calpe* and *Fernie* will be command ships. *Calpe* will carry Captain Hughes-Hallet and Major-General Roberts. General Truscott, an American observer will be on board, *Fernie.'*

Manley's hand immediately shot up.

'Yes, what is it?' said the admiral, sounding irritated at being interrupted.

'You haven't mentioned *Helix,* or *Albrighton,* sir,' Manley replied, giving Lieutenant Commander Hanson a furtive glance.

'All in good time,' the admiral replied, picking up a pointer. 'The raid will consist of two phases. Phase one will take place at 0450 when Number 3 Commando will land on Yellow Beach and capture a battery here, near Berneval. Lord Lovatt's commandos and fifty US Rangers are to neutralise the Hess battery on Orange Beach. The South Saskatchewan Regiment will land on Green Beach and attack the western headlands overlooking Dieppe. The Royal Canadian Regiment and elements of the Canadian Black Watch will land on Blue Beach and attack a battery on the eastern headland. These are, in effect, flanking attacks to allow phase two to take place. If they fail, the main landings could be put in jeopardy. This will begin at 0520, when Canadian Fusiliers, the Canadian Essex Royals, the Royal Hamilton and Royal Marine Commandos, followed by the fourteenth Canadian Regiment's Calgary tanks will form a frontal attack on Red Beach, in front of Dieppe. This particular landing will be supported by *Helix* and *Albrighton,* who will, by that time, have detached from the other four destroyers, leaving them to bombard the headlands. I hope that answers your question,' the admiral added, staring at Manley.

'Perfectly, thank you, sir,' Manley replied, shooting a quick grin at Lieutenant Commander Hanson.

Romuald Tyminski, the tall, distinguished-looking captain the Polish frigate, *Slazak*, stood up, and in almost perfect English, asked, 'Will the RAF be doing a preliminary bombing, sir?'

Once again, the admiral appeared to look uneasy. 'The answer to your question is no. Air Marshal Harris refuses to send heavy bombers as he considers the collateral damage would outweigh the strategic benefits. However, Leigh Mallory is sending sixty-seven squadrons of fighters, mainly Spitfires, to attack the headland. The only problem is the Spits and Hurricanes are seventy miles away from their bases in England and have only a limited endurance.'

Lieutenant Commander Frederick Peters, raised a hand. 'Excuse me, sir,' he said, nervously licking his lips, 'in 1938 my wife and I did a motoring tour of Normandy, and stopped at Dieppe. As I recall, it's a large fishing port near the mouth of the River Arques.'

'Yes, yes,' the admiral impatiently interrupted, 'what exactly is your point?'

'Well, sir, Dieppe has a horseshoe beach that is mainly shingle. On the eastern side is a medieval castle that commands a perfect view of the port and sea. And as I recall, there's a large casino on the eastern side of the harbour, which is dominated by a rocky headland. So seems to me, that if there are batteries are on either side of the harbour, it will make any landing very dicey, to say the least.'

'Your observations are very perceptive,' said the admiral, 'as subduing the enemy fortifications on both headlands is the key to success.' He paused, and with an edgy smile, added, 'If this is not achieved, then, as you say, it could be dicey indeed. Perhaps you should have been on the planning staff.' His remark immediately provoked a moment of uneasy levity. The admiral stopped talking and said, 'Would someone would be kind enough to open a window, as it's getting rather stuffy in here.' Straight away an officer at the end of row stood up, and managed to prise open a window, allowing a warm breeze to freshen up the room.

'Now,' he went on, 'after the flanking attacks, the bombardment will cease and all destroyers will attack individual targets. Now, before I go on, any more questions?'

'Yes, sir,' said Manley, 'just how close to the beach is my ship and *Albrighton* allowed to go?'

'That'll be up to you to judge,' the admiral replied, 'and use your initiative.'

'What are the objects of the raid?' asked Lieutenant Commander Byron, the captain of HMS *Brocklesby*.

'Good question,' replied the admiral, 'these are as follows; the destruction of enemy airfields radar, power and dock and petrol dumps in the vicinity of Dieppe. Capture barges for our own use. Obtain secret documents and to capture prisoners. How does that sound?'

'Not a great deal, considering the number of troops involved, sir,' Byron replied, glancing sceptically to those officers near him.

'Nevertheless, there they are,' the admiral replied. 'Anything else?'

'Just one, sir,' said the commanding officer of HMS *Calpe,* Lieutenant Commander Porter, 'besides being well dug in, how strong are the enemy troops?'

'Intelligence reports the presence of the fifty-seventh regiment that consists of second-rate troops and conscripts from occupied countries.' (In fact, the 10th Panzier Division was based at Amiens 80km away.)

'I'm sure that must be very reassuring to the Canadians and Lovatt's men, sir,' Manley answered, 'but isn't that what was said about the Turks at Gallipoli?'

'Maybe,' the admiral replied tersely, 'but remember, the Gallipoli landings took place thousands of miles away from England.' After a momentary pause, he added, 'Before I hand over to Captain Storey, who will fill you in on the movement details, any more questions?'

'Just one, sir,' said Manley. 'I notice you haven't mentioned *Dulverton or Eridge.*'

'Ah, yes,' replied the admiral, 'I'm afraid *Dulverton* has to have a new boiler and *Eridge* is urgently required elsewhere.'

'Thank you, sir,' said Manley.

The admiral sat down at his desk and poured another glass of water. Captain Storey stood up and took centre stage.

'Good afternoon, gentlemen,' he said, straightening his jacket and clearing his throat. '*Calpe,* will lay a smoke screen to protect the allied forces and shipping. 'H' Hour will be 0450. At 0300 on the19th, the commandos will join the transport, *Prince Albert,* at Southampton, for the crossing. Seven miles from France, they will transfer to LCAs for the run to Orange Beach. He paused, picked up a glass from his desk and after taking a good gulp, continued. 'The Royal Regiment of Canada will embark at 0200 at Portsmouth and cross in two Channel ferries, the *Prince Astrid,* and *Invicta*, supported HMS *Garth.* Six miles from the French coast, the troops will be transferred to LCIs for the run in to Blue Beach. At 0300, the South Saskatchewan and Cameron Highlanders will cross in the channel ferries, *Invicta* and *Prince Astrid.* Seven miles from the enemy coast, the troops will embark in LCAs and land at Green Beach.' Before continuing he took out a handkerchief and nervously mopped his brow. 'As you have heard, the landings on Dieppe itself will be the province of the Royal Marines along with battalions from the Canadian Fusiliers Mount Royal, Essex Scottish and Royal Hamilton. They will cross in three transport vessels, *Glengyle, Prince Charles* and *Prince Leopold,* and will, be in their LCAs by 0320to land at Red and White Beaches. As stated earlier, four destroyers bombard the beaches and headlands, any questions?'

'What about minefields, sir?' asked Lieutenant Commander Byron, *Brocklesby*'s commanding officer.

'I'm pleased to say, that the minefield from the Pas-de-Calais to Le Harve, offers very little danger to the shallow draught drawn by the LCAs, and the minesweepers have made a pathway for the transports.'

'What about reserves, should they be needed, sir? asked Manley.

'Ah yes, reserves,' Storey repeated. 'Major Roberts has a battalion of Royal Marines and Fusiliers Mount Royal at his disposal, should he require them.'

Lieutenant Commander Hanson raised a hand. 'What arrangement have been made for a withdrawal from the beaches, sir?'

'Another good question,' Storey replied. 'The code word to withdraw is *Vanish*. This order will be given by Captain Hughes-Hallet whenever necerssary. Rather appropriate word, don't you think?' he added with a weak smile.

Hanson didn't reply. Instead, he cast a dubious glance at the officer next to him and slowly shook his head.

'Thank you, gentlemen, do you have anything to add, sir?' he added, glancing across at the admiral.

'Just one thing,' said the admiral, standing up. 'I received a medical report on Captain Penrose from the PMO in BMH Gib. I'm sure you'll be glad to hear he's making good progress. You will each receive top secret instructions concerning Operation Jubilee within the next two days. Officers only to be informed. Oh, and congratulations to *Commander* Manley, who I notice,' he added, giving Manley a warm smile, 'is out of the rig of the day.'

His remark brought a ripple of laughter as several officers turned and grinned at Manley. 'That's being rectified, thank you, sir,' Manley replied with a slightly embarrassed smile.

'Well, good luck and Godspeed, gentlemen,' said the admiral, 'now, please carry on.'

Once again, chairs grated on the floor as everyone stood to attention. The admiral and Captain Storey picked up their caps and left by the side door.

'That's good news about your old captain, Hugh,' remarked Lieutenant Commander Petch.

'Yes, indeed,' Manley replied, 'and I'm sure his wife and family will be pleased. But I think his seagoing days are over.'

As the officers filled outside the room, Manley looked at Lieutenant Commander Byron, and said, 'What do you make of it, Jim?'

Byron gave a quick, nonchalant shrug of his shoulders and said, 'All we're being asked to do is land thousands of troops on a poorly defended coast without strong sea or air support. Nothing to it, really.'

CHAPTER THIRTY-TWO

Manley arrived on board *Helix* at 1630 and was met by Lieutenant Powers. Liberty men were fallen in on the quarterdeck and Powers had just given senior ratings permission to go ashore.

'How did the meeting go, sir?' Powers enquired.

Manley returned Powers salute, then frowning slightly, said, 'All in good time, but you'll be pleased to hear Captain Penrose is recovering well.' He walked across the quarterdeck and unhooked the tannoy and informed the ship's company about Penrose. Afterwards he re-joined Powers. 'As you know, Number One, I'll be leaving the ship tomorrow. When I return, I'll address the officers about the ship's movements.'

'Sounds rather ominous, sir,' replied Powers.

'It is,' Manley answered coldly. 'I'll be in my cabin if you need me.' Then made his way to the citadel, unhooked the hatchway and disappeared.

Shortly after eight o'clock, after an enjoyable roast beef dinner, Paddy O'Malley and Joyce, together with Harry Johnson and Ethel, went to the White Hart. They managed to find a table in the parlour, which was heavy with tobacco smoke, stuffy and warm. During the next two hours, the beer and port wine flowed freely, as accompanied by a grey-haired lady pianist, they joined the crowd and sang every song from *Lili Marlene* to *We'll Meet Again*. The singing continued after closing time as the four linked arms and ignoring the blackout, walked to Harry's house.

Later that night, sitting alone in Joyce's house, Paddy looked into her emerald green eyes and said, 'Joyce, me darlin', will you do me the honour of being my wife?'

'Of course I will, Paddy,' Joyce cried, and hugged him so hard he thought his ribs would break. The next day at tot time, Harry promised to be Paddy's best man.

The following morning, after taking "colours", feeling slightly self-conscious of the cluster of silver on the brim of his cap, Manley left *Helix* and climbed into the tilly. Under his Burberry he wore his number one doeskin uniform and carried his steel helmet and respirator over his left shoulder. The dark, low cirrostratus clouds partially hid a pale, early morning sun, and a stiff, chilly, westerly breeze blew downriver from the Solent.

Ten minutes later, he boarded the 0900 train from Portsmouth and almost three hours later, after an uneventful journey, arrived at Waterloo a little after 1145. He bought a copy of *The Times,* then made his way through the sparse crowd before taking the Bakerloo tube to Paddington. He managed to down a mug of strong tea and buy a cheese sandwich from a mobile canteen, before catching the 1230 Cornish Express to Penzance.

Except for a large contingent of noisy service personnel and some civilians who occupied the third-class section, the train appeared to be empty. Manley found a vacant first-class compartment. He slid open the door and after taking off his Burberry and placing it along with his respirator and steel helmet onto the rack, sat in corner near a grimy window and opened his newspaper.

Despite the stark headlines telling of the decimation of Convoy PQ 17, when most of the thirty-three merchant ships were lost, and the appointment of General Bernard Montgomery in command of the Eighth Army, Manley's thoughts kept on turning to Laura. With a worried sigh, he folded the newspaper and sat back, imagining her lying in bed, worried about the future. The shrill sound of the station master's whistle and the slamming of compartment doors interrupted his reverie. This was quickly followed by a sudden jerking as the train slowly shunted forward and gathered speed.

The gentle rocking of the train and the steady *rickety-rick* as the train passed over the sleepers had a somnolent effect and he nodded off. The sound of a male voice shouting, 'Tickets please,' abruptly woke him up. He looked up as a small, grey-haired ticket inspector slid open the compartment door. After checking Manley's travel warrant, he said, 'The next two stops are Dorchester then Plymouth. We should arrive in Truro about five-thirty.' He closed the door and carried on down the corridor.

The time was 1330. Manley sat back and watched lines of rain angle against the window, obscuring the view of the countryside. 'Four hours to go, four long bloody hours,' he muttered to himself. So much had happened since he and Laura had driven through this same countryside. How, he wondered, would she react when she saw him. He closed his eyes and prayed she would welcome him with that dazzling smile he remembered so well.

When the train arrived at Bournemouth, Manley left the compartment and along with a queue of sailors, managed to buy a mug of steaming hot tea from a trolley.

'Plymouth, sir?' asked a two-badge gunnery rating, who insisted Manley went ahead of him.

'No, a spot of leave,' Manley replied, and after accepting his drink from an elderly, grey-haired woman, returned to his compartment. As the train rumbled on, Manley, realising he was hungry, remembered his cheese sandwich and ate it while enjoying his tea. He closed his eyes and dozed off. He dreamt he was alone on *Helix*'s bridge. Laura was standing next to him, smiling as spray from an exploding bomb saturated them. When he woke up the he was soaked with sweat.

By 1500, the rain had stopped and the compartment was bathed in warm sunshine. Looking outside the window, Manley's attention was drawn to the dark silhouettes of a small convoy escorted by two destroyers, standing out against the glittering waters of the English Channel. Heading for Portsmouth or Hull, Manley thought. What happened next seemed to Manley, to be unreal, and was over in a matter of minutes. From out of a clear blue sky, two twin engine bombers appeared about a thousand feet above the convoy. At the same time, several sticks of black objects fell from their undercarriages. Almost immediately the bombs exploded around the convoy. In an instant the ships disappeared under a huge wall of white foam. At the same time, the high angled guns of the warships opened up. Suddenly, the sky was decorated with tiny bursts of black smoke. One of the bombers was hit, and streaming a cloud of yellow flames, plunged into the sea; no parachutes, no survivors. However, as the convoy emerged from the watery curtain, Manley saw that none of the ships appeared to be damaged. At that moment, the compartment was momentarily engulfed in darkness as the train sped through a tunnel. Daylight quickly emerged, causing Manley to blink rapidly. The ships had disappeared leaving no trace of their presence. Manley sat back, wondering if what he had witnessed had really happened or was it another dream.

When the trains stopped at Dorchester a small, stout grey-haired priest entered the compartment. He wore a black overcoat and carried a small brown leather suitcase. 'Good afternoon, commander,' he said, glancing at the three gold rings on Manley's sleeves. 'I hope I'm not disturbing you.' His accent was distinctly Devonian and as he spoke, his pale blue eyes set against a pallid complexion, lit up into a warm smile.

'Not at all, Padre,' Manley replied, 'as you can see, there's plenty of room. Hugh Manley,' he added, proffering a hand.

'Henry Goodhall,' the minister replied. 'On your way to Plymouth, or shouldn't I ask?' They shook hands.

'Truro, actually, to see a friend,' Manley replied.

The minister took off his overcoat under which the whiteness of his clerical collar he wore contrasted sharply against his black shirt and sombre charcoal grey suit. 'Well, at least we've got lovely weather for travelling,' he said, placing his overcoat on the rack. He then sat opposite Manley, crossed his legs and relaxed into his seat.

Throughout the journey along the picturesque Devon coast, they discussed the war, the effect of the *Blitz* on Londoners and the U-boat menace. Manley welcomed the minster's conversation, as it took his mind off Laura.

'According to the eight o'clock news, Stalin is pressing Winston for a second front,' the minister remarked, 'although where we're going to find the troops to do it, only the good Lord knows.'

'Quite so,' Manley quietly replied.

Upon arriving in Plymouth, the minister shook Manley's hand and wished him Godspeed. Then, gathering his overcoat and suitcase, he left the compartment.

After crossing over the River Tamar, on Brunel's magnificent bridge, the train entered Cornwall and arrived in Truro half an hour later at 1800. Manley put on his Burberry and his cap, then, gathering his steel helmet and gas mask, he opened the door and left the train. Before leaving the station, he asked a station official when the last train to London was due and where he could find a taxi.

'Cornish Express from Penzance to Paddington, stops here at eleven o'clock, my 'andsome,' replied the official, 'and there's a few taxis outside the station.'

Manley thanked him, and on his way across the concourse, he saw a buffet and realised he hadn't eaten properly since breakfast. He went inside and ordered beans on toast and pork pie and a large mug of tea. He paid the bill then then made his way across an almost empty concourse to an archway marked "Exit". He hurried through and saw two black taxis parked alongside each other. The drivers, two elderly men wearing baggy trousers and jackets, stood leaning against the bonnets, smoking a cigarette.

Upon seeing Manley approaching, the smaller of the two looked at him. 'Where to, sur?' he asked, stubbing his cigarette on the cobbled ground.

'Truro Infirmary, please,' Manley replied, 'how far away is it?'

'Just outside the city. Hop in, sur, it won't take long,' said the driver, opening the passenger door. Manley climbed inside and sat down then placed his steel helmet and gas mask by his side.

There were very few people about and traffic was sparse. After driving down a quiet high street and passing Truro's imposing Gothic cathedral, they soon left the city behind. Shortly after seven o'clock, they arrived outside a high, red-bricked wall. Manley looked out of a side window and saw an open gate and a wide gravelled path leading up to a four-storey building constructed in white granite. On either side of the pathway, small gardens, clusters of long stemmed red and yellow roses added a dash of colour to the sombre surroundings.

They drove down the pathway and stopped near the bottom of four flights of granite steps. Nearby, a few dark blue ambulances were parked while the drivers stood around, smoking and charting.

'Well, here we are, my bird,' said the driver, 'as you can see, the main entrance is through that big oak door at the top of the steps. And I hope the person you're visiting is keeping well.'

'Thank you, so do I,' said Manley. 'How much do I owe you?'

'That'll be one and six, to you, sur,' said the driver.

Manley gave him half a crown and after telling him to keep the change, asked, 'What time do you finish?'

'About twelve, or sooner if business is slack,' the driver replied.

'I have to catch the eleven o'clock train,' Manley said. 'Could you pick me up here at, say, ten thirty?'

'Ten thirty it is, sur, and me name's Bert.'

'See you then, and thank you, Bert,' Manley replied. He climbed out of the taxi, and hurried up the steps. He stopped and after pushing a highly polished brass knob, he opened the door and was immediately assailed by the pungent mixture of antiseptic and mansion polish. The entrance hall was quite spacious. Painting of local dignitaries lined the wainscoting and two imposing chandeliers hung from a ceiling stuccoed in white.

On his left, a pretty, dark-haired receptionist sat a desk. She had just finished talking on the telephone and was placing the receiver down when she saw Manley.

'Can I help you, sir?' she asked, flashing him a warm smile.

'Yes indeed,' Manley answered, 'would you be kind enough to tell me which ward a Miss Laura Trevethick is in, please?'

'One moment,' she said and opened a thick ledger. She quickly found the appropriate section, and after running finger down the page, said, 'Yes, here she is. She's in a private room in ward eight. That's the woman's ward. If you look across the floor, you'll see three corridors. Ward eight is down the one in the centre. Now, I must ask you to sign your name,' she added opening a smaller ledger.

Manley took out his fountain pen and did as she asked. After thanking her, he made his way across the black and white tiled floor, passing closed doors marked "Physiotherapy", and "X Ray". The walls of the corridor, painted in pale green, were hung with small paintings of some of Cornwall's picturesque scenery. Upon seeing him, three young, off-duty nurses, wearing dark blue cloaks, gave him quick, shy glances, before hurrying past him in a fit of girlish giggles.

Manley arrived outside ward eight and was about to go inside when the door opened and out came a tall man with thinning fair hair and a pallid complexion. From a side pocket of his white coat dangled part of a stethoscope. Upon seeing Manley, he stopped and said, 'Good evening, I'm Mr Frobisher, one of the orthopaedic consultants, can I help you?'

'Yes,' Manley replied, noticing the dark smudges under his brown eyes. 'I'm looking for a Miss Laura Trevethick, I've been told she is in ward eight'.

'Ah, yes, Laura, a lovely young lady,' replied Mr Frobisher, 'she's one of my patients. Are you a relative?'

'No, my names Hugh Manley, and one day I hope to marry her,' he replied. As he spoke, they stood aside to allow a nurse to leave the ward.

'Do you know about her accident?' the consultant asked.

'Yes, her father wrote and told me,' Manley answered, 'how is she?'

'The leg is healing nicely,' the consultant replied, 'and she's putting on a brave face, but she's naturally worried about the future. Are you on leave?

'Just a few hours before catching the train to London,' Manley replied.

'Then I'm sure your visit will be just the tonic she needs,' said the consultant. 'Now you must excuse me. I have a few rounds to make. Nice to have met you and good luck,' he added, shaking Manley's hand. 'I'm sure Sister O'Malley will look after you.' He turned and hurried down the corridor.

Manley took off his Burberry and placed it over an arm, then opened the door and went inside.

CHAPTER THIRTY-THREE

The ward lights were on and the blackout curtains drawn across the windows. A small, stout woman, wearing a dark blue uniform, stood near a white door marked "Ward Sister", painted in red. She held an open book in both hands and was talking quietly to two nurses. All three turned and looked at the tall, dark, handsome naval officer standing by the door.

'Saints preserve us,' said the stout woman, 'what can I do for you?' Her brogue was distinctly Irish and as she spoke, her round pale features broke into a warm smile.

'I'd like to see Miss Laura Trevethic, please,' said Manley as he removed his cap.

'And you are…?' she asked.

'Commander Hugh Manley,' he quietly replied.

'I'm Sister O'Malley, are you related to Laura?'

'No, a close friend,' Manley answered.

'Have you come far, or shouldn't I ask?'

'About two hundred miles,' Manley replied.

'Well, now, it's way past visiting hours,' Sister O'Malley replied, 'but I'm sure we can bend the rules for you.' Turning to the nurses, she said, 'You two carry on with bed making, and stop gawking.' After giving Manley a quick, bashful glance, the nurses turned away and walked down the ward.

'Is Laura expecting you, Commander?' asked the sister.

'No, I want to surprise her, and I'd prefer it if you didn't mention my name. Just say a friend is here to see her,' Manley replied.

'Very well, if that's what you want,' Sister O'Malley replied, 'and are you aware what has happened to her?'

'Yes,' Manley said, 'before I came in, I met a Mr Frobisher who told me she had lost part her leg just above her left ankle. How is she bearing up?'

'She's doing well, considering what she's gone through,' the sister answered. 'Now, wait here while I go and see her, and tread softly, she's still rather weak.'

'Thank you, Sister, I understand,' Manley replied.

She turned and hurried down the ward and stopped outside a side door. After knocking gently, she went inside.

As the door closed Manley glanced around the ward that smelt strongly of antiseptic. Ten beds and lockers rested on either side of a rectangular shaped ward.

Central heating was provided by small pipes discretely placed on the floor behind the beds. The walls were painted in pastel green and shiny brown linoleum covered the floor. At the end of the ward, next to the bathroom, stood a set of white curtained screens. In the centre of the ward, a tall glass vase containing long stemmed red and yellow roses resting in the middle of a well-polished oak table, added a touch of homeliness to the impersonal surroundings.

Ear phones and an emergency chord hung behind each bed. Two patients lay in bed with their legs encased in plaster of Paris, suspended on a series of traction pulleys. A few patients lay in bed asleep. Others, wearing an assortments of dressing gowns, sat on armchairs. They stopped talking and stared inquisitively at Manley, no doubt wondering why he was there.

The side door opened and Sister O'Malley beckoned him inside. The room was small, but well equipped. At the foot of the bed hung a chart showing Laura's temperature, blood pressure and pulse. Then came a dressing table, wardrobe, chairs and a door leading into a bathroom, tiled in white. The floor was covered in pale green carpet and the blackout curtains were drawn across a solitary window.

Laura was sitting on a tall, wing-backed chair reading an *Everybody*'s magazine. Close by was a white enamel locker on which rested two books and a glass tumbler, inverted over a water carafe. Under a pale green dressing gown, she wore a pink nightdress. As the door opened, she looked up. Upon seeing Manley, a startled expression came into her eyes. She dropped the magazine and her hands shot to her face.

'My God, it's you,' she cried. 'I told father I...'

Manley quickly interrupted her, and kneeling by her side, took hold of her hands and said, 'But, darling, not hearing from you was driving me insane, I was sick with worry and had to see you.' As he spoke, he couldn't help but notice the left, lower part of her night dress was empty, in sharp contrast to the fluffy, pink slipper on her right foot. He also noticed that she had lost weight and her face was pale and drawn. Her auburn hair, normally worn in a neat chignon, hung loose around her shoulders, and the dark smudges under the lovely violet eyes he had dreamt about so often, showed the strain she was under.

'I must look a mess,' she said, touching her hair, while averting his gaze. 'I thought you wouldn't want to see me like this, a cripple for life.'

'But, darling,' he replied, gently stroking her face, 'I would love you even if you were cross-eyed and bald. But, more important, how are you feeling?'

'I don't remember much about the first week as I was given regular injections of morphia,' she replied, 'but things have now settled down. The leg is dressed twice a day and the physios are teaching me to use the crutches.' She paused, and for the first time, noticed the three gold rings on his sleeves. 'Congratulations, darling,' she said admiringly, 'I see you're now a commander.'

Manley went on to tell her about Penrose. 'And I've been given command of *Helix*,' he added with a touch of pride.

'I suppose that means more sea time?' she said, with a sigh.

'I'm afraid so, my love,' he replied. Now,' he went on, staring intently at her, 'I want to know exactly what happened. Who was driving the car?'

At that moment the door opened and Sister O'Malley came in carrying two cups of tea. 'I go off at eight thirty so I thought you'd like a cuppa,' she said, placing the cups on Laura's locker top. 'And I thought I'd pop in to say cheerio.'

'That's very kind of you, Sister,' Manley replied, 'and thank you and your staff for everything you're doing.'

'Sure, tis a pleasure,' she replied, 'but before I go, I'd better make sure the curtains are correctly drawn So far we haven't had an air raid, but there's always a first time[7].' She then reached past Laura and checked the curtains. She then stood back and giving Manley a confident smile, went on. 'Now, I'll say goodnight, and don't worry, sir, while you're away we'll take good care of Laura, so God's blessing and come back safe.'

As soon as Sister O'Malley left, Manley drew the chair from under the dressing table and sat facing Laura. He took hold of one of her hands, and giving it a gentle squeeze, said, 'Now, darling, what happened and who was driving the car?'

---

[7] On August 6 1942, Truro experienced its first air raid. 65 people were killed including women and children. Part of B wing of the hospital was damaged and 9 members of staff were killed.

CHAPTER THIRTY-FOUR

Laura withdrew her hand from his and took a good gulp of tea. With a weary sigh, she sat back in the chair, and averting Manley's stare, said, 'It all began when Susan and myself were given a long weekend commencing the following Friday. On the Thursday, we were in the wardroom having a drink when I asked her to come to Helston with me to visit father. FP, who had taken a shine to Susan, was standing nearby. He overheard me and offered to drive us down.'

'FP!' exclaimed Manley. 'That pompous ass.'

'Please, Hugh,' Laura replied, reaching for his hand, 'this is difficult enough so please don't get angry.'

'Sorry, darling,' Manley said, 'but FP, of all people,' he added dolefully shaking his head.

'At first Susan and I refused his offer, but you know FP,' sighed Laura. 'He persisted, saying he could borrow a friend's Austin Eight and how it would be quicker by road.'

Manley gave Laura a rueful smile. 'Yes, darling, I remember,' he muttered.

'Well, Susan and I agreed. We were all in uniform and he picked us up at eleven o'clock the next morning.' She paused and finished her drink. 'The car looked pretty old and FP insisted Susan sat next to him and I sat behind, and I remember having difficulty closing the door. It was a lovely morning with a clear blue sky. We made good time and at one o'clock, we stopped at Poole and had lunch...

Manley interrupted her and said, 'And I bet FP had a few drinks.'

'Yes, all of us did,' Laura replied. 'Sue and I had gin and tonics and a chicken salad, I'm not sure what FP had to drink, because while we were eating, he stood at the bar, talking to someone.'

'Hmm...' muttered Manley, 'knowing FP, I'm sure he had a couple of Scotches on the sly. Anyway, go on.'

'We arrived in Plymouth sometime around five,' said Laura. 'Susan and I needed the toilet so we stopped at a pub.'

'Where FP had more to drink, no doubt,' Manley said.

'Well,' Laura replied, lowering her voice slightly, 'his breath did smell strongly of alcohol. But he seemed all right. Would you pour me a glass of water, please, darling?'

Manley reached across and removed the tumbler off the carafe and poured half a glass of water then handed it to her.

After taking a few sips, she placed the tumbler on the locker. She took out a white lace handkerchief, and after dabbing her mouth, sat back in the chair.

Noticing how tired she looked, Manley took hold of her hand and said, 'I wish we could stop there darling, but I have to catch the eleven o'clock train.'

'You poor thing,' she replied, reaching across and stroking his face with her free hand, 'you must be all in.'

'I'm fine,' Manley replied, 'now, what happened after you left Plymouth?'

'After we crossed the bridge into Cornwall, the heavens opened and it started to pour down. Now, as you know, the roads in Cornwall are fairly narrow and winding,' she quietly answered.

Manley gave her a suspicious look, and said, 'Yes, I remember, darling, what about them?'

Laura withdrew her hand from his and began toying nervously with her handkerchief. 'I think the accident happened after we drove through St Austell.' As she spoke her voice faltered slightly. 'The road was wet and I remember looking out the window and seeing a cottage painted white.'

Noticing her hand trembling, Manley placed his hand over hers, and said, 'I know this is painful for you, darling, so take your time.'

'Everything happened so fast. The car swerved and I remember hearing Susan screaming. The car must have hit something as it tilted up. The door opened and I was flung out onto the ground. I looked up and saw the car lying at an angle close to me. Then...' She stopped and grasped Manley's hand so tight, he saw the whites of her knuckles. 'Oh, Hugh, it was like a nightmare. I... I watched as the car slowly began to topple forward. I tried to move, but before I could do so, the car fell onto my leg. I felt a searing pain shoot through me and passed out. The next thing I remember was feeling terribly cold and being lifted up and being placed on what I now know, was a stretcher.' She paused then, nervously licking her lips, said, 'could I have another drink of water, please, Hugh?'

Manley withdrew his hands from hers and poured out half a glass of water. 'What a terrible ordeal, no wonder it seemed like a nightmare,' he said, watching her hand shaking slightly as she drained the glass.

'When I eventually woke up, I was lying here in bed, wearing an operating gown. The curtains were dawn and a light was on and a nurse was sitting by my bed. The foot of the bed was raised and I seemed to be lying at an angle. My mouth felt terribly dry and I asked her for a drink of water. I asked her what time it was and she told me it was eight o'clock at night. That was when I remembered the car falling onto me. I tried to move my foot and was about to ask her how badly I was injured, when the doctor came in.'

At that moment, a knock came at the door and nurse came in carrying an enamel tray containing dressings, surgical instruments, a fluted bottle of antiseptic, a pair of latex gloves and a surgical mask.

'Sorry to interrupt you, 'she said apologetically, 'but it's nine thirty and I'll have to ask you to wait in the sister's office while I attend to Miss Trevethick,' she added, giving Manley and apologetic smile. 'Sister O'Malley has left a packet of sandwiches for you in her office, sir, you can collect them before you leave.'

'Thank you, nurse,' Manley replied. He gave Laura quick kiss and stood up.

Manley picked up his gas mask and helmet and left. The ward lights were dimmed and the patients were in bed. A nurse carrying a bed pan covered in a cloth emerged from behind a screen and disappeared into the bathroom.

Manley quietly opened the office door and switched on the light. The office was neatly furnished and compact. Curtains were drawn across a solitary window. Manley sat down on a chair facing a desk, on which rested a telephone, an ink stand and several fawn coloured folders. A small parcel wrapped in brown paper lay on a leather-bound blotting pad next to an old copy of *The Daily Mirror*. Manley smiled, thinking how thoughtful it was of Sister O'Malley, who must have known he had a long journey ahead of him. The clock on the wall above the desk read nine thirty-five. The headlines on the front of the newspaper reported the success of General Auchinleck's forces in North Africa repulsing Rommel's latest attempt to reach Cairo. This was a stark reminder to Manley of the forthcoming raid on Dieppe. Ten minutes later, the door opened and the nurse told him he could go back in and see Laura.

Laura was sitting up in bed. Her shoulders were covered by a woollen shawl. She had combed her hair and the touch of lipstick she wore was in sharp contrast to the paleness of her face.

'Everything all right?' he asked, pulling the chair by her bed.

'Yes, darling,' Laura replied, 'the nurse said my leg is healing well.'

'When did the doctor tell you how severe your injury was?' he asked, taking both her hands in his.

Laura nervously bit her lip and took a deep breath. 'That was the worst part. He told me the bones in my ankle were completely shattered, and he had to amputate it above the ankle. It took some time to sink in. And when it did, I immediately thought of you. Oh, darling,' she said, clutching his hand, 'I thought you'd…'

'And you were quite wrong, my love,' Manley replied as he kissed her hands. He then looked at her and asked, 'But tell me, what happened to FP and Susan?'

'Susan, poor thing, injured her head and had a badly bruised face. FP had some sort of head injury and bruised ribs,' said Laura, 'both of them were kept here for two days. Apparently, the hospital informed RNB and they sent transport to take them back to Portsmouth. Susan is now on leave. I received a letter from her and FP. He didn't say where he was. I didn't reply. They came to see me before they left but I was asleep and Sister O'Malley wouldn't allow them in.'

'And your father…'

'The poor dear's been worried sick,' Laura replied, 'he's been in every afternoon.'

'Did he mention sending you to see a prosthesis specialist when you've recovered?'

'Yes, he did,' Laura replied, 'and a private physiotherapist to help me walk.'

The door opened and a nurse popped her head around. 'Sorry, sir,' she said, apologetically, 'but it's gone ten and…

'Thank you, nurse,' Manley replied, 'I understand.'

She gave a quick smile and left. Immediately the door closed, their arms went around each other. Their kiss was hard and passionate and in doing so, Manley felt her tears wet and warm against his face.

'Oh, Hugh, darling,' Laura gasped as they broke their embrace, 'if anything happened to you, I think I'd die.'

'Nothing's going happened to me,' Manley replied, using a finger to wipe away a tear from the corner of one of her eyes, 'so please try not to worry.' They slowly removed their arms from each other. Manley stood up and gathered his Burberry, steel helmet and gas mask. Looking into Laura's tear-stained eyes, he said, 'Remember, darling, I'll always love you.' He opened the door, and with the heartrending sounds of Laura's sobs ringing in his ears, slowly walked away.

CHAPTER THIRTY-FIVE

Manley returned to *Helix* shortly after 0700 on Monday 3rd August. The journey had been long and tiresome but he was able to catch a few hours' sleep.

'That was some round trip, sir,' said Lieutenant Powers, who greeted him as he stepped over the brow. 'How do you feel?'

'Not too bad, thank you, Number One,' Manley replied, returning Powers' salute, 'but I'll feel much better after a shower and a good breakfast.'

An hour later, after colours, he was sitting at his desk flitting through the signal log, when he heard the pipe, "all ratings going on leave fall in on the quarterdeck". He closed the log and went to the quarterdeck, passing on the way, ratings carrying small brown cases and canvas holdalls.

'Not going on leave, then, sir?' Asked a rating.

'Next month,' Manley jokingly replied. 'And I hope you're not taking to many duty-free cigarettes ashore.'

'As if we would, sir,' another rating answered, laughing.

Shortly afterwards, Manley and Lieutenant Powers watched as most of the ship's company left the ship. Throughout the rest of the morning, the officers also went on leave.

'How many ratings, living locally, who volunteered to remain, are on board?' Manley asked Powers.

'Thirty, sir,' Powers replied. 'The chief engineer, the chief stoker, the chief cook and bosun's mate, Petty Officers Hardman and PO Frost, Steward Turpin and twenty-three ratings.'

'Good, and tell them I'll make up for the leave they've lost whenever possible,' Manley answered, 'and as I'll be remaining on board, I suggest you go ashore tonight and see that popsy of yours.'

'Thank you, sir,' Powers replied, feeling slightly embarrassed, 'I'm sure she'll be more than pleased. And by the way, I've left a signal on your desk for approval, sir, it's for additional ammunition.'

'Indeed, Number One,' said Manley, giving Powers a searching look. 'That sounds like you're expecting us to sea rather soon.'

With a wry smile, Powers answered, 'Well, sir, I have an inkling that something's in the wind, so it's better to be safe than sorry.'

'Quite so,' Manley calmly replied, and walked away.

The rest of the morning was spent checking signal lists for stores the heads of departments had submitted to him. Among them was a request for additional supply of 4.7 shell and ammunition for the Vickers and pom-poms. Manley sat back in his chair, looking at the request form and wondering if Powers had more than an "inkling" that something, indeed, was in the wind.

In the afternoon, Manley and Powers went ashore and checked the ship's moorings. This was followed by a walk around the ship, ensuring everything was secure. Except for a few ratings engaged in cleaning duties, the ship looked deserted.

'The words "skeleton crew", seems very apt, eh, sir,' Powers remarked as they walked down the main corridor towards the quarter deck.

'Yes, I must admit, it does feel odd,' Manley replied. 'If it wasn't for the sound of the generators, we could be in dry dock.'

That night, Manley lay in his bunk listening to the soporific hiss of the air circulating in the punkah-louvres and imagining Laura, lying in bed, hoping she wasn't in pain. Finally, he fell asleep, feeling her arms around him and her warm lips on his.

The next morning, Manley was sitting at his desk writing up the ship's log when Lieutenant Powers knocked on the door and was told to enter.

'This just arrived, sir,' he said, handing Manley a signal. 'It appears we're getting a new first lieutenant.'

'And about time, too,' Manley replied. However, as he read the signal, he felt the blood drain from his face. Unable to believe his eyes, he reread the signal.

From C-in-C Portsmouth.

To Commander H. Manley, R.N. HMS Helix.

Date 5th August 1942.

Lieutenant Commander, The Right Honourable Basil Foster-Price, R.N., has been appointed to H.M.S Helix as First Lieutenant and will report for duty on Thursday 6th August, 1942.

'My God, FP,' Manley muttered as he slowly closed the log. 'Bloody FP.'

'The Right Honourable, eh, sir,' said Powers, 'how are we to address him?'

'You can forget the title,' Manley angrily replied, 'just plain Number One. Is that understood?'

'Yes, sir, have you, err… served with him before,' Manley answered, noticing the obvious animosity in the captain's voice.'

'No,' Manley replied, 'but we met briefly some time go.'

'Are you all right, sir?' Powers asked. 'You've look rather pale.'

'Err… yes, thank you,' Manley managed to reply, 'carry on and ask the steward to bring me a strong cup of coffee.'

'Very good, sir,' Powers replied, taken aback by Manley's strange reaction to what he thought would be good news.

No sooner had Powers left than Manley began wondering how he could get rid of FP. This was the man he was almost sure was responsible for Laura's accident. Suddenly, the thought of seeing FP every day and night for the foreseeable future made him feel physically sick. But he asked himself, what could he do? The contingencies of war meant experienced officers were in short supply. Therefore, any request to the C-in-C would certainly be refused. Furthermore, any excuse for doing so on personal grounds would almost certainly meet with disapproval. So, his hands were tied. Still lost in thought, he hardly heard the steward come in and place a cup of coffee on his leather-bound blotter. And more importantly, he reflected while sipping his drink, it was vital not to allow his personal feeling for FP to cloud his judgment and affect his responsibilities.

That night he hardly slept. Every time he closed his eyes, he saw Laura's tear-stained face and the tall, fair-haired figure of FP standing by her bedside, looking at her with his beady brown eyes. He hardly heard "call the hands" at 0600 or notice the steward standing by his bunk, holding a cup of tea.

FP arrived on board *Helix* shortly after 0900. Lieutenant Powers knocked on Manley's door and was told to enter. The door opened, and seeing FP standing behind Powers, Manley felt his heart rate increase.

'Lieutenant Commander Foster-Price, sir,' said Powers.

'Yes, I can see that,' snapped Manley, 'carry on and close the door.'

No sooner had Powers left, than FP's slightly tanned face broke into a wide grin. He stepped closer to Manley's desk, and proffering his hand, said in that plummy voice Manley remembered so well, 'Hugh, old boy, I can't tell you how good it is to see you.'

Ignoring FP's hand, Manley remained seated, and staring coldly at FP, replied, 'I wish I could say the same.' Then, doing his best to control his pent-up anger, Manley raised his voice, then went on. 'And remember, I'm your commanding officer and you will address me as "sir" at all times. Now stand to attention.'

Taken aback by Manley's outburst, FP's face turned crimson. 'But I thought you'd be glad to see me... *sir*,' he cautiously replied, shuffling to attention.

'Glad to see you,' Manley seethed, 'if I had my way I'd have you off my ship before you'd unpacked your gear.'

'But, why?' FP asked, looking somewhat puzzled.

'Because,' Manley grunted, 'it was due to you that Laura is now in hospital having had part of her leg amputated.'

'Nonsense,' FP answered hotly. 'It was an accident. It had been raining pretty hard and the road was slippery. The car swerved and...'

Manley interrupted him. '*Because you were drunk and lost control of the car,*' he thundered.

FP lent forward, and placing both hands on Manley's deck, narrowed his beady brown eyes and staring keenly at Manley, said, 'No, I wasn't drunk, and even though you are my commanding officer, *sir,* you've no right to accuse me of such a thing, so, I suggest you contact the C-in-C's office and ask for me to be to reappointed.'

'You know bloody well personal problems wouldn't be accepted as a valid reason to get you removed,' Manley replied, 'but I suppose you could always use your father's influence...'

'And you know I wouldn't do that,' FP answered, then standing back from the desk, added, 'so it looks like I'm stuck with you.'

'And unfortunately, I with you,' Manley replied firmly, 'but one hint of inefficiency, or anything else, and I'll have you removed. Do I make myself clear?'

'Perfectly, *sir*,' F P answered bluntly.

'I haven't received your service documents, so what was your last ship?' asked Manley.

'I've recently finished a gunnery course at Whale Island,' FP replied, 'prior to that I was navigating officer in *Airedale* on escort duty in the Atlantic.'

'Good,' Manley said, 'so you'll be familiar with the Hunts?'

'Very much so,' replied FP. 'But may I ask what the ship's movements are?'

'As you are aware, the ship's company are on leave,' Manley replied. 'When they return tomorrow, I'll be briefing the officers. That's when you'll receive your answer. Understood?'

'Yes, sir,' FP replied curtly.

'Right then,' said Manley, 'as the Chief Bosun's Mate Harris is on board, I suggest you find him and have him take you around the ship. Now,' he added, dismissively, 'carry on, and remember what I said.'

'Before I go, sir,' said FP, putting on his cap, 'how is Laura? I did write but haven't received an answer.'

'I wonder why,' Manley replied sarcastically, 'but if you must know, she's as well as can be expected, now get out.'

After FP had gone, Manley realised his hands were shaking and he was covered in sweat.

Just before morning "stand easy" was piped, Sub Lieutenant Brownlow arrived carrying a buff-coloured envelope marked, "Top Secret".

'Thank you, Sub,' said Manley, accepting the envelope, 'I trust you had a pleasant leave?'

'Yes, thank you, sir,' Brownlow replied, 'but like the rest of the officers, I'm dying to know what's brewing.'

'Well, you'll soon know,' Manley answered with a smile, 'now please carry on.'

As Manley thought, the envelope contained the details of Operation Jubilee, and for the next half an hour, he carefully studied its contents.

During the evening, ratings and officers began to return from leave and by 0900 on Friday 7th August, everyone was on board. At 1300, all officers stood up as Manley, followed by FP, entered the wardroom.

'Stand at ease, gentlemen, and smoke if you want to,' said Manley, who, like FP, stood in front of the officers, whose faces he had come to know as well as his own. After giving FP a quick glance, he went on. 'Before I go into our future movements, I would like to introduce you to Lieutenant Commander Foster-Price, our new first lieutenant.

'Good afternoon, gentlemen,' FP said, in his unmistakable plummy voice. 'I won't keep you long, only to say that I intend to meet each one of you over the next few days. In the meantime, if you have any immediate problems, don't hesitate to come and see me. Thank you.'

During the next half hour Manley explained the details of Operation Jubilee, adding, 'Dieppe is about eighty miles from Portsmouth. At 0100 on the nineteenth of August, *Helix*, in company with *Albrighton*, *Berkeley*, *Brocklesby*, *Bleasdale* and *Garth*, will leave Portsmouth and rendezvous with the Polish destroyer, *Slazak*, five miles west of the Solent. Lieutenant Commander Byron in *Brocklesby* will be Captain D. Now, as it will be British Summer Time, the clocks will be advanced one hour and it will be almost daylight when you leave. I must stress that surprise is essential; if the invasion fleet is spotted, then we're in trouble. That's why, as I've said, the flanking attacks have been set for 0540. The six destroyers will proceed to the coast and bombard the headlands overlooking Red and White Beaches. *Helix* and *Albrighton* will detach from the destroyers and support the landings directly in front of Dieppe. Any questions?'

'I have one, sir,' said Lieutenant Powers, 'how long will the bombardment last for?'

'Captain Hughes-Hallet will determine this,' Manley replied, 'and send a signal to Lieutenant Commander Byron, who will inform the other destroyers. Meanwhile, individual captains are to use their initiative, and get as close to the beach as possible.'

'Excuse me, sir,' said Lieutenant Weir, 'but I'm somewhat concerned. You said the only support the landings will have will only come from the destroyers and a few attacks by the RAF. Surely the four-point shells from our destroyers won't be powerful enough if the enemy are well dug in.'

'Your question is a good one,' Manley answered, feeling slightly uncomfortable. 'But I can't give you an answer. We'll just have to wait and see.'

'Will you be addressing the ship's company, sir? asked Sub Lieutenant Milton.

'As security is paramount, I'll be doing so when we put to sea,' said Manley, 'now, if there's no more questions, I suggest you carry on.'

Half an hour later, Manley and OOD Sub Lieutenant Jewitt were watching PO Hardman overseeing seamen practicing raising and lowering the port lifeboat.

'Everything all right, PO?' Manley asked Hardman.

'Well, sir,' Hardman quietly replied, 'I'll feel a lot better when we get back from this bloody place, Dieppe.'

'How the blazes do you know that?' snapped Manley, glancing furtively around. 'That's supposed to be top secret.'

Hardman shook his head and gave a slight laugh. 'It seems the rating who was on duty outside the room where you had your meeting with the admiral, overheard everything that was said. Now, he's married to one of the women in the NAAFI, and he told her everything. Now everyone knows what's happening.

Manley took a deep breath, and giving a quick roll of his eyes, glanced at Jewitt, and said, 'So much for security.'

The news of the forthcoming raid on Dieppe quickly spread throughout the ship. In the senior ratings mess Paddy O'Malley looked at Harry Johnson, who, like Paddy, was getting ready to go ashore, and said, 'Be Jesus, Harry, do you know where this place Dieppe is?'

'Yes,' Harry replied, making sure his shoes were properly shined, 'I think it's some small fishing port on the French coast.'

'Maybe the Frogs will throw some fresh fish our way,' chimed in Dai Evans.

'I've a feeling we'll get more than a few fish thrown at us, Taffy, my son,' Bob Shilling replied warily.

'Och, I hear those French partys, don't shave under their arms,' Jock Forbes said to Dutch Holland. They were in the seaman's mess, finishing of mugs of tea before going ashore.

'I don't care,' Dutch replied, giving Jock a salacious grin, 'as long as there's plenty between you know where.'

Throughout the next week, the ship was a hive of activity. Stores were replenished. Lighters came alongside and ammunition taken on board. Manley watched as FP supervised everything, and was secretly impressed with his efficiency. One morning, Manley met the thick set figure of Chief Bosun's Mate Charlie Jackson, on the quarterdeck.

'Morning, Chief,' Manley said, feeling the warm breeze fan his face, 'how are you getting along with the first lieutenant?'

The Buffer's weather-beaten features broke into a wide grin. 'All right, but he don't half speak posh, like one of those BBC announcers.'

'Yes, I know what you mean,' Manley replied with a smile.

'Anyway, sir,' the buffer went on, 'he seems pretty strict. Yesterday he put the guns crew through their paces, but wasn't satisfied, and told Lieutenant Powers to give them extra practice, so he did.'

'Indeed,' Manley muttered to himself. He was about to walk away when he heard the ringing of the quarterdeck telephone.

'Excuse me, sir,' shouted duty QM Able Seaman Buster Brown, holding the receiver, 'there's call for you.'

How odd, thought Manley. Usually, telephone calls for him were put through to his cabin, 'Thank you,' Manley said, taking hold of the receiver.

'Commander Manley, who is this?'

'It's me, darling,' cried Laura.

'Good Lord,' said Manley, 'it's wonderful to hear you, but how did you get through?'

'Sister O'Malley let me use the phone in her office,' Laura replied. 'I told the operator in barracks I was your sister and it was an emergency.'

'How enterprising, darling,' Manley said, smiling. 'But tell me, how are you?'

'Goods news,' she replied. 'The doctor's told me I'll be going home in two weeks. Father has arranged for a daily visit from a nurse and Doctor Pascoe, our family GP.'

'That's wonderful,' Manley said, then added, 'but I'm afraid I must go, I have defaulters in ten minutes.'

'Oh, darling, do take care. I love you so much, and…'

'Try not to worry,' Manley said, and feeling a lump come into his throat, added, 'I love you also, darling, and one day you won't have to lie about being my wife. Goodbye, I'll see you soon.'

CHAPTER THIRTY-SIX

Shortly before 0030 on 18th August, FP went to Manley's cabin, knocked and was told to enter.

'The ship is ready for sea, sir,' he said standing smartly in front of Manley who was sat at his desk. 'Special sea duty men closed up, Chief Coxswain Barnes at the wheel and all deadlights secured.'

'Thank you, Number One,' Manley replied firmly, 'I'll be up top presently.'

Half an hour later, with *Brocklesby* in the van, the six destroyers slipped their moorings, and sailed silently out of Portsmouth harbour into the Solent. It was daylight and a chilly northern breeze rippled an otherwise calm sea.

Like everyone else on *Helix*'s bridge, Manley wore a duffle coat over his uniform. He was sitting on his chair, closely watching *Albrighton'*s foamy wash churning up the dark blue sea, a hundred yards in front his ship's bow.

'Fall out special se duty men, Number One,' Manley said to FP, who was standing near the binnacle, 'I don't want to get too close in case we have to suddenly increase speed.'

No sooner had he spoken, than PO Signalman Spud Tate cried, 'Warship approaching one mile to port, sir.'

'That'll be the Polish destroyer, *Slazak*,' said Manley, 'she'll come with us, before breaking away to protect the eastern flank of the convoys.'

'*Brocklesby* flashing, sir, '"all ships increase speed to twenty knots".'

Just then, Sub Lieutenant Brownlow came onto the bridge. 'Excuse me, sir,' he said to Manley, 'I've just picked up a signal from Dover. A German convoy has been sighted heading down channel.'

'Then here's hoping it doesn't discover Number Three Commando approaching Yellow Beach,' Manley replied, thoughtfully stroking his chin.

'Star shells exploding about five miles to port, sir,' reported Able Seaman Dusty Miller from the crow's nest.

Everyone on the bridge looked away to their left and saw small bursts of yellow explosions lighting up the night sky.

'With a bit of luck, the Germans will think it's only a small raid,' FP said to Manley.

'I hope you're right, Number One,' Manley, replied, 'or else we've lost the element of surprise and the bastards will be waiting for us.'

Shortly after 0400, Manley, using his binoculars, saw a long, shingle beach and roof tops of houses, glistening in the early morning sunshine. He then focussed on the rocky headland overlooking the western side of the beach. This was the target *Helix* had been given. He recalled the question raised at the meeting with the admiral concerning the effectiveness of the destroyer's 4.7 shells against a well dug enemy. Nevertheless, he was determined that *Helix* and her crew would do their best. Manley then looked around, and saw through the grey, morning mist, *Albrighton*, a few miles on *Helix*'s port beam.

'Enemy coast roughly fifteen miles away, three assault ships and dozens of landing craft dead ahead,' Able Seaman Dinga Bell reported from the crow's nest. Simultaneously, Dolly Gray reported a large cluster of small and large black dots on his pale green radar screen.

'That'll be *Glengyle, Prince Charles* and *Prince Leopold,* who have just disembarked from the Canadians into the landing craft,' Manley said to FP, while focussing his binoculars on dozens of landing craft heading towards Dieppe.

'Better sound action stations, Number One, and hoist the battle ensign.'

In a matter of minutes, PO Yeoman Tate had raised the large union jack to the top of the mainmast. A sudden gust of wind made it flap defiantly as if announcing its presence to the enemy. Meanwhile, each department reported they were closed up. Manley unhooked the tannoy and in a calm voice, said, 'We are about to open fire as we escort the commandos inland. I will keep you informed.'

Most of the ship's company had a fairly good idea what awaited them, nevertheless, Manley's words immediately increased the tension that had been felt since the ship left Portsmouth.

'Keep us informed, he says,' said Dutch Holland to his oppo, Dinga Bell, both of whom were manning the port pom-pom. 'From where we're sitting, we'll have a bird's eye view of everything.'

'Aye, including the fuckin' Jerry planes,' Dinga sardonically replied. 'Now, look what's happening, *a bloody smoke screen.*'

As he spoke HMS *Calpe* appeared a few hundred yards in front of the LCIs laying a long stream of billowing white smoke.

FP gave Manley a sideways glance and said, 'Bloody good idea, sir.' While adjusting his steel helmet over his anti-flash gear, he said, 'but it'll disguise our fall of shot.'

'Well, Number One,' Manley replied with a sardonic grin, 'Guns has been given the details for shelling the headland, so here's hoping the smoke will clear away in time for him to hit the target.'

The time was 0450. Suddenly, the ear-splitting barrage from *Berkeley, Bleasdale,* and *Garth* rent the air. All four were broadside on, allowing all their guns to bare. Ripples of explosions sprung up on the headlands. Debris, sand and bits of stone flew into the air as shells erupted along the beach. The casino disappeared under a cloud of dense black smoke. The barrage continued for over an hour then, abruptly stopped, leaving the air thick with the acrid smell of cordite.

On *Helix*'s bridge everyone watched as four lines of twelve LCAs, each one carrying up to forty Canadian troops, disappear into the billowing smoke screen.

'Sound action stations, Number One,' ordered Manley, 'and hoist the battle ensign.' Manley immediately contacted Lieutenant Powers who was on the gun direction platform, situated above the bridge. Seconds later *Helix* rocked heavily as all her 4.7 guns opened up.

'Up five degrees,' Powers shouted to the gun aimers. This was followed by another barrage and the inevitable jerking motion as the guns fired again.

Using their binoculars, Manley and FP saw puffs of black smoke explode onto the western headland and medieval castle.

'Starboard five, revolutions ten,' snapped Manley.

Almost straight away, *Helix* heeled to the right and headed into the smoke screen. Suddenly the daylight disappeared as *Helix,* passed through a miasma of white smoke. Seconds later the ship emerged some two hundred yards behind the fourth wave of LCAs. Flashes of gunfire from inland were quickly followed by jets of water as shells exploded all around the LCAs. Sadly, two of them suffered direct hits and began billowing palls of yellow and red smoke. Suddenly one of them exploded. Jets of yellow flames shot into the air. In seconds the stricken vessel slowly sank leaving the sea a swirling mass of debris and dead bodies. Another LCA was hit and then another. But undaunted, the LCAs pressed on towards the beach, two miles away.

'Turn five degrees to port, Number One, it'll enable all our heavy guns to deliver broadsides.'

'But won't that make us easier targets, sir?' asked FP. As he spoke a shell exploded about twenty yards away on the ship's starboard beam.

'Those Canadians are taking a helluva pounding and they need our help,' Manley shouted. 'So that's the chance we'll have to take.' A few seconds later *Helix* heeled over to the left.

'*All guns open fire*,' shouted Manley.

Immediately, *Helix*'s 4.7 guns, pom-poms, and Oerlikons began firing at prearranged targets on the beach and further inland. The cacophony was deafening as the acrid smell of smoke filled the air and stung the eyes.

Gradually the breeze dispersed the smoke, allowing the enemy to have a clearer view of the oncoming craft. Everyone on *Helix*'s bridge watched anxiously as the first wave hit the beach. The ramps were lowered, allowing the Essex Scottish to hurry ashore.

Manley adjusted his binoculars and said, 'Many of them appear to be bogged down in the shale, but most have reached the sea wall, lying between the town and the beach, Number One.'

'Yes, I can see them, sir,' FP shouted over the intermittent roar of gunfire, 'but I'm afraid quite a lot have been hit by gunfire and haven't made it. It's almost as if the bastards were waiting for them.'

'Yes, you're right, Number One,' yelled Manley, 'the poor beggars seem to be pinned down.'

Training his binoculars left, close to the casino, Manley cried, 'Good Lord, the Royal Hamiltons on White Beach have landed directly in front of a pillbox and are being mown down like flies. Those that have made it are crammed against the sea wall.'

The men manning the 4.7s and machine guns could also see what was happening.

'Where the fuck is the RAF,' Tansey Lee said to Bob Rose, as he closed one of the breeches of B gun. 'Those poor bastards are being pounded to buggery.'

'I don't know about the RAF,' shouted Rose, 'but what we really need is the heavy guns of a cruiser or monitor. Our 4.7s don't seem to be making much difference, especially if the sods are well dug in.'

Those closed up in the claustrophobic atmosphere of the engine and boiler rooms were not so fortunate. All they could do was wait, listen and pray that a bomb or shell wouldn't suddenly hit the ship. At least the first aid party, mustered on the canteen flat and in the sick bay received reports of the landings from the medical officer, who occasionally ventured onto the bridge before returning below deck.

On the bridge, Manley adjusted his binoculars and saw the bodies of men strewn in front of the sea wall. 'The poor sods are being massacred,' he cried.

'So much for the second-rate soldiers the powers said would be defending the town,' FP yelled. 'Whoever they are, they want locking up.'

'I couldn't agree more,' shouted Manley, 'but where the hell are the tanks? It's now almost 1000. They should've been here earlier to support the infantry.'

No sooner had Manley stopped talking than the high-pitched voice of Dinga Bell in the crow's nest reported three lines of LCTs (Landing Craft, Tank), approaching two hundred yards on *Helix* and *Albrighton*'s port beam.

'Thank the Lord for that, Number One,' Manley shouted.

'Better late, than never, I suppose, sir,' FP replied, 'their extra firepower should help the Canadians to get off the beach.'

CHAPTER THIRTY-SEVEN

The time was now 0530. Despite shells exploding all around *Helix* and *Albrighton,* both vessels continued to keep firing at the enemy's positions. In between dodging squalls of spray, Manley was able to see the first wave of LCTs arrive on Red Beach. Each LCT carried three Calgary tanks, equipped with bundles of wooden palings to grip the shingle. At first this seemed to work perfectly as each tank landed safely. Unfortunately, one LCT lost its track and was so damage and holed by shellfire that it sank.

'I see the second wave of troops have got off and are heading towards the town,' cried FP, who, like Manley, was watching the LCAs arrive.

'Yes, but tone of the LCAs has lost its bow door,' retorted Manley, 'and I can just about see many of the crew lying in the water and on the ramp. It looks they're all dead.'

'Third wave is coming in, sir,' cried FP, as another shell exploded thirty yards away on the port beam.

'Yes, and one of them has been hit and has lost its tracks,' Manley replied loudly.

Both officers watched as a second tank was hit by mortar fire and began billowing clouds of black smoke. Manley heard himself shouting, *'For God's sake, get out.'* One by one, the tank crew scrambled out of the gun turret, only to be hit by machine gun fire.

The LCTs now came under intense mortar bombardment and machine fire. One LCT made three attempts to beach before landing her three tanks. The first tank managed to reach the beach, but as the ramp went down, many Canadians were raked with machine gun and never made it to the sea wall. The third, was hit by mortar fire and began to spew clouds of black smoke. Most of her troops were either killed or wounded. The last LCT landed safely but due to engine failure, became grounded in the middle of the beach. Luckily most of the troops managed to get ashore just before the craft was hit by mortar bombs.

Manley watched as the LCTs managed to land a dozen tanks. Looking like beached whales, some slipped their tracks and became bogged down in the soft shingle. Others lay burning, surrounded by the bodies of their crews. Those tanks that managed to get over the sea wall and onto the promenade were prevented to do so by anti-tank obstacles. Braving the deadly fusillade of bullets, the Canadian sappers engineers tried to remove the obstacles but were instantly cut down by machine-gun fire. The rest of the tanks remained on the beach, engaging the enemy positions with their 6-pounders, until they ran out of ammunition and had to surrender. (Of the 169 sappers that went ashore, 152 were killed or wounded.)

Manley and FP looked on in horror and saw Red and White beaches littered with dead. Some of those wounded were seen to try and crawl up the beach only to be picked off by snipers in the casino.

'Jesus Christ, sir,' FP uttered to Manley. 'What a bloody shambles.'

'Bloody is the right word,' Manley replied. He was about to continue speaking, when Dinga Bell's voice in the crow's nest interrupted him. '*Enemy aircraft approaching from the east.*' Straight away Manley and FP trained their binoculars upwards. The time was 0600. A stiff warm breeze blew from the south and clusters of white, fluffy clouds raced across a pale blue sky.

'Focke-Wulfs and Messerschmitts, this time, sir,' said Sub Lieutenant Baker. 'About two hundred of them.'

'They'll probable make for the civilian ships,' Manley remarked, as one by one the enemy planes peeled off and headed downwards.

'Spitfires and Hurricanes approaching green four thousand feet,' cried Dinga Bell, 'roughly fifty, of 'em.'

Shielding their eyes from the sun's glare, everyone on the bridge watched the Spitfires, followed by the Hurricanes, peel off and dive towards the enemy. Suddenly, the *rat-tat-tat* of machine gunfire rent the air.

'Go on, me hearties, give 'em hell,' yelled Wacker Payne, the port lookout as the enemy planes broke formation.

'Looks like the Spits are outnumbered, sir,' shouted FP, as he watched a dozen or so Focke-Wulfs dive towards the civilian liners.

'I agree, Number One,' retorted Manley, 'and we can't open fire on them because we'd hit the Spits as well as the enemy.'

'About a dozen Focke-Wulfs are diving towards the beaches, sir,' yelled Sub Lieutenant Baker.

'Yes, I see them,' shouted Manley, 'pom-poms and Oerlikons, open fire.'

Seconds later, streams of bright yellow tracer and machine gun bullets streaked from the guns as the enemy planes came within range.

'Enemy bombers approaching, red five thousand,' yelled Able Seaman Payne.

'Dorniers and Heinkels, sir,' Sub Lieutenant Baker cried, scanning the sky with his binoculars.

'The bastards are making for the liners,' cried FP.

Sticks of bombs, twirling angrily, fell towards *Prince Charles* and *Glengyle*, lying three miles off Red and White Beaches. In an instant, both vessels disappeared under walls of white water as the enemies bombs exploded all around them. As the spray gradually settled, a thick plume of black smoke from *Glengyle* could be seen curling wildly into the air. Luckily, *Prince Charles* appeared to be unharmed.

Meanwhile, a bitter dog fight ensued during which time several Spitfires were hit; two, burst into flames, three streaming black smoke went into a steep dive. Everyone watched anxiously as parachutes burst open and floated seawards. Two Spitfires broke away from the fighting and dived down and raked the headland with cannon fire, then soared upwards and re-joined the melee. Minutes later, a Spitfire broke off the engagement, and produced a smoke screen along the edge of Red and White Beach.

'Fat lot of use that'll do,' bellowed FP, 'they'd be more use giving support to the poor devils being pinned down on the beach.'

To everyone's surprise, one by one, the Spitfires broke off the engagement and headed west with a dozen Messerschmitt's in hot pursuit.

'I say, sir,' shouted FP, 'I wonder why the Spits are leaving, surely they can't have run out of ammunition.'

'Running short of fuel, more likely,' Manley, yelled. 'You see, the Spits are eighty miles away from their base and only have limited endurance.'

Suddenly, their attention was diverted by Dinga Bell's voice coming over the bridge intercom. *'Berkeley on fire. Looks like she's hit a mine.'*

Moments later, PO Signalman Tate reported, 'Signal from *Brocklesby,* sir. "*Berkeley bombed and is sinking. Albrighton to take off crew then scuttle. Helix to remain on station".'*

Seconds Dixie Dean, the port lookout yelled, *'Enemy aircraft approaching on the port beam, sir.'*

All heads immediately turned from focusing their binoculars on *Berkeley,* and saw a Messerschmitt swoop over the ship, its black crosses clearly visible on the underside of the fighter's pale green wings.

'Hard a starboard, coxswain,' yelled Manley, watching intently as the bomber dropped a stick of bombs. At the same time, *Helix* heeled precariously to the right. Manley clutched hold of the arms of his chair to prevent himself toppling onto the deck. However, this didn't prevent him and the others being drenched with warm spray as the bombs exploded some ten yards away.

As the ship slowly righted itself, FP picked himself up off the slippery deck and cried, 'That was too damn close for comfort, sir.'

'Quite so,' came Manley's understated reply. He focussed his binoculars onto the beach. 'My God, Number One,' he cried, 'Red and White Beaches are still taking heavy fire from the eastern headland, and the men remain pinned down.'

'And I can see men crouching in a ditch between the sea wall and the promenade,' said FP. 'Most of the poor blighters look either dead or wounded.'

'Aircraft approaching about five hundred yards on starboard beam, sir, looks like a Messerschmitt,' shouted Sub Lieutenant Baker.

All eyes turned and saw the fighter streaking towards them, almost at sea level. From the edge of both its wings, pairs of yellow flames blazed away.

'Everyone, take cover,' yelled Manley, as the sharp crackle of gunfire rent the air.

'*You as well, sir,*' cried FP, launching himself in front at Manley. Seconds later the sharp sound of bullets peppering the starboard side of the bridge, and the tinkling of glass as the bridge consort shattered into little pieces.

Unfortunately, Manley's warning came too late for Wacker Payne and Wiggy Bennett, whose bodies lay crumpled and bleeding on the deck of the port and starboard wings.

Suddenly, with the exception of the dull throb of the engines, everything was quiet. That was when Manley became aware he was lying on his back with FP on top of him.

'Thank you, Number One,' Manley grunted, looking at FP's face lying against his left shoulder. 'You can get up now, I'm all right,' he added trying to push FP away. In doing so, he put his arms around FP, and felt his hands warm and wet. He slowly withdrew them and saw them covered in blood. '*Number One, how are you?*' cried Manley, turning his head and looking at FP's glazed eyes and ashen face. '*For God's sake, speak to me.*' Seeing FP's lips moving he placed his head close to FP's mouth.

'T… tell… Laura,' muttered FP, his voice almost incoherent against the sound of gunfire, 'I… I'm sorry.' His eyes then closed and his head lolled, lifeless, to on side.

Just then, Sub Lieutenant Baker and Lieutenant Powers appeared. 'Don't just stand there,' Manley shouted, 'the first lieutenant's been injured, send for the doctor.'

'I already have, sir,' Baker replied. He knelt down and felt for the carotid pulse in FP's neck, but sadly, found none. 'But I'm afraid it's too late for a doctor, sir, he's gone.' Baker manged to say, over the ear-splitting gunfire from A and B guns.

While *Helix*'s heavy and light armament continued to pound away, FP's body was draped with a blanket by PO Steward Sandy Powel. It was then taken by some of the first aid party to Manley's cabin and placed in a corner and covered with sheet. A blanket was placed over the blood-stained corpses of Wacker Payne and Wiggy Bennett, and taken by the rest of the first aid party, and secured to stanchions on the quarterdeck.

Meanwhile, Manley, badly shaken by FP's, sudden death, was finding it hard to concentrate on fighting the ship. Despite the ongoing sound of battle, he kept on hearing FP's last words before he died. Regaining his composure, he looked at PO Tate and said, 'Better get a signal off to C-in-C, Portsmouth.' Tate took out a pad and pencil. 'Say, *"Regret to inform the death of Lieutenant Commander, the Right Honourable, Basil Foster-Price, RN, killed in action on board HMS Helix on 18 August 1942. Able Seaman Bennet, Able Seaman Payne also killed. Please inform next of kin"*.' Manley paused then added, 'Insert their Christian names and official numbers of Bennett and Payne.'

'Very good, sir,' Tate replied quietly and hurriedly left the bridge.

'How close is the ship from the shore, Pilot?' he managed to ask Baker, while doing his best to focus his binoculars on a group of Essex Scottish, who crouching low, were weaving their way up the promenade in an attempt to join small contingent of their comrades, who were also under heavy fire.

'Just over two hundred yards, sir,' Baker shouted, 'and five fathoms clear of the bottom.'

Manley was about to order the ship to move fifty yards closer to the beach, when PO Tate reported, 'Signal from *Brocklesby*, sir. *"Calpe informs, Essex Scottish, Fusiliers Mont Royal and A Commando Royal Marines being sent to land on Red Beach. Ships to continue support"*.'

'They must be the reserves,' said Manley. 'Thank you, PO, acknowledge.'

'Here's hoping this will tip the balance and allow the Canadians to move inland, sir,' shouted Powers.

'I hope you're right,' Manley answered, giving Powers a dubious look.

The time was 0900. 'A dozen LCAs approaching about half a mile behind smoke screen,' Dinga Bell reported from the crow's nest.

Everyone on *Helix*'s bridge watched as a ragged line of LCAs emerged from the smoke screen and immediately came under fire. 'Two LCAs have been hit by mortars, sir, and are sinking, sir,' Powers shouted.

'My God, now, they're being slaughtered!' cried Manley, seeing men desperately throwing their arms up and disappearing under the dark blue water. The remaining eight LCAs managed to land the Essex Scottish, who immediately they stepped onto Red Beach and came under blistering fusillade of machine gunfire.

'Second and third waves coming in, sir,' shouted Lieutenant Powers.

'That'll be the fusiliers and the marines,' Manley muttered to himself. However, they fared no better than the Essex Scottish. Everyone on the bridge watched as the battalion was reduced to scattered groups, clinging to holes in the shingle, in an attempt to protect themselves against the deadly hail of bullets.

A similar fate awaited the two LCMs and five LCAs approaching White Beach carrying the marines.

'Jesus Christ,' blurted Lieutenant Powers, 'one of LCAs has ran aground and has been hit by mortars.'

Manley was too occupied watching the ship's 4.7 shells explode inland and lines of yellow gunfire from the Oerlikons and pom-poms rake the enemy's expertly concealed positions in the casino, and headland. It was when Powers yelled out, saying that two LCAs were hit by mortar fire, that he turned his attention to the marines who had had managed to reach the beach. As the marines stormed ashore, Manley winched as he saw the marines come under intense, accurate machine gun fire and mortar bombardment from both headlands. In a matter of minutes, the beach was littered with prostrate bodies as black smoke and flames curled skywards from the burning LCAs.

The time was now 0930. 'Signal from *Brocklesby*,' shouted PO Tate, 'It says, "*Message from Calpe. Commence Operation Vanquish. Withdrawal to begin 1030. All ships to increase shelling both headlands. Reduce enemy's ability to hamper essential*".'

Manley gave Powers a grim look, and said, 'Thank God for that, Guns.'

'I agree, sir,' Powers replied, 'I thought Dunkirk was bad enough, but this is a bloody disaster.'

However, the withdrawal from the beaches proved to be equally disastrous.

CHAPTER THIRTY-EIGHT

Shortly before the order to evacuate, Manley and everyone else on *Helix'*s bridge watched as a Spitfire, darted along the beaches, thickened the smoke screen laid down earlier. But bedlam reigned supreme. As *Helix* moved closer to the beach in order to give support to the men, the ship came under accurate enemy gunfire, and with every near miss, the ship rocked like a child's cradle.

'I can't see how more smoke can help them, sir,' Sub Lieutenant Baker yelled over the deafening din caused by A and B guns. 'The Jerries on the headland can see every move we make.'

'Well, here's hoping our guns will shut them up,' Manley replied.

'Excuse me, sir,' cried Sub Lieutenant Baker, 'but as far as you know, are there any specific plans for the getting the men off the beaches?'

'None whatsoever,' bellowed Manley, 'but no doubt, the LCAs and the barges captured by the marines, will be used, but it'll be very dangerous.'

'Signal from C-in-C. sir, said PO Tate. '"*Hearse to meet on arrival to take Lieutenant Commander's body to local undertaker to await collection by parents for private burial. Able Seamen Bennet and Payne to be taken by ambulance to mortuary at RNH Haslar. Next of kin have been informed*".'

'Thank you, PO,' Manley quietly replied.

Manley's prediction proved to be correct. While *Helix*'s guns continued to pound away, four LCAs were seen emerging from the smoke screen heading towards Red Beach, only to be met with a storm of mortar and machine gun fire.

'How far away are we now from the beach, Guns?' Manley shouted.

'Just over a hundred yards, sir,' Powers replied.

'It looks like the Germans have moved forward and have reoccupied the surrounding slopes, sir,' shouted Sub Lieutenant Baker.

'Then let's move fifty yards nearer. This will allow our small arms to concentrate on them,' Manley bellowed, as a hail of water from a shell exploding twenty yards away, drenched him and everyone on the bridge.

'Isn't that a bit close, sir?' Powers replied, glancing warily at Manley.

'Perhaps,' Manley answered stoically, 'but we've got to give those poor beggars all the possible support, besides,' he went on, 'I was told to use my initiative.'

'The LCAs have made it, sir,' barked Lieutenant Baker, 'and they're beginning to take off the men.'

'One of them is so overcrowded that it is beginning to sink,' Manley replied, 'and there's sweet bugger all we can do to help them.

The gun's crew and everyone on the bridge watched as one of the LCAs managed to turn and head towards *Helix*.

Manley immediately unhooked the ships tannoy. '*This is the captain speaking*,' he said, doing his best to sound calm. '*All hands, including the doctor and first aid party, muster on the upper deck, ready to receive men from the landing craft.*'

Manley grabbed a loud hailer and went onto the starboard wing. He watched anxiously as the LCA, crowded with men, came along the ship's starboard side. Many men wore blood-stained slings; others had their heads half covered with bloody bandages, while several lay on stretchers, covered with great coats and blankets. Those standing, still wore their steel helmets and carried rifles. The remainder were bare-headed. All of them looked pale and drawn.

Manley gave a quick wave to an army officer who, despite a heavily bandaged head, stood holding a megaphone.

'Glad to see you, how are things ashore?' Manley shouted.

'Bloody chaotic,' yelled the officer.

'Then the quicker we get you and your men on board, the better,' Manley replied.

In a matter of minutes, guard rails were removed. Scrambling nets were placed over the side and hoists were rigged ready to receive the stretcher cases.

Despite the constant gunfire coming from the beach and enemy shells bursting nearby, the wounded were brought on board. Strong hands then helped soldiers onto the deck.

The injured were quickly attended to by Surgeon Lieutenant Latta and SBA Wright, while the chief cook and his staff dished out mugs of warm tea. A second LCA arrived, and by 1200, corridors, and flats, were crammed with Canadians and Royal Marines, all of whom still had their rifles. Men lying on the quarterdeck were too exhausted to notice the bodies of Wacker Payne and Wiggy Bennett, after all, they had just seen many of their comrades lying dead on the beach. Others, glad to be away from the carnage ashore, simply sat quietly and sipped their tea.

Manley turned left and saw *Albrighton,* half a mile away, also taking off soldiers from another LCA.

'Better do a quick round, and see if there're any more casualties,' Manley shouted to Lieutenant Powers, who nodded and quickly, and left the bridge.

At that moment, a tall, army officer came onto the bridge. The left side of his steel helmet had a slight dint and the khaki battle dress he wore was covered in sand, as were his boots and gaiters. From under the flap of his brown holster he wore on his left side, the handle of his Webley revolver could be seen, ready for use. His dark blue eyes were bloodshot and his unshaven features looked pale and strained. A single gold crown on either shoulder epaulet indicated his rank.

'Major MacDonald, South Saskatchewans, sir,' he yelled, giving Manley a smart, parade ground salute. His throaty Canadian accent sounded tired. 'I know how busy you must be, sir, but I thought I'd come and thank you for rescuing myself and what is left of my company.' As if to confirm his sentiments, they both instinctively ducked as a deluge of water from a near explosion swept over everyone on the bridge.

'Not at all,' Manley replied, wiping water from his face with the back of his hand. 'The beaches look in a terrible state.'

'Yes, and the smoke screen didn't help much. There are dozens of wrecked landing craft, and scores of dead bodies all over the shingle. The Jerries in the headland must have had a perfect view of everything. All communication with the command ship was lost when our radio car was hit by a mortar. Most of my company are dead. Lieutenant-Colonel

Menard, my adjutant, and several officers have been either killed or taken prisoner. It really is chaotic.'

Manley was about to speak when Lieutenant Powers arrived. 'Other than a very tired crew and a few cuts and bruises, nothing serious, sir,' he yelled, 'but we are dangerously low on shells and ammunition for the pom-poms and Oerlikons.'

'Then I think we better leave before we're blown out of the water,' Manley shouted. 'Port ten degrees, revolutions five, increase speed ten knots.'

Digger Barnes repeated the order, and seconds later, the ship slowly turned around. Manley unhooked the ship's tannoy. 'This is the captain speaking,' he said in a clear calm voice. 'We are now returning to Portsmouth. As you can see the ship is crammed with troops, I'm sure you'll do your best for them. Everyone is to remain at action stations. Well done all of you.'

The time was shortly after 1330, by which time the smoke screen had been dissipated by a fresh northerly breeze. As the ship increased speed, Manley turned and gave a final look at the beach. The scene that met his eyes was one he would never forget. Bodies supported by their life-jackets, lay floating in the sea or rolling about in the waves. Body parts washed to and fro on the edge of the shingle. Tanks and half-trucks were on fire and the beach was wreathed in smoke. With tears welling up in his eyes, Manley slowly lowered his binoculars, and walked onto the port wing.

In company with the remaining destroyers, all of whom were also packed with soldiers, *Helix* headed across the Channel. The sea was calm and grey clouds partially hid the warm August sun. The warships were surrounded by numerous civilian ships also loaded with military personnel. Half an hour after leaving the beaches, the ships were attacked by Focke-Wulfs and Heinkels. By the time a squadron of Hurricane arrived and attacked them, nearly all of the civilian vessels and the destroyers had suffered damage.

The convoy arrived off the Hampshire coast a little after 1700. Every vessel was packed with soldiers, many of whom had died of their wounds. An hour later, *Prince Leopold*, *Invicta* and *Prince Astrid* sailed into Portsmouth harbour and tied up alongside Fountain Lake Jetty. They were followed *Calpe, Fernie, Albrighton, Brocklesby,* and *Helix,* who had been instructed to tie up alongside Kings Wharf, while *Bleasdale, Garth* and *Slazak* also made their way to berth at Fountain Lake Jetty.

'Thank God, the nightmare is over,' sighed Manley, watching from the bridge as the special sea duty men removed a section of the guard rails on the ship's port side, ready to receive the gangways. *Helix,* being the junior ship, was the last to enter the harbour. Many of the soldiers, their white bandaged heads and slings standing out among the drab khaki, laughed and joked, no doubt glad to be in England. *Helix* nosed her way past Fort Blockhouse and tied up alongside Kings Wharf, aft of *Brocklesby.* For the first time in days, Manley thought of Laura and made a mental note to telephone the hospital ward and tell her about FP and his final words before he died.

No sooner had the gangways been lowered into position, than medical staff from the civilian and naval ambulances came on board. Manley saw Surgeon Lieutenant Latta and SBA Bamford speaking briefly to a white coated doctor. They seemed to come to some arrangement and shook hands. Manley and Lieutenant Powers left the bridge. Powers went to the port waist to ensure the ship-to-shore telephone line was rigged. Manley made his way to the quarterdeck and accepted a grateful handshake from a few officers and soldiers. Shortly afterwards, any soldier who could stand, stood up as some of their comrades, who had died during the crossing, were taken off on stretchers. The seriously wounded were either helped down the gangway by medical staff or stretchered off. Then came the walking wounded, followed by the remaining military personnel, including the officers. As each soldier stepped off the gangway, they were met by a member of the WVS, (Women's Voluntary Service), smiling, while handing out bars of chocolate and cakes. A similar scene was taking place on the other ships. Soon, convoys of ambulances could be seen driving along the wharf, heading for either the local hospitals or the Royal Naval Hospital at Haslar, at Gosport.

As the last soldier left *Helix,* Major MacDonald, met Manley at the top of the brow.

'Once again, Commander, thank you and your crew for all you've done. I'm sure Canada won't forget it,' he said, as they warmly shook hands.

'It's us who should thank Canada for her sacrifice,' Manley replied sombrely, remembering the carnage he had witnessed on the beaches[8].

The major snapped to attention, and after giving Manley another of his smart, parade ground salutes, he turned and walked down the gangway and climbed into a coach full of soldiers that immediately drove off. The only vehicles remaining near the foot of the gangway, were a naval ambulance and gleaming black hearse with curtains dawn across the side windows.

Manley said to Lieutenant Powers who had returned from the fo'c'sle, 'Better go and tell the Chief GI to have the first lieutenant's body brought to the quarterdeck. Pipe for the side party. Clear lower deck. Officers and senior ratings fall in on the quarterdeck and stand by to have the jackstay flag lowered.'

Meanwhile, Manley watched several able seamen mopping up dried bloodstains and pools of vomit from seasick soldiers.

'To be sure, what a fuckin' mess,' Murphy, remarked to Dutch Holland.

'Shit in it, you two,' snapped PO Mills, 'and just be glad you're not one of those poor buggers lying on the beaches in France.'

Five minutes later, Chief GI Digger Barnes arrived along with four ratings carrying FP's body on a stretcher covered with a dark brown blanket, and placed it near the top of the gangway.

'Ship's company, attention. Off caps,' shouted Manley.

PO Mills, two ratings, each holding a silver bosun's call, were fallen in by the side of the gangway. Opposite them, OOD Sub Lieutenant Milton, Manley and the rest of the ship's officers stood in line, stony

---

[8] Footnote. 6,086 troops landed at Dieppe. 4,963 were Canadians. Only 2210 returned to England. 913 were killed and the rest captured. The Royal Navy lost 33 craft and one destroyer. 6, U S Rangers were killed and the RAF lost 106 aircraft. The only success of the raids was Lord Lovatt's Number 4 Commando, who, as his LCA pulled away, sent a message to Mountbatten: 'Hess battery destroyed, all enemy guns crews finished with bayonet – is this OK with you?' No answer was received.

faced and silent. Close by, stood two elderly undertakers wearing morning suits, and four SBAs.

All eyes were concentrated on the three stretchers. Suddenly, the ship's bell rang out and the white ensign on the quarterdeck's jackstay was lowered.

Manley gave a quick nod to side party who piped "the still". The SBAs carefully picked up Bennet and Payne and carried the stretchers down the gangway and slid them into the open back doors of the ambulance. The undertakers bent down and slowly lifted up FP's stretcher. After a momentary pause, they took it down the gangway and placed it into the back of the hearse then climbed inside. As soon as the hearse had driven away, Manley shouted, 'Ship's company, stand at ease. On caps. Carry on.'

Gradually the officers and crew turned and left followed by the senior ratings. Manley turned to Lieutenant Powers, and was about to speak when he heard the quarterdeck telephone ring.

'Call for you, sir,' QM Knocker White said, holding the receiver in his hand.

'Thank you,' Manley replied, accepting the receiver while wondering who could be ringing him. 'Commander Manley,' he snapped.

'Oh, Hugh, darling, don't sound so official, it' me,' cried Laura.

'Laura, how wonderful to hear you,' Manley said, doing his best to keep his voice down. 'How are you, and how on earth did you manage to get through so soon?'

Laura gave a short laugh, then said, 'I'm fine, but I heard on the wireless three men had been killed on your ship. I was sick with worry, so I told the operator I was your wife. What happened, are you all right?'

'I know I shouldn't say this over the phone, but it was FP and two ratings who were killed. FP joined the ship shortly before we sailed and I intend on recommending him for a Victoria Cross.'

'Good Lord, poor FP, I'm so sorry. He must have done something really brave.'

'Yes, he certainly did,' Manley said quietly. 'I'll tell you more when I see you, but I must go, now. I love you and one day you won't have to lie about being my wife, goodbye darling.' With a sigh, he replaced the receiver. Manley walked over to Lieutenant Powers, and said, 'I'll be in my cabin, I have three letters to write.'

'Very good, sir,' Powers replied, glancing up at the mainmast, 'shall I order the battle ensign to be taken down?'

Manley didn't answer straight away. Instead, he looked up at the white ensign, fluttering from the mainmast, and feeling his throat contract, replied, 'Yes, Guns, I intend on sending it to the first lieutenant's parents.'

'But, sir,' Powers replied, 'it's full of bullet holes and looks rather worse for wear.'

Manley gave a quick, nonchalant shrug of his shoulders, then, with a wry smile playing around his mouth, said, 'Just like the ship, eh, Guns?' Then slowly walked away.

EPILOGUE

Hugh Manley and Laura were married in St Michael's Parish Church, Helston, at midday on Saturday the 25th of October, 1942. Despite a chilly western breeze, the sun, half hidden by grey clouds, bathed the crowd gathered outside the church in warm sunshine. After returning from Dieppe, *Helix* had undergone a two-week refit, during which time the ship's company enjoyed a week's leave, thus allowing Manley and Laura time to arrange the wedding.

Inside, the church was full of relatives and the friends of the Trevethick family as well as Harold and Martha, Manley's parents. Several of *Helix*'s ship's officers and crew, transported from Portsmouth by a coach, occupied two rows of pews. Among them sat Sub Lieutenant Baker now engaged to Janet, his childhood sweetheart, Chief Stoker Harry Johnson, CERA Paddy O'Malley and Joyce, recently married in Gosport's registry office.

Suddenly, the melodic sound of the organ blaring out Felix Mendelssohn's *Wedding March*, heralded the end of the ceremony. The stout, oaken door of the church opened. Seconds later, to the delight of the crowd, Manley and Laura appeared, their faces wreathed in smiles. Behind Laura stood Susan, her maid of honour, wearing a lovely white dress. Then came Manley's parents, Laura's father and the Reverend Timothy Feneck, whose cassock hung around his small, portly figure like a miniature bell tent.

Laura, looked dazzlingly beautiful in a high-necked, long-sleeved silver wedding gown. Her auburn hair was done in a chignon and behind her veil, Laura's face was wreathed in smiles. Her left hand, complete with her shiny gold wedding ring, clasped hold of Manley's right hand, while her left hand held a small bouquet of red roses. The tip of a white handkerchief poked discretely out of the breast pocket of Manley's immaculately tailored uniform, above which, his recently awarded Distinguished Service Cross was proudly displayed. At first, Manley was bareheaded but was handed his cap by Lieutenant Powel, who was his best man.

Finally, the traditional wedding photographs were taken by a tall man wearing a dark suit and horn-rimmed glasses. Then, to the sound of loud cheers and clapping coming from the crowd, Laura took tight hold of Manley's arm. After carefully negotiating the four steps leading to the wide, gravelled path, the happy couple, covered in confetti, walked under an arch of shining swords provided by Lieutenant (E) Logan, Surgeon Lieutenant Latta, and Sub Lieutenants, Baker and Milton. As they arrived at the rusting wrought iron gate, Laura stopped and threw her bouquet over her head into the crowd, causing even more cheering as it was caught by Susan.

Parked on the road opposite the gate, a chauffeur, an elderly man wearing green livery, stood holding open the door of the sliver limousine that would take them to Trevithick House, where the wedding breakfast was to be held.

'Congratulations to you both,' said the chauffeur, in a thick Cornish accent. 'And may you have a long and happy life.'

Manley thanked him then helped Laura, who, picking up her gown, gave a quick glimpse of the metal prosthesis on her left leg as she climbed into the back seat. Manley removed his cap, bent down and followed her inside. As the car pulled away, Manley gently lifted Laura's veil, and looking into her moist, violet eyes, said, 'Alone at last, how are you feeling, Mrs Manley?'

'Wonderful, Mr Manley,' she replied, then grasping his hands, she smiled and added, 'darling, if our first child is a boy, can we name him after FP?'

'Of course,' Manley answered, 'I'm sure he would have liked that.'

'Now kiss me, my love,' Laura answered, as a tear ran down the side of her face, 'because now I really do know love laughs at locksmiths.'